CW00557740

About the Author

Jenny Dawson was a radiographer in the NHS for most of her working life. She lives in Lincolnshire.

Donation to the Prisoners' Education Trust
reg charity no 1084718

Jenny Dawson

THE POOR MAN'S PHYSICIAN

AUSTIN MACAULEY
PUBLISHERS LTD.

Copyright © Jenny Dawson (2015)

The right of Jenny Dawson to be identified as author of this work has been asserted by her in accordance with section 77 and 78 of the Copyright, Designs and Patents Act 1988.

All rights reserved. No part of this publication may be reproduced, stored in a retrieval system, or transmitted in any form or by any means, electronic, mechanical, photocopying, recording, or otherwise, without the prior permission of the publishers.

Any person who commits any unauthorized act in relation to this publication may be liable to criminal prosecution and civil claims for damages.

A CIP catalogue record for this title is available from the British Library.

ISBN 9781785541209 (Paperback)
ISBN 9781785541216 (Hardback)

www.austinmacauley.com

First Published (2015)
Austin Macauley Publishers Ltd.
25 Canada Square
Canary Wharf
London
E14 5LQ

Printed and bound in Great Britain

Acknowledgments

I would like to thank: my writer friends for their inspiration, York Library and Archives for their invaluable help with primary and secondary materials, the staff at Gainsborough library for their amazing patience and kindness, my sister for her encouragement – and, last but not least, my longsuffering proofreader.

PREFACE

THE APOTHECARY is the poor man's physician. When times are hard, and indeed when times are not hard, the poor will seek him out in the belief that a measure of the physician's wisdom will be distilled into the tincture that he dispenses.

I say this because there were those among the fraternity of physicians in the fair town of York who were apt to suspect me, at worst of devilry and at best of following the calling of the charlatan, so ready was I considered to be with the diagnostician's patter.

Nor was I prepossessing in person, having the brooding looks and accent of the French, to such a degree that some thought I was an emissary in the pay of Napoleon Bonaparte; and I have to say not without their own reason, for there is much to be deduced from the physiognomy before so much as a word passes.

And there were yet others, and here I come to the soul of this matter, who thought my sympathies to lie with certain insurrectionists from the hill country in the county of York itself, who, seeing their livelihoods falling off, took to breaking the machines that so robbed them. For in straitened times no man is above suspicion.

Yet it fell to me, the least of men and a foreigner withal, to leave a record of the time of the insurrection.

And I did the best that I could, having collected from my witnesses that which each considered to be the truth. For who is to know what truth is? It is variable, as the patterns of the sunlight on the hills are variable, and though it may be seen by all is seen variously from various places. All saw their truth according to their several places, and were each to tell their own tale according to their own truth in the words that they had, which I gathered from my patients and others, being representative of the times yet not exhaustive. For no man could comprehend all the interests abroad in those days, least of all myself, who was but an apothecary practising from rooms in the shadow of the Monk-bar in the town of York.

Nevertheless, my calling brought to me many from the hill country where the hand loom weavers and finishers had their living, yet made no living but rather went out by night to break the frames. And the same calling brought to me those of the King's men whose heavy task it was to keep the peace. For in this life there are many callings, and it is given to each to follow his calling according to his conscience.

And these were numbered among my witnesses:

Hannah Mary Gaut

Zephaniah Gaut, her husband, hand loom weaver

Robert George Gaut, their son

Luke Bower, my scribe

Simon Horridge, hand loom weaver

Elizabeth Horridge, sister to the above

Martin Gathercole, master of Clywold mill

Ellie Bright, housekeeper to Martin Gathercole

Domenico Jommelli, musician and the brother of my soul

Thomas Hayward, officer of the King's men

Jane Pearce, mill-hand

Susan Knowles, mill-hand, who also found grace at her life's end

Jem Bailey, sometime nurse in our household

Richard Born, magistrate

Grace Born, his wife

Rosie Todd, maid to Grace Born

Whose names I have altered only in some respects where I deemed it necessary to protect the identity of the so-called malefactors, as I have changed also the names of the places where they dwelt and laboured, for that same reason.

And others there were of divers callings whose names are in this record who also played a part in the history; and lastly also myself, though I wished it not that I had a part.

The record beginning at the close of the year of our Lord 1811 in that time betwixt the birth of our sweet Saviour and the next year's dawning, when the Dog Star burns low in the eastern sky by night and the sun describes but a narrow arc by day.

At which season I saw under the Monk-bar and meagrely sheltered from a keen north wind a man and a woman standing, whom I took from the decency of their dress to be hill folk; who presently made their way in some bewilderment to the street gate of the dispensary, seeming to confer one with another, and all the while studying a morsel of paper, attempting as I thought to match the writing on it with the name of John Rivaulx, my own, drawn on the plaque. Yet I liked not to open the door in readiness lest I cause alarm, for their looks even from afar told of the misery of the times; there being in the town of York at divers times many such, come from the hill country beyond Clywold, not least at the times of the assize, for the law fell heavily on those who broke the machines that reft them of their living, of which more in its proper place.

And the man and the woman thus arrived I took to be the first of my witnesses.

I

And indeed, I could hear the good man before I saw him, so laboured was he in his breath as he climbed the dispensary stairs, and seeing also his shadow and that of his wife rest on the way up before continuing the ascent.

'Thas Mr ... ?' he said.

'Reevo,' I said. 'Tis a strange spelling, from my ancestors.'

'Ah,' he said, 'ancestors.'

'Family,' I said. 'They were of the land of France.'

'Tha meaning like Napoleon Bonaparte?'

'Before him.'

'Ah, before Napoleon Bonaparte,' the man said.

'Zephaniah,' the woman said, 'please, less of thy thoughts.'

'Thas Romish then?' he said.

'Yes, that I am,' I said.

The woman's face was marked by dark circles under the eyes, which themselves were large and shone bright like the stars on a winter's night. I observed moreover deep hollows below the bone of the cheek, and lines etched below the corners of the mouth. Her face in repose bore the stamp of affliction and the chill had laid hold on her fair features; that in spite of the fire of coals we kept in the dispensary.

The man was somewhat stooped about the shoulders, a common enough variant I have observed often among certain of the hill people who work the hand loom, as I thought this good man to have done. He was some fifteen years older than the woman. His brow was lined with much thought, and exhaustion sat deep in his eyes.

4

'Tis the bairns, I tell her,' he said. 'She's ever hearing the cries o the bairns.'

'Zephaniah, please,' said the woman. 'Let the gentleman find out my complaint.'

'Hannah,' said the man, 'tha knows our means are but limited. I were but helping en cut to the point.'

'It may be that we can look to your complaint without the necessity of a tincture,' I said. 'There is no fee in a few words. Our words are dispensed to us freely by the Lord God and it is for us to dispense them again freely.'

'Then that as you Romish folks think,' said the man.

'Tis what I think,' I said. 'I cannot answer for my brethren.'

'Happen there aren't too many Romish folks hereabouts,' said the man.

He said their name was Gaut, Hannah and Zephaniah. They dwelt out beyond Clywold. He had brought his wife to me, he said, because she was ever hearing the cries of the bairns, which were no more, for all but one had been delivered to her untimely.

The woman sat quietly in a chair looking down at her hands. The man's hands meanwhile accompanied the rise and fall of his speech, alternately resting on his knees and ploughing the air around him. I observed in him moreover clubbing of the fingers, which were otherwise slender, as was his person, and near as tall as I. And I saw also the sign of cyanosis about his lips.

'Mr Gaut, my good man, before we look to your wife's ailing I will pray you to come to my study upstairs,' I said, to which he agreed, albeit in some bewilderment.

It was with him as I suspected, and indeed, though he looked to his wife his malady was the greater. He was hard pressed to climb the stairs, which though few in number were steep more than the custom, and he had need to pull himself up by the rail. I bade him be seated and drink a draught of water to which I added in the dispensary a tincture of Digitalis purpurea, of which he partook and then fell to singing under his breath, laboured though it was. Then I prepared while he was thus seated a quire of paper and a measure of ink, having perceived that the good woman, Hannah his wife, in common with many of her sisters from the hills, was possessed of a natural modesty in matters relating to childbearing; and indeed, I would not that she should speak to me of such and be put to shame.

'Happen we're hindering thy work.' Zephaniah had already risen from his chair and was making for the staircase.

'No, no,' I said, 'be seated and recover thy breath, my good man. I would if she pleases that your wife records on this paper in the seclusion of her dwelling house what she wishes me to know of the sounds she hears.'

'Happen thas noticed how I gab,' he said. 'The poor lass canna get a word in.'

'You are a good man, Zephaniah Gaut,' I said.

'The lass has a fair hand. She'll write for thee,' he said. 'Thas given me a draught of restorative, tha has done the lungs a world o good an I mus pay thee.'

'I gave you water,' I said, 'and asked you to sit down to recover the breath that was hard pressed to catch up with you. Tis a poor physician who demands a fee for water and a minute of his lifetime.'

Then to the woman I said, 'Will you write down what you can of the sounds you hear, what they are like and when you hear them, as much as you wish to impart? No other will read your thoughts save my scribe, who is an honest soul.'

And seeing what manner of question was writ there behind her eyes I said to her that her affliction was not the madness, which she surely feared, but the condition called tinnitus. And I asked her then if there were any children who yet lived.

'Thas Robert,' said the man, 'and tha name's like as much as we know o him these days, the names he were baptised wi, Robert George Gaut.'

Then I said no more, having been as I ever fear important to myself; for learning is a gift of the sweet Saviour and must be given humbly as the sun and rain are given, to all men.

So I watched through the window of the upper chamber as they went, leaning into the wind and rain, the good man with his words and the good woman with her silence, knowing nothing of them but their names, the afflictions they brought with them and the innocence of their souls.

For I found in them no guile. He carried no more than his years at the loom and she no more than her sorrow for each year she had delivered out of time, her sorrow for the narrowness of her frame, and her sorrow that she carried sorrow for all to see, that it sat in her eyes and in the lines around her mouth, in her thin hands and in every step she took along the path of her life.

II

'You're melancholy again, sir.'

'I was but thinking,' I said. 'How is it that you may enter a chamber though the door is closed and see my face through the back of my head? Pray tell me what I'm melancholy about, Luke Bower.'

'You are comparing the situation of the folks you have lately seen with your own and thinking that although they have sorrows enough they are not labouring under the burden of guilt as your Romish beliefs compel you to do, sir.'

'That might well be so, Luke,' I said. 'One day you will tell me the nature of my guilt. Until then we must resign ourselves to the task of recording these patients, when it pleases you.'

'You may begin, sir. I see you have been making up the ink for your sooty fingers tell me so. Pray give me their names.'

'Hannah Mary Gaut, Zephaniah Gaut.'

'Spelling, sir?'

'I leave that to you, Luke, as I leave all other intricacies of the English tongue to you. Hannah, she hears sounds, which her husband attributes to the cries of her untimely delivered bairns. Diagnosis: Tinnitus aurium. We have begged the patient to record on paper in the seclusion of her dwellinghouse and from day to day that which she hears.'

'Write it down, sir? Tis like a tale, not a record.'

'Zephaniah, he is naturally garrulous but wishes to spare his wife the immodesty of talking in the present company of the untimely delivery of her infants. I observed expansion of the finger ends and requested that the patient should accompany me up the stairs to the study, when my suspicion of exhaustion of the heart and lungs was confirmed.'

'Tis a tale you've asked of her,' said Luke.

'By writing down what she hears she will grow to understand her condition, for which there is no cure. Her husband will allow himself a rest and a draught of water when he is exhausted, which I fear is frequently from the appearance of his hands and the cyanosis that sits around his lips.'

'Tis but a part of their troubles, sir.'

'How mean you, Luke?'

'They bear the troubles of the hill folk, sir. I meant no more. Tis true that writing of troubles will serve as a remedy, sir?'

'Tis but a theory, Luke. Your wrist, it is scorched. It has been exposed to fire or some other mischief.'

'Sir?'

'You know as well as I where the tincture of elm is.'

'I apply a costly tincture to a trifling lesion on my wrist, for which I thank you, sir. Meanwhile you prepare to go out in the storm, which is gathering though it is yet but a patter of rain on the casement.'

'I have given no indication of going out in a storm. Yet you say rightly, Luke. I am going out later. You may consider yourself at liberty for the remainder of the day.'

'Sir.'

'Luke?'

'Sir?'

'Might it be that I am full of my own importance, Luke?'

'Happen, sir. But you will not be again.'

'Go in peace, Luke.'

And indeed, a winter storm broke while I was yet in the town of York; and the night fell early and with equal gloom and rancour on street and field and on hill and vale, discriminating little between the dwellings of man and beast and rich and poor.

I followed the lantern, at times gleaming bright and at times guttering to blackness, as it led through the by-ways at the end of the town and onto the road that stretched up beyond Potterton into a waste I did not know, accustomed though I was to waiting on patients far and wide; joining at length the coach, which I left at the sign of the Spread Eagle. Being then led by another who walked steadily at some half of a furlong distance, neither stopping nor quickening his pace. The rain, which had been heavy as we alighted from the coach, enough to sodden my cloak, became lighter, but the way was rough and stony with sudden rifts and gulleys. Sometimes there was the lowing of a beast, the smoke of whose breath I could see rising into the same raw air that I breathed; sometimes the glimmer of the sheep seated in the lee of an outcrop of ulex. Yet I met no man and passed no dwellings save those of the beasts, and I heard no sound but the plash of their hooves, the peaceful chewing of the cud, and the suck of my stick and the measure of my feet on the path. Thus until a crack of grey dawn appeared in the eastern sky and a rough dwellinghouse rose up out of the darkness.

The light that I had so far followed came to a halt and my guide, for such I took him to be, motioned me to keep silence and, knocking twice, pushed open the door of the dwelling.

A soft woman's voice spoke out of the darkness.

'Tis the apothecary come to see thee, Simon. Tell the gentleman what ails thee. We canna.'

'Tha mus.' The voice of a man broke painfully from, as I understood, near sealed lips, and remained adrift on the close air of the room, beyond the hearing and yet not dying away.

'Tha mus.'

'We canna, Simon.'

Presently in the darkness, which was not darkness all for the blessed light of the day crept in through many a breach in the walls, I made out a pallet in the corner on which a man lay. In the opposite corner was a hand loom. On a chair by the loom a cloaked figure whose age and gender I could not discern. Seated on the ground beside the bed of the man Simon, the woman who had first bidden him to speak.

'Tha mus tell him, Simon. We canna. Wha tha tells a third party mus come from thine own lips.'

Her voice, like his, hung on the air, diminished yet undying.

'Tis not for us to tell on thee, Simon.'

'Nay, tis not.'

'He mus know, to help thee, Simon Horridge.'

Thus I learned the man's full name. I learned also, waiting there, the man's calling and his affliction. The room was rank with the scent of the weft; not new, as I understood while I yet waited inside the door of the dwellinghouse, but such sour weft as had been lying for some weeks and had not been put to the loom. There was in the room moreover the odour of scorched flesh and the fainter odour of putrefaction.

This I deduced, that the man Simon Horridge was a weaver but he no longer had work. He had been touched by fire or by some kind of corrupting material. As I stood there his few words became the more distant, even as is the voice of he who calls to his sheep on the hills.

'I pray thee, send for a light, my good woman,' I said. 'I fear Simon may not be long for this world. The tender membranes around his nose and windpipe are swelling as we talk, and presently he will no longer draw breath. Where is the guide who brought me here? Let me have his lantern, I beg you. Be assured that whatever I find when I see him remains with me as far as the grave and even into the next world.'

And thus I prattled, knowing not what I said. Yet I gathered this much, that there was some mystery afoot surrounding the condition of the patient, which accounted both for his reluctance to speak and for the delay in summoning help. He who had been seated by the loom rose and went out, brushing by me as he went and leaving the door open so far as to admit a panel of the wan dawn which fell across the pallet where the patient lay.

Some small attempt had been made to bathe his face, which was yet blackened and all over covered with putrid welts of raw flesh, charred at the edges and exuding blood and plasma. The tissues around the nostrils and lips were grievously oedematous, scarcely admitting the passage of air, and over all there was a nauseating odour such as I have never encountered in all my life.

The man was trying to speak, but the passage between his poor lips was encrusting with a rank yellow matter even as we looked.

'Pray bid your attendant bring some water, my good woman,' I said.

'Thas left,' the woman said. 'Thas only messenger unknown to us. I'll get thee water. I'll hand thee thy medicines.'

'This will hurt thee, Simon.' I said. 'Be a good man and stay with us and you'll breathe yet.'

I extended his neck and introduced a pipette between the encrusted lips. He made no sound. We waited.

'I fear he's going. He should rightly have cried out with the pain.'

'Nay,' said the woman. 'He canna speak but he's nay going. We dunna speak, folks such as us, but we're not like to give up. Neither will you give up, sir, I pray you.'

I introduced more tincture and yet more. The man did not show signs of life, nor yet did he die. While we waited a new day had come to being in the sweet world outside, and needles of sunlight pierced the gloom.

'I've given him as much compound as I can. A small dose is medicine. A large dose is poison.'

'Nay,' said the woman, 'whas to lose?'

She was bathing the man's face, washing away the encrusted matter, gently pressing the frayed and charred flesh back in place. A thin line of blood ran from the corner of his mouth and down the chin, pooling in the hollow above the collar bone. He coughed and took in a draught of air, struggling to raise himself onto one elbow as he did so.

'The swelling has begun to subside. I will leave a lotion for you to bathe your husband's face.'

'Thank you gratefully, sir. Simon's sister, na his wife.'

12

'Will he talk to me?'

'Try, sir. I canna speak for him. Simon, lad, canst thou hear me?'

'Aye.'

The man sank down on the pallet and pulled the cover up to his chin.

'Simon Horridge, I will tell no one,' I said. 'Your secret goes with me as long as I shall live. Pray tell me what ails you and I will know the tincture to leave with you.'

'My sister may tell thee,' said the man. 'Liz, thou mayst tell the gentleman.'

'He blacked his face, sir,' said the woman, 'wi some foul sludge he fell upon nigh the drainage. Happen you've seen loom in corner o the room tha doesna work. Folks like us being destitute, sir, an all the work gone to frame looms. Happen tha knows folks canna do aught but break the frames.'

'Aye an be hanged,' the man said. ''Tis that or starve for want o work, an they o the brethren wi bairns an all.'

'I will not tell any soul,' I said.

'Thanking ye, but we canna hold thee to tha promise,' said the man Simon, 'can we, Liz? Frame breaking being a hanging offence like, an the same for they that abet.'

The sun was well up when I left the dwellinghouse of Simon Horridge, and that after having declined to tarry for refreshment seeing the poor state of their larder. So I left, thinking to find the drainage in the case that there might be growing some remedy, for where nature plants her ills she often plants there also her succour.

And looking back when I came to the crossroads I saw the woman Liz Horridge yet standing in the doorway, her cloak wrapped closely around her, waving me in the direction of the path that led to the carriageway to the town of York; who seeing that I took the right path went back inside, leaving to the hills and the sky with its chequered clouds an emptiness such that I have rarely known.

So I walked until the sun was little short of its zenith, all the while searching for the area of the drainage, yet knowing not what to look for, and searching moreover for that substance which proved to be all but the death of Simon Horridge, yet not finding it. But seeing instead, some two furlongs ahead of me along the road that which I took to be a company of the King's men, a sight such that I knew to be all too common in those parts.

And having given me by the grace of God two furlongs' ground in which to weave a deception, they stopped, gathering around me, with their horses stamping and snorting after the manner of their kind. Then one of their number, whom I took to be the captain of the men, though looking little inclined for the task, dismounted and gave me a perfunctory salutation.

'What fellow are you to be on the King's highway in the dress of a common charlatan? Where do you come from?'

I told him my name and the place of my lodgings close by the Monk-bar in the town of York, whereupon he cuffed me lightly with an ungloved hand; and all the while behind his shoulder another, well made and comely, uttered ill-concealed oaths.

'I asked you where you came from. Where have you lately been?'

The other spat upon the ground.

My quest for the drainage which I hadn't found had taken me far out of the way of the dwelling of Simon Horridge. I said I had been to the lodging of a man whose name I did not know.

'Who needs a charlatan to dress his wounds, eh? We'll know where he lives now,' the officer said.

To which demand I gave precise but inaccurate directions, round the shoulder of the hill, through a half furlong dense in the summer season with agrostis, and across a fast running beck, thereafter following the pathway on the other side which led I knew not where.

'An easy catch, I tell you then,' he said, at the same time fingering the cord of the scrip around my neck.

'Now you'll divulge the exact nature of the malady of the patient,' he said; and with his nearness I detected the odour of grievous decay of the dentition, observing also that the fellow was badly on his feet, such a one indeed who was like to be dismayed and prostrated by talk of sickness.

'An inflammation of the lymphatic glands accompanied by some discolouration and exquisite pain until the buba erupts,' I said, 'typical of the disease commonly known as the plague. I would beg you to bathe in the beck as your unprotected flesh has been in contact with mine. And your fellows also, as a precaution,' I added. 'Fare thee well.'

At the end of the day who has not erred in the sight of God? Even a man who sits alone in his dwellinghouse without intercourse with the world may yet give the thoughts of his mind to wander along forbidden paths.

For, more than deceiving an officer of the King's men, I had dwelt inordinately in my mind on Elizabeth Horridge, in whose sweet eyes were writ all the kindness and grace of they who are of the hill country; yet I wished it not that I should be partisan in those troublous times.

And I thought of her many times for the remainder of the waking day and into the eve, long after the fire of the setting sun had flashed and died in the windows of my dwelling close by the Monk-bar in York.

And it came to me moreover that in times of unrest, as I have seen oft at the time of the terror in the fair land of France, each man believes he has right on his side, though he may care little by what means justice might be had.

III

From then on my scribe Luke Bower took pains to hide from me the lesion on his wrist, a matter I would scarcely have noticed but that one day going to the dispensary shortly after he had completed his work I thought I could detect in the air, hardly discernible though it was, the odour of decay, which resurrected in my mind's eye the dwellinghouse I had lately attended, the man on the pallet, and the woman by his side, to whom my mind returned at every waking moment and yet again in my dreams at night.

The sum of our morning's work was lying on the desk, the ink not yet dry. It was, as always, exquisitely done, minutely tabulated and without error, far surpassing in exactness my poor dictation. At the foot of the page was a stain the colour of straw streaked with blood. I carried the page over to the window to examine it more closely.

'Luke Bower! Are you there?'

The injury, which had first appeared on the dorsum of the wrist, had surely spread, at least to that part called the ulnar margin, and had now turned to putrefaction; the tincture, although effective in the short term, had made the mischief worse. And the hand loom weaver Simon Horridge, to whom I had given the selfsame remedy, was in all likelihood in a perilous state, getting not better but worse, with the affected area extending to the precious tissues of the eyes and running up into the hair.

Luke Bower appeared below the window at which I stood, emerging from the iron-gate under the lodging-house and turning into the Monk-bar. When I reached the place he had vanished into the milling crowd.

Then I resolved to go back to the hill country beyond Clywold to seek again the so called drainage, which resolve had fled quite from my mind after the manner of they who are long in years; yet knowing that wherever nature finds a pernicious substance she will plant a remedy, as indeed every small boy stung by the Urtica dioica will straight away look for a broad leaved dock and will invariably find it growing nearby to salve his wounds. And for which reason I doubted not that somewhere near the source of the foul substance that Simon Horridge had used, for what purpose I did not presume to ask, there would be an antidote.

It was towards the eventide when I found the place or some other place like to it, too dark indeed by then to see the damp earth, but evident from an acid taste to the air, being otherwise heavy with the breath and the sweet smell of the sheep's fleece, which poor creatures noticing me huffed and turned away after the manner of their kind. The last flare of the sun was fading and Polaris already glimmered in the northern sky. At my feet was a pool of water, encrusted with ice at its edges and fed from a thin rivulet running down a shallow hill, the earth lying rank and cloying all about; from which I collected a portion, and from the pool a phial's length. Then I was minded to set off and trace the noxious stream to its source, following it round the heel of that hill I knew as Borthwick, along the side of the sheep path and into the higher level of the plain, all the while tasting its poison on the still frost air which sat ill with the sweet sharp tastes of the night.

Presently the path of the stream rose sharply, passing between outcrops of stone and scree and becoming increasingly inimical to life; all, I noticed, but a type of sow thistle which grew consistently alongside the stream far from its customary dwelling, and indeed out of season also for the ice bristled at my feet. Yet I had seen it in full summer and wondered at its peculiarity, having happened upon this same

17

place in the yester year. And then as now I was surprised by the great mill which rose of a sudden out of the bright night covering every star as high as Arcturus; and noting also then as now the noxious substance that seeped from its foundation as from a suppurating wound.

And on that same night in the last summer I saw lights that flickered and danced in the tall windows, and for some while until all was dark. Then a line of men passed by me on muffled feet, so close that I could have reached out and touched them each one, yet I could see nothing of them, so like were they to the darkness that surrounded them, dark in their dress and darkened in their flesh, melting into the speechless night as an owl called from Kessle-wood and a meteor glided down the sky and sank into Borthwick-hill.

And for a reason unknown to me a stray thought of my scribe Luke Bower came then into my mind and lingered there. I sat down against the wall of the building, sheltered by a buttress and away from the effluent, Luke Bower being yet present to my thoughts. I knew nothing about him. I might never have known him but for the fact that I had fallen upon him among a company of urchins and others as he drew a hopscotch on the pavement in the shameful shade of the gallows-tree. It was a remarkable drawing, executed with the left hand and ornamented with exquisite calligraphic figures.

'Pray what are you doing here?' I asked, knowing full well that the spectacle of the gallows-tree would hold no terrors for lads such as he.

'As you see, sir, writing.' The voice accorded oddly with the ragged garments he wore.

'Can you not write somewhere else?'

'I can write well nigh anywhere, sir.'

'Then you may be my scribe. You must tell your parents,' I added, for there were surely those who had given him words.

'I have no parents, sir, no more than you have parents or any other kin.' That was the first I knew of Luke Bower's acuity.

The victim, for I will ever so think of such persons, was a young woman, sentenced for heaven knows what slight misdemeanour; she who would walk out of the black door, take her last gasp of the sun and the sweet air, and then pass silently out of the world. Luke Bower continued to write on the ground as the crowd melted away.

'You may go in peace,' I said. 'The deed is done.'

'Then you may go also, sir,' he said. 'But you do not. You linger here. Not for the same reason as those who came to witness a spectacle. There is some other reason why you should be drawn to a scene like this. You have the bleak look of the newly dead on your own face, sir, though you do not know it.'

And while I was yet in my thoughts outside the gaol of York on the day I first set eyes on my scribe Luke Bower, and while it was still dark, the first of the workers came up, soundless and covert to the mill. For they who had employ also carried with them the dishonour of gaining a livelihood when others did not; though I say not myself that one man is more worthy or less so than another, for all are made in the image of God Almighty.

And I set off down the hill, following the way of the effluent where it seeped out along its course, dyeing the earth black as sable and running round the basal leaves of the plant I had observed in the summer of the yester year; which was much like to the Sonchus arvensis in that it carried its life cycle on a single flower stem from bud to seed, and yet the petals, though vivid yellow for the most part were on some flowers edged in violet. I collected then one of these strange deviants from the common and observed that the sap from the broken stem, which otherwise would have been milky, was faintly off hue as if the Creator had allowed a purple pigment to run into the white.

Then, since nothing in nature is random, but all is plotted and planned to an infinitesimal degree, I understood that the plant grew there as a remedy against the noxious drainage from the manufactory. Which plant I knew, but had not understood its gracious purpose, thinking it to be but the humble sow thistle. And for want of a better name and for my own record I called the plant the Sonchus hesperus, as it appeared in my life that second time at the evening season, and moreover had about it the same deep blue as the eyes of the hand loom weaver Liz Horridge, whose station in life was humble yet who put me in mind of the peace of the evening and of the dying light and of the fire of all the stars in heaven.

IV

The cart which I had seen at the sign of the Blue Boar south of Withersedge came to a halt at the foot of Capcar-hill. For indeed in that country a man may stand on any hill and see, to the north, south, east and west, the towns and homesteads far and wide, as I did on that morning, being Clywold, Beckwith, Tindercliffe and Withersedge, and the great mills also, being three in number but no doubt yet more yonder of the horizon.

The driver was a thick set man, muffled against the cold in spite of the temperate air. For that day in the year of our Lord 1812, early in the season though it was, saw a pale sun insomuch as the mist rose from every beck.

'Ah can do wi company,' The driver's voice was light for all his worn and heavy aspect. 'Thas a long rooad for a fellow on his own. If tha doesna mind the plague, ha!'

'Why plague?' I climbed up. 'We haven't seen plague in these parts for nigh on a hundred years and fifty.'

'Well tha has noo. Tis all abroad at the sign o the Blue Boar. Them King's men them sez some physic fellow ont rooad ha seen plague ovver yon side o hill. Ha ha! We all gotta goo some way. Thas what ah telled en.'

'What are you carrying in the back?' I said.

'Ye dunna wan to noo,' the man said.

The sight of a rigid sheep's leg, ill-concealed as it was and black and muddied, had already answered my question.

'How long dead?'

'Dunno,' the man said. 'Fellow said en found en on hill. I these times, sir, a wise fella doesna ask no questions. What a fella doesna noo a fella canna tell again. Thas wha they say.'

The cart lumbered over the Lendal-bridge in the town of York and stopped. I thanked the driver and jumped down. When I looked again the cart was there no longer. It had neither melted into the throng because there was on that day no throng, nor had it taken a turning to the side, the way from the Lendal-bridge being open on every side, save at the mouth of the great drain of the town of York; which place I had a long time wondered at, oft fearing that a pestilence might arise from it, exposed as it was to the thoroughfare.

'You're asking of yourself where all the market folks are no doubt, sir,' said Luke Bower, who was even then at my elbow, having arrived out of nowhere. 'Are we to suppose it's the rumour of the plague? Foul news travels fast.' He laughed. 'The town of York is unusually empty today because the good citizens are at their dwellinghouses saving themselves from the plague. You look none too good yourself, sir. I would suggest that your present haggard and disordered condition is the result of your journey from the foot of Capcar-hill in a cart, which cart may have held associations for you, sir, if I might be so bold as to say.'

'There were dead sheep in the cart,' I said.

'Is that so?' said Luke.

'And heaven knows what else,' I said.

'And you judiciously did not pursue the matter, sir,' said Luke. 'What a man doesn't know, that he cannot be compelled to tell again.'

'We may have found a remedy for the mischief on your wrist, Luke.'

'It is better, sir.'

'It is not, Luke.'

'No, it is not, sir. I believe I will try the remedy, thanking you, sir.'

'I will try it on myself first.'

The water collected from the noxious stream flowing down from the mill was straight away inimical to the tissues on the back of the hand, the dried earth less so. An application of the blue-white exudate from the broken stem of the

Sonchus hesperus, a sample of which was indeed laid by in the dispensary though as yet without a purpose, healed the area within a half day. So I resolved to give Luke Bower a tincture of the same.

'It could be a candle burn, sir,' he said. 'It is good of you to take pains on my account.'

'You are usually more subtle than that, Luke.'

'Sir?'

'I know a candle burn when I see one.'

'A fellow came by after you were gone, sir. I asked him to come back after the midday.'

'What manner of fellow was this, Luke?'

'Nothing remarkable, sir. You're most likely to have seen him in the course of your journeys.'

The unremarkable fellow, whether Luke Bower knew it or not, was that same officer of the King's men who had accosted me on the highway as I returned from the dwellinghouse of Simon Horridge.

'I'm here,' he said.

'As I see,' I said. 'I was expecting you. Pray be seated.'

'I will stand.'

'As you please, sir.'

'I have the plague. I have something on my foot.'

'Pray show me.'

The fellow sat down on that same chair he had refused but a moment before, unlaced his boot, and showed me a simple naevus under the heel.

'And pray how did you find this out? A man cannot see easily under his own heel.'

'That's none of your business.'

'That may be so, sir,' I said, detecting the reek of the bedchamber on his person. 'But it's the business of the poor young woman you've been with who is even now at her wits' end waiting for the first signs of the bubonic plague.'

I noticed also on the feet the unshapen digits not uncommon among the militia who must needs make do with ill-fitting boots, and moreover often go wetshod; and I noticed also swellings of the end joints of the fingers.

'They were naught but common women from Clywold,' he said.

'They?'

'Jane Pearce and Susan Knowles. They work the power loom. Happen they've already lowered themselves in the eyes of their kin.'

'So they deserve the plague? It behoves you as an officer of the King's men and a Christian to tell me where they dwell.'

The fellow gave cursory directions to a tenement building at the north end of Clywold.

'And your own name?'

He said his name was Thomas Hayward.

'Will I die?' he said.

'Yes,' I said. 'You will die.'

The sweat ran fast down his face but his mouth was set firm, and I pitied indeed the poor fellow for he showed the true grit of they who are fearful. For what man in his youth, looking at his own death, does not fear?

'You will die,' I continued, 'because we will die, every one of us. Most do not know the hour of their death. That is the greatest mystery and grace God has shown us, to keep from us the knowledge of the time of our death.'

'Is there not a remedy?'

'No, there is no remedy. What you have, Thomas Hayward, is a simple naevus under your heel. There is no remedy, but neither will it cause you harm. You do not have the plague.'

'I do not have the plague.'

'No.'

'I am not going to die in a sennight then?'

'I do not know when you will die, Thomas Hayward. Only God Almighty knows that. All I know is that you do not have the plague.'

'Then I am a fool,' he said.

'No,' I said. 'Not only did you seek the assistance of a practitioner you no doubt regarded as your natural enemy, but you divulged the names of those you believed to be affected, who may yet stand in need of remedies for other ills. That is great wisdom.'

'You misled me because you were at pains to spare the folks you'd tended.'

'Yes.'

'I could apprehend you.' Thomas Hayward was long lacing his boots.

'Yes.'

'I could take you in and get my fellows to screw the names of the loom breakers out of you.'

'You could but you will not.'

'No.'

'Go in peace then, Thomas Hayward. Return to me if you wish for a tincture to alleviate the fire in your toes and finger ends. The war will be lost while they are waiting for you to lace your boots.'

V

There were those who said at the time of the terror in the fair land of France that the knock on the door had been heard through all generations of mankind; that they who were within the hovel, the dwellinghouse or indeed the great chateau had been waiting for it since the beginning of time, wondering as every new day lightened in the east when it would come; whether it would wait until night after the candles had been quenched or whether it would be in the bright noonday when the city was athrong with folks going about their business, knowing naught of the ill-intentioned figure who approached because he was one of their own, lately hidden in the crowd of men and women.

And, for myself, as my cloak was got ready for the journey to seek out the dwellinghouse of Simon Horridge and my scrip prepared with that remedy I believed to be effective against the burning malady, the door of the dispensary was thrust rudely open.

She who entered was a woman of some forty summers, haggard of feature and unkempt. There were moreover the steps of others on the stairs, which surprised me not, for she herself had not the look about her of a woman who had thus arrived of her own free will.

'What brings you here, my good woman?' I said, it being ever my habit to fill my fearfulness with words. 'How far have you walked, and your feet in that condition?'

For indeed her boots were no more than meagre strips of sacking bound over and over and tied at the ankles.

She told me she was from Clywold. She had come to beg my assistance for one Jane Pearce who had given birth and was in a fever and the bairn none too wholesome either, sickly and puny as ever a child was, and opening his mouth into a small letter of "o" from which came ceaselessly the most piteous thin wail, she said, herself making mewing sounds as of the bairn. And his mother, Jane Pearce, was expected back at the loom that very day, and the women too frighted to appeal to the mercy of the master.

I asked the woman to be seated and take a draught of water.

'And where are your shoes, pray?'

She said she had sold them to another woman, being too sick to work and fain to do anything to earn her bread.

'And how come you to be sick?'

'It is not seemly for a woman to speak to a gentleman of such things, sir,' she said.

'Then if that's the case I will put some salve on your feet, my good woman. We all have feet, men and women both.'

She told me that she had been touched by the devil and now had a manner of canker. The devil's touch was at first no more than a lump the size of a coney's dung. Then it became larger and blackened and then broke out onto the surface of the flesh, weeping red and yellow matter and stinking something awful, which she knew not for herself but there were certain rough folks who had told her so.

And she knew not for a truth what she had done to be touched by the devil, lest it be her lewd conversation with the soldiers of the garrison, but what was a woman to do in hard times when hand weaving no longer paid than to turn to the power loom, and then only to be laid low and unable to work the loom, being that she was sick and had no pay. 'For it is hard work,' she said. So yes, she supposed she had done enough and more so as to entertain the devil, on those two counts if on no others, but what otherwise could she have done.

So I gave her a sweet-smelling poultice of agrimony, bugle and groundsel for the mark of the devil, to apply it herself in the secrecy of her dwellinghouse; knowing that this was a malignant canker against which there was no remedy once it had reached the state of putrefaction, the only salve being to make the patient comfortable and to ameliorate as far as it were possible the odour of it, which indeed had arrived with her as she entered the room in spite of the shawl she held tightly around her shoulders, of which odour she, having it with her all the time, could have had but little knowing; all this taking place in less time than the telling of it, for she had great anxiety to be away as I could observe by her repeated and affrighted looks towards the door.

'Begging your pardon, sir,' she said, 'but the cart is waiting and I was bidden to bring you without delay.'

'You were bidden? Then you did not come here of your own free will?' I said, 'or that of your friend Jane Pearce with the sick bairn?'

The woman looked towards the door again and was, as I could discern from her hesitation and the rising colour in her face, about to deliver a false statement and thereby give her poor mind yet more reason to believe she had been touched by the devil, when the door opened as if of itself and let in the darkness of the staircase, which from the look of terror on the poor woman was none other than the shadow of Satan himself.

'Sir?'

'Yes?'

'It is not the plague, sir?'

'No, it is not the plague.'

'We're waiting, Susan. Make haste.' The voice from the stairs was neither hillsman nor townsman, nor yet Satan, who though I was ever of the papist persuasion I had yet to meet in the town of York.

There was by the Monk-bar not a cart but a closed carriage drawn by two ill-fed horses, awaiting my boarding of it.

The air inside, such as it was, was rank with reeking straw and the sour breath of humankind, and indeed the contours of a fellow passenger at length emerged out of the darkness as well as those of the woman Susan, who remained in silence.

'It is nigh on five hours to Clywold,' I said. 'Might we draw open the blinds?'

'You're welcome to try,' the other passenger said, 'but you'll find them set closed. You're welcome to try, as I say. Happen you don't favour this manner of transport, sir, tumbling over the rough cobblestones of the town et cetera. It is like to upset the equilibrium in the head and make the subject bilious.'

And indeed the suspension on the carriage was poor; either that, or I had been touched by the poor woman's fear.

'Or happen there have been like journeys to stir the memory, sir,' the passenger continued. 'There is many a reason a body may turn to biliousness.'

When I awoke the carriage door was open and the woman Susan was gone into the blinding light of the sun, which was already in the decline. An acid water rose in my mouth.

'Answer me, sir.'

No doubt they around me were speaking the King's English yet I understood not a word.

Presently, though I had no knowledge of being taken to such a place, I found myself to be laid out on a trestle in some kind of outbuilding, bound across the thorax and knees, with a fellow on each side holding down my arms, whose faces I could not see.

'Are you going to answer?'

'What was the question?'

'I asked you the names and whereabouts of those scum of the earth you went to, charlatan.' He spoke of a day, which I heard as from a great distance. 'Or are we going to give him some encouragement? Encouragement, sir?'

A gust of mirth echoed briefly around the dark space, then subsided.

'This is likely to last out a chain of tallow.' There was a further gust of mirth.

'For the third time of asking ... But we forget, he's a papist. No doubt he don't know that formula. What is thy name, papist?'

'Don't forget he's a bad handler of the facts. Whatever the fellow says won't be the King's truth.'

'Aye, an he's a Frenchman.' There was another wave of merriment.

'Give the Frenchman some assistance. No doubt he ain't averse to the stink of charred flesh.' He addressed by name (a name I thought I knew well but have ever since forgotten) another figure who, as my eyes became accustomed to the darkness, I could discern standing at the far end of the place.

'Look at the light, sir. There, that didn't hurt, did it? Once again now ... and again ... and again ... and again ... I told you it wouldn't hurt.'

And I was as I thought climbing up steps, much worn and splintered, and uneven in height so that at every third step I faltered and stumbled, so often that I doubted if I would reach the top. The steps themselves moreover were blistered by the mid-day sun, so that my feet were as on fire. All around, yet becoming the more distant the higher I went, were the jeers and taunts of a crowd. And although I knew that the Lord God had appointed to the sky the hue of lapis lazuli and the whole scene was washed indeed in brightness I could see nothing for the blind-fold tied tightly around my face. And all the while a voice, measured and melodious enough, said the words ... 'and again ... and again ... and again ...' at each step until I could climb no more, at which extremity there was a great crash about my ears and I fell, hurtling down the steps until I believed I was again on the sweet earth in the land of England in the summer season. A stem of charlock grew nearby, lovely in the simplicity of its gold petals and dark leaves and beaded seed cases, and the sky was dazzling as the common alkanet is dazzling, and every blade of grass was made silver by the sun.

'There's nothing more to be screwed out of him.'

'A papist withal.'

Someone spat.

'Did I say anything?' The sound of a voice like to my own rose up to the rafters and returned thinly to the trestle on which I lay.

'He's trying to speak. What does the fellow say?'

'He's wanting to know if he gave anything.'

'You did, sir.' The fellow shouted as if I were scattered in my wits, which indeed I was. 'You gave the necessary. Under coercion, of course, sir. We have taken the liberty of applying one of your own salves to repair the mischief. Be on your way now, sir. You will find the dwellinghouse of Jane Pearce nigh on a furlong's journey south by the sign of the Stag.'

The woman whom I knew by the name of Susan looked away when I entered. Another woman was there, seated on a low stool nursing a bairn. A third person was seated by the table, a fellow whom I understood by the cut of his dress to be of some account. The room was ill-aired and had the odour of fever and vomitus, as well, faintly, of the fungating canker the poor woman Susan had described as the devil's touch. I took it that they present were accustomed to it and held their peace.

The man stood up. He was of some fifty summers, and as tall as I.

'Then I'll be away, my good woman.' A blessed breath of gathering frost entered the dwellinghouse as he left.

'You summoned me to see the bairn, Susan.' I said. Still she averted her eyes, and motioned to the other woman.

'Are you Jane Pearce, pray?'

'Yes.'

'Then I am come at the behest of Susan to see your bairn, Jane Pearce.'

She handed the child to the woman Susan who, still unable to meet my eyes, busied herself with laying the bairn on the table and removing such poor cloths as covered him. The little legs were puny and showed early signs of bowing, and the small face was puckered into a soundless misery.

'It is allus with them as works the looms.' Jane Pearce spoke for the first time. 'The same wi others an all. Thas bairns turn out to ha bad legs. Tis summat catching among them as are wi child.'

The doorway darkened and the man who had previously been in the room entered.

'How do you find the bairn, sir?' His manner carried a certain diffidence.

'It is a case of the rickets.'

'Rickets?'

'The bairn has need of sunshine and fresh milk. His little bones are not making. I have seen it before in bairns whose mothers work in the manufactories, who have scant sun for themselves or their bairns.'

'Susan Knowles and Jane Pearce have not been at my mill this last twelvemonth, sir. I understand they are among those women who have an alternative source of livelihood. It is a practice I care not to tolerate. However, we are bidden to care for the sinner though we despise the sin.'

For the first time Susan Knowles raised her head.

'Happen that were the case, Mr Gathercole, being as them that's unequal to the work at loom mus do other things or else starve, asking your pardon, sir. But at this moment in time me an my friend Jane Pearce we can't do neither one thing nor tother, being laid low wi the sickness like. We mus even bring ourselves to degradation an do badly to them as helps us.'

Which saying I took to be the contrition of Susan Knowles, who indeed, after she had uttered the words, was minded to look me in the eye, as I looked into hers, in which dwelt all the sorrows of the times.

And her speech was the gentle speech of the hill country. For though the music of the English tongue has ever been a mystery to me, I discern the various tunes of they who dwell in the hill country and they who dwell in the fair town of York. Yet he who delivered the coercion, whose name was said and indeed though I heard it I lost it in the instant, was neither of the hills nor of the town of York, being melodious in speech and like to no other.

VI

'Here we have the record of him as could not remember his own name, sir.'

'You may call me John, Luke. I've told you that before.'

Something about Luke Bower had begun to suggest to me that in the gracious gifts of the intellect he might be infinitely my superior, the more so as his attitude of humility became the more marked, as indeed he was my better in the agility of the pen.

'Thank you, sir.'

'So you have it here. Thank you, Luke . It is, as always, exquisitely done.'

'Thank you. Sir?'

'Yes, Luke?'

'I have a message, sir, relating to one Simon Horridge, to thank you for sending the preparation. The patient has improved greatly.'

Luke's shadow, picked out by the sun coming in through the open window, looked over my shoulder as I read; for the day was mild and indeed I had noted in many places in the dispensary garden the filling of the bud contrary to the early season's habit.

'Simon Horridge is welcome,' I said.

Luke Bower knew as well as I that the preparation intended for Simon Horridge was yet in my scrip, and that hanging behind the door in the dispensary.

'And how come you to have this message?' I said.

'From the selfsame fellow, him as could not remember his own name, sir, whose records you have in your hand.'

'And how did that fellow, who is as yet nameless, come by this message, Luke?'

'From some as who had been at the sign of the Blue Boar outside of Withersedge, sir.'

'And they?'

'From some itinerant musician fellow, sir.'

'Is this all God's honest truth, Luke?'

'Not all, sir.'

'And which part is true?'

'That a hand loom weaver by the name of Simon Horridge has received at the hands of a person unnamed a preparation which has been beneficial in soothing certain burns to his face, sir. You will let me know if there are any errors, sir.' Luke nodded towards his script which I held in my hand. 'Your hand is shaking, sir, more than the day's chill breeze would explain. You are not recovered quite from the mischief done to you. I suggest you be seated, sir, and lay the record on the table to read.'

Which I did, my eyes delighting the while in the cursive script which seemed to me to be dancing joyously across the page in spite of the heavy content it carried, which said thus:

"Record of him as does not know his own name ... who being a poor tinker found in the common way close by the Monk-bar in the town of York on the day of Hilary and in a bad way with certain of the finger nails wrenched most cruelly from their beds and no little sign of the Thumb Screw either was brought to the dwellinghouse of John Rivaulx apothecary by certain artisans going to their labours.

"Who had also clutched in his poor, maimed hand a rough and bloodied script the burden of which is appended hereto.

"Who being asked his name delivered nothing but a bloodied spittle and could say naught of any sense.

"And the fellow in question appeared but a poor tinker who might well have been dragged through the Kessle-wood backwards, so much leaf and twig he had about his person and so little of the natural converse of men.

"Wrought by injury to the person and the fright to the body and the draining away of the blood from the vital organs so that the poor fellow's face was white as the sheep on Capcar-hill and as senseless was he withal.

"Who receiving those remedies specific to the hurts he had borne was sent forth and asked to return on the morrow to see how he fares and to discover if his name had been restored to him."

'You do well, Luke,' I said, 'though your manner is a trifle archaic, more so than your customary manner, if I might say. How so?'

'I was aiming for consistency with the appended script, sir, which I have taken the liberty of unbloodying, though of a truth it turned my stomach, and I have smoothed it out so that it might be read. Here, sir.'

'Will you read it, Luke, if you would be so good, since you have familiarised yourself with the text.'

' "I ..." This is what be writ, sir, and tis lacking in learning. " ... of my own free will and A coard declare and solemly sware that I will never reveal to aney person or persons aney thing that may lead to discovery of the same Either in or by word sign or action as may lead to aney Discovery under the penalty of being sent out of this world by the first Brether that may meet me. Furthermore I do sware that I will punish by Death aney Trater or Traters should aney arise up amongst us. I will persue with unceaceing vengeance should he fly to the verge of Statude. I will be grist true sober and faithful in all my dealgs with all my brothers SO HELP GOD TO KEEP THIS MY OATH UNVIOLATED AMEN." Tis done now, sir.'

'Is that what I think it to be, Luke? I have not set eyes on such a tract before.'

'Tis the oath, sir. Tis all over the world.'

'How do you make that out, Luke. All the world?'

'It was but a figure of speech, sir, no more. It was to say that tis known.'

The fellow whom Luke had described as a poor tinker returned the next day in no greater command of his tongue than previously. The wounds on his left hand had responded to an application of elm, but the binding had been removed from the right thumb, and the wound, far from mending, had begun to fester.

'Why think you this has happened, Luke?' I said. 'See, the wounds that have been covered up are doing well but those uncovered are doing ill.'

'I would say, sir, that exposure to the air has had some contrary effect.'

'And would you say that the common dirt of the town of York has any bearing on this case?'

'I would say the mischief is more like to have been done by exposure to the air, sir. Everyone knows that a body as is indisposed must be confined to his bed. The same with a wound; it must needs be hidden from sight. Think of the plague, sir, where those as had it were shut in their dwellings.'

'We will leave nothing to chance in this case, Luke. Pray bring some water and we will bathe the wound first before applying the elm again and also bugle for the fester, and then we will replace the binding.'

Meanwhile the poor fellow was trying to speak but was making no better progress than the day before. Indeed he was faring the worse, since on the yesterday he had opened his mouth a little, but now no more than a florin piece, and there came on his breath also a most foul and noisome odour.

'Luke, pray bring some warm water,' I said, since my assistant had made no effort to do so. 'And pray bring some cold water for the patient to drink.'

Then I bid the poor fellow try as well as he might to open his mouth and tip his head so that the crown was resting on the back of the chair, for although his speech was defective his understanding seemed not so, and indeed a spasm of terror passed over his face as I approached with the candle.

'It is but to look, my good man,' I said. 'Do not take fright.' For I was put in mind of my own ordeal in the outbuilding nigh to Clywold.

It was as I thought. Instead of the poor fellow's tongue, as far as I could see, for he could open his mouth but little, was naught but a gaping void and the blood so bubbling up from the hurt that he was like to choke upon it.

'Where does this poor fellow live?'

Luke Bower had placed a basin of water on the table and was standing at a distance with his arms folded.

'Sir?'

'Where does he dwell?'

'Why do you ask me, sir?'

'Because you know most things, Luke.'

'Well then, sir, since you ask, the fellow dwells here. I know not where he dwelt last week, sir, and I know not where he will dwell in a twelve month. But I can follow the convolutions of your thoughts, sir, which run to the conclusion that the fellow seated here, who cannot remember his own name, sir, must if he wishes to stay alive in this world be offered some safe haven. That being the closed off chamber of your own dwellinghouse, sir. That is what you are thinking, is it not? Though I would not mention it to another living soul,' Luke continued. 'Happen you took this lodging for the selfsame reason, namely that there is a part of it accessible from the tallow chandler, though that fellow knows it not, and a part also from the house of mercy, which no persons else need be aware of, sir. Which is, in short, a secret chamber.'

'Then how does Luke Bower know of it, pray?' I said.

'Sir?'

'And presumably I now have no need of a secret chamber, Luke?'

'One never knows for certain what fires might reignite over yonder' (Luke jerked his head in a direction which I took to be that of the fair land of France) 'but you are safe for the present time, sir, lest danger lurks in giving salves to him as cannot remember his own name, which eventuality is not for me to say. If it pleases you, sir, I know of a good woman who will with a good heart tend him as cannot remember his own name.'

The subject of this converse was meanwhile looking from one to the other of us. And I have to say, because he had lost the faculty of speech, we, as is the common manner among all folks, talked in his presence as if he wasn't in his right mind, and loudly withal as if he were deficient in his hearing.

'Come, my good fellow,' I said, still as if he were slow of wit, 'we will show you where you may dwell in safety until you have recovered your strength. There is a good woman who will nurse you back to whatever health of body and mind the Lord God Almighty sees fit to give back to you.'

All, to my shame, as if the poor fellow had not been seated there for the past half of an hour hearing what we spoke of, whereupon he made a feeble gesture with his maimed hand.

'He asks for the means of writing, sir,' said Luke. 'With your leave I will bring him a quire of paper. Twill keep him occupied, sir.'

It was at that moment in time, as the tinker, as so we called him, rose to his feet and stood there faltering, a sorry spectacle in a shaft of the declining sun, which I have ever considered to be the most melancholy, that the intention came to me: namely to glean such writings as I could, not only from the good Hannah Gaut for the reason of her modesty but also from whatever witnesses came my way, and to preserve them as a record of those troubled times.

And I have to say that simultaneously I had a less than charitable mindfulness of my scribe Luke Bower, nimble of wit as he was, and always one step in front of me, as runners in a race. Which mindfulness was justified when he returned to the dispensary after settling the poor fellow in the secret chamber and accessing the help of the good woman he had spoken of.

'Sir?'

'Luke?'

'Him as cannot remember his own name, sir, he's as well as may be and the woman will nurse his hurts and prepare whatever he can take in the way of refreshment.'

'Who is this woman, Luke? She must be paid.'

'Regarding the former, sir, she is to be relied upon. Regarding the latter, she is resident in the house of mercy and the deed she does is sufficient recompense. So she says. Sir?'

'Yes, Luke.'

'It strikes me, sir, though happen it meets not with your approval, but you may wish to preserve a narrative of the present times, sir. Which asking your pardon is only but a thought and may not be pleasing to you. For trouble may be afoot, sir, if you take my meaning.'

VII

I know not what mischievous angel gives men and women changefulness of mind, or by what means, divine or otherwise, the crowd is one day brought to the foot of the gallows-tree and the next sent dancing in the streets.

For in those sombre times when dawn saw many an ashen face catch the last of the world's light any spectacle out of the ordinary ushered in the excuse for merriment. And indeed I suspected it was because of the shadow of the gallows-tree rather than in spite of it that the throng looked for diversion wherever it might be found.

'Did you ... you know, sir ... yesterday?' Luke said on such a morrow

'You know I did, Luke,' I said. 'It is my custom and my duty. To ignore such a practice is to condone it.'

'And what did you find, sir?' he said, no doubt wishing me to believe that his habit of sitting in the shadow of the gallows-tree had fallen off since he had been in my employ.

'Another poor young woman arraigned for heaven knows what trifling misdemeanour and sent out of this world before she had time for amendment of life,' I said.

'That way of speaking does not sound papist, sir, begging your pardon, though I know not what papist is, never having been in such a place.'

'You know I attend where I can, papist or otherwise, in a spirit of enquiry. The words of the service, whatever they be, cling like the seeds of the dactylis on a summer's day. What else did you wish to know, Luke?'

'If the young woman had any maladies or distortions that you observed, sir.'

By which I knew that my scribe Luke Bower had been present on the yesterday, though for what purpose I knew not, and I liked not to ask.

'She did, Luke, as you yourself know,' I said. 'She manifested a certain lowness in stature by which I deduced that she had shortening of the limbs caused in turn by the softening of the bones characteristic of the condition known as the rickets, which suspicion was later confirmed when I paid a visit to her place of rest. I do not know what the answer is, Luke. For nowhere I believe in the scriptures does it say that the life of a young woman may be required of her at any hands save those of the Father who deals mercifully with all at their appointed time. And indeed to reft another of life is putting on he who does the act of execution a burden too great for any man to bear.'

'Sir? You have said that the condition is prevalent among those young women who work in the manufactories who lack the gladdening rays of the sun. I have writ it in the records.'

'That may well be, but I was referring to the other matter, Luke. It is a wonder that the gallows-tree has not fallen down for all the custom it gets. Pray open the window and tell me what there is abroad. If it is the dregs of yesterday's spectacle I want none of it.'

For indeed there was a cacophony more than usual in the thoroughfares around the Monk-bar, and it needed not that the window should be open to hear it; such was the noise of it.

'Come and see, sir.'

Into the distance, in Jewbury and the Ald-wark, and indeed as far as Peter-gate the throng surged and swayed like a primitive living organism, rippling and seething as it moved forwards. In the centre, looking taller than all around, was a fellow of foreign appearance similar to my own, dark haired and dark browed, and carrying on his back a case much like the casing of a viol but infinitely larger; and all the while they in the crowd were making to touch the object as they would a sacred thing. And a merry noise rose up on all sides as if the folks had not been those very ones that crowded underneath the gallows-tree the day before.

Yet I must say that I, and I could tell by the kindling of his eye, Luke Bower also, was minded to join the throng and follow after the stranger. For in those times, and in every time before and after, humankind would seek out any diversion from the arduous journey of the soul. And I was minded to ask Luke Bower's opinion, because I knew not what this extraordinary musical instrument might be named or indeed who was the stranger labouring with it through the crowd, jostled and importuned as if he were Christ the Saviour himself. Yet I knew that if I held my peace Luke Bower would without any prompting from me deliver the information I sought, having, as I have noted before in these pages, the faculty of looking into my head.

'If it pleases you, sir, we will venture forth to hear the music of the double bass, for so they say it is though I would not have known it myself,' said Luke. 'And, sir, if I might be so bold, pray secure the door to the dwellinghouse, since he as cannot remember his own name is there, sir. And, sir, if we follow those' (he jerked his head towards the throng) 'we will be in the presence of the great Domenico Jommelli, repeating only, sir, what I have by hearsay for I know not of such matters myself,' he added.

Which Domenico Jommelli we could see amid the slow throng more than a furlong ahead of us, so tall was the case he carried, looking for all the world as if it were a giant of a man he bore on his back.

'It is to be hoped that the room is spacious enough, Luke, for such a throng will be starved of breath if they are all to crowd into one place.'

'It will be, sir,' said Luke, 'for most of these folk have come abroad only for the excuse of making holiday. Happen they have not come to hear the great Jommelli play, which for all I know, though I know not, will sorely try the ears of they who hear.'

'You have heard talk of his music also then, Luke,' I said.

'No, sir,' said Luke. 'Not yet. If I am not mistaken, sir, there will be someone near at hand needing assistance before too long. It is a happy chance that we ventured out, is it not?'

'Then I rely on you to find that person needing assistance,' I said.

Which Luke Bower did, before we had travelled another furlong's length, seeing with his sharp eyes at a far distance from us a knot in the crowd like to an eddy in a stream, accompanied by a commotion of voices raised above the rest.

'The falling sickness! Give her room!' yet surging the more about the afflicted one on the ground.

And it was no great wonder that any one should fall, pressed on all sides by the throng with their odours of body and breath. For when we reached the patient and little enough space had cleared around her I perceived also that she was slight in habitus and stature and would have been most easily overwhelmed.

She was opening her eyes and attempting to sit up, assisted by two women. In her plain but decent dress she could have been a servant in a privileged household. She had a cloud of bright hair like the fire of the western sky at sunset. My scribe Luke Bower whistled under his breath.

'Luke, pray make space in the crowd,' I said, for he was indeed disabled by the sight of the damsel. 'The patient is oppressed by all of us hovering about her. We will give her bryony for the falling sickness, which if the malady proves to be something other can do no harm.'

'They will go, sir,' said Luke, coming to himself. 'They will be away when they see she is alive.'

Which surely was the case; for the crowd thinned, seeing that the young woman was awake and sentient, all but the two good women who had offered assistance, and a gentleman, whose person I had not noticed in the mêlée, but who now came forward and most tenderly helped the young woman to her feet.

'We must needs return home, Ellie,' he said. 'I will not subject you to the press of the crowd and cause you to take ill.'

'I am myself again, Martin,' said the young woman. 'Pray let us go on. See, the crowd has cleared now.'

'What think you, sir?' The young woman's companion paled slightly as he addressed me. 'The young lady wishes to hear the great Jommelli and yet, as you can see, she is scarcely equal to the rigours of the journey.'

'You also wish to hear the great Jommelli, Martin,' said the young woman. 'You as much as I if not more.' She turned to me. 'What say you, sir?'

'You may go to hear the great Jommelli,' I said, 'so long as the gentleman is in agreement. The crowd has thinned and you have more air. I will leave with you some thyme to be held to your face in the event that you take ill again. She will grieve the more, sir,' I said to her companion, 'on your account as well as her own, if she goes back home having come so far.'

'So far?' he said. 'Why so far?'

'It was but a manner of speech, sir,' I said. 'I know not how far you have journeyed. All I know is that my scribe and I have travelled this last hour of the day and have made little enough progress, though we could have gone three leagues in the time.'

And indeed, he whom they called the great Jommelli had fared little better. Ahead of us he was still visible with the double bass on his back, impeded by the throng and yet taking the throng with him, for all the world like a swarm of bees clinging to his person as he laboured towards the stationers' hall.

'Luke, I fear that your enthusiasm for the music of the double bass runs ahead of you,' I said, for I could see that my scribe was minded to follow close on the heels of the young woman, and was about to cover on swift feet the distance between ourselves and her. 'What an error of judgement, having warned her against the press of the crowd, if we ourselves were to hem her in and cause her more hurt.'

'You have made your case, sir,' he said.

That which they called the double bass stood in the vestibule of the stationers' hall outside its great housing, looking much like that which I knew as the violone, with the lights of the coloured glass windows glancing off its wooden surface, and surrounded on all sides by folks who, from the appearance of their dress and the manner of their speech, and indeed from the simplicity of their curiosity, seemed to have come from the hill country, hesitant as they were and timid, as of a wild beast.

Jommelli stood in their midst, the bow in his right hand, addressing them thus,

'See the three strings of the double bass, that is the warp. And see the bow, this is the weft which will weave the music ...' and with words of that ilk, until I marvelled how he knew of the concerns of the hill dwellers of these parts and their livelihoods. And I would have made a remark to that effect to Luke Bower my scribe, but seeing the spark in his eye, which was searching the crowd for the young woman who was lately our patient, I held my peace.

VIII

So I was minded, after Domenico Jommelli had finished playing and before the crowd gathered again to escort him beyond the city wall, to seek him out and ask him how he, a native of the land of Italy by name though his speech contradicted the fact, knew of the livelihoods of the hill dwellers. Having this in my thoughts, I looked for Luke Bower but could find him nowhere; and indeed, as I considered when I had seen him last I concluded that it was before the proceedings had begun; and so rapt was I in the extraordinary music, gruff as it was and as from a place under the ground, though at times reaching heaven itself, that I had not given so much as a passing remembrance to the truth that I was not in the hall on my own and the sole witness to such alchemy. For indeed the word had spread and right up to the last note they of the town of York and the hills afar off continued to press into the stationers' hall.

And I know not what the melodies were for they were neither of my gracious compatriot Marais, nor yet of one Bach whose name I had heard but seldom his airs, he being of a grey teutonic cast and inimical to the ears of a Frenchman, and I have to say also more to the protestant liking. For there were those of my own country, who caring little for melody lest it be that of Rouget de Lisle and his like, knew this, that they would flee a hundred leagues from those tunes issuing out of the protestant chapel.

Yet my intention to speak with Domenico Jommelli came to naught for there was another with a like mind, who even as I had gathered up my courage to speak to the musician, had engaged him first, and I made to go away. Though not without taking in the whole scene, that a man who from his dress and demeanour was a hand weaver from the hill country, whose face indeed bore a resemblance to one I had seen but recently, had trod where I feared to.

For I will say this here, as a reason for seeking out Luke Bower, that though he is oft an irritant even as the sting of the Urtica dioica is an irritant, he has this grace, that he will go where I fear to go on account of a natural timidity which has pursued me from infancy, and also on account of a reluctance to manifest myself in any other role in the theatre of life than that of a common apothecary; the Urtica dioica having this property also, that it revives even as it irritates.

Both the musician and the young man from hills, seeing me, gestured that I should wait. But I did not. Instead I left forthwith, taking away with me the sudden imprint of their faces on my mind: Jommelli, the eloquent musician whom all supposed to be a Tuscan, whose sleeve had slipped during the rendering of the music to reveal for all to see the marks of some manner of coercion; and the young man from the hills, who, as I had perceived from the stooped posture already evident about the shoulder girdle, was a hand weaver; having this in common that, though they were separated in age and station, each carried with him the trappings of eternity.

And I know not whether it was the breeze springing up that caused a door to clang, but I was again on a topmost step, blindfolded and with the baying crowd below, awaiting a final cataclysm which would surely propel me into the next world; having no more awareness until I was once more outside the stationers' hall and Luke Bower was at my side.

'... from which I gather that the music of Domenico Jommelli was something out of this world since it has landed you in such a trance,' he was saying. 'And before you ask my thoughts on the occasion' (Luke jerked his head towards the stationers' hall where they were even then closing the doors) 'which, sir, you are about to do as soon as you have recovered yourself, I will tell you that I heard not a thing of it, with the result that I have reached this present place in the Goodram-gate with my patience and my powers of intellect untried. And

I will now escort you home, sir, since the pallor on your face indicates that you have had a vision of the next world, which from the look of you, sir, is not a place I would hasten to visit myself.'

Luke jerked his head towards the luminous sky where a flight of rooks was going home to roost. And it came to me in passing that the winter season was done once more and the sweet spring was come, for I am ever thankful to have lived so long in this fair world as to see the earth wake again.

Thus my scribe continued his patter all the way from the stationers' hall to the lodging close by the Monk-bar, though I knew not what he said. Nor did I know in all of that time with any certainty where I was, whether climbing towards some final and deafening sound or in a place beneath the sentient world where the music of the double bass had its birth.

'Sir, we are preceded,' said Luke as we approached the Monk-gate. 'You will have to return from whatever next world you have been in and attend to the patients at present waiting outside your door.'

'I am not deaf, Luke,' I said, 'nor am I lame.'

'That may be so, sir.' Luke was still speaking at the utmost of his voice and pulling me along by the sleeve. 'But you have heard not a word this last quarter hour, nor would you have found your way back had I not assisted. The young woman as had the falling sickness and the gentleman are waiting at the apothecary's door. Begging your pardon, sir, you are the apothecary. I thought I might bring that situation to your notice, sir.'

I bade Luke approach the dwellinghouse through the concealed entrance and make ready the dispensary, though he was so unwilling to let go my sleeve that I was bound to admit to myself that he might after all be a fellow of good intentions.

There are some that will come to the apothecary by night, waiting for the whisper of the dark to bring their maladies and forgetful in their shame of the fact that underneath the skin all are the same and are prey to the same maladies. Others will come in the brazen daylight hidden by the raucous throng, out of sight because they are seen by many.

Ellie Bright was of the latter; or I might say Martin Gathercole, since left to her own devices she may not have thought sufficiently of herself, or had the means to venture on her own; or indeed had she not been in the throng that day it is likely that her malady would have been passed by.

'Martin Gathercole, sir.' The visitor held out his hand. 'And this is Ellie Bright.'

'John Rivaulx,' I said. 'The pronunciation perplexes many people. It is from the French, spelt R I V A U L X but pronounced Reevo.'

My tongue was running away with me to such an extent that I wondered indeed if my wits were scattered also and that my scribe had said the truth.

'We have met before, Mr Gathercole, I seem to remember, though I cannot recall quite where.'

'Why, sir, it was but a few hours since on the way to hear the playing of the great Jommelli. My companion had fainted owing to the press of the crowd. Perhaps, sir, your mind was so bent on restoring her to health that you scarce noticed me.'

'That may well be so, sir. I am sure you say truly. My assistant will prepare a draught for your refreshment,' I said, all the time trying to gather my scattered wits as one would the teasel plant by the beck side at the back end of the year. For I had gone far in search of my wits. Indeed, I had gone the day's journey up to Clywold and to the dwellinghouse of Jane Pearce and Susan Knowles, where I had discerned in the deep shadow in the corner of the room the person of Martin Gathercole, who even now was present in the dispensary.

Meanwhile the young woman at his side was addressing me in the voice of an angel from heaven.

'Sir, I thank you for making me better. If it had not been for the remedy we would have returned home with great disappointment. And we are grateful to your assistant also.'

For my scribe Luke Bower, whom I judged from the length of time it had taken to come to the front entrance had been engaged in a lengthy one-sided conversation with he that we called the tinker closeted in the secret chamber, had returned with a draught of water.

The young woman carried on her person the insignia of the condition known as the rickets, having a forward deformity of the spine and shortness of stature which I deduced to be the result of bowing of the bones in the leg rather than achondroplasia, her arms being adequate in length. I also observed a hammer deformity of the third finger of her right hand unlike any contracture I had previously seen, though this did not appear to cause her concern any more than did the condition of rachitis. Rather she was concerned only about the fact that she had importuned her companion and wished not so to importune him again.

'Even though I don't venture out to any great extent, sir' she concluded.

I gathered also, looking at Ellie Bright's fair face, and noting her pallor and the violet shadows under her eyes, that it was the time of her courses. For much is to be understood without giving the offence of words to a patient.

'My assistant will dispense more of the remedy which restored you today,' I said. For Luke had fallen into a transfixed state and stood much in need of employment. 'And I prescribe also the gladdening rays of the sun to strengthen your frame, as I perceive you have suffered some hurt to your spine, for which mischief we must give you the medicine of the tamarisk and the ash.'

'It is nothing of note in my back, sir,' said the young woman. 'Indeed, I stay much in the house for fear of falling, do I not, Martin?'

'Miss Bright's health is protected as far as possible.' Her companion said this uneasily, and as he did so straightened his neckerchief with the right hand, at which insignificant gesture the very same deformity which I had observed in the young woman's third finger became visible. And I reflected not for the first time that anomalies will replicate themselves in several generations of patients, indeed sometimes missing one generation and reappearing in the next. I perceived also, in

Martin Gathercole's face, a sudden access of the blood, which was neither anger nor shame.

'You are in pain, sir?' I said.

'You must tell the gentleman, Martin,' said the young woman.

'Nay, Ellie,' he said. 'It will pass. But you may tell the gentleman if it pleases you.'

'He is in pain in his side, sir,' the young woman said, 'sometimes to the extent that he is rolling on the floor with it and I am fearful when he is in that condition he will breathe his last.'

By which I understood that the good man was afflicted with the stone, for such is the agony of it that they suffering will writhe even on the floor, as well as manifesting a sudden access of blood to the face, which I had lately noticed in Martin Gathercole.

I bade Luke take him to the dispensary and provide him with a preparation of tansy and white saxifrage for the relief of the stone, for having returned with the young woman's remedy he was again leaning against the door frame in a state of abstraction.

'Recently, sir,' the young woman continued when he was gone, 'there have been events up beyond Clywold which have caused great distress and have brought on the illness.'

And I observed that the more she gave her account, even though it was of others and not of herself, the colour returned to her fair face, which caused me to reflect yet again that there might be great good to the patient to be drawn from the talking remedy. So much so that I resolved to extract what I could of the stories of other patients also, but only insofar as I considered the practice beneficial to their treatment.

'What is happening beyond Clywold hardly touches us here in York,' I said, knowing that she needed but little to continue her discourse.

'There are those in the hill country who are obliged to shut themselves up in their homesteads after dark, sir. I've heard tell of men with blackened faces and their tunics turned outsides in for fear of recognition, who go out by night bent on doing mischief to the shearing frames. And indeed, sir, I fear that the lips of all in those parts are sealed on account of reprisals.'

'Are you afraid, my dear young woman?' I said, knowing not how to address her rightly, for I judged her to be part servant and part angel.

'Not for myself, sir,' she said, 'but there are many round about who despise Martin for adopting the shearing frame, and would do him harm if they had the means.'

'And who are these people?' I said.

'I do not know, sir,' she said. 'Some say they are trouble makers brought in from over the hills. Others say they are of the selfsame folks abroad in the town who will pass the time of day as if nothing ailed.'

'How has this come to pass?'

'Why, sir, some say it is the machines that take the work from the small masters because more cloth is finished where there is the machine. But whether or not, Martin is a good man who does no ill to his workers, and there are many who earn their daily bread at the mill who would else starve.'

Then I asked the young woman if she had aught of pain about her person, and gave her again thyme and also lavender, bidding her to take rest at those times when she was like to faint away, knowing that she understood well the prescription. Having done which I bade Luke Bower accompany the patients to the Monk-gate, which indeed I would have done myself but that my scribe was scarce able to bide his time until he was in the sweet presence of Ellie Bright again.

IX

I thought again of the woman from the hill country, Hannah Gaut and of the shadows under her eyes, which surely with the much derided knowledge of hindsight were the result of hunger and grief in equal measure. Though how the faces of Hannah Gaut and her husband came back to me I did not know until the next day , my assistant Luke having leave to see his kindred, yet I knew not that he had any. Indeed, I knew little of him in any respect for all his talk, less than he knew of me, though I had told him but little.

Certain pages were lying on the table in the dispensary, which I perceived were the first from "him as does not know his own name" as the heading in Luke's exquisite hand indicated. And having lifted the first I had no little surprise in finding some degree of penmanship, I knew not how, whether done with the maimed hand or the sound; and I wondered also, how such was acquired in persons otherwise of a reduced state.

"I was yonder of Endcliffe-tor by night three weeks gone or so," the poor fellow had written, "taking rest as it be my custom at the foot of stone wall when I was waked by a great hord of menfolks with blacked visage awearing motley and hatted so as I knew not ther faces only from the aspex of them I surmised they were those as follow the trade of cropping tho weavers was among them perchance and each having an hamer and ax and trampint wi not a word among the lot o them and making as far as I were concerned for mill at Beckwith."

The remainder had, I noticed, been transcribed by Luke Bower, as the hand of the tinker became little better than an

53

arachnoid wandering drunkenly across the page, so many blots of ink were there, and I fear also splatters of blood, as if the poor fellow's mouth had fallen open with the mental and physical ardours of telling his tale. And I have to say also that Luke had extracted some sense from what were random excursions of the pen, more than I could have done myself; and I resolved to tell him so before he had further occasion to nettle me and the inclination to do so left me.

"I thought I was not seen," Luke's transcript continued, "and I ventured out of my resting place at the foot of a stone wall to watch the croppers and others with blacked faces. But one of the number lingered in the cover of a growth of gorse as I believed for the course of nature and saw me yet said not a word. And I slept not a drop that night for fear but kept myself close into the wall seeing all kinds of mischief arising like spirits out of the bushes and the rocks and with blacked faces which when morning came returned back to themselves. And the terror were still on me …"

Luke's narrative here came to a close and I feared there was no more to be understood from the tinker, as so I called him without any firm reason. But Luke, when he returned from seeing his kinsfolk or for whatever other reason he had taken leave, assured me that him as could not remember his own name was willing to write more, and indeed appeared to be restored in health by imparting his recollections, having been promised that anything he wrote would not be passed to any other soul save my scribe Luke Bower and myself, even though the act of committing words to paper taxed his little strength.

So I resolved to visit the patient and put Luke's assertion to the proof, that the telling of his story had indeed assisted the poor tinker fellow in his recovery. And I found his mouth repairing and clean, whether by means of the remedy I had given, or the healthful agency of the patient's own saliva which I have observed on many previous occasions is a powerful restorative, or else the effect of committing to paper the fearful sufferings he had undergone.

I did not notice at first, so bent was I on visiting the patient, that a figure stood half concealed in the shadow cast by the low beams, who, as soon as I started examining the patient, slipped covertly away without my knowing, for she was no longer there when I looked again. I say she, for I presumed the figure to have been that of the good woman from the house of mercy whom Luke had engaged as nurse, and whom, if I had had the opportunity I would have thanked from the depths of my heart, for few could have been trusted with such work, or indeed could have viewed with equanimity the amputation of the tongue.

Neither did Luke appear to know the name of the woman, which ignorance I doubted as he knew the name of well nigh every man and woman within a five furlong radius of the Monk-bar.

'She is from the house of mercy, sir,' he said.

'I know that, Luke,' I said. 'You have already told me.'

'She is to be trusted with a secret, sir. She won't talk.'

'I'm not disputing it, Luke. How is it that you know of her goodness and yet have not found out her name?'

At which Luke's face closed and there was nothing further to be gained from him.

'By your leave, sir,' he said, 'a change of linen will be sent from the house of mercy for him as does not know his own name. By your leave, sir, they are delivering it at this moment.'

Which simple requirement had not passed through my mind, so unfamiliar was I with the uses of a hospice.

'Forgive me, Luke, I had not thought of the practicality of linen. You have done well. I will take it down to the poor fellow.'

She from the house of mercy was not there, having done, as I thought, what was required of her in attending to the patient and his lodging place. Had she been there and offered her assistance to the patient in easing the sleeve of the clean shirt over his maimed right hand the fact may have remained hidden from me, namely that for such a reduced fellow the muscles of the right arm, in particular m.biceps and m.triceps, were developed to the extent that a working man's are developed. And I observed moreover that the sinews of the maimed right hand were the same. And moreover that if the fellow were recently a tinker, of which indeed we had no confirmation but word of mouth and not from the fellow himself, he had been for many years a working man.

'My good fellow, you have fine muscles,' I said, whereupon the tinker, though indeed he had never said he was such for he came to us in a state of voicelessness, made as well as he might the action of the cropping shears in dumb show; leaving me nonplussed and ignorant as to who should be perpetrating such torments to the poor fellow in my presence and to others, and indeed to myself. And it came to me that the practice might well be random and used indiscriminately, and no man may ever know the truth. For it was not impossible that the same might be done by both sides, whether they be cloth workers driven by hunger and grievance or those burdened with the task of suppressing the so-called rebels, or indeed they ordering the militias.

'So you are a cropper?' I said. 'That is a fine trade and a worthy one, though in truth and to my shame I know little enough but that certain of they are reft of their livelihoods.'

And I believe he whom we had lately thought to be a tinker would have attempted an answer of sorts in dumb show but that the door opened and the veiled woman from the house of mercy stood there, who seeing me still to be present went silently away. Yet not before something in her carriage and in the directness of her gaze, albeit that the veil covered the most of her face, evoked in me the most tender remembrance.

'How does that good woman call herself?' I said to the patient, 'she who cares for you?'

Whereupon the poor fellow took up the pen in his left hand, dipped it in the vessel of ink, and would have made, I believe, to form a name. But at the last moment he did not, laying down the pen and shaking his head.

'What do they call the good woman who tends that poor fellow?' I asked Luke again, thinking he might have forgotten that I had already asked the very same question. But again he said he did not know, and said moreover that we need have no fear on account of her trustworthiness for she would not talk.

'Will not or cannot?' I said.

'Begging your pardon, sir,' said Luke, 'there was a knocking on the door while you were with him as does not remember his own name' (jerking his head towards the concealed chamber) 'and I asked the party to come back two hours after the noonday, sir.'

'And who is this party, Luke?'

'You'll know him, sir. That is to say, very likely you will not know him, but when you hear the speech of him and look into his face you'll have encountered him before.'

'Did he say what ails him?'

'Not in so many words, sir. He will no doubt have settled himself by two hours after the noonday. Or he might not, if you follow my drift, sir.'

Which I did not, not the least ripple of it.

'Meanwhile I will prepare the remedies, sir,' said Luke.

'You don't know for certain what the patient's complaint is, Luke.'

'That I don't, sir,' said Luke, 'but begging your pardon I will prepare the remedies. He will tell you about a dream he has had. I said to him, sir, as you might be interested in his dream.'

'And since when has my speciality been dreams, Luke?'

'That I know not, sir,' said Luke, 'but nevertheless the party will tell you about his dream.'

The fine face and the quiet voice of the patient told me of a certainty who he was, and I was once more struck with wonder that the human flux should carry in it the die of life. For this young man carried as surely as if an artist had painted him, for indeed the Lord God is an exquisite artist, as I have only to see the flowers of the field to confirm, half the nature of his mother and half that of his father. He held out his hand.

'Robert Gaut.'

The finger ends of the other hand, I noticed, showed the signs of early callus, and the whole hand appeared unnaturally stretched.

'That will mend,' said Robert Gaut. 'It is early days.'

'I was fearing mischief,' I said, 'as happens more than enough in these times. How came your hand like that?'

'I am a student of that they call the double bass.'

'Ah, indeed, pray let me see, my good man. If you will permit me I will give you a preparation of groundsel which will ease the fire in the sinews of your hand. As will the healing balm of time, since you say it is yet early days.'

'That is not what I came here for. I saw you waiting after the recital and would have spoken to you then, but you did not stay.'

'I wished not to interrupt your converse with Domenico Jommelli.'

'It was about nothing of consequence. I was sorry you went away.'

'Neither was my query such that the great man should have been detained,' I said. 'I wished but to ask him how he knew to talk with the hill people of their own livelihoods. But, sir, forgive me, I am letting my prattle get the better of me.'

For my words were running away with me even as I strove to cleanse my mind of the vision I had had of him, and indeed of the musician, as I waited in the stationers' hall, as marked out for eternity.

'I came here for my parents,' said Robert Gaut.

'At their behest?'

'No, they do not know I am here. You would wish to see them, sir?'

'Indeed yes,' I said. 'But go on, my good man. There may yet be some counsel you might carry to them. You will be speaking with them on the morrow?' For I gathered he had come a day's journey from the hill country.

'No.'

Robert Gaut, after some hesitation, related accurately and in some detail the ills of Hannah Gaut and her husband

Zephaniah, saying that his mother was oppressed by the cries of her untimely delivered bairns and other morbid soundings in her ears until he sometimes feared for her reason, and that his father Zephaniah though somewhat past the prime of his life was losing his strength and vigour daily, and it would now be the journey of seven hours to carry the weft whereas it had formerly been but four hours.

'If the weft were there for the carrying,' said Robert Gaut, 'for the small masters are losing ground to the mills.'

And I perceived a great bitterness in his voice, whether directed at his father Zephaniah or at the calamitous times, I knew not.

'And there is surely no blame in heaven or earth in using such means as there are,' continued Robert Gaut, 'but happen you are of the opposite persuasion.'

'A physician is neither of one persuasion nor the other,' I said. 'As to blame, on earth there is blame enough, as you are no doubt aware. I cannot answer for heaven. But pray be seated, my good man.' For all this time he had remained on his feet, restlessly picking up and putting down Luke's pen which lay on the table. 'Tell me your story, I beg you.'

'One night I approached the homestead,' began Robert Gaut. 'It was some little time before dawn. I knew that by the lightening of the sky east of Holmroyd. Yet there were stars, as bright as ever I knew them, with the great Orion stretched out over my head like a vast sheet of cloth on the tenter. There was a dim light inside the homestead, by which I knew that he within had already risen from his bed and was preparing to walk over the hills to collect the weft. I could see his shadow moving around inside, for the shutter was open. The man was singing under his breath, a tuneless ditty which drove me to distraction the longer I listened to it. I can't tell you how much this senseless tune enraged me, so much that I would have laid violent hands on the singer and taken him by the throat and throttled the tune out of him. I willed him to stop his singing but he did not. Rather it grew the louder as he walked to and fro across the room eating a crust of bread to break his fast and donning his outer garments, for indeed his eating did not still the tune.

'The singing grew so loud to me that I could bear it no longer. I threw my weight against the door, which yielded easily and flew back, upsetting the singer so that he fell heavily to the ground. Before I could muster any gentle and forgiving thoughts my hands were fastening around his throat, and as I just said, sir, squeezing the tune out of him. Which singing continued, not in any way inhibited by the throttling it was suffering, but, indeed, it was as strong as before and I could not stop it, though the singer's head was lifeless in my hands and the eyes had rolled up and the tongue lolled out as in a cadaver.'

Robert Gaut stopped speaking and buried his head in his hands. When he looked up his face was drained of the last vestige of colour and the sweat gathered in great drops on his brow. He viewed me with some perplexity, as if he had forgotten where he was and to whom he had lately been speaking.

'My good man,' I said, 'your narrative has worn you out,' for the sake of uttering some commonplace words to break the terror that had come upon him. 'I will draw you a little water.'

When I returned with the draught of water he was as before, looking for all the world like the cadaver he had described in his discourse, so blanched was his face and vacant were his eyes.

'Thank you, sir.'

I have oft observed that the saying of simple words learned in the earliest childhood has a most healing effect, even if the speaker is unaware of the words he has said. And such was the case with Robert Gaut, that the simple involuntary act of gratitude restored him to his wits, inasmuch as his wits came back from the scene in the homestead to where he was yet seated, in the apothecary's lodging.

'How far did I get?' he said.

'The singer of the song was lying apparently lifeless on the floor of his homestead, and yet the song he was singing could not be stopped.'

'Then I have told you all, sir,' said Robert Gaut. 'You have offered a draught of water to a murderer.'

'What do you wish me to do, my good man? Tell you it is not true?'

'Yes, sir, I wish to believe it is not true.'

'When did the murder take place?'

'I lose time, sir. I know not when.'

'Do you have this dream every night?'

'Yes, sir.'

'My good man, pray be at peace. Your narrative was grounded in reality as long as you were outside the homestead watching he inside preparing for his day's journey. As soon as his song began to prey on your spirit you lost the thread of reality and your narrative turned into your dream, a dream you both wish for and greatly fear. You will not know this, because to you there was no difference between the one state and the other. To one watching you, the change in state was made manifest by the movement of your eyes, by which I concluded that the latter part of the narrative, where you broke in and reft the singer of his life, was but a dream. You have not murdered your father. I suggest that you and your father have profound differences. Your reasoning mind reached the end of its capacity to understand these differences, and the hidden part of your mind took up the cause, namely how you were to live with the presence of this man, your father, and his song. You have told me your dream and now it is broken.'

'I no longer live with my parents,' said Robert Gaut. 'I said to them that there was little enough work for three and I would make a living as a musician, picking up that trade as I went along.'

'And what think your parents?'

'They think I am a machine breaker,' said Robert Gaut. 'But better a machine breaker than a patricide, sir,' he added.

'Do you love your mother?'

'Yes, sir.'

'And your father?'

'Yes, sir.'

'Then you may go in peace, my good man.'

'But I must pay you, sir.'

'You must not,' I said. 'I have given you naught but my words, which the Lord Almighty gives freely to all men. You, similarly, have given me your words, for which I thank you. My assistant will furnish you with the remedies for your parents.'

Then I asked leave of Robert Gaut to write down such words as he had given me to which he assented and made to leave, but on reaching the door of the dispensary he turned.

'You do not ask me if I am a machine breaker, sir,' he said. 'And though you do not ask me yet I will tell you, that happen there are they who … but it matters not, sir. I have mislaid the words.'

And I begged the young man be seated again until such words as he was about to utter either returned to him or fled quite away; for indeed I wished him not to say that which later he would regret. So I said as much, and there was naught from him to break the silence.

X

Robert Gaut sat yet in the dispensary, gazing with uncomprehending eyes at the remedies my assistant Luke Bower had placed in his hands.

'What are these, sir?'

'You asked for assistance for your mother and father.'

'But I understood that the remedies could not be given unless the patients were present.'

'You understood rightly,'

'Then I will leave the remedies outside the dwellinghouse, sir, and my mother and father will presume them to have been brought by some messenger.'

'You may go in peace, my good man.'

But still Robert Gaut stayed, as if he lacked the will of mind and body to rise from his chair and leave, all the while looking around as if he sought the presence of one that had been in that place before.

'Might I ask you for another draught of water, sir?' he said, 'then I will be on my way.' He was trying in vain with his right hand to loosen his neckerchief. 'You will have other patients and I am delaying you, for which I apologise, sir. A momentary faintness came over me. I seemed to see some other here, but it matters not.'

'Luke will help you with that,' I said. 'I am all fingers and thumbs, though I lack the full quota of both; I will do no better than you if I offer my assistance.'

'I have noticed your hands, sir,' he said, 'for which I am grieved. This garment fitted me with ease earlier in the day. Now it is so tight I can scarce get my breath.'

And indeed his face, which had been pale at the start of his narrative, was showing signs of cyanosis, so much so that I wondered if it had been present all the time and had gone unnoticed by me. For it is not unknown that even young men will show precocious evidence of those ailments that affect their fathers. Luke had meanwhile loosened the knot. I knew not how, but I had ceased to wonder at his skills.

'Will you have Luke remove your neckerchief for a while to give you some air?' I said, for the patient seemed anxious to keep it about his neck, holding on to it indeed with a desperation at odds with his general debility.

Luke, who was yet standing behind the patient, caught my eye and jerked his head towards the side of the patient's neck, where the neckerchief had fallen away, and where the flesh was a deep purple, engorged with lines of blood and festering where the skin was broken. And still the patient endeavoured, with diminishing pertinacity, to cling to the garment and keep it in place, while all the time the cyanosis was gathering in his face; until his grip failed and the neckerchief fell to the ground. Luke picked it up.

'I ask you no questions, my good man,' I said, 'but pray let us offer you treatment for the mischief on your neck, which as we speak is causing rapid swelling and impeding the flow of air to your lungs.'

'It is of no account,' said the patient. I believed it to be no more than a minor accident.'

'But now it is turning to bad, and if you have no remedy you will before the day is out have ceased to live. Is that what you wish?'

Robert Gaut, for all his debility, appeared to be giving the matter some consideration, although it was no more than a rhetorical question I asked. For all men will clutch at the sweet air and the golden rays of the sun as long as they might.

'No, no,' he said, albeit with some hesitation. 'I believe I wish to live. I have always known that I wished to do one good thing while I am yet in this world.'

'And what would that be, Robert Gaut?' I said, willing the poor fellow's windpipe to be maintained if only by the simple breath of words while Luke Bower prepared a tincture of Sonch. hesp; for I had seen, and Luke my scribe also, evidence of burns in the tissues of the patient's neck, whether of the rope or of powder I knew not.

'And what might that good thing be?' I said again, for he was fighting for words.

'I don't rightly know, sir. I will know when it happens, no doubt.'

'Have you heard of the Sonchus hesperus?'

'No, sir. Though my mother knows much about plants, she does not talk of that.'

'My assistant has been preparing the tincture while you have been fighting for your breath.'

'What is it for?'

'It is for the effects of burns,' I said, for there is nothing to be gained by concealing findings from patients. 'Pray drink it, and we will apply a balm to the lesion. We ask no questions, nor will we pass on any knowledge we have of you or indeed of your presence here. When you feel restored you may go in peace. Luke will give you some more of the remedy.'

But still the patient Robert Gaut made no attempt to rise from the chair, even though, as I had observed on those other occasions, the preparation of Sonch. hesp. had rapidly reduced the symptoms and the patient's breath now flowed freely.'

'I was not burned,' he said. 'Leastways, I have no recollection of it. Why have you delivered a treatment for burns, which has made me better, and yet I have not been burned?'

'A man cannot see his own neck,' I said, 'save by looking in a glass, which you may not have done, my good man.' Here I might have added that beauty requires no looking glass to confirm itself, though I did not. For indeed, the young man was fair to look upon, and into my mind, unbidden, came the image also of Ellie Bright, who though humble, and likely for that very reason, was as an angel from heaven. 'The condition of the tissues is such that it is impossible at the moment to detect what has caused the mischief,' I continued. 'A burn is not always caused by fire. It may be caused by the rope, or by powder, or any other malevolent substance. All could look like burns. We ask you no questions, my good man. You may go in peace.'

But still he made no attempt to leave, taking elaborate pains to tie the knot of his neckerchief.

'Do you know of the oath?' he said at length.

Luke jerked his head in the direction of the concealed chamber where he we called the tinker still languished.

'We know of the oath,' I said.

'I would not take it, for then I would have been bound by the practices,' said Robert Gaut, after which, and with expressions of profound yet unmerited gratitude he rose and left the dispensary.

'What caused that?' said Luke. 'I have to say, sir, when you engaged me as your scribe you didn't say there would be so much mischief, as you quaintly put it, sir, with folks and their innards displayed to view. It turns my stomach at times, sir, to be quite honest with you.'

'You forget where I first saw you, Luke.'

'At that place the folks are clothed and there is no blood, sir, besides which though I was present I did not look,' Luke said, recovering somewhat his usual colour; yet not altogether, for I could see that this latest spectacle had disquieted him, though not I thought for the reason he wished me to understand.

'That mischief was but a mischief of the flesh,' I said, 'and may be healed if God Almighty so wills. They that inflicted it, and indeed they that send poor folks to the gallows-tree, suffer a sickness of the soul, and I know not how it is to be amended. What do you know of the oath, Luke? Is it a sickness of the soul or is it justified to redress the grievances of those who lose their livelihoods in these times?'

'I know no more and no less of the oath than you, sir; that is, what we gleaned from the document' (Luke jerked his head in the direction of the concealed chamber) 'which document him as does not remember his own name had in his hands when he was brought to our door.'

'And when you address the poor fellow, Luke, as I assume you are bound to do as you visit his abode with some frequency to collect his writings, what do you say? By what name do you greet him?'

'Why, Will Cantrell, sir, that being the name of him.'

'And his means of livelihood, Luke?'

'That I don't know, sir,' Luke said, after which his countenance closed and there was no more to be gained from him on the matter, though I could see he had not yet run to the end of his words.

'Sir?'

'Yes, Luke?'

'Begging your pardon, sir, had you come to any conclusions as to what caused the mischief?' He jerked his head in the direction of the door through which Robert Gaut had lately passed on his way out.

'I have, Luke, as I am sure you have, and I told the patient my thoughts. But the less discussed the better. We will leave the matter and trust to the recovery of the patient.'

'Whom we have not seen the back of, sir,' said Luke.

And indeed I was of the same opinion, not least for the reason that each man wishes to conclude his own story.

'He left with the rest of his tale untold,' I said. 'He will be back.'

'Begging your pardon, sir, but he as cannot remember his own name ...'

'Whom you call Will Cantrell.'

'... has been awriting, sir, which by your leave I will copy out as best I might, though the sight of blood and spittle is abhorrent to my stomach, sir, and well nigh makes me vomit.'

'Then the more credit is owing to you, Luke, for undertaking a task so far at odds with the comfort of your stomach,' I said, for I wondered that a spirit so doughty in every other respect should be dismayed by the sight of a little blood. And not for the first time it occurred to me that there might be another reason for Luke wishing to transcribe the narrative of the tinker, for as such I still thought of the poor fellow.

'If it pleases you, I will go to collect the writings myself and spare your stomach.'

'It does not please me, sir,' said Luke.

'Nevertheless I will go on this occasion. I wish to see how the poor fellow does.'

'You wish to see the poor fellow's attendant, sir.'

'If you say so, Luke, then I do. That is not the same as believing she wishes to see me.'

Which indeed she did not wish, for there was another nurse in her place, who announced herself as Jem Bailey and said she had been sent from the house of mercy, as the first nurse was gone.

'Gone?'

'Yes, sir,' said Jem Bailey.

'And do you know where?' I said, though in truth I did not want an answer of any description, preferring that Jem Bailey, who was as bright-eyed and bonny a young woman as ever there was, should keep her counsel.

'I know only that she's away, sir. I was asked to take her place, though I know not how to be a nurse, and the sick gentleman talks only with his hands and his eyes and I know the language of neither, sir. And though I am of a willing disposition, sir, I do not well.'

Here she stopped and was ready to shed the tears which had been gathering in her bright eyes.

'And that, sir,' Jem Bailey continued, 'is the history of my life. That I am of a willing disposition, though I do not well and I know not how to do better.'

Whereupon she began to weep bitterly, covering her face with her hands; which I let her do for some time until I perceived that the storm was subsiding and her sweet soul was sailing once more into calm waters.

'Jem Bailey,' I said, 'there is not one of us who does not fall short of the glory of God.'

'Yes, sir,' she said.

'What makes you say that you do not well?'

'That I was found in the company of soldiers of the militia, sir, and so sent to the house of mercy for my own protection.'

'Your own protection?'

'You may not know, sir, living in York as you do, the griefs of the hill country. There are those among the cloth workers who would force information, and indeed the same among the militias. In a different way,' she added. 'Though I would not give the names.'

'And you will say nothing about the patient, Jem Bailey?'

'No, sir. I can keep a secret.'

'Then you do well,' I said. 'One cannot do well in everything in this life, but one can do well in some things. To keep your counsel is a thing of great merit, as is the care of this patient.'

Who, all the time Jem Bailey talked, followed her with his eyes and remained in a state of some consternation after she fell silent. And I have to say that her own consternation was scarcely less, watching the poor fellow mouthing mute words and rolling his eyes and gesticulating wildly with his hands.

'You will tell the patient what you have told me, Jem Bailey,' I said. 'Although he cannot speak his wits and his hearing are unimpaired.'

Whereupon she approached the poor fellow and gave her promise, namely that she would keep her counsel; so that his face cleared somewhat but not all, as a summer day when rain threatens, yet enough to strike me that if his peace were restored to him he might have the face of an apostle.

'As for nursing the patient, my good woman,' I said, for there was no end to my prattle, 'there is little needful but to ensure his nourishment and help him with such clean linen as the house of mercy kindly gives, for as you will see his hand is hurt as well as his speech. If you do these things you will have done well.'

So having said much and achieved, I fear, little in the way of comforting either the patient or his nurse, I gathered up such pages of his writings as were lying on the desk and left with a heavy heart.

'Why so, sir?' said Luke. 'For the fact that you left him as cannot remember his own name and his attendant in no better state than you found them you are downcast, sir?'

'I fear I was pompous, Luke.'

'You did your best, sir. You can do no more. Did you know there was a letter?'

'A letter?'

'So to speak, sir. With the papers.'

'I gathered up such writings as were on the table, Luke. For your attention.' For I had lost the will to look over the writings of Will Cantrell before Luke came upon them. 'Will you be so good as to read the letter, pray?'

'I would rather you do so first, sir,' said Luke. 'And, sir, it was forward of me to tidy up the writings of him yonder before you had seen them, sir, and henceforward I will bring them to you for your perusal first, sir.' And so he went on in the most contrary way, yet confirming my suspicion that he had access to my soul.

'As it pleases you, Luke, I will read the letter first: "Sir, do not think ill of me should I take my leave and do not fear for me. Sig. E. Hor".'

'This has been written under duress, Luke.'

'How so, sir?'

'The body of the letter and the signature do not match, although the writer has made a fair attempt to emulate the writing of a young woman.'

'Young woman, sir?'

'Why, Luke, this is the poor fellow's attendant who was there previously.'

'If you say so, sir.'

'But written elsewhere. See, the ink is of a more dilute quality. Luke?'

'Sir?'

'Tell me, they that work the looms, can they read and write?'

'I never knew one as could not, sir, though that is not to say the whole as I never knew many such folks in my life.

They as can read and write, sir, they cannot be rendered mute, if you get my drift, sir'

'Then if you prepare the Sonchus hesperus, Luke, I will arrange to see the patient who suffered the burns to his face.'

'Him as just left, sir?' Luke jerked his head towards the door.

'No, the patient Horridge. He who dwells beyond Clywold. Why think you of the patient Robert Gaut?'

'Because there was powder about his person, sir.'

'And?'

'You surmised that the fellow had had the barrel of a musket or some such thrust into his neck, sir.'

Which indeed I had surmised though I could not recollect imparting my thoughts to my assistant.

'You say rightly, Luke.'

'Then you will exercise caution on your journey, sir.'

XI

It is said that the face of a man is a window into his soul; that a man with a louring and unprepossessing visage will entertain a dark and baleful spirit; that he whose eyes are narrow or set close will show deceit and cunning; that he who is possessed of full lips will be possessed also of a louche and sensual nature.

I say this is not true. Not only because an angel may dwell within a poor and broken temple and a devilish spirit within a palace, but because the premise takes no account of the hope of redemption, as if the pattern of a man's life were set at his birth.

If any man caused me to reflect thus, it was the magistrate of the parish of Holmroyd. Though if truth be known when I first set eyes on him my thoughts were neither on what shortcomings he may or may not have had, nor yet on redemption; for all manner of men and women enter the dispensary, and indeed sickness turns many a gentleman into a churl, and also the opposite.

His name was Born.

'B O R N,' he said, noting that I was not an Englishman. 'Have you got that? You're writing it down, I trust?' All the time with his voice raised as if I were both impaired in hearing and scattered in my wits, which latter I sometimes suspect I am.

'My scribe is at present away,' I said. 'He will make a fair copy in due course. Pray take a seat.' For the man was pacing to and fro in the dispensary enough to set the bottles of tinctures ringing like a peal of bells at Eastertide.

'Richard Born and Grace Born,' he said. 'Have you got that? My wife will sit down. I will stand.'

He continued to pace the room.

'You may know that I am a magistrate.'

And indeed, his dress marked him out from the common run of men, being well cut and little worn, and the linen clean. His face also was little worn and comely, and his voice, though addressing me as if I were deficient in my intellect, was melodious enough.

'I come to you for my wife here,' he said. 'In short, she has ceased to interest me. When I enter her chamber it is no longer with me as is the manner with men, and I believe the fault to lie with my wife as all was well before. She ails in some way, though I am not blaming her. Am I, Grace, my dear?'

'No, Richard dear. You have patience with me, I do believe,' the young woman said, inclining her head towards her husband slightly, yet sufficiently to render visible, whether by design or accident, a livid haematoma on the side of her neck below the mandible. The husband, following my eyes, coloured.

'I fear that your wife may have spontaneous bruising,' I said. 'There are several possible causes. We will treat the symptoms first, and then look to the reasons for the condition, for they are many and various. If it pleases you, sir.'

'As long as I might return home with her in a recovered state,' said the husband. 'What do you mean "spontaneous"?'

'I mean in this context, though begging your patience, sir, as you will have realised that English is not my mother tongue,' for he yet addressed me in a loud voice, 'that the bruising has occurred for reasons not apparent.'

Saying which it pleased my purpose to confirm him in the opinion that my wits were scattered, for I knew well enough the cause of his wife's bruise and have seen it oft in women who are unhappy enough to be blamed for a husband's impotency.

Yet I could not dismiss him entirely as a brute, as indeed no man is, having detected in his speech, albeit that it was delivered at a high volume, a possible cause of his misery; and misery it surely was in a man accustomed to mastery, as indeed his demeanour and his station in life and his readiness to inform me of such confirmed to me.

'You tell me that all is well with yourself, sir,' I said.

'So I did,' he said, still loudly though the window stood open and anybody passing in the street below might have heard his intimate account of himself and his bed chamber. 'Which is why,' he continued, 'I believe the fault to lie with my beloved wife, as I know there can be no fault with me.'

'As you have said before. And when was the precise time you noticed this change in your wife?'

'I can tell you exactly. It was almost to the day when certain laggards and ne'er-do-wells were brought before me. Since which time the tykes have arrived at my door with some regularity. A devil of a job to get them to talk.'

'So you fear you are not fulfilling your role as a magistrate if the fellows won't talk?'

'On the contrary. They'll talk eventually.' A smile flickered across his face. 'Thy have no alternative.'

'So, as I understand, you may congratulate yourself as to the success of your endeavours?'

'Yes.'

'Yet all is not well.'

Richard Born continued to address me loudly.

'I am not here on my own account, my good fellow. I am here on my wife's account. There is something amiss with her. She will no longer admit me willingly into her chamber, and when I do gain entry I am not interested in her. What do you say to that? If you cannot assist me I shall be obliged to go elsewhere.'

'I can tell the apothecary, Richard.' Grace Born had removed her gloves and was looking down at her fingers. 'I can tell him why we have no conversation of that kind. I cannot be in the presence of my husband, sir, when I see the blood under his finger nails and sense the odour of men's fear about his person.'

'Do not heed her. She is a sick woman. Hold your noise, Grace.' The husband made as if to stop her mouth with his hand.

'I have not finished yet, Richard,' Grace Born continued. 'One day, sir, and my husband, thinking I was indisposed with the head ache and confined to my chamber, yet having recovered towards the setting of the sun when the air turned cooler – unlike my normal habit, sir, as I am usually indisposed for three days at the least, but this time after only two days – I went for a walk under the lime trees which on a summer evening shed their scent on the earth like the most sweet benediction, and even at the spring of the year burst into leaf like a blessing from heaven; and approaching the hawthorn hedge I was aware of several persons standing in the cover of it on the footway the other side, on our side there being outhouses used for the keeping of the plough and other implements of the land. And hanging on the hedge were some outer garments which as I approached seemed in appearance to be those of my husband, as well as of others unknown. And all the time the other side of the hawthorn hedge there was sound as of a rustling of women's dress, and low whispering voices.

'Then presently, while I was yet a way off so I could not hear distinctly, if there was indeed anything to be heard, the door of the last of the outhouses was opened and a woman brought out scarce able to walk, with her mouth bloodied and awry and swollen. I did not dream this, sir, though I remember no more, as I must have suffered some manner of forgetfulness since the next I knew I was in my chamber laid out on my bed as if I were still there with the head ache. And it was confirmed by my husband that I had been at the bottom of the garden yet not recovered and had walked inadvertently into the low branch of a lime and fallen down. Though, sir, the limes had no low branches that I knew of lest they were shorn for the purpose of letting traffic in and back from the outhouses. I ramble, sir'

Here Grace Born opened her reticule and brought out a torn and dirtied piece of paper.

'I'll have that!'

Richard Born, who during his wife's discourse had not ceased to pace the room, seized her wrist and wrested the paper from her.

'It is nothing more than the poor woman's name, which my husband well knows, which was delivered into the hand of my maid in the days following. So, sir, as I have tried your kind patience long enough I will conclude by saying that, through my maid, who is from the hill country and knows many there, it was arranged that the woman, who, sir, had at the hands of my husband, whether he did it himself or had others do the deed for him, had her back teeth drawn and her jaw put out of socket and sorely broken in the process, be put in the house of mercy in York. And, sir,' said Grace Born, for I perceived that she was yet a way from concluding her story, 'I know not the rights and wrongs of the machine breakers, though I know the wrong of the hill dwellers going hungry through lack of work, as I hear from my maid, and I know the wrong of hurting a woman, being my sister in affliction, whatever her station be in this world.'

Which discourse, finishing as it did with Grace Born closing her reticule and rising to her feet, would have brought the sudden and violent hand of her husband down upon her person, but that his arm was stayed by Luke Bower who had appeared out of the thin air when he was supposedly on leave of absence in the context, so he told me, of seeing his kin.

Richard Born let his arm drop and turned to Luke.

'Thank you, my good fellow. I would have sinned again but that you saved me.' Then, addressing me, 'You see, sir, to what my wife has driven me.'

'It is a pity he has not always folks there to save him from his sin,' said Luke as we watched the husband and wife Richard and Grace Born leave the Monk-bar; together yet not together, for she made certain that not so much as the skirt of her gown should touch the hem of his coat.

'By your leave, sir,' said Luke, 'I have begun the record.'

'You surely mean without my leave, Luke,' I said. 'Pray read me what you have written.'

'...."Richard Born, being magistrate of the parish of Holmroyd," ' read Luke, '... "suffers an aversion to his good wife. Grace Born suffers aforementioned aversion towards husband Richard Born." '

'Though the patient spoke to me in such a way as one would to a fellow scattered in his wits, as I could well be, I did not hear that he is of the parish of Holmroyd, Luke. He did not say it. Therefore we do not record it. How come you by this knowledge of him?'

'Then I will score that out, sir,' said Luke.

'Have you written any more?'

'That you gave him ...' (Luke jerked his head towards the window) '... basil for the melancholy, sir, though tis too good a remedy for the likes of he, and his good lady wife elm for the bruising and feverfew for the head ache, sir.'

'And tell me again, what condition did you record for Mr Born, Luke?'

'I wrote nothing more, sir, because he does not merit your ink nor my labours, save that you gave him basil for the melancholy, that being what basil is for, and you know best, sir.'

Then perceiving that there was no more to be gained from Luke in his present frame of mind, for I could see his whole being was bent of visiting retribution on Richard Born, I asked him if he knew the name of Grace Born's maid.

'Yes, sir, tis Rosie Todd,' Luke said, and went on to give me her entire pedigree from birth to her present state, that being of the hill country and of a family of croppers she had been sent out to service when the machines were brought in and work declined among her kinsfolk. And indeed she had been wed, though Luke knew nothing of her husband, whether he be deceased or no, nor for how long she had been wed.

'And, sir, Mistress Born and Mistress Todd have time enough to air their grievances one to another during the braiding of the hair,' Luke added.

For indeed Grace Born had elaborately braided hair, which sat at odds with her otherwise self-forgetful and modest demeanour.

'And, sir,' Luke concluded, I have prepared the remedy for your journey.' By which I understood that there was no more to be had at present on the subject of Rosie Todd. And it came to me yet again that I might ask Luke about any number of folks in the whole county of York and he would know the pedigree of each one; yet he had chosen to withhold the name of the former nurse of Will Cantrell.

'You know where you're going, sir,' he added, at the very moment the thought crossed my mind that although I knew where I was bound I was at a complete loss as to how to reach the dwellinghouse of Simon Horridge, having journeyed there by night after leaving the Clywold coach at the sign of the Spread Eagle and having a guide also, who was doubtless leading me on a circuitous route.

'Thank you, Luke, I know where I'm going,' I said, 'which is not the same as knowing how to get there.' For I knew well enough by now that few matters escaped Luke Bower.

'I thought as much, sir.'

So saying he jerked his head in the direction of the concealed chamber, muttering something to the effect that he was going to collect more of the writings of him as could not remember his own name.

A guide with a lantern, whether the same as before or another, was waiting at the sign of the Spread Eagle as such passengers as wished to break their journey stepped down from the coach.

The evening was low and overcast with the sweet scent of gorse and new meadow grass on the air, the end of a day hot enough for the season of the year and dry withal, for the tired prints of travellers lingered in the dust. And the whole was redolent of a peace and tenderness out of step with the troubled times, in a country of unsurpassed loveliness which yet daily bore witness to the secret uses of coercion, and no doubt other ills that I knew not of.

I followed the guide at a distance of some two furlongs, proceeding on a path uneven and stony, climbing steeply then of a sudden dropping into tumbles of scree, and all the time the poor sheep alarmed and jostling and scattering after the manner of their kind.

The first light of day was glimmering in the east, and the morning star yet ablaze, when the guide stopped as if to enable me to gain ground, he being sure of foot and familiar with the way whereas I was clumsy and stumbled oft, being much impeded by my cloak. And not for the first time that night, seeing the slender figure bearing the lantern, though not to reveal the face, it struck me as before that the guide could as likely be a woman. Though I had no opportunity to verify the notion, as seeing me approaching my guide, whether man or woman, directed me to a well-defined path up the hill ahead, and herself, if indeed a woman, yet I knew not if it were a woman, left me, descending to the foot of the hill through a growth of gorse. And all this before I might offer a word of gratitude.

There was yet left a steady climb of some three hours before the dwellinghouse came into sight, and I could see others far off on the shoulders of the hills, and occasionally the white of a tenter; though few enough, which confirmed Grace Born's account of the falling off of domestic cloth work among the hill people. And the whole world at this early hour would rightly have been wrapped in silence but for the solitary cry of the curlew and the soft cropping of the sheep. Yet I could hear, distinctly, the sound of men's voices, though not the words they said; first from the right then from the left, ahead, or behind me down the hill, sometimes louder as the breeze carried the voices, sometimes lulled to a barely audible whisper; sometimes a single voice, sometimes many; sometimes also the sharp metallic rasp as of a firearm being primed. And indeed, the hill path was so disposed that a walker could not see into the valleys either side, or ahead, or below, owing to the acute angle of the terrain on every side.

The door of the dwellinghouse of Simon Horridge was answered by a youth of some twelve years, tousle-headed and ruddy of complexion, though thin and wasted in the limbs, who said he had been instructed to give the gentleman visitor some refreshment and to say that Simon Horridge would be back. Yet seeing the poor lad I deemed him to stand in greater need of refreshment than myself and begged him to partake of what was offered to me, but he did not, so we drank water companionably enough; and he would say nothing of the whereabouts of Simon Horridge, nor did I press him, or indeed divulge that I had witnessed the hills in conversation one with another. Thus we sat together for some half of an hour until he questioned me on the contents of my scrip, whereupon I explained the principles of the remedies to him.

And we were so seated, engaged in a lesson on the labours of the apothecary, when Simon Horridge returned, though I would not have known it was he, so little like was the young man who entered the dwellinghouse to the sufferer I had attended; only that he had the same violet blue eyes as his sister. He shook me by the hand, pressing refreshment upon me, which I declined knowing the hardships of the hill dwellers, and answering such questions as I put to him in the most gracious manner. The remedy had indeed restored him and his recovery was greatly advanced by the application of the second treatment which had been delivered by an unknown person and which he believed to come from the dispensary in York. Regarding the initial reason for blackening his face he said nothing, nor anything of his late whereabouts, and I thought better than to question him, knowing that his previous openness had been born out of pain and the fear of death; and moreover the boy whom he called Matthias was yet in our presence.

XII

Having ascertained that Simon Horridge was sound in body there was little cause for me to stay. And yet I was like the patient Robert Gaut who had lately appeared at the dispensary, insomuch as I could not muster up the will to leave. Neither did I feel it fitting to stay, as Simon Horridge had the air of one waiting to be gone as soon as courtesy allowed; though I could see from the whole district around that there was no cloth in the making, where indeed it was only the morning sun that fell as in great tenters on hill and vale. And all was at peace as if the sweet heaven had not lately witnessed the priming of muskets and the harsh voices of men.

'And your good sister, how does she fare, Simon?' a voice said, though not my own. A woman stood under the lintel of the door, who, noticing my presence, added that she could see he had company.

'I will come back later,' she said, and would certainly have gone in the instant had I not made steps myself to leave the dwellinghouse.

'My sister fares well enough, Rosie Todd,' Simon Horridge said. 'Her late hurt was healing when I saw her last, and I trust she continues to mend. This gentleman is an apothecary who has been good to me. He is bound by the secrecy of his profession. You may talk freely in his hearing.'

If the young woman had not been thus addressed by Simon Horridge, and indeed had she not given evidence in her subsequent speech of her situation I might well have known her as Rosie Todd, Grace Born's maid, by the same elaborate braiding of her hair. She eyed me with some curiosity, her gaze moving from my face to my hands, which seeing she nodded.

'He is the gentleman,' she said, by which I understood that Grace Born had delivered a full account of her visit to the dispensary into the sympathetic ears of her maid while undergoing hair dressing. Yet for all that she heard much and appeared at first glance as if she might be a giddy and unguarded woman, judging her solely, may I be forgiven, on the braids in her hair, I could see that she would say nothing. Which habit I gathered was the habit of the hills, and which no doubt made Richard Born's task the more arduous.

'So where go you, Rosie?' said Simon Horridge, and I knew that all talk of his sister was finished as soon as it started. To which Rosie Todd answered something and nothing which I did not hear the finish of as I left the dwellinghouse in the company of the lad Matthias.

'On my way up I heard the hills conversing one with another,' I ventured.

'Yes,' said the boy. 'I hear likewise though they speak in a foreign tongue and I know not what they say.'

'No more do I,' I said. 'And I will not tell any living soul about the hills conversing one with another as they will no doubt conclude that I am an old man who has lost his wits.'

'Thank you, sir,' said the boy. And I knew that he would carry this back to the dwellinghouse and that Simon Horridge might know, both that I had been witness to some kind of drill taking place among those who were like to be machine breakers, and that the knowledge was as safe as it could be given the frailty and fear of all men.

The boy Matthias continued by my side as I pursued the path down the hill, which I remembered from my previous journey though I knew not whether I was leading or indeed being led.

Thus until we reached the shoulder of the hill and the lad, seeing that I would have followed the pathway down, indicated that I should follow him, striking off to the left through the gorse to a cluster of homesteads until then concealed by the curious disposition of the landscape. For as I have noted before in these pages, at one minute a traveller in such a country is as by himself under the wide canopy of the heaven and at another in the midst of the homely dwellings of folks.

Outside the dwellinghouses the tenters stood empty, and they whom I saw, though few in number, bore all of them the same marks of hunger I had first observed in the face of Hannah Gaut. And as if to confirm my observation, although I had not uttered a word, the boy Matthias said, 'There's not the work, you see, sir, and the folks they is anhungered. All the work is gone to the mill.' He made a vague gesture to the north west, but there was nothing to be seen but the hills dotted with the yellow of the gorse and the white of the sheep, which poor beasts indeed fared the better, being fed by heaven.

'We're here, sir,' he added, and entered one of the homesteads without so much as a knock, closing the door behind him.

He appeared again presently and gestured to me to follow him inside, where, seated in the corner and half concealed in the shadow cast by a casement was, as I thought, my guide of the previous night, the former nurse of the patient Will Cantrell, and the sister of Simon Horridge. A shawl partially covered her face. By the side of her, on a low stool, was a bowl.

'This is the gentleman,' said the boy Matthias, not otherwise addressing her in any way which might have indicated his relationship with her.

'Thank you, Matthias.' She said, in that same sweet voice as was yet in my mind, albeit that she spoke with a difficulty which suggested, for all that she held the shawl over her mouth, a gross malady of the face and throat.

'Am I to go?' said Matthias.

'If the lad has no other call upon his time he may stay.' I said, 'if that suits ...' and I finished indecisively, knowing not how to address her.

'She has something amiss with her face, sir,' said the boy, by which I perceived that he might speak for the patient if she could not. 'It pains her to talk, and if you look, sir, her face is not equal one side with the other. And, sir, she can do no better than a spoon of thin gruel and that not often for it pains her to eat. Though the rest of her is in health, sir,' he said. ''Tis only her face. And now if you'll excuse me, sir, I'll away for I canna stand the sight o blood and she'll forgive me for she knows it well enough. Though I would have stayed, sir, believe me I would.'

'You have done your good deed, Matthias,' the patient said. 'Go now, and blessings on you.'

I asked her if I might open the casement to admit the light, and then asked as well as I might though clumsily enough as befits a foreigner how I might address her, which question was lost in the opening of the door and the entry of the young woman Rosie Todd.

'I am come to assist you, sir,' she said, adding that she had passed the young rapscallion in the way, who sent her hither saying the gentleman within had need of a nursing assistant and he himself could not stand the sight of blood. 'So here I am,' she finished, as she busied herself in removing the shawl from around the patient's face; which was indeed grievously unequal, as the boy Matthias had said, bearing a dark taut swelling under the angle of the jaw on the right side and to a lesser extent on the other.

'Did you ever see such a sight?' said Rosie Todd, with more ferocity of manner than regard to the patient's sensibility. 'Because I didn't, I'm sure. Did you, sir? And you from foreign climes, sir.'

I knew not whether the latter question needed an answer, as the English tongue has never ceased to mystify me, and does so to this day. So I said nothing, but was taken back to the bloody habits of certain of my republican brethren, and for all I knew those of the King's party also. For cruelty copies cruelty and in times of unrest all are equal in guilt and innocence. I begged of Rosie Todd a bowl of water and clean cloths, and she hastened to oblige; and for all her words and braids she was a kind and dutiful soul.

'Let the gentleman see, Liz,' she said, solving not at all my anxiety as to how to address the patient; yet in other respects Rosie Todd was already proving to be my voice, as well as my eyes, and my hands and feet.

'Open wide, there's a brave girl. She knows you will be obliged to cut into the place, sir. She is not afraid. She only wishes to be rid of the agony. There is water aboiling to wash the lancet, sir.' With which, had I placed in her hands, I believe Rosie Todd would have accomplished the operation herself.

The patient uttered not a word while all this talk was passing, and without any ado submitted to the opening of a large abscess on the right and a lesser one on the left. And although she remained silent I knew the operation to entail exquisite, albeit fleeting, pain. Yet she made no complaint. Even as I waited and the good Rosie Todd assisted her in spitting out the pus and blood from her mouth I could see her face resuming its former loveliness and a smile lighting her violet blue eyes.

'Thank you, sir,' she said. 'Thank you.'

I bid her then call me John, knowing not what I said, and she bid me call her Elizabeth, though I doubted that I would ever call her in that free manner, being now bound by the gracious custom of my profession in relation to the patient.

Then after leaving a preparation of bugle for the fester and salix against the fever which would else follow such a mischief, and instructing the patient as to their application, I joined the boy Matthias outside the door, and though looking green enough he accompanied me through the gorse to the high path; and to whom I gave on leaving a preparation of bistort for the settling of the stomach, for he was a good lad and a kindly. Knowing also that there was little to be gained in giving sorrel to restore the appetite, for in times of hardship appetite is not a blessing but a curse.

The path climbed sharply upwards before it fell down to the valley. It then turned an acute corner from where the whole of the valley and the hills on yonder side stood open to view. And the he morning was as the first morning in the creation of the world, with the pale sun climbing the sky and a soft mist in the valley, the white puffs of the gentle sheep on the slopes and the dark green and yellow of the gorse; yet, in spite of the peace lying over the land I noted again from the clusters of dwellinghouses clinging to the lower rungs of the hills that few were white with tenters and I knew then what hunger and hardship lurked within; and that many there were who woke each morning with the gripes at the pit of their stomachs and shadows under their eyes, and who daily saw the flesh falling from their frames. And as I so reflected the top of Clywold mill rose up out of the mist afar off.

Thus I stood, idling away yet more of my allotted span of life which was now, according to men's supposed time in this world, well nigh three quarters spent, when I noticed emerging from the mist onto the pathway at the foot of one of the hills opposite a figure labouring under a burden carried on his back; which burden looked for all I could make out like the body of a man, it being so heavy that he carrying it was obliged to stop many a time, resting it upon the ground and resettling it across his shoulders. Yet so far away was he and so obscured by the drifting of the mist and the sudden glances of the sun that I could not be sure whether he I took to be a man was after all an apparition.

Whether man or ghost, he vanished from the landscape as suddenly as he had walked into it, either enveloped by the mist or by a dwellinghouse, or indeed by the configuration of the hills. And something about the figure disquieted me, labouring as he was under a weight, which I construed from the slow progress he made was as heavy on the mind as on the body.

My own mind was meanwhile diverted, such is the custom of they who are long in years, by the notion that since the mill was visible, albeit far, there might be growing in the proximity of its effluent the plant Sonchus hesperus; which indeed I found, further down the hill by the side of a dark and turgid beck, and my mind was thrown back to the last patient I had attended, whose name was Elizabeth, whose silence under duress and whose loveliness came upon me as a benediction.

So occupied was I with these reflections, and with gathering the basal leaves of the plant, which grew there in profusion and would do so more as the season progressed, that I had not noticed the shadow of a man stretched out upon the earth before me as a felled giant might be, with a great tumour arising out of his head.

'I hope I do not startle you, sir.' The voice was that of Robert Gaut, whose history was writ vividly upon my memory, as indeed were the histories of all my patients to the extent that the services of my fine scribe Luke Bower would hardly need be called upon, but that I lacked the facility of committing words to paper; that and the fact that Luke Bower, for all his youth, was of the world and knew the ways of mankind.

'No indeed,' I said, 'though I must confess that your shadow did, looking over my shoulder, for I was seeing not only you but also your double bass, which I mistook for an extension of your head.'

'It is good to see you, sir,' Robert Gaut offered me his hand, giving me cause to wonder yet again at the restrained courtesies of the English. The hand was hot, and unnaturally dry for one who had laboured on the hill path carrying so heavy a burden.

'You are not over your recent malady,' I said, 'and the double bass is heavy. Pray let me take a turn with it, as far as the Clywold road at least.'

Robert Gaut was declining my request with some vehemence when his speech was cut short by an event taking place far below in the valley, which indeed I had not noticed. I followed his gaze to where it was fixed, on a sombre procession of eight black clad mourners following after a horse drawn cart with a dissenting minister following on behind, as I could detect even from afar off by the white ribbon about his neck, such was the sweet clarity of the air.

'Tis he,' said Robert Gaut.

His face, in which I had observed the dull flush of fever but shortly before was white as the mist drifting in tatters across the valley. And I concluded with a heavy heart both that my remedy had not effected a cure and that my words, for all their pomposity, had not driven away his dream, which would no doubt still hover over his fitful nights in the presence of fever.

'Tis my own fault,' Robert Gaut continued as if he had seen into my thoughts, which I have to say are sometimes none too subtle. 'I had occasion to give away the medicine to a soul whose need was greater than my own, knowing well, sir, that to be effective, the course of treatment must be followed to its end. Which I have not done, sir. I am to blame.'

Meanwhile Robert Gaut's eyes were upon another pilgrim, for such are we all in this life, this other making his way along the selfsame path as the company of mourners but in the contrary direction, who stood back from the path and removed his hat as they passed by, and then continued walking with the difficulty of one who could not get his breath.

'Tis he.' A dull red fire flared in Robert Gaut's face. 'Tis Zephaniah. He lives yet.'

Then I bade him let me see the lesion on his neck which he did, undoing the knot of his neckerchief with more facility than previously, by which I understood that the hand was recovered and that he might yet resume his livelihood. The hurt on the neck was, however, grievously inflamed and suppurating, and I could see also the beginnings of a cavity opening, which would if left unattended soon lay bare the tender structures beneath the flesh.

'You shall have more of the remedy, my good man,' I said. 'And so that you do not give it away, I ask you to send the other sufferer to me to be treated. It could be that the remedy I gave to you doesn't suit another and might even cause harm. You need not to tell me their name.'

For I knew well enough not to ask.

XIII

So reluctant was Robert Gaut to go on and so wearied that I made the suggestion again to him that I might shoulder the double bass as far as the Clywold road, assuring him also that I was bound for York and would await the coach, so that the good fellow might know for how long he would be burdened with my company. This indeed had the effect of reassuring him somewhat, and he took up the double bass with a renewed energy, and made to strike out along the path with so ready a step as to lead me to suspect that the case was now empty.

'And likewise, sir, if my presence does not importune you, I will be honoured to have your company,' which saying I took to be merely a courteous figure of the speech, as folk in general are downcast rather than honoured in the company of the apothecary, since his presence presupposes the visitation of some indisposition of the body or mind, and he is generally a fellow to be avoided.

We continued in silence for some time until the Clywold road, which had been for an hour of the day far below before disappearing entirely from view behind a growth of ash, was now above us and travelling along a ridge some furlong's walk away; which sudden contortion caused me to wonder again at the curious disposition of the hills and their converse one with another, and I said as much to Robert Gaut, remarking on the variableness of the hill country, yet not its converse, to which he answered, 'Aye.'

And as my companion had said nothing more I was beginning to think myself mistaken in supposing that he had something further to say. Certainly his step was lighter, as was the weight he carried, yet I knew not whether to think it a reflection of his frame of mind or because the case was in truth empty. And it came to me that the casing of the double bass might easily conceal heaven knows what else in the stead of the gracious instrument, the more so as I detected two small apertures the neck through which air might pass.

'I must rest a while, sir. I need to recover my breath, as does the double bass. It breathes as we do.' And Robert Gaut, as if he had seen into my mind, indicated the apertures which I had lately noticed, causing me to marvel yet again at the way my thoughts could so easily be scrutinised, to the extent that I resolved to consult the glass in the dispensary as soon as I may to determine if indeed I carried around on my cranium a window into my mind.

'How so?' I said.

'These small holes enable the pressure to be maintained within as without. Otherwise tension is exerted on the strings and they will break.'

'It breathes and it sings,' I remarked, merely for the purpose of continuing the conversation with Robert Gaut, as his custom was to start a long way off when he had matters to disclose.

'I do not understand the mechanism fully, sir. The French musician tried to explain as well as he could, though I am a rough tuned man.'

'Yet the name Jommelli is Italian, surely.'

'Yes, sir, but he is from the land of France. Happen he believed that they in England do not take kindly to the brethren of Napoleon Bonaparte, sir, yet I know not.' Robert Gaut had meanwhile leaned the double bass against an outcrop of stone and was himself seated by the side of it. 'The double bass needs air as a living creature needs air,' he continued. 'Has news reached you in York of any burnings, sir?'

I begged Robert Gaut to explain to which matter he referred, but he said little enough, only that there had been burnings, and he feared worse and more, and he cared not what manner of man it might be who was the victim of such, for none deserved to see his homestead up in flames not knowing if those of his household were within. Which had so far not come to pass, yet he feared the day when a homestead would go up and those without stand helplessly by hearing the screams of their kin trapped within.

Having said which he rose to his feet, with the appearance of one wishing to be on his way, and he said he had been too free with his speech as it was and would say no more, by which I understood that he referred to his talk of the burnings. So I said in my turn that I would divulge nothing of the talk that had passed.

Yet my mind was thrown back to an event in my former life which I cared not to remember when, but for the saving grace of a fire igniting in certain abutting outhouses my hands would have been in a more broken condition than they were; for those about me fled in the act, leaving me free to exit, albeit with fire at my heels; and another there was also undergoing some means of coercion in a contiguous room and I knew not whether he also had lived.

And arriving back in the town of York late towards evening I saw all the windows along the Spurrier-gate aflame in the setting sun as if portending the times to come.

The thought of which, and the late conversation with the musician and weaver Robert Gaut, must surely have accompanied me to my chamber for towards morning I was again climbing steps, to the tune not of a baying crowd but of a single blackbird carolling close by, and all the while I reflected that no rooftop could be so high as to accommodate the blackbird, yet he they call the merula will seek out the highest point in the land from which to pour forth his music, and indeed will do so while the earth is yet sunk in darkness. So far had I climbed, and yet I kept on, with the sweet creature no less present to my hearing, until that which I knew to be a dream ended in the sound of the blade rattling earthwards; and I came to my senses hearing still the blackbird's song, which song indeed I would hope to hear in the last moments of my journey in this world.

It was on that same morrow that I recalled the words of Robert Gaut, and that he had seen into my thoughts as I was speculating on what appeared to be breathing apertures in the casing of the double bass. Then, it being early and my scribe Luke Bower abroad somewhere as was his habit, I thought to look into the glass in the dispensary to see if indeed there was a window into my mind, as Robert Gaut and Luke Bower and others were wont to detect; all the time reflecting that there was another patient to whom Robert Gaut had given the remainder of the remedy, which might not be right for him, and which might indeed be harmful also.

I have heard it said often that he who consults a looking glass finds a man quite other than the man he believes himself to be. So it was with me in the early morning on a day in the month of April in the year of our Lord 1812. The fellow who looked back at me, framed in the doorway on the far side of the dispensary, was rough-hewn indeed with the rime of old age already scattered about his hair, raw boned withal and sunken about the eyes, and altogether unlike the fellow whom I thought to encounter, though I had little enough notion of how he would look. Yet for all that the rough fellow in the glass looked back at me and indeed scrutinised me for no little time I could not detect a window into his mind; and I was still thus searching, whimsical though I knew the quest to be, when I observed that the door of the dispensary, visible in the glass, was opening.

'You will forgive me, sir. I thought to find you here.' The voice was that of Martin Gathercole, the companion of the young woman with the rickets, Ellie Bright; yet not his person, which was so unlike that I doubted for a moment the soundness of my memory. 'And I was right, sir,' he added. 'You are indeed here. You will forgive me for intruding upon you at so uncivilised an hour, and a foul one at that.'

I bade him come in and be seated.

'How did you know I would be here in the dispensary, looking like a half-witted fellow into the glass to see if there is a window in my head?'

'It was easy enough, sir. I have been in the town of York since the small hours of the day, waiting for your casement to open, by which I might deduce that you were risen from your rest and not yet gone out on your morning's affairs. But I would beg of you a draught of water, sir, for my throat pains me somewhat and I find my breath does not come as freely as before.'

And truly, Martin Gathercole's aspect bore the marks of one scarce of air, for his complexion, naturally high coloured, bore now the purple mottling of incipient cyanosis.

'Yet I am better than I was, since the medicine,' he continued, 'otherwise I would be in a pretty pickle, if not standing before my Maker. Forgive me, sir, I talk too much. This garble is as unlike me as the attire you see me in, sir, which is not mine, as my prattling is not, though I can neither alter my dress nor my speech at the present moment. In short, sir, we have been in extremis, Ellie and myself, and she has not a part in it. It is an accident of birth that placed her in the same household as a mill owner and I fear she will burn for it yet.'

'Where is Ellie Bright?' I said, not so much to elicit the fact as to steady Martin Gathercole's mind, for he seemed to me as a man going into a delirium, whether as a result of some mischief that had befallen him or because of an insufficiency of air in the lungs, I knew not.

'The young man who took her would not tell me,' said Martin Gathercole. 'What a man does not know, that he cannot divulge. There is many a one who has said those same words. Ha. He would have taken me also but that I stayed to quench the flames until help came. He gave me the medicine, sir, without which I would be in a pretty pickle and no doubt either, and as I said, as like as not standing before my Maker in the clothes I appear before you in, which were put together for me by certain of my mill hands; and I fear they gathered of the Sunday best of those good fellows.'

And here Martin Gathercole's prattle as so he called it was interrupted by a paroxysm of grief such as I have seldom witnessed in a grown man; after which he was more nearly himself and partook of a draught of the Sonchus hesperus.

And although the clothing the mill hands had given him was clean and decent, and indeed of the Sunday best of those good fellows by the look of it, the breath of fire was in his hair and yet clung to his flesh.

'The medicine will help your breathing, Martin,' I said. 'It is from a plant I have named the Sonchus hesperus, which I believe to be a variant of the Sonchus arvensis, but with violet blue on the petals as like to the peaceful sky at twilight. It is useful for conditions where the lungs may be swollen and the windpipe constricted and the breathing impaired,' prattling in my turn to render the patient silent while the remedy took effect; yet I did not say where I had found the plant, close by a beck carrying the noxious effluent from a manufactory.

'It is helping, sir,' said Martin Gathercole. 'I feel restored to health and I must settle my account with you and leave the day to you for you are a busy fellow,' saying which he produced a charred pocket book and begged the use of a pen. And I was hard pressed indeed in my efforts to convince him that the lilies of the field grow freely under heaven, and that I was not in the habit of exacting payment from my patients.

'But you had to prepare the medicine,' he said, 'and, sir, you may argue all you like that water comes freely down from heaven in the way of rain, but I know from my hands that time is work and work is time and must be paid,' and so on in the manner of the fellow of affairs that he was.

So seeing that he was like to relapse into his former hectic speech I suggested to Martin Gathercole that his account of the mischief, as much as he wished to impart, was worth more than any payment, at the same time harbouring in my mind a doubt that he was a fit subject for the talking remedy, being but a bluff man; and reassuring him also that anything he said would be addressed in the same spirit of confidentiality as a mischief to the health of any patient might be.

After which words he quieted somewhat and thus began his tale:

'It may be that you know, sir, that there are those dwelling in the hill country that loathe the mill. They have their reasons. They argue that the mill has reft them of their livelihoods, mainly the folks called croppers that were used to finish the cloth. Now we have the machine, sir. What we formerly did in a hundred and eighty-eight hours we now do in eighteen.

'The fellows lay the blame for their loss of livelihood on the machines. They don't see the big picture, sir. Tis the closure of foreign markets due to the war, you see, sir, saving your presence, for I see you are not from these shores. And you only need on top a bad harvest to see the price of bread go sky high. They don't see the big picture. Tisn't just the mills. They're only part of it.

'And, sir, once a process is invented no man can uninvent it. They don't see that. The shearing frame, it's here to stay, and likewise the power loom, whether they like it or not. And the mill gives work to the folks, sir.

'So they starts wi their threats. An uncouth filthy scrap posted through the door, what they're intending, sir, though folks say some o the fellows are lettered like as you an me are lettered men, sir.

'So I'm not going to let the …' (here Martin Gathercole used an oath, and apologised profusely for it, to the extent that I feared the former delirium would descend on him again; and I begged him to carry on, using whatever words he might to best express what had befallen him, whether or not oaths, though he did not so again) '… I'm not going to let them affright me,' he continued, 'with their burnings and their arsons. So I did not mention the fact to Ellie.

'And thus it carried on, sir, a letter through the door betimes in the mornings when I would find it on the way to the mill. Until a day I went out before the sun was risen and the bushes in the garden were seething although there was not a whisper of a breeze, it being that time before the dawning of the day when all the world is peaceable. But yet the bushes they were aseething, and as I passed by I caught sight of certain fellows with blackened faces who I would not have known as critters of the Lord's creation but for the whites of their eyes. And I have heard tell of such, sir, and now I have seen such, sir.

'And it came to me, sir, that this was the day when the fellows might act. So I made to go to the mill but didn't. Only in the way I encountered the musician fellow with the double bass, for he is half crazed to my mind and walks about o nights, though on this occasion he was bound for my house, which as we stood was already alight with the south room gone. And the musician fellow, sir, he asks where the young woman is and I say perchance she is attending to the affairs of the kitchen, for I am distracted and I know not what I am doing; so he goes off round the back of the house looking, with me running after, but the lintel of the door comes down between me and him.

'And to cut to the ending, sir, for I know the ending more rightly than I do the middle of this tale, which the musician wouldn't part with, Ellie Bright is in a place of safety unbeknown to me; and my bay mare Yolande, I know not where she is gone for I found the door to the stable down and her gone. And I know not aught else.'

And here Martin Gathercole covered his face and wept again; and it occurred to me that the talking remedy might like the mistaken medicine make certain patients the worse, in particular those whose naturally robust exterior might well have carried them through their afflictions.

But the good man recollected himself, and his face, now cleared of the signs of cyanosis, resumed its customary ruddy hut.

'It is but a dwellinghouse, sir,' he said, 'no more than a house. And Ellie lives yet, though I know not where. And the musician fellow, who I believe is of a cloth-making family, lives yet. And for all I know he may be of the opposite persuasion if you get my drift, sir, and be opposed to the workings of the mill. Yet having delivered Ellie Bright from danger, though I know not where she is, he came back to see how I fared. And he gave me his medicine, sir, therefore I fear he has gone without, for which cause I am here.'

After which Martin Gathercole fell silent, turning back the cuff of his borrowed surtout in some bewilderment then righting it again

XIV

He then rose, taking up and laying down his hat, which was not his, for at first he did not know it and looked vaguely around the dispensary for any peg upon which a hat he might know as his own should repose; until, realising the object of his search, I conveyed into his hands the borrowed hat, noticing at the same time that the nap was new and that it was clean about the inside and must have been of the best his mill hands had to offer. So with his garments, which were clean and little worn though simple, as if the tenants of such were accustomed to wear them to the dissenting chapel of a Sunday. From which I was led to suppose that the mill owner, for all that he had his enemies, was well regarded among the hands.

I followed him down the staircase, begging him to mind his head on the low beam at the turning which has met with my own head many a time when I have not been vigilant. At which turning he stopped and took out of his pocket fragment of paper.

'This is one o them, sir,' he said, 'one o them letters,' thrusting the same into my hand. Then when I made to protest that it represented evidence in his case he uttered words to the effect that the King had declined into an early dotage and was no more likely to take up his case than one of the witless sheep on the hills above Clywold.

For in truth, though I knew much, I had no wish to harbour about my person or in my dwellinghouse anything that might be turned to evidence, having had enough of the ways of both England and France in extracting the truth, which is itself variable.

And there was moreover that which I held in my head knowing not if I had imparted anything under duress, and knowing also that it was the manner of some to lead those under coercion to believe they had broken in their extremity; for many a man believing he has given away his secrets will give yet more.

'Have it, sir,' said Martin Gathercole. ''Tis better in your hands than mine.'

So saying, he took his leave, having given into my keeping not only his letter but also his words of disparagement of the King, and having felt, I did not doubt, the better for parting with the words, both written and spoken.

And it occurred to me that I was like as not to descend into a man of fear, precious of the health of his mind and body, and indeed of his life in this world. Which thought drove me, though I know not why, to the place in York they call the popish church of St Clare, taking Martin Gathercole's letter with me in my scrip. Where, finding outside a body of the King's militia questioning the faithful on the way in, I would have abandoned the idea and repaired back to the dispensary, but the very reason that had so driven me, namely that I was sinking into a man of fear, returned from I know not where except that it was of the dear Saviour; and I approached the door where certain of the King's men were stationed. For this I did rather than confirm to myself that I was indeed a man of fear.

That officer I knew as Thomas Hayward stepped forward, though he gave no sign of remembering me, and begged to examine my scrip, questioning me on the medicines it contained, what they might be and how prepared, and for what manner of ailments, and how effective the treatment might be; all the time regarding the letter, which he looked over in a cursory manner and afterwards returned to the scrip. Which would likely have been the end of the matter, but that the letter was seized from the scrip by a fellow officer and scrutinised, obliging Thomas Hayward to return to it with more application.

'What is this, my good fellow?'

'A letter.'

'Read it to me, I pray you.'

'... "Let him beware who dwells herein". '

'Is it yours?'

'You see it is in my possession.'

'Is it yours?'

'It is in my possession, as you see.'

'Then you had best to keep it in safety, my good fellow, lest it fall into the wrong hands.'

Thomas Hayward looked me in the eye and gestured to the officers of the militia that they should stand back and let me pass into the church; yet for the life of me I could not call to mind the occasion that had brought me there and I left through the eastern door without seeing either my confessor or the men of the King's militia, who for all I knew were yet stationed at the south most door until the ending of the mass, waiting for me, which thought gave me no little comfort.

'I perceive that you are in some kind of pickle, sir,' said Luke Bower on my return, by which I supposed that he had seen Martin Gathercole in the way, as I had not heard the expression used by Luke before, or indeed anyone but Martin Gathercole that very day, and again I reflected on the curious usings of the English tongue.

'Why think you that, Luke?' I said. 'Have I the appearance of one that is in a pickle?'

'You have been to the popish church, sir. Therefore I assume that you feel yourself to be in a pickle. And before you ask another question, sir, you bring the aroma of frankincense with you on your person. Thereby I suppose you to have been to the popish church. And thereby I suppose that you suppose yourself to be in a pickle and seeking the confirmation of your confessor that you are a sinner.'

'Yes indeed, Luke, that has all the ingredients of the truth. And now you will tell me what a pickle is.'

'It is a sorry plight, sir.'

'Am I in a sorry plight, Luke?'

'That is for you to tell me, sir.'

So seeing that this talk was likely to progress in ever decreasing circles I gave Luke the letter Martin Gathercole had left with me.

'This could have landed you in a pickle, sir, if any officer of the King's militia had found it on your person.'

Then, although Luke appeared already to know what had befallen me during the morning I related to him the details of my recent encounter with the patient Thomas Hayward, who was an officer of the King's men, and what might have been his apparent willingness to overlook the letter, had not a fellow officer seized it and scrutinised it.

'Whom I would remember well,' I concluded, 'as I observed a carbuncle on his neck which had already become grossly inflamed by the chafing of the neck of his tunic. Otherwise a tall fellow and well looking enough but for a hordeolum developing on the left lower eyelid.'

'That's Caleb Sawney,' said Luke. 'Those fellows think they can see off Napoleon Bonaparte and yet are too fearful to go to the physician.'

'Then the physician must send a remedy to this fearful fellow,' I said. 'We will not wait for him to come to us. We will have a tincture of Ajuga reptans conveyed to the garrison.'

'Only so long as I am not required to do the conveying, sir,' said Luke.

'Then you are acquainted with this fellow, Luke, either in person or by repute?'

Luke returned that he was not and I saw that there was no more to be gained from him on the matter, for he was busying himself searching among the patients' records.

'It is gone, sir,' he said after much searching, and with a contortion of the features which suggested that he still dwelt on the officer Caleb Sawney as well as on his fruitless search.

'It is gone because I had the selfsame thought as you, Luke, and removed the document from Will Cantrell's record in order to compare the script with that of the letter given to me by Martin Gathercole. It is the same script. Either the mischief was done by the same fellows; or not, if several applied to the same scribe to write for them. What think you? It is to be hoped that he who writes rinses his hands in the beck after handling this ink, which I suspect is noxious, for a foul stench arises from the paper.'

'Caleb Sawney is a vicious fellow,' said Luke. ''Tis no marvel he has a carbuncle with that much poison in his soul; tis the evil of the man bursting out.'

'A carbuncle is an acute burning in the tissues under the skin leading to multiple eruptions, Luke. It happens in the angel and in the devil alike. No doubt the poor fellows in the garrison are ill fed and make up with whatever scraps they can get.'

'Nevertheless, the fellow seeks preferment and will seize at it wherever he can find it; most likely in the very boots Hayward wears now, if they fit him coming from such a cripple.'

'He has the gout,' I said, 'which appears in the hands and feet,' though Luke Bower knew this well enough. 'Thomas Hayward will return to the dispensary when he is ready.'

'Until such time he is prepared to overlook the pernicious document in your possession in case you should spread the word about the plague under his foot, sir.'

'Which I would not do, Luke. He is a patient and we don't spread idle talk about patients.'

'I know that, sir,' said Luke. 'But happen Hayward doesn't. Folks think all men are as themselves with the same vices and the same virtues. Why think you that the fellow Gathercole gave you the letter?'

'I know not, Luke.'

'Well, sir,' said Luke, 'he gave you a cup of poison as like as he handed you a cup of hemlock. He no doubt suspects you of sympathising with the machine breakers, sir, and was bent on foisting the evidence upon you. I'll convey the remedies, sir, as you asked. Henbane for Hayward and bugle for the carbuncle fellow.'

Which I prepared forthwith, while trying to recover to my mind my assistant's recent talk and the degrees by which he had arrived at a change of mind; for I feared him subtle beyond my comprehension, though a well-meaning fellow in his way.

XV

Meanwhile the good young woman Jem Bailey continued at her post in the concealed chamber tending the patient Will Cantrell, who showed no eagerness to leave his place of asylum. Rather he showed a degree of agitation when the possibility of release was aired in his presence, to the extent that although both his poor face and his hand had healed I suspected that the shock of the mischief yet lingered in his soul and was like to do so for the remainder of his earthly life. And I reflected not for the first time that although men generally fear death as the greatest calamity, yet it brings the end of all earthly terrors; as I had on many occasions witnessed in the fair land of France when those approaching the blade did so with no fear, seeing as it were the doors of eternity flung wide open and the end to their afflictions. Yet there is far to travel between the first condition and the second, and we are but pilgrims, journeying either slowly or with haste towards our end as the case may be.

Suffice to say that no further effort was made to persuade the poor fellow to leave, and the terrors of Will Cantrell continued to inflict themselves on Jem Bailey. Indeed, as he had failed to respond to the tincture of betony for the madness I began to suspect that the poor fellow's wits were beyond recall, and my assistant Luke Bower made to confirm this by remarking that there was generally no hope for them as could not remember their own names. Though I gathered by now that Luke must know the cause of his speechlessness, namely that his tongue had been torn out by the root as a tare is pulled out of the field.

It became evident to me also, and no doubt to Luke though he made no mention of it, that Jem Bailey's "faults", though I would not call them thus, had found her out and she was with child. And I have to say that Will Cantrell, for all that he had carried on a rough and heavy trade, behaved to her now with the courtesy commonly expected of a more lettered man; the fastness of his tenure in the concealed chamber no doubt also having some bearing on his more settled behaviour.

So it was with Jem Bailey, and I knew not what to do since all around me held their peace on the matter; until a day when the good soul detained me as I was leaving Will Cantrell after inspecting his hurts, and stood before me with an outward defiance which I could see would soon dissolve as she told her tale.

'Sir,' she said, 'when I told you before that I was too willing that was a mistruth, for which I beg your pardon. I was not willing, sir, though I dared not say so because he who did this to me said he would visit retribution upon my father, who is in the same line of work as Mr Cantrell here. Indeed, they know each other, sir, as all in the cropping profession know one another, either in person or by repute. And he who visited this upon me told me what he would do to my father, sparing no detail, so that I had no alternative but to comply with his demands. So here I am, sir, and you can see that I am with child, and I thank you and Mr Cantrell here and Mr Bower that no mention has been made. Though you can't have failed to notice, sir,' she added.

And here Jem Bailey broke into loud and bitter weeping, so that her whole frame was shaken and she was hard pressed to get her breath; and, as if in sympathy, tears rolled down the honest face of Will Cantrell.

Then I bade Jem Bailey be seated and take a preparation of honeysuckle and thyme, though in small doses as I knew her malady to be of the spirit and I feared also to do harm to the bairn which, for all its cruel beginnings in this world, had no part in its own conception.

'You are now going to ask me who did this, sir,' said Jem Bailey, and a simple thought came to me that at the least Jem could not see into my mind, as nothing was farther from my intentions than to extract from her the name of the fellow and thus subject her to more misery. So I told her as much, but asked leave to tell her plight to Mr Bower, he being my scribe and assistant and keeper of the records of medicines in the dispensary, which she readily agreed to.

'Sir,' Jem Bailey went on, 'I fear I'll be hard pressed to cherish the bairn as I ought, remembering its beginnings.'

So I said what was lately in my thoughts, namely that a child is in no way responsible for the circumstances of its conception, trying as I might to pacify the poor young woman, yet in a pompous way as is my habit, I fear; and knowing also that, besides the bodily malformations and idiosyncrasies of the parents a child might also take on elements of bad habits from a parent in spite of good care given to its nurture, as I have oft remarked with sorrow in my sojourn on this earth.

'Who did this?' said Luke, which I suspected rightly would be his first words on the matter, and suspecting also that he knew the answer to his question.

'These matters are often resolved when the infant appears in the world with no question being asked,' I said. 'But even should that be the case we would not spread the fact abroad for fear of bringing about reprisals.'

To which Luke Bower assented though I could see from the contraction of his brow and the set of his mouth that the injustice done to Jem Bailey smouldered within him and would no doubt manifest itself in some other way, as is the manner of ills harboured in secret.

And so the matter rested, and neither Luke nor I spoke of it, nor of Jem Bailey's plight, for I believe we trusted to the good offices of those at the house of mercy to watch over her and replace her with another nursing attendant when her duties became too arduous. For this reason, and because Luke Bower and I were rough-hewn bachelors and entertained a natural awe in the presence of women's affairs, we resolved in a tacit agreement between ourselves not to make our persons present in the concealed chamber at times when we believed Jem Bailey would be there.

And so it was thus, until a day when a message was conveyed by way of Will Cantrell when Luke attended him to collect his writings, which were still coming up to the dispensary though little and seldom, namely that the young woman humbly asked for help in a plea writ at the foot of a page of Will Cantrell's script, and though haltingly in as pretty and neat a hand as was ever seen; which effort must have caused much time and pain, and that of her mentor also for I could detect in the formation of certain characters the influence of Will Cantrell.

So I took to the concealed chamber tinctures of lavender for the pain of childbirth, though I knew not at what time the bairn would come; and also carrot for a speedy delivery, bistort for sickness, and basil to cheer the heart and drive away the melancholy, knowing all young women to be melancholic at this time, mindful that in bringing a life into the world they might forfeit their own. For which reason I have ever held in the deepest respect young women in this condition, who are equal in bravery to any young man who goes to war. And for a better purpose, for a young woman bears life into the world whereas a man of war seeks to drive life out of the world.

She who greeted me was little like the young woman I had seen before, being now pale and sunken eyed, though but a month of the year had passed since our last meeting; and noting her malaise I asked how she fared. To which she answered that there were none competent in the mystery of childbirth in the house of mercy, being all aged women and never wed, though kind enough if kindness meant to make as if all was well and there was no bairn on the way. She said moreover that she feared she might not be safely delivered of the bairn now that she was not well, and she feared that she might not long be welcome at the house of mercy in her shameful state.

When all this talk was done, and perceiving that the poor young woman was sinking into the most melancholic state oft seen when a child is expected, I did my best to persuade her that such a condition of the mind was not uncommon, though I fear that I did not convince her fully, both of us being mindful that her situation was, though I fear common in those times, one that could hardly be borne. Nevertheless, Jem Bailey took a tincture of lavender for her comfort and a further tincture of basil for quietness of mind, and presently seemed better. Then knowing that she was without a companion in her ordeal I said to her that, with her leave, I might find a good and trusted woman to call on her and give whatever help necessary. To which Jem Bailey readily assented and her melancholy lifted; and I saw then that the worst of such an ordeal, or indeed of any ordeal, is to have to go through it without the companionship of another human soul.

'Do I know this nurse you have in mind?' said Luke Bower, to which I made no answer, as there was scarce a living soul in the county of York he did not know, either personally or by hearsay. 'If it pleases you, sir, I will be myself in the parish of Holmroyd and if the nurse you have in mind lives near that place I will deliver a message,' by which I gathered that Luke had seen through the window in my head the intention to ask Rosie Todd. 'I only say this, sir,' he added, 'to save you the journey, as you were needed, sir, while you were in the company of him as cannot remember his own name,' (Luke jerked his head in the direction of the concealed chamber, as had become his habit) 'and I informed them that they could wait on you this day after the noon. If it pleases you, sir.'

'Then I will write a letter for you to take, Luke, if that is the case.'

For in spite of the fact that I knew little enough of Luke Bower for all his talk, I knew this, namely that I trusted him to bring any mission or errand to completion. Neither would I have felt it necessary to seal the letter but that Luke insisted upon it, saying lest the epistle fall into the wrong hands.

So I begged him to please be rid of the letter to its destination before embarking on whatever business of his own he had. For I never knew what manner of commerce he was engaged in when he left the dispensary; except I trusted he was safely housed and with some creature comforts, as he was ever neat and clean about his person and did not ail overmuch, which all led me to suppose that in the straitened times in which we lived, with the long war just ended, he fared adequately if not luxuriously.

The same could not be said for Hannah Gaut, who with her husband Zephaniah presented herself at the dispensary on the afternoon, and who appeared as harrowed as at her last attendance, and complained still of the hammering in her ears.

'Which I know is the tintinnabulation, sir,' she said, 'as you told me before, though to my mind it is in these days the knocking of nails into the gallows-tree, and I hear it every day of my life, sir, and more often than not of a night when I wake in the thin hours before the dawn.'

'I tell her tis the tintinnabulation as you said, sir,' said Zephanaiah. 'An she knows it in her mind but not in her heart. Thas the fix we're in. Tho for myself, sir, I'm restored a little an I thank thee. Surely I do, sir, and for the medicine tha came as an angel's gift outside the door.'

Having said which Zephaniah took up the aimless song which Robert had described, and indeed which I had noted on his first visit to the dispensary; and having concluded a line of it he cast a glance at his wife.

'Hannah,'

'Nay, Zephaniah, I canna.'

'But ye can, lass.'

'Nay.'

'The gentleman's waiting on ye, Hannah. Let me do the deed for ye, lass, if ye canna.'

Whereupon Hannah Gaut handed over to her husband Zephaniah her reticule, and he drew forth from it a sheaf of papers.

'Tis my writing, sir,' she said. 'Tis my soul.'

'I will take care of your soul, Hannah,' I said.

'Tis jus as I told her' said Zephaniah, 'Ye han no need to fret, lass.'

Then I gave to Zephaniah a tincture of digitalis and to Hannah a tincture of basil to cheer the heart, though I doubted greatly that the tender green leaf would be such as to drive away the gallows-tree. Then, because Zephaniah was intent on paying me from the little he possessed I took the good folk down to the garden at the back of the dispensary under the great wall of York so that they might see for themselves that their remedies were provided by none other than the Lord Almighty. And whether it was the peace of the garden resting under the sun, or the scent of the new basil and lavender rising into the warm air and the soft green spikes of the foxgloves pushing up from the earth in that sheltered place I knew not, but Hannah Gaut resumed a former self which I had imagined yet not seen, becoming a woman of great quiet, and fair of face; and seated on a low wall in the shade of an ancient nutmeg tree she spoke thus:

'Sir we fear we have wronged you and misused your kindness. We gave you to believe that we came here on account of our own ills, which we did to an extent, for my husband is hard pressed to catch his breath and I have the tintinnabulation ever present in my head, though it sounds to me, sir, like the building of the gallows-tree. But our intention has ever been to ask you on behalf of our son, who some say has half lost his wits and wanders, which we well know, around the hill country above Clywold in the company, they tell us, of certain men they call machine breakers and makers of fire.'

Having said which, and indeed having scarce begun their tale, Hannah and Zephaniah rose to their feet and courteously bade me farewell, not having asked for a remedy for their son, which indeed I could not have given as he was not present.

But I believed the telling of her woes lifted Hannah's spirits and, I have to say, silenced Zephaniah's song, which I thought to be an expression of the torment of the mind, much as another man will gnaw at his finger ends.

That same night I had a dream. It was, as always, that I was climbing, higher and higher into the sun, which was dazzling my eyes. I continued climbing until I could no longer hear the baying crowd beneath, though I could see them way below standing expectantly, looking not towards me but towards a fellow whom I saw clearly, being manhandled into their presence. I watched as they stripped him of his tunic and placed a blindfold over his eyes. One of those who had lately been leading him had in his hand a scourge which he appeared to be offering to a company of militia standing by, as if appealing for a volunteer to carry out the chastisement on the poor fellow, whom I knew well by the kerchief yet in place round his neck, though I could not remember his name. None was willing to take up the scourge, and although I could hear nothing I could see that the crowd was becoming restive, calling for one who was man enough to take up the challenge; though still I heard nothing. Then I saw a fellow, taller than all others, shoulder his way through the crowd, take up the scourge and commence the affliction; which sound rose to my ears in a sharp spasmodic beating though I could hear naught else.

And my dream ended, for a strong south wind had arisen in the night and loosened the casement, which was riding back and forth upon its hinge and beating the frame of the window.

XVI

Neither did the wind abate, not at the dawn nor as the day turned from violet to white with dark rags of cloud driven across the sky as if fleeing a pestilence. And abroad in York there were great branches down across the thoroughfares of Peter-gate and Collier-gate, and many a casement loose on its hinges and like to fall; and already, early though it was, men, and women also, clearing glass lest the poor beasts should be lamed, all with a great measure of perseverance because the wind was enough to topple a grown man. I saw also linen from lines wrapped around trees and many a hat bowling along the carriageway, not least my own hat, which was lifted from my head as I left the Monk-bar and set down, as I thought, behind the outbuildings of the tallow chandler.

Also the poor horses were agitated by the wind, tossing their heads and giving the coachman trouble enough in calming them lest they rear and upset the coach entirely, which indeed could have done with more of us travelling, and all of they present meagre of build, as was I myself. For in those days few I believe ate their fill, and it was seldom that I saw an apoplexy or one with the morbidity of corpulence.

And all talk in the coach was of the weather and the great havoc occasioned by it, and of the sign of the Bee-hive flying off its moorings and carried the length of the Stone-gate and by a hair's breadth coming to ground short of the night watchman at the end of his labours, which they said was a miracle if ever there was one. And several other tales there were of miraculous escapes which filled the time and diverted our thoughts from the buffeting of the coach, which was indeed enough to turn a traveller bilious; and which happened ere long in the case of one of my companions, to whom I gave a tincture of bistort.

Then arriving at Holmroyd boundary at two hours after the mid-day I requested to be set down, though I knew not why I was come there, only that the dream of the previous night had unsettled my spirits and caused me no little anxiety on account of he whose name I could not bring to mind in the dream, who was as I thought about to be subjected to the scourge, and also on account of my scribe Luke Bower who was, I trusted, on a mission to the same place.

The southerly wind had abated somewhat but was yet enough to carry on it the secrets of mankind, namely some converse between the coachman and a messenger handing in certain packets to be conveyed yonder to Beckwith, which was brought to my hearing as I alighted; from which I understood that the magistrate Mr Born was called to the Sheep-close nigh Holmroyd to deliver justice to one who had been seen at an arson, which, the speaker said, though confidential in nature, was abroad in all the valleys just as if the hills themselves were whispering the news one to another; and he pitied the poor fellow, for whatever he had done was little to warrant the justice delivered by Richard Born, for he was a hard man and a cruel one, though with charm enough to spare and a honeyed tongue when affairs went his way.

It is a curious phenomenon, and I believe common to many men, that given the name of a place the feet will travel thither without ever having been in that place before. So it was with me, that I set off along the path at the heel of a hill, observing the cotton grass flattened onto the ground with the late force of the wind and the sheep so crowded against the briar hedge that drifts of fleece had caught on the thorns like the winter's snow.

And turning the heel of the hill also I saw from afar a huddle of folks on the yonder slope as if watching a spectacle in the valley, to which I hastened, finding the space known to those who dwelt about as the Sheep-close; and lying prone on the ground the poor fellow, stripped of his tunic yet still wearing a kerchief about his neck. And all about stood bands of the militia, and in their midst the magistrate Richard Born with a scourge in his hand, appealing as I surmised, for I was still some fair distance away, to the men of the militia in a manner of dumb show, for the wind was such as to carry his voice away from me and up the valley even though I knew well his loudness from the time he had attended the dispensary.

And, although I could not hear his words, I understood that Richard Born was appealing for any one of the militia to take up the scourge and deliver the affliction to the poor fellow; though none would, each man looking down at his boots or up at the scudding clouds, anywhere but into the eyes of the magistrate, who became the more vehement, waving his arms and approaching each man in turn. Until from the back a member of the militia shouldered his way through and stood in the centre facing the magistrate. Some dialogue passed between the two, after which the officer removed his coat and made to offer it to a fellow to hold, though the fellow would not, but placed it on the grass as if it were a contaminated thing. And all the while the magistrate demonstrated in wild gestures how the affliction was to be delivered; this all, as I have said, taking place within the silence of distance.

Yet even as I approached a rider bore down on the scene at a canter, jumped from his horse and threw the reins on the ground. And as he, whom I knew to be Martin Gathercole yet wearing no longer the dress of a common man, came near, the magistrate indicated, in that very instant, that the affliction should begin. And though I heard naught else I heard the crack of the whip, like the report of a firearm echoing around the hills, and I saw gouts of blood spring up from the poor fellow's back. Meanwhile Martin Gathercole stood pleading with the magistrate for mercy and attempted to lay hands on the persecutor, but was pushed aside as easily as a wisp of cotton grass, for all that he is tall and a well made man.

And this as I approached, yet did not, for I was as in a dream trying to run yet tied to the spot and going nowhere, while the lashes continued to be delivered to he who was on the ground, as silent as if he were dead, and the crowd looking on the while, both in the Sheep-close and on the hill above.

Until hidden by the broad day a cloaked and hooded man, in the interval that the persecutor stopped to flex his arm, felled him from behind and fled again into the bright day. For many a man who is found out in the cover of darkness may yet do an ill deed in the light of the noon day.

Then as I drew near I saw that the persecutor had been helped to his feet, and I could see that his right arm, which had lately wielded the scourge, hung loosely as if by a sinew and would likely never fulfil such an office again. And indeed, he in charge of the militia, whom I recognised as my patient Thomas Hayward, was commanding that the fellow's coat be torn up and used as a stanch, and the rest to cover the wounds of the prisoner, who was yet lying face downwards, and as I observed on nearing the scene was senseless and twitching spasmodically in the upper limbs. Then seeing the folks come down from the hills Thomas Hayward ordered his men away. And the magistrate also was gone, although I did not see him leave, nor, I believe, did any other.

For when Martin Gathercole asked no man knew of the magistrate's whereabouts, or were not admitting it if they did know, but rather ignored the question, recognising Martin Gathercole from his dress if for no other reason as a mill owner, even though, as I understood for I could not hear the discourse, he had pleaded on behalf of the prisoner.

Meanwhile the good folk from the hills noticed the apothecary, though I have to say that I was scarce awake to myself, and made way, gesturing to the poor fellow on the ground who was becoming sensible and attempting to move, and was being restrained by certain good souls lest he cause himself the more hurt. To whose wounds, by the grace of God, for I knew not to whom else to attribute the matter, being both short of breath with running and sick at heart into the bargain, I applied tinctures of elm and agrimony for their healing; all the while being conscious of a considerable shadow falling over the proceedings, which I feared to be some dark contingent of the law. Until looking up I saw it was merely a horse, nuzzling the poor fellow's face after the manner of their kind.

'Tis my bay mare Yolande, sir,' said Martin Gathercole. 'As you see, she came back, and she will take the young fellow home to wherever his dwelling is,' which I truly believe was said in good faith, though the folks from the hills, no doubt interpreting the fine gesture as a device to seek out their dwellings, said they would not importune him. But as all were bewildered as to how to raise the wounded man to his feet, let alone convey him to his dwellinghouse, Martin Gathercole bade his horse to kneel, which the gentle creature did, and the young fellow was assisted onto her back. And the hill folk marvelled, saying they had never seen a horse behave so, quite forgetting then that Martin Gathercole was a mill owner and thus a man engendering suspicion.

So the company went forward at a slow pace, until coming to Holmroyd and a cart being to hand the poor fellow was transferred and taken off to I know not where. Nor did I wish to know for there were too many seeking him; and what a man does not know that he cannot tell again. Suffice to say that his name came back to me once I saw his face.

Then Martin Gathercole said he was intending to repair to the sign of the Ram's Head, where, he said, he would obtain oats for his bay mare Yolande. And he said also that she had learned to get down low so that Ellie Bright might easily mount up on her, though Ellie did so seldom as she went abroad little enough being conscious of her malady, and when she did venture abroad she preferred that it be on foot. And he knew not where she went but some there were who had seen her following after the musician fellow, even he who had been lately afflicted in the Sheep-close, though he himself doubted on account of her bodily ills that she could walk more than half a furlong.

So I accompanied the good man to the sign of the Ram's Head, saying little but hearing much, until arriving there he bade me farewell. But before going on his way he said he had been in receipt of another letter, this time offering mischief against Ellie Bright; not, he said, that she had done any offence to anybody because she was as an angel from heaven, but because they who wrote it knew she was nearest to his heart in all the world. And I feared that Martin Gathercole would give me the letter as he did the last. But he did not.

All they in the public room of the Ram's Head fell silent as I entered, who indeed were few in number since all of the other guests who, by reason of the clamour they made seemed many, were in the private apartments. And I could not but be aware from the conversation when it started up again in the public room that certain soldiers of the militia had commandeered the private rooms, having brought with them one of their number who was sorely wounded and like to meet his Maker that very night. But as to the nature of the wound none had any true knowledge. Some supposed it was his head, and another his heart, and yet another his legs, and all had a lively opinion on the matter. For all men are fascinated by the presence of death, just so long as it is not their own or that of a cherished one.

Thus I reflected, looking into the fire blazing in the hearth though the day was become warm, and I thought of the fire that intervened to save me and another from certain death in Paris at the time of the terror. Yet my mind could not envisage the future life of the other, and it came to me, seated by the hearth at the sign of the Ram's Head, that my fellow captive had surely perished; and I believe I had always known it but unconsciously, which thought sank me into a great desolation of the spirit. And I was in that low condition of the mind, believing I yet lived when my brother in affliction had long deceased, when one belonging to the militia awakened me out of my reverie, indicating that I should follow him into the private apartment of the hostelry.

For which recent train of thought I had cause to feel greatly ashamed when I saw the plight of the patient lying on the billiard table, whose face was white as the snow on Brancliffe-tor in the winter season, and whose right arm, though unrecognisable as such, so drenched in blood was it, seemed hardly to belong to the fellow. And in truth there were several in the room who were ready to pass out at the sight, for all that they had seen worse many times over on the field of battle. Though not Thomas Hayward, who, for all his groundless fear of the plague, proved himself to be as staunch a man as any.

'You'll recognise the patient here as Caleb Sawney, sir,' he said. 'He agreed to take the scourge to yon prisoner when none else would, nor would they hold his coat while he did the deed. And then, while in the act of it, some fellow came upon him of a sudden and delivered this hurt, sir.' And Thomas Hayward removed the cover from the patient's arm with no more distaste than if her were uncovering his couch at night. 'It is a sorry mess, sir, as you can see. I sent some men after the villain but on a fool's errand no doubt as no man saw where he went.'

Meanwhile Caleb Sawney's eyes were fixed on mine in a most pitiful way, and for all that his deed was an ill one his plight disconcerted me greatly, and I had no doubt that his pain was extreme. For which I administered poppy to provoke drowsiness, and lupin in the case of a subsequent gangrene which would of a certainty set in before the sun was gone to rest that day.

'You will wonder, sir,' continued Thomas Hayward, 'at the nature of the wound, since the mischief delivered to Sawney was over and done before anyone knew it had begun so to speak, but the limb has the look of having been hacked about as if the villain were at the task a half hour. The reason being, sir, that Sawney here, when the guard stepped outside to relieve himself, attempted an amputation, and as I say, sir, we have a sorry mess here. And what you're expected to do for him the Lord only knows.'

Which indeed was well said by Thomas Hayward, for of a truth I knew not what to do myself.

'He will stay here if the host permits,' I said, 'and we will give salix for the preventing of the fever. And if one of your men will be kind enough to assist me to dress and make stable the wound until he be removed to a surgeon he may yet do well.'

But no man of the militia would, whether it was for the sight of the mischief or on account of the patient being Caleb Sawney I knew not. But none either would meet my eye, nor that of Thomas Hayward, who looked to each of his men without finding any willing to assist; and all the time, for the poor fellow was sore with the gout, shuffling from one to another foot as if he could bear to put neither to the ground.

'Then it must be Mistress Todd,' he said.

'Tis no work for a woman,' I said, and would have said more but that even as I spoke the door opened and Rosie Todd was ushered with little ceremony into the room.

XVII

She looked at the patient lying on the billiard table with some equanimity, less discomfited by the sight before her than any man of the militia.

And the poor fellow in turn directed his gaze towards her, focusing as well as he might, for the tincture of poppy had taken effect and he had sunk into a state of drowsiness, though not I feared sufficiently to blunt the pain of the procedure awaiting him.

'As you see, Mistress Todd,' said Thomas Hayward, 'we have here a sorry mess and the apothecary needs assistance in dressing the wound. For which reason you were brought, and for which we thank you heartily since, in short, every last one of my men lacks the stomach to undertake such a task, and I also, and that is the truth of it as God is my witness.'

With which Thomas Hayward lifted the cover from the patient's wound.

'That's like to turn to mortification,' said Rosie Todd. 'Your ligature is on too long.'

'That or the other, Mistress Todd,' said Thomas Hayward.

And all this conducted in a low whisper, though I had no doubt that the poor fellow could hear it every word, as all men know that the faculty of hearing remains after every other has taken flight; which I know well from those times when such has been the case with me. And my mind would have returned to my late dark thoughts, namely that though I had escaped the burning dwelling in Paris he who was undergoing the same affliction in a neighbouring room had not, but that Rosie Todd's voice had returned to its customary volume and was addressing me.

'There is water aboiling for thy lancet, sir, and I have ordered fresh linen to be brought. For you know better than I, sir what it behoves us to do.'

And indeed I did for already the flesh of the lower arm had paled and I fancied I saw a creeping discolouration affecting the hand though it was in shadow, and between the living part of the arm and the mortified a red line, though I could not be sure on account of the whole area being soiled with the fellow's blood.

'Caleb Sawney, doest thou hear me?' Rosie Todd leaned close to the patient and called loudly into his ear like any keeper of the beasts in Clywold market, in spite of her braids. 'Caleb Sawney, hear me. Thou art not afraid. The gentleman here will wash thy wound and cut away the bad.'

The poor fellow rolled his head about on the bolster which had been placed under it for a pillow, and for all the influence of the poppy his eyes were wide with comprehension.

'He is not afraid, sir. And now I will make sure of the water and clean linen while you prepare for the operation, and also I will ask for candles as they out yonder will all be looking in if we don't make fast the shutters.'

And I could see that Rosie Todd was right, for already when she left the room there were certain folks behind the door intent on finding out what was going on within, and indeed also lined up at the window.

'I have told them to be off, sir,' she said on entering with the linen, and bearing a parcel also, the contents of which I liked not to inquire into. 'Tis not a theatre that they should stand and gawp. A basin of water will be brought in presently. Now, sir, your silence informs me that you have not performed such operations. But I have heard of the like from my husband, may the Lord rest his soul, and I took to heart the tale never knowing when it might come in,' having said which in hushed tones she went again to the patient and called into his ear.

'The gentleman has done many such operations, Caleb Sawney, and will see you well. I know tis a fable I just told, sir,' she whispered, 'but the Lord will forgive me for tis either the operation or the gangrene and no way in between.'

The host himself carried in the water and I believe would have stayed for the spectacle, so long did he linger, but that Rosie Todd bade him go and heat more water and see to some gruel for the patient, who would stand in need of it after the proceedings.

Meanwhile the poor fellow had fallen into an uneasy slumber under the influence of the poppy, of which I had given him a further dose while Rosie Todd was absent seeing to the water.

'I will remove the cover for you, sir, and you will inspect the hurt and begin by swabbing the area with water, sir, before we loosen the ligature.'

All of which led me to understand that the good woman was about to guide me through the operation.

'And happen you'll need a ligature for the vein and indeed a suture for the outside, and a more substantial lancet than you carry with you, sir, which we have to hand,' having said which she unwrapped the parcel and displayed a goodly array of kitchen oddities, which she set out on a cloth atop the mantle shelf beyond the sight of the patient should he awake.

'Please God the wound is less severe than we anticipate,' I said, more to reassure the good woman that I was still in charge of my wits, of which I had a doubt.

And as if to confirm that which I did not believe, namely that the wound would prove to be less grievous than we expected, I saw that the assailant had done little, making a laceration on the inner side of the upper arm, which nevertheless had gone deep enough to bite into the brachial artery, and there was much blood, which had run down the arm and set brown, apart from the later wound where the poor fellow had tried to cut off his own hand.

I bade Rosie Todd to bring the candle near in, which confirmed what I suspected, that the typical red line of demarcation betwixt the dead flesh and the living was indeed an illusion which had washed away, as had also the discolouration of the patient's hand for, and I had observed this before in my dealings with him, he was none too regular in bathing.

'Then you will have no need of the suture, sir,' said Rosie Todd, and I believe she was dismayed that the great event was turning into a small one. So I placed two sutures in the area of the self-inflicted injury, and asked the good woman if she would please to improvise a structure by which we might elevate the arm in a sling and prepare to loosen the ligature; which she did by tying a sheet to the high back of a chair.

Then all this done and all the basins of soiled water and bloodied linen removed from the room she called into the patient's ear.

'Caleb Sawney, you may wake for tis finished and you have done your part like a soldier of the King.'

Whereupon the poor fellow awoke, and looking for his wounded arm which he thought to be lying on the table beside him, and not finding it there, broke into loud and bitter lamentations, until the good woman, after letting him so think for a while, drew his attention to the sling.

'There's thy arm, Caleb Sawney. Tis as good as ever it was. And some may say that's a misfortune for that it wielded a scourge this very day. And let this be thy lesson. The good Lord, with the help of this gentleman here, has restored thy arm, and if at any time this arm goes to the bad thou wilt lose it for sure.'

Saying indeed what my profession denied me, even had I wished to use such words; since all men, malefactors and saints alike, are dealt with equally by the apothecary, who, if this were not so, would have more than sufficient opportunity to deliver poison to those he considered the world to be well rid of.

Then the host, having been summoned to ask if the wounded man might pass the night at the sign of the Ram's Head, said in categorical terms that no, he might not stay there on any account, the reason being that it had come to his knowledge how the fellow had gained his hurt and there would no doubt be reprisals from the hill folks, to the extent of an arson in the night. For he knew well the ways of the hill folks, that they would not let a mischief to one of their number go unremarked. And the young fellow of the militia must join his men and they would do well to convey him as they might to his folks at Beckwith.

Which talk informed me that all around knew Caleb Sawney, for good or ill, and I have to say mainly the latter. So they of the militia who had stayed behind, Thomas Hayward among them, who for all his fear of the plague and the pains in his feet, looked to the good of his men, were brought in from the public room with no little reluctance, expecting to see the sawn off remains of the limb. And indeed I saw them searching with their eyes for any receptacle on the floor which might have contained it.

'His arm is sound,' I said, 'and the host asks for him to please be conveyed to the bosom of his family, as others are expected at the sign of the Ram's Head on the morrow and all chambers will be needed,' for which invention may the Lord forgive me.

'Why, that's the first in the history of the Ram's Head,' said Thomas Hayward, 'for it is known in these parts to be a lonely and unfrequented place. But it will be done if the host wishes. Though I have reservations about the bosom of the family you refer to, sir, for it is a hard bosom if ever there was one and not one I would like to be abed with, be I never so desperate.'

'And he's a desperate man,' said one of the fellows, which occasioned much merriment; and all the while Caleb Sawney was looking from one to another, though none looked at him.

'I will give officer Sawney a preparation of bugle should the wound fester, and salix against the fever,' I said, for I had no doubt from the brightness of his eyes that he was heading thereto, 'and I beg you to ask those at his dwelling place to give the remedies to him daily, though he might appear sound, for fever can yet strike even though a patient may look recovered.'

'Which I will do myself, sir,' said Thomas Hayward, 'for they at his dwelling place are far gone in liquor and it would surely slip out of their minds.'

To Thomas Hayward also I gave, though in privacy for fear of the ridicule of his men, henbane and tansy for the joints of the feet for he had an arduous journey up the hill road to Beckwith and the fellow Sawney in a cart withal; the driver of which, for it had meanwhile been summoned, struck me as oddly familiar though I was at a loss to place him, or her, for in those afflicted times there were many who went abroad so muffled in cloaks and hats that whether they were men or women none could know. And in the latter half of the cart was a rude cloth covering heaven knows what, and I preferred indeed not to know, for that which a man doesn't know he cannot tell again; save that there was a poor sheep's leg protruding which from the looks of it was long since it had trodden the sweet grass of the upland, being yet the most meek and most humble of the Lord's creatures.

All the while, as the rest of the company were thrown into some confusion by the events in the Sheep-close and the fearful anticipation of an amputation, Rosie Todd's braids remained as neat and elaborate as ever they were; and indeed her person itself remained unruffled, though I have to say that she was the only soul who was so.

I found her seated thus, with her braids and her dress neat and clean, in the public room awaiting the return of the good host, who had told her that as a measure of his gratitude to her and the apothecary for having removed from the sign of the Ram's Head the incubus, for so he called the wounded man, he would bring in plain refreshment before our journey hence.

And though I like not to hear ill of any man, the good host, when he returned, continued to regale us with the ills that Caleb Sawney had done from his birth onwards, until I fairly believed that the host must be without sin himself to have cast so many stones, and I believe Rosie Todd also thought thus for she reminded him that they who tend the sick do so regardless of the patient's moral nature and that had always been the case since the time of Hippocrates, whereupon the good host, finding such learning concealed beneath braided hair, ceased his diatribe. And I myself reflected with some shame that at the first I had been ready to think Rosie Todd a light and frivolous woman on account of her braids; which she was not.

But the good host had not even then finished his discourse, and asked me where I came from, whereupon he mentioned another traveller not cast in the English mould who had lately been that way, with a musical device out of the ordinary, who had regaled the guests in the public room with astonishing and mysterious airs, from the very depths of the world yet not gloomy, the host said, which fellow looked like a kinsman to me so near was he in his dark colour of hair and eyes. And indeed, before he went on his way carrying the great musical device on his back he had inquired of the host if he knew of an apothecary in the county of York who happen looked much like himself, not that he was kindred but that he was from a southern place where the strong sun lends all folks their dark looks.

'Be that as it may,' continued the host, 'I told the fellow no, for at that time I had not set eyes on you, sir, if you be he that the other was searching for. And it is only but weeks past and he may yet be on the fair soil of England. Not that it is so fair at this precise time,' he concluded, 'with the likes of they at the Sheep-close, if you get my drift, sir.'

Having said which the host departed, and none too soon for Rosie Todd, since she had for some minutes past been at excessive pains to rein in certain words of her own.

'He is gone, sir,' she said.

'He has other guests to attend to, no doubt,' I said.

'I did not mean him,' said Rosie Todd, indicating the door by which the host had lately left the room. 'Him, sir. Mr Born. He has not come back home.'

In answer to which, as I was not certain how much Rosie Todd knew of what had passed in the Sheep-close, though I feared that she, and Grace Born also, knew much if not all, I said nothing.

'And we know not whom to ask, sir, being neither friendly with the King's men nor with the hill people, Mr Born being the magistrate, sir; and I have to say though I would not in front of Mrs Born, for when all is said and done she is tied to him, that Mr Born is not well regarded hereabouts on account of his station in life.'

I suggested then to Rosie Todd that perchance he had gone to some other place as his calling demanded, but she said no, he would always have his wife informed what he was about, even if it were not the Lord's truth he was telling. For, she said, there were those who had reported seeing him about the stews in York when he was supposedly attending to his calling.

And she fell silent, by which I understood that her tale was told and she knew I could do nothing even if Richard Born returned to the dispensary, not so much as to inform his wife that he was yet in the world.

So after a while, and Rosie Todd adding nothing more, I ventured upon the sorry plight of Jem Bailey, saying nothing but that she was residing at the house of mercy among women who, though they meant kindly and would no doubt cherish the little bairn when it arrived, knew nothing of the matters between now and then, so to speak, namely how a bairn comes into the world; stumbling around among my words like a blind man for I had no wish to cause offence to Rosie Todd, being alone with her in the room.

Whereupon she said she had been in attendance at the child bed many a time, which I had no doubt of as she had done all else in the way of nursing, and would wait upon the young lady at my earliest convenience, adding that it was a low deed the fellow had done, though I had indeed told her nothing of it, and she said moreover that she hoped she was spared to give him a corner of her mind.

So it was set that on the way from Clywold, for I intended to call upon Jane Pearce and Susan Knowles before returning to York, Rosie Todd should wait at the sign of the Ram's Head and accompany me back in the carriage.

XVIII

'I am much the same as before, sir, thanking ye. I can't complain. Leastways, I might complain but that I know all of my ills to be consequent upon my own wicked doings, for which reason I must be patient and rejoice that I have received my deserts; yet less than my deserts when I consider the extent of my ill doings, sir, as you well know.'

Which latter I took to be a further confession from the poor woman Susan Knowles. And I feared that as long as she lived, which from the look of her would be but a short time, she would in her oblique way continue to pour out to me her griefs.

'You must take a remedy for your breathing, Susan,' I said, for the poor woman was so near the end of her journey, though she appeared not to know it, that I had no scruples about calling her by the earliest name she knew. Indeed, she seemed lightened by hearing her name, which was a sweet one and suited her well, for she was a dear soul who had suffered much and been tempted much, and I had no doubt that there had been many a young man with a fancy for her before she fell into misery.

'You see, I am no worse, sir. I like not to use your remedy when others may be in greater need,' she said.

'One day I will take you to see the plant I am going to give you, Susan,' I said. 'And you will see you have deprived no one for there is so much centaury yonder of Kessle-wood as to provide for the whole county of York.

'I shall look forward to that day, sir,' said Susan Knowles, 'and I could wish it were today that I was walking in Kessle-wood, but my breath fails me and I cannot get far.'

Then I told her also of the lesser centaury and its flowers, the hue as of the gentle clouds on a summer's dawn, and how the plants were related even as if they were kindred, asking her at the same time if she had any who might be sister or brother to her. To which she answered I knew not whether in the affirmative or no, only that she said her present ills forbade her converse with folks other than Jane Pearce who was the sister of her soul.

'After you have taken the greater centaury, Susan,' I said, 'your breath will come easier, and that within a space of hours, please God, for I can see that you suffer much.'

'Yes, sir,' she said, and this latter out of the hearing of Jane Pearce, 'though I try to keep it from my friend who has troubles enough of her own. How long do I have, sir?'

Then I saw that it was neither use nor kindness to withhold the gravity of the illness from good Susan Knowles, for indeed she knew it herself, and was indeed like to have done so all along.

'My dear Susan, the illness has entered your lungs,' I said, 'and the most I can do for you is beg you to confide the troubles of your soul, for I have known long that the griefs of your spirit weigh on you more heavily than the sickness of your body, which is but temporary whereas your spirit you will take with you, and I would that you travel light on your journey.'

Whereupon she confided to me what I knew, that she had told certain persons where I dwelt, who suspected me of sympathies with the machine breakers, and who had then taken me off for interrogation, of which I was well conscious every day from the abiding stinging in my feet. And she said that though she knew I had overlooked her perfidy, else I would not be with her at that moment attempting to ease what little she had left of her life's journey, yet she could not so forgive herself and would carry her pain into the next world.

And talk as I would in whatever clumsy manner I might I could see that Susan Knowles was right, that in this life there would be self-recrimination beyond her deserts, for indeed the doing of the deed weighed more heavily than the outcome.

'See, I can walk,' I said. 'They did no lasting hurt and for all I know, for my wits were scattered at the time, I said what I should not have said.'

'That you did not, sir,' said Susan Knowles, 'for I heard it noised abroad and I know it to be true that you gave nothing, though they were at pains to make you think you had; that is their way.'

'You have taken away the worry I had, Susan,' I said, 'and may you also be comforted.' Yet I knew she would not.

And I sought afterwards Jane Pearce and the bairn, noting with no little surprise that the dwellinghouse, which had been disordered before, was now neat and clean; though neither poor Susan Knowles, nor Jane Pearce, were likely to have had the time or the inclination for household work. And the bairn also was fair to look upon, and wrapped in a newly knitted shawl, the work on which would have entailed many a candle, and which was folded and tucked in under the little feet, concealing the deformity of the lower limbs.

'You may pick him up, sir,' said Jane Pearce. But I did not, fearing that the small body might slip through my clumsy hands to the floor, yet fearing also that she would take my hesitation amiss.

'Leastways, sir,' she said, 'you will sit down and I will hand the bairn to you'

So I sat, awkwardly enough, with the bairn, who soon sensing as I supposed my unease, set up a wail enough to raise the rafters, which disconcerted Jane Pearce not a little, for she said that the bairn was thus all the time and would not be pacified. From which I understood, and from the light weight of the bairn, that the poor young woman yet suffered from an inflammation of the mammary glands; though I could not ask for fear of causing offence. And I gave her groundsel, which she understood well enough.

Then I would have made to leave the dwellinghouse, fearful that good Rosie Todd would be waiting long at the sign of the Ram's Head, but that Jane Pearce, knowing that she had little time to say her few words for I would shortly be gone, spoke.

'You will wonder that I have a bairn, sir, since I am not wed.'

Which indeed I had not wondered, for there were many such in those days, and more to be pitied than despised, for all that the world poured its scorn upon them.

'He that did this to me dwells at Beckwith. And I was a willing participant in the act, being the price I paid on condition that he should leave my kinsman alone. For though I work at the mill, sir, that is anathema to my folks, among whom are machine breakers. And that is the reason I entered into this wicked converse, which indeed did not achieve its end for they at home have had no tidings of our kinsman this quarter year past, and we fear him gone from this world. And, sir, the fact I do not call him by his name tis not that I mistrust you, but that which a man doesna know he canna tell again, which is the maxim by which we order our lives. Though I know you would not tell, as my friend Susan Knowles has assured me.'

Yet even though I knew who the kinsman was, and indeed his features were writ clear on the face of Jane Pearce though in a fairer form, my profession bade me hold my peace. And Jane Pearce expected nothing in the way of words from me, for she had not finished her own, which, once started, continued to flow as water from a spring.

'There is yet one thing more, sir,' she said. 'God has blessed my friend Susan Knowles and me in our extremity, and hers is worse than mine by far, by sending us an angel from heaven, though she thinks not of herself as an angel. If indeed angels are to be found in the dwelling of a mill owner,' she continued, 'and if indeed angels suffer the curse of womankind, sir, if you get my drift; for I am of the opinion that is her malady, yet I should not say so in front of a gentleman. She has the falling sickness, sir, which I think is not the falling sickness but the other, you understand, and so thinks my friend Susan Knowles. To conclude matters, sir, while you are yet under our roof, would you be so kind as to give her some remedy against her faints, if you please, sir.

You will find her yonder in the scullery, and please to mind your head on the low beam, sir.'

'You will be surprised to see me here, sir,' said Ellie Bright.

Though I was not, having expected at every turn of every day that she would appear, if hope were any guarantee of its own fulfilment. And neither was she surprised to see me.

'I am surprised and I am not,' I said, 'for I perceive the dwellinghouse to be neat and clean beyond the strength of these two good women. How came you here?'

'I was carried here,' said Ellie Bright, 'and more I cannot say, for I fear he who brought me has been taken in by the magistrate and cruelly done to. And whether he lives or not I cannot discover, for there are none I can ask.'

'Good Jane Pearce asked for a remedy against your faints, Ellie,' I said. Yet I found the young woman on the contrary in good health and without the pallor I had previously observed. 'Do you suffer?'

'No, sir,' said Ellie Bright. 'Leastways not at this moment, though it does happen. I keep the remedy you gave me for such times. I bid Jane Pearce ask your professional advice, but what I stand most in need of are tidings. I am full of deceit and duplicity, you see, sir.'

'Indeed you are, Ellie Bright,' I said, 'for I have never met an angel who pretends to be more duplicitous with less success than you.'

Then mindful of the anguish of her sweet soul I recounted as much as would give her a scrap of consolation, namely that the young man lived yet, in part because of the intervention of Martin Gathercole who pleaded with the magistrate; though I did not tell her of the hurt done to the young man or to he who inflicted the supposed retribution, or that the magistrate had not been seen since. For I had no doubt that any mind less tender than Ellie Bright's could readily conjure up Richard Born out of the thin air in all kinds of disguises and in all unlikely places, knowing him to be abroad.

'And Martin Gathercole, though he does not know you are dwelling in this place, nevertheless would wish you to know that you dwell in his mind every day,' I concluded, not knowing the relationship in which Ellie Bright stood to Martin Gathercole; yet I understood she believed that I did know, and that Martin Gathercole had told me.

Then like any of my patients aforementioned who concludes their story and immediately launches upon another I told her of the bay mare Yolande, wishing to bring some sunshine to Ellie Bright's sweet face, yet noticing that tears stood in her eyes. And she then told me that Martin had been to every market in the county of York until he found the bay mare Yolande, whom he was at great pains to instruct to kneel upon the ground to be mounted.

'And it hurts me in my heart,' said Ellie Bright, 'that I would ride upon Yolande's back only infrequently, not liking to be seen abroad, though Martin always urged me to experience the healthful rays of the sun.'

And so she went on, mourning her perceived ingratitude, as if she would never again see Martin Gathercole in this world to repair matters.

'But, sir,' she continued, 'now you will believe that I am indeed deceitful, for though I was ever unwilling to go abroad when Martin urged me, I have since been abroad on my own account and without his leave, though I know well if it had not been granted it would only have been for my own weal. And since I have told you the half, sir, and knowing you would not ask the rest, it is this: that since the day I first heard that strange music I must needs search the earth until I heard it again. But in truth, sir, I know not whether it is the music or the pupil musician, whose name is Robert Gaut, for both are one to me. I blush to say these things, sir, yet to a physician such as yourself I may, that it is an offence against the whole of nature for such as I to entertain such wanderings of the mind. There are some who say that Robert Gaut conveys muskets and the like to the machine breakers in the casing of the double bass, as he appears at times to be labouring under a heavy weight, and at other times to carry the case lightly. You will know now, sir, that I am frivolous and a gossip.'

And indeed, frivolity and gossip became Ellie Bright exceedingly, for her complexion was by then that of any young woman in the best of health, though I could see that as soon as the last word had settled into the silence of the room she was at pains to draw so much as the next breath for shame.

'I have spoken out of turn,' she said. 'I pray you to say something, sir.'

'Ellie, you have not spoken out of turn,' I said. 'You have spoken of nothing I did not ponder over already. Indeed, you have said less, for I have reflected often on your journey from the burning house of Martin Gathercole to the dwellinghouse of these good women, and I have come always to the same conclusion, that you travelled in the casing of the double bass, though you would strenuously resist, believing yourself, as you do, to be a burden to all the world. And for the other matter, that Robert Gaut is suspected of carrying muskets up to the hills, I think that is not so, for I believe I know how such weaponry travels. But it is true, I have also noticed that Robert Gaut sometimes walks as under a heavy weight and sometimes not, and I have entertained the opinion that the weight is the weight of the spirit.'

For I knew that whatever I said Ellie Bright would not say again, since in the hill country in those times there were many who laboured under the burden of their secrets. And I thought also that I would not touch on her fascination with the young man, only that I would talk of him by name and that might be a solace to her, which indeed it was, for the trouble cleared away from her sweet face.

'And, dear Ellie Bright, you might help me,' I said, 'for I have been given to believe that the older musician whom some think to be an Italian, but who is from France as I am, has been at pains to search me out and I know not where I might find him.'

But Ellie Bright knew no more than I, only saying that the bass player Domenico, and unable to remember his second name for the strangeness of it, would stand out from others as a Gulliver among the people of Lilliput were he to walk through Clywold, for there were many such as she dwelling there, she said, who suffered the same affliction of the bones, though to a lesser extent, but were nevertheless short of stature.

So we conversed pleasantly enough about Gulliver and other like works of literature until Ellie's spirits were quite restored; and she revealed that Martin had ever encouraged her in reading, though with a taste more inclined towards boys than girls, and would moreover set every broadsheet that came his way before her for the furtherance of her knowledge, whatever be the subject. From which she knew a little of the fair land of France and the uprising there.

'Which is why, I think,' she said, 'the machine breakers are so much feared, as if they would set up that terrible blade in Clywold market and deal so with those who work the mills.' For neither side would converse with the other, she said, until one side starved and burned dwellinghouses and the other side used the scourge to draw out secrets. And she feared that the apprehending of the musician would draw forth reprisals, though I had been at pains to spare her the details of his afflictions.

So I left poor Ellie Bright sailing again in troubled waters, and I left also the dwellinghouse; yet not before Jane Pearce had set before me a portion of bread and Ellie had entrusted me with a letter to be sent to Martin Gathercole, and I had said farewell to Susan Knowles, thinking no more to see her in this world, yet assuring her that one day we would walk to Kesslewood to see where the centaury grows, to which she readily assented, knowing well what I was saying.

Then I made my way down the Clywold road to the sign of the Ram's Head, having been taken some way in a cart, malodorous enough, with a poor sheep's legs protruding from beneath a rude sack, until I wondered how long the same sheep's legs could be carried back and forth before they returned to the dust from which we all came and would in the Lord's good time return.

And it was with these thoughts that, having alighted from the cart and travelled some two furlongs on foot, I beheld from afar, for the path was downhill and unimpeded by gorse, some folks gathered at a place where the beck came to rest in a rancid pool; which folk seeing me coming near stood back as if there were a spectacle to be seen in the pool.

Which indeed there was, though I saw nothing until I was a quarter chain's distance, only the faces of those who stood by, known to me by sight indeed, as some of their number had been present in the public room at the sign of the Ram's Head on the day Caleb Sawney had been carried to that place.

'Tis past your help, sir,' one of the men said. 'See.'

Then I looked into the pool and saw dimly, for the water was both rank with stagnation and foetid withal, the remains of a poor fellow's body reposing there.

'And we would have called for the magistrate, sir, had there been a magistrate to call for but there is not, he being absent, sir, so we must needs do the deed ourselves.'

XIX

Then they repaired to the hostelry for whatever could be found in the way of instruments for the retrieval of the poor fellow in the pool, coming back with little enough: a length of rope, a pallet of wood which had once done service as a door from the look of a rusted hinge yet clinging to it, and a pitchfork with one prong absent. Yet none would go into the pool on account of the foetor and the stink of it, which hovered above the water and rose up to our nostrils as the water was disturbed.

And the whole operation was set to be let go entirely, when the single prong of the pitchfork gained purchase in the back of the stock yet around the neck of the unfortunate fellow, and he was brought to the edge. Then preparations were made to draw him forth from the pool, but that in doing so the poor fellow's remains rolled so as to reveal the face, which was not a face, for what had once been set there in the image of the Lord God was sorely defaced by the violence of man and the sojourn in the pool, so that there was but a mask, pared almost to the bone and bearing the likeness of no man. Indeed, much of the poor fellow's remains had suffered the same fate, and there were but clouts of dress by which he might be known. For the Lord quickly takes back the temple once the spirit has fled and we have but our rags of possessions by which men might know that we have ever walked the earth.

Reflecting thus and at pains to assist in the retrieval of the deceased I was slow to see that but four of those from the sign of the Ram's Head remained there, one being he who had first spoken.

'They are sick and they have gone, sir,' he said. 'And we are sick and we have not gone, for the deed must needs be done.'

So by and by we hoisted the remains onto the bank of the pool, all of us being sullied by the foul water in the process; until what was left of the poor fellow lay there on the board, roped fast and ready for removal; yet not before the head had swung over to one side, emitting a stream of noxious effluent and leaving lodged between the teeth some kind of tract. And I envied not they who must presently deliberate on the case, for we were all of us by then sick at heart and all but bilious, not least on account of the stench we carried on our persons.

Which whole process reft me for a short space of time of the belief in a divinity guiding the affairs of men, until I observed while assisting to lift that there grew in the proximity of the most desolating scene I had ever beheld the Sonchus hesperus, which even then, though it was but the spring of the year, grew at the water's edge in that dead place.

And it was a thankful thing also that the sweet breath of the hills dried and freshened our dress, for else we would have been less than welcome at the sign of the Ram's Head; and we were unwelcome enough, but that the matter must needs be followed to its conclusion. For which purpose a rude outbuilding at the rear of the premises was made ready with trestles on which the deceased was placed.

And a debate ensued between those at the retrieval and the host as to whatsoever way to proceed. And none knew, for there was no magistrate. Yet what was most apparent to all was left unsaid, namely that the vestiges of dress which yet clung to the remains denoted by their cut and cloth a wearer of some standing; until he who had so far taken charge of the proceedings, who was a worthy fellow, spoke.

'Tis our duty to inform the magistrate, which we cannot do on two counts, first because the magistrate is at present known to be absent from his dwelling, and principally, sirs, because this is the magistrate.'

Then all agreed that it was the case, for indeed which other man was so clothed that his dress could withstand the noxious water of the beck when the flesh could not, there being those also who spoke of seeing him in the very surtout which yet clung to him.

And I said nothing, it being far from me to judge in the matter, which I could see was fast being decided by those present, namely that this was indeed the magistrate Richard Born whom we saw before us, which personage should rightly be the subject of scrutiny by his nearest of kin; but that there was little of his mortal remains left to scrutinise, God rest his soul, though it had been a cruel one, they said.

'What say you, sir?' The man, whose name I found out to be Kit Swain and who was a keeper of the sheep, turned to me. 'You are a stranger in these parts, sir, having no acquaintance with the deceased. What say you? There be many as pass from this world secretly and are laid in the earth secretly. Do we thus with the magistrate here and spare his good lady wife? Happen there is another among us who could read the office for the dead, for I myself am an unlettered man.'

And, in retrospect, that course of action might have saved many a trouble in troublous times, but that while the company were so deliberating, though indeed there was not one man among them who would admit to the faculty of learning sufficient to read the office, a messenger came to the door saying that Mistress Todd was in the public room and had been for some time past and was sending to inquire whether the apothecary was yet there, for it was noised abroad that he was, and in attendance upon a patient at the rear of the hostelry. Having said which, and having cast an eye over the remains, the messenger would have beat a hasty retreat, but that Rosie Todd was there at his back and he had no recourse but to come himself into the room with the good woman following. Whereupon Kit Swain stepped forward, attempting to place his frame, which was but a spare one, between her and the deceased; yet to no avail for she was of a sudden in our midst inspecting with equanimity, as was her wont, that which we men could hardly call upon ourselves to look at.

'Tis a case for the magistrate,' she said, 'but he is not at home.'

'Happen this is the magistrate we have before us, Mistress Todd,' said Kit Swain. 'Tis only guessing as his face is gone. We are minded to lay him to rest privily to spare his good lady.'

'Thou shalt not, Kit Swain,' said Rosie Todd. 'Thou shalt leave thy quaint notions here and go to seek the opinion of the justice of Tindercliffe.'

And whether it was the change of air in the room occasioned by Rosie Todd's entrance, or that the ropes binding the poor fellow had slackened during his travel to the Ram's Head, the left arm fell and the contracture of the fingers loosened, to display a further tract similar to that lodged between his teeth. Which fearful event was sufficient to dispatch those present to Tindercliffe in search of the justice, and the good fellow Kit Swain to repair to the host to ask for a sheet with which to decently cover the remains. Who, having returned with the linen, asked leave to join his fellows making ready a cart for the road, he being the chief witness; and I had no doubt anxious to be gone from the presence, being no less bilious, yet stouter of heart, than the others.

So once again I found myself in the company of good Rosie Todd, having thought until then that no watch could be less wholesome than that over Caleb Sawney; yet this was, not least for the stench in the close confines of the room, and the constant seeping of the vital fluids from the remains; and I feared also the dispersal into the air we breathed of the noxious effluent contaminating the beck. Yet Rosie Todd showed no sign of distaste and arranged over the remains the linen, which I observed to be a table cloth, much used and ready for laundering.

'They say tis the magistrate, sir,' she said.

'That is what they say.'

'And how say you, sir?' For although the others knew not that I was acquainted with Richard Born, Rosie Todd knew well that he had accompanied his wife to the dispensary. 'Is this Mr Born?'

'You know as well as I, Rosie Todd,' I said. 'The others believe that what remains of his dress agrees with a man of some standing. Therefore they say this is the magistrate.'

'It is without doubt his dress,' said Rosie Todd. 'But is it he?'

And though I said nothing I had my doubts for the fingers that had been closed around the tract carried long and unkempt nails, whereas I had observed that Richard Born's were pared down to the finger ends, I feared on account of his wife's talk of the blood of they who had been coerced lodged there.

'I believe this is some other,' continued Rosie Todd, 'for the finger nails are long and Mr Born keeps his short. Unless nails are known to grow after death. Do you know if that is the case, sir?'

'I think it is not the case, Rosie,' I said, 'unless you have evidence to the contrary.'

'And I do not, sir,' she said. 'What say you is the best to be done at this time?'

'For myself I can neither do nor say anything,' I said, 'for my profession bids me be both impartial and secretive. Therefore even were I asked I could say nothing. Yet it is doubtless I will be asked as I am regarded as a stranger in these parts who has never set eyes on the magistrate.'

'Then I will do as you do, sir,' said Rosie Todd. 'Pray, sir, has it been remarked that the deceased had tracts about his person, one of which has fallen out of his hand and is now on the ground?'

'That I do not know,' I said. 'If any have noticed the tracts they have not said in my hearing.'

'Then I will not make mention of them either, sir,' said Rosie Todd. 'We will leave all to the magistrate of Tindercliffe parish. And I will say nothing to Mrs Born, who believes me to be on a journey to York to see the young lady you told me of, sir. Though no doubt Mrs Born will hear soon enough, if she has not done already, for the hills talk even if they who dwell there keep their mouths tight shut.'

And I wondered if Rosie Todd had heard the strange converse of the hills and yet seen no person, or if she indeed was using some trick of the speech as the English are apt to do, and which has ever confounded me.

So we remained there for upwards of two hours as I noted by the declining sun slatting through the casement, saying little else. For I know not whether it was the sombre presence of death or the effects of the noxious fluid which yet seeped out from the remains onto the earthen floor, but I had little inclination to converse, and I believe Rosie Todd also; who I supposed had fallen into a slumber, as when the messengers were heard returning she started suddenly and made to attend to her braids, though she need not have done as there was no hair out of place.

'They are back, sir,' she said.

'I believe so.'

'They have been gone but a little time.'

'Tis upwards of two hours,' I said.

'Then I must have been asleep, sir,' she said, 'for which I beg your pardon. It is poor manners to fall asleep in the company of a gentleman and an educated one at that. What will you think of me, sir?'

I assured Rosie Todd that nothing could detract from my good opinion of her, and she would, I believe, have made some gracious reply but that Kit Swain came in with no great ceremony and, without looking at the remains, said that word had arrived from the justice of Tindercliffe to send the deceased fellow up yonder in a cart.

'For the justice is abed having an attack of the gout, and I thought as much,' he continued, 'which happen is for the best as we'll be rid of the matter since we are all of us well-nigh sick by now, some more than others. Best send the papers as well. Better there than here.' With which Kit Swain picked up the tract lying on the floor and placed it on top of the remains, neither he nor any other have paid previous attention to the papers.

'Tis not uncommon in these parts,' he said addressing me, 'that when a mischief is done to a body there will be a paper nearby. Tis the oath of the machine breakers, sir, though I say it without the evidence of my eyes for I am an unlettered man.'

'You may take with you a tincture of henbane for the relief of the good man's gout, Kit Swain,' I said.

'Thanking you, sir,' he said, 'but I have not let it be known that you are present at the sign of the Ram's Head lest the Tindercliffe parish magistrate should demand your attendance, for he is an irascible man.'

'I will be well on the way to York by the time you reach Tindercliffe,' I said.

'Be it so, sir,' said Kit Swain, 'yet I will say no more but that the remedy was sent by a physician then lodged at the sign of the Ram's Head and merely passing through. And if you'll excuse us, sir, we must be gone for night is falling and the justice will be the more irascible to be awoken from his slumbers.'

The coach bound for York was waiting and the horses changed, and certain curious folk were watching under the first stars the cart being loaded with a noxious collection of cloths, to whom Kit Swain said it was a deceased bound for Tindercliffe and no man knew the manner of his demise, which caused no little consternation among the onlookers, who, covering their mouths with their hands, scattered all ways. Yet on the low slopes of the hills going northward folks were gathered in the twilight to watch the cart leave. And I fancied I saw at their back and somewhat higher in order to gain a view the same figure who had inflicted the hurt on Caleb Sawney. Yet I was not sure, and there was no sign in Rosie Todd's face to indicate that she had seen aught amiss.

So we journeyed back to York as the dawn was breaking, there being nothing more disheartening to the spirit than to come suddenly upon a new day when the affairs of the one just gone still linger in the soul. Yet Rosie Todd showed no such perturbation of the mind, having slumbered on the way; and to halt her apologies which I knew would be long and many I asked her how she had done and apologised myself for having slumbered in the presence of a lady, which indeed I had not done as the sight of the remains of the poor fellow whoever he be was before my eyes and the stench lingered on my person; for which also I apologised to Rosie Todd, who said she did not notice. And I reflected that there is much merit to be found in false statements made with kind intentions.

Though my scribe Luke Bower showed no such kind falsity and began forthwith to throw open every window in the dispensary until I bade him go down and take Rosie Todd to the house of mercy where she might rest and refresh herself; knowing that during his absence, which was likely to be lengthy as he was never away without finding some body or other to converse with and some news to gather, I would have time to put the offending cloak to steep in the scullery.

'So, sir, you have been present at a retrieval,' he said on his return, drawing in the window.

'Why say you that, Luke?'

'Because my nostrils inform me so.'

Then, understanding that there was nothing more to be gained from Luke on the subject at the present time I asked him what news had passed.

'That fellow has been here,' he said.

'There are many fellows in the world, Luke. Which one are you referring to?'

'Him as plays the double bass, sir.'

'You mean the young fellow with the neckerchief?'

'No, sir, the one who could be mistaken for one of your countrymen, sir. I told him you were away, sir, and said you'd left no word when you would be back.'

'Did he say anything?'

'To tell you the truth, sir, and with all respect for I mean no offence, his speech is more confusing even than yours, sir, and I led him to believe my wits were awry to spare his feelings. For tis easily done to persuade others that my wits are awry.'

'You are a man of many parts, Luke.'

'Thank you, sir. There is one other matter. He's gone, sir.'

'The musician?'

'No, sir. Him as cannot remember his own name, sir. I went down to see if there were any writings, though there have not been any such to speak of for many weeks, and found him gone, sir.

Luke placed a paper on the table.

'We will read that later, Luke. What of the young woman?'

'She is at the house of mercy, sir, where I have taken Mistress Todd. So it was the magistrate's remains, sir?'

'Why say you that, Luke?'

'It is all over York, sir. Others say it, not I.'

XX

'What do they noise abroad all over York, Luke?' I said.

'This and that, sir,' said Luke.

'Which is no kind of answer.'

'Meaning, sir, a fellow hears this from some folks and that from some folks else and all together it is a pretty tale. Meaning, sir, since you are about to comment on the expression, it is not a pretty tale at all.'

'And you will tell me the pretty tale in your own good time, Luke,' I said, 'until which time I suppose I must be patient.'

'I will tell you it now, sir,' said Luke. 'Folk say that the magistrate of the parish of Holmroyd, Richard Born by name, was found this day a week gone in the beck by his wife Grace Born, who not liking her husband resolved to leave him so until others came by. Which by and by folks did, they being certain of the King's militia, who finding the magistrate Richard Born in the beck sent to the justice of Tindercliffe who apprehended into custody awaiting questioning the wife of the said magistrate and her maid, believing them to be co-authors of the evil deed. And if not they, certain machine breakers whom the magistrate dealt harshly with, and if not they the fellow you have mentioned, sir, with the neckerchief. For the magistrate had dealt ill with all and tis in the nature of folks to seek redress.'

'And how much of this is your own fabrication, Luke?'

'Well-nigh all of it, sir,' said Luke, 'for I could see you wanted a tale.'

'And how much of the tale is God's truth, Luke?'

'Little enough, sir,' said Luke, 'save that you have been at a retrieval as my nostrils inform me, therefore a fellow is deceased; and Mrs Born has been here searching for the apothecary, that being you, sir, and saying that Mr Born has not been seen by his hearth these two weeks gone. Therefore there is a deceased fellow gone from his hearth side.'

'I pray you say nothing outside these four walls, Luke,' I said.

'You know that I would not, sir,' said Luke. 'But what of the tale? Was it near?'

Whether Luke expected an answer or no I could not tell, nor indeed could I conjure one up, for I knew not myself what the answer was.

'And the young woman, Luke, how does she fare?'

'By which I conclude that you have caught my malady, sir, in forgetting a question was asked if it be an awkward one. But as to the young woman, sir, that I do not know,' he said, 'for him as cannot remember his own name, sir,' (Luke jerked his head in the direction of the concealed chamber) 'being gone she has no patient to wait upon, therefore she confines herself to the house of mercy, and a doleful time she has of it, I'll be bound, for they there will talk to her of all other things but those which concern her the most.'

And hereby Luke hit upon a truth which had fairly passed me by, namely that kindness might lie more in curiosity than discretion; but I had no doubt that Rosie Todd would dispense both in judicious measure, where Luke and I could not or would not.

So I repaired to the house of mercy for the first time in my life, for though we were neighbours since my arrival in the fair town of York, I had not stepped inside, nor indeed had I ever cause to.

And I knocked with some trepidation, not for myself so much as for the good woman, whoever she be, who might answer and see a Frenchman and a papist withal there before her, assuming they inside to be of another persuasion, though I knew not which.

Yet when the door opened I was at a loss to see anybody whatsoever until, casting about, I beheld a young woman grievously afflicted with the rickets, whom I may not have noticed, being so much the taller. And it struck me that here indeed was a doorkeeper in the house of the Lord, who had found refuge from the ribald habits of the world; who may not there be alone of her kind but may be one of many suffering divers maladies. So I resolved to ask if they in the house of mercy would accept remedies, being also mindful that there be many that are afflicted who regard their afflictions as the cross they gladly bear, and do not wish to be made whole.

Reflecting thus I was conducted into a small chamber leading off a panelled hallway, where I found good Rosie Todd and the young woman Jem Bailey. For it was she, though I would scarce have known her for the same, so drawn was she, and her pretty face disfigured by a recent haematoma. And presently she who had answered the door brought in wine and a loaf of bread, pressing Jem Bailey to partake, and Rosie and I also, though I could see that even the homely act of mastication must needs be painful to Jem Bailey, who yet said, 'Thank you, Melody.' And I thought I had never heard so sweet a name in all my born days.

But as to how she came by the hurt, Jem Bailey did not say, nor did I ask. Nor did she say much of anything, it being also painful to speak. Though I could see from the looks of her and the pallor of her that she was untimely delivered of the bairn, which Rosie Todd understood well enough, as I perceived when I caught her eye.

And after a while spent thus more or less in silence I entreated Rosie Todd to accompany me to the dispensary for the remedies of ragwort to cleanse and feverfew for the melancholy and dizziness, and whatever else Rosie Todd would recommend, for I had long thought that were she in my profession she would have done better than I.

But she said little, except to remark on the variety and extent of the remedies and their neat classification, which I said, for the sake of putting her at her ease and making pleasant conversation, was wholly the work of Luke Bower my scribe. And she asked if he came of the Bower family of Beckwith, to which I knew not the answer, as I believed him to have no kindred alive in this world. Then thinking Rosie Todd slow to mention the patient's condition, I was minded to speak when she herself spoke.

'Is the young lady always thus, sir?'

Hearing which I realised that Rosie Todd, though a servant in the magistrate's household with braids in her hair, was indeed as fine and knowing a physician as ever there was, to inquire thus about the patient's normal condition, which, indeed, is the first office of the diagnostician.

'If you are asking, Rosie, does she habitually wear a pallor the colour of meadowsweet and a haematoma the colour of the nightshade I can tell you that she wears neither, but has the prettiest complexion you ever saw. And I fear, Rosie,' (since I saw I must make mention of the fact to spare her from doing so) 'she has delivered the bairn out of time and suffered some hurt beforehand; for a little bairn, who is but an idea in the mind of the Lord God Almighty, will yet cling tenaciously to the life that awaits, whatever that life may be.'

'You are right, sir,' said Rosie Todd, 'that the young woman Jem Bailey delivered her bairn out of time, and it is a calamity to see any bairn thus, no matter what the course of events. For she told me so far, and she told me about the patient she was called upon to nurse in the concealed room, who is now gone. Though she did not tell me, sir, how that came to be, or how she received the hurt to her face.'

Then I asked of Rosie if she knew what else might help Jem Bailey's recovery apart from the feverfew and ragwort, and she said no, unless it be the elm for the wound, as she had seen it given to those with the broken bones while her husband was yet alive in the world. To which I assented, although I had thought that Rosie would advise on the matter of untimely delivery, but she did not. And I thought moreover that she was not quite herself and had some concern on her mind, more than the fatigue of the journey and the plight of the young woman would have occasioned, for Rosie Todd was inured to both.

'Begging your pardon, sir,' said Luke, 'but have you looked over the writings of him as cannot remember his own name?' Luke jerked his head in the direction of the concealed chamber, although he had told me himself but a few hours earlier that Will Cantrell was gone. 'For if you have not, sir, you might look over them now, with more enlightenment than I have done, sir. Tis not the King's English. Happen it's the French tongue, sir.'

'No, Luke, it's the King's English,' I said. 'It's writ backwards, which is not to say the poor fellow writ it backwards for no man can do so with fluency. I think he was writing, and rather than sand his manuscript placed another paper on top, for it is also smeared. We will examine it with the help of the mirror.'

In which task we were so engaged, beholding Will Cantrell's manuscript before the very glass in which I had but a minute before, for such is human life that weeks may pass by in the twinkling of an eye, fancifully examined my own head to see if indeed there was a window into my soul, when I perceived through the same mirror the door behind opening and the person of Grace Born emerging out of the shadows which lingered on the staircase at all times of the day.

'You must come to the conclusion that our wits are quite scattered,' I said. 'Either that or we are become vain. We are trying to decipher a script written backwards, hence our preoccupation with the mirror.'

And my words ran on, for I thought not to see Grace Born so suddenly in this manner, not yet having resolved in my mind how to address her on the matter of her husband, and not knowing if any word from the justice of Tindercliffe had reached her. For indeed she looked as if she carried the weight of the world with her.

'Pray be seated,' I said, 'and we will leave our antics for a later time.'

'We did that as children,' she said. 'We became quite adept at writing and reading backwards.' And a sweet smile lit her face.

'So we may turn to you if we cannot solve this mystery, Mrs Born,' I said, 'but in the meantime we will cast off our childish ways. Pray be seated.' For she stood yet, twisting her reticule in her hands; and I thought again how oddly her braided hair sat with such melancholy.

'My husband is not at home,' she said, 'and he has not been at home these weeks past. And that is the end of it.'

Yet I could see from her attitude that indeed was not the end of it, and I had but to wait for a tale which I knew already, as Grace Born was more than aware. For there is great merit to be had in hearing the same tale told by many, as all have their own ways of telling.

'You will know, sir, that my husband deals cruelly with men, and women also,' she continued, 'and there are many that bear rancour towards him.'

And though I am but imperfect in the English tongue I remarked this use of the present, that Grace Born believed her husband to be yet alive. Which turn of phrase I resolved to store up in my mind though all else might flee.

'My husband was in attendance at a chastisement in the Sheep-close, and I remember not the date but that it was a day of blue sky and white clouds as if all the sheep on Capcar-hill were grazing in heaven, and yet what was happening on earth was an offence to all the angels in heaven. For my husband, so I hear and I know that this is true, offered the scourge around and found no one willing to take it up but a man of the militia who comes from Beckwith, who did the deed, or as much to cause great hurt to a poor weaver who is also an itinerant musician, though they say he uses the case of the instrument for other purposes. So I hear, sir, and I know what I say you will not tell again. And while this affliction was running its course, and indeed there were many watching from the hill, one stepped out of the crowd and inflicted a grievous wound on he who wielded the scourge. Then during the mayhem that ensued, for they of the militia were exercised to aid their colleague, though none other would take up the scourge, and as the folks came down from the hill to attend to the poor musician, they fled, both he who had imparted the wound to the militia man, and my husband also, whom I have not set eyes on since that day.

'Then I heard it said, sir, that there had been a finding close by Holmroyd in the beck and I examined my husband's wardrobe, finding nothing gone from there but what he stood up in on the day at the Sheep-close, and one other suit of clothing. And I heard it said also, sir, that an apothecary had been in attendance at the retrieval, a Frenchman like yourself. Though I knew the articles of your profession forbid you saying anything.'

There Grace Born stopped, and finding she had come to an end of what she was minded to say for the present I asked Luke for a tincture of thyme to settle her fears, though she had much to fear.

'I may say what you will yourself hear in the course of time.' I said. ''Tis best to hear the truth if a tale is to be heard at all.'

Then asking Grace Born if she felt herself strong enough to hear, and her answering in the affirmative, I told her of the finding and that the matter had been placed with the justice at Tindercliffe. And knowing the question Grace Born most wished to ask but would not, namely if it had been the magistrate of Holmroyd parish so found, I told her that as yet no identity had been established, though not the reason, yet she knew well enough.

'Then I will be summoned to bear witness,' she said, not so much as to elicit an answer as to speak the fear uppermost in her mind as I understood, that she would be required to look on the face of her husband again; and it mattered not whether he was alive or dead, it was nevertheless he, whom she wished never to set eyes on again, be it in this world or the next.

So I asked if there were others of her kindred who might go with her if she were called upon to bear witness and she said no, for the reason that her shame at being so misused by her husband, whom they had warned her against at the outset, prohibited her from asking their assistance. For, Grace Born said, she had been headstrong in her girlhood and flighty also, and had run away with Richard Born, which she now regretted every minute of every day. Yet then he had a honeyed tongue and beauty enough in her eyes, though lately she was hard pressed so much as to look at him.

'And to tell you God's honest truth, sir,' she said, 'if it were he retrieved from the beck it would be for the best.'

'Have you mentioned this to others?' I said, in as light a way as I could, for Luke's tale yet drummed in my ears.

But whether it was that I was but an indifferent actor, or that Grace Born repeated what she had already said to others to gain my opinion on the matter, she knew well what I was saying and started to weep. And I wished wholeheartedly that good Rosie Todd were there, but she was not; so I bade poor Grace Born take the tincture of thyme to steady her fears, and prayed her to be of good cheer, for at times like these all manner of things were said and not meant or indeed even heard. Which I did not believe and neither did she. For words once said cannot be reeled in again and may remain moreover dormant in the minds of they who hear, ready to awake at any time.

And from then on I debated within myself how to protect Grace Born for I could see that a turn of speech made without thought had placed her in the greatest jeopardy, even of her life which was sweet and blameless; and indeed she had suffered much.

'What am I to do, sir?' she said. 'I am without protectors, having only my maid Rosie Todd and they who tend the house and garden at Holmroyd.'

Which question would I believe have been occupying my mind to this hour had not Rosie Todd appeared in the doorway, and having heard the end of our converse assured Grace Born that he who was retrieved from the beck was likely not to be the magistrate but some other poor soul.

'For I observed,' concluded Rosie, 'that the poor soul kept his finger nails long whereas Mr Born's nails were always short, and if a maid can deduce from a simple circumstance that the deceased, God rest his soul, was some other and not the magistrate how much more the justice of Tindercliffe, being a worldly man, will deduce that also. For they all did know Mr Born and his attention to his manicure.'

Then if I had not known it before I realised the true worth of Rosie Todd, that although she could have called upon me to support her statement, nevertheless she did not, knowing that I could not divulge even on pain of death the fact that Richard Born had been my patient. Which indeed I was glad of, for though he had great cruelty, no man deserves the intimacies of his bed chamber to be noised abroad.

'Sir,' said Rosie Todd, 'the poor young woman Jem Bailey will yet do well if she may be persuaded not to take the ills of the world upon her shoulders. For she believes herself to be at fault for conceiving the bairn and for the event which caused her to deliver untimely, though she does not say what it was, and she believes herself to be at fault also for the disappearance of her patient. But in her body she will grow strong again. Therefore, sir, I would wish to accompany Mrs Born home and return again to Mistress Bailey having done so.'

And though I had concerns for the safety of Grace Born, Rosie Todd was confident in her sweet soul that the good judgement of the magistrate at Tindercliffe would prevail and that the remains would be proven not those of Richard Born but of some other.

So I bade them farewell, having walked with them to the sign of the Jester where they were to take refreshment and await the night coach. And I also promised to make a call on Grace Born, with her leave, on my way back from Beckwith, for I proposed a journey to call upon my patient there.

XXI

If Grace Born and Rosie Todd knew who was my patient in Beckwith they did not say; or if they wondered who it might be they did not ask; or if they suspected they gave no indication of such. Yet Rosie Todd had been present at the dressing of Caleb Sawney's wound as he lay on the billiard table at the sign of the Ram's Head and, even if she had not been there, would have known enough, namely that Caleb Sawney was of the family of Sawney of Beckwith who were known throughout the hill country as drunkards and rough livers. And I knew not what greeting I might receive, yet Caleb Sawney was my patient and I was bound by my profession to call upon him and see how he fared.

It was a low and scudding day with a thick grey mist hugging the ridges of the hills, and the faces of the poor wan sheep peering through. And high above on the road leading northwards from the town stood Beckwith mill, which I could see from afar had been much ravaged, and the glass broken and the walls fired by the successive night time visitations of machine breakers. Yet at my feet growing close to the beck with its roots in the rancid black earth was the Sonchus hesperus coming into its first flower, whose violet-edged petals would for ever bring back to me the sweet memory of Liz Horridge; whom indeed I had neglected as my patient, being much occupied with others, though I had no doubt that if she fared ill word would have reached me. For though each one in the hill country kept their own counsel and would not speak even on pain of death, yet all knew each others' affairs.

And reflecting thus with little in my head but the wanderings of an ageing man I became only slowly aware of

155

the thin mewing of a raptor hidden in the mist but nevertheless making an accompaniment to my thoughts, and an unwanted one at that. For though all creatures upon earth are fashioned by the merciful hand of the Almighty, the raptor is supposed by men to be the bringer of bad tidings; and even though that office were indeed ordained by the Lord God the raptor is nevertheless feared and despised in equal measure. Which feeling I have to say is reciprocal, for the poor maligned creature no doubt sought an opportunity to come down, but that a fellow, namely myself, was in his very path.

And having heard the fearful cry I knew that nearby would be an answer, for though men may act without reason there is none else in all the Lord God's creation that lacks a cause for his every action; and the poor despised creature led me presently to the place, a hollow ringed by gorse wherein was a rough dwellinghouse little bigger than a sheep fold. Which on entering I found to be inhabited by a woman of the most forsaken appearance, with scarce any breath left in her and her whole flesh running with sores, who seeing me cowered away into a corner, covering her eyes with her hand. For the poor soul had been cooped up for so long that the blessed daylight, although it was dour and little enough, was hurtful to her to behold. And I knew not whether her mind was sound for she, like the raptor covered by the mist, made no sound but a constant mewing as if she were calling to the bird to come to her.

For indeed, had she stayed half a day longer as she was her soul would surely have departed, so slender did her hold on life appear to be.

'Have you anything to drink?' I said, not so much to elicit an answer for I expected none, but to break the unearthly sound coming from her. She indicated a flagon by her side, which I saw had once contained strong liquor, and a cup also which was empty.

'No water?' I said. She answered not but continued with her fearful sounds, so that, as my habit is, I fell into aimless talk, for my own benefit more than hers, as my spirit was breaking with the loneliness of her mewing.

'You have no water, my good woman, and you are sorely in need of refreshment. If you will allow me I will bring you water, for the gorse yonder is full of fleece, which is saturated with mist, and I dare not bring you from the beck for I know it to be unwholesome.'

And indeed, the humble sheep had left enough fleece caught on the gorse to hold as much fluid as the poor woman could take, for her frame was shrunken through lack of water, and more than the merest sip would come back.

The poor creature took the cup from my hands and drank, the very act of which made her doleful sounds to cease, for which I was truly thankful, being by then frighted to the last degree. And fearing that she would start mewing again I was ready to fill the silence with my idle chatter when she spoke.

'What hour is it?'

I told her it was nigh on two hours after the mid-day, and asked her how long she had been living there.

She looked at me without comprehension, taking occasional sips of water.

'What did you say?'

'I asked you how long you have been living in this way, my good woman,' knowing even as I spoke the futility of the question, for mere hours in isolation will cause the mind to lose the homely thread of time.

'I do not know,' she said. 'What is it to you?'

Then I told her, for I realised that her mind was sound, though slow to comprehend, that I was on my way to Beckwith to see a patient and had come upon her dwellinghouse, without telling her of the raptor overhead.

'No doubt you saw the bird also,' she said.

I told her that in truth the mist was so thick that not only the birds of the air, but also the sheep that walk on the earth, were hidden by it.

'So you travel to Beckwith to see a patient? If the name of your patient is Caleb Sawney that is my son. For, sir, seeing that my time is near I left the dwellinghouse on account of there being too many to feed already, even though a man of the militia helps. And my folks, who have little understanding, sir, for all are as I and worse, think me, if they think at all, to be seeking work. For they at Beckwith are laid off mill work since the machine breakers went in. And if you will leave me, sir, you will be doing me a kindness. For to tell the truth, sir, since I have not had recourse to strong drink my mind is less foggy and, although my flight began under the influence of liquor, I still see it as for the best, being now in my right mind.'

I gave the poor woman juniper for the itch and the scab, for I could see the eruptions were caused by excessive scratching of the skin, and I begged her also to take part of a loaf of bread, for she was already reaching and clutching onto the life she had decided to leave, though she knew it not. She told me her name was Sarah, which she said was well chosen, for Caleb was the son of her old age, she said, though that was as far as her association with the holy book went for she had lived a wayward life, and though she said it herself, and may the Lord forgive her, Caleb her son was no credit to her and reflected shamefully on her offices as a mother.

So she went on talking, her mind clearing with each sentence, until the darkness in the dwellinghouse was as light as broad day to me and my nostrils were no longer offended by the foetor therein.

Then I ventured to ask her if she would direct me to the dwellinghouse wherein her son Caleb lay, which she said she would, for though he had done ill, and all of Beckwith and indeed the hill country round about knew it, he was still her son and she wished him better in body even if his spirit were beyond reclaim.

And as we came out into the air the mist was clearing and I saw the town of Beckwith but a short step hence, and also, though I did not say so to the poor woman, her late companion the raptor but a spot in the white sky.

'The bird has gone,' she said, 'which means my time is not yet come, so I must live, and I must go home.'

'Happen it was not you he was looking for but some poor sheep out on the hill,' I said.

'No, he was looking for me,' she said, 'and he will come again one day, but not today. We are here, sir. You may go in.'

She had stopped in front of a dwellinghouse, and poor withal, yet no more so than all the others. Seeing my hesitation she pushed open the door.

'You will find my son inside.'

The room was rank with the odour of the human body and the lees of sour liquor, which so occupied the space that my foot nudged in the darkness against certain pots set down on the floor.

'Mind those, Hayward. If you can break anything you will, you clumsy fellow.'

And I was half minded to keep my peace in order to hear what else in the way of incivility Caleb Sawney was ready to hurl at he whom he supposed to be his senior officer, who of his own free will had volunteered to see to his welfare.

'Haven't you anything to say for yourself, Hayward? You've been to the stews, I'll be bound. Nothing more calculated to reduce a man to silence than failure in that department, eh?'

'I'm not Thomas Hayward,' I said, 'and if I were I'd be questioning my presence here if I were constantly the recipient of such ribaldry.'

'Well I'm damned if it isn't the Frenchman,' said Caleb Sawney. 'You'd better open up the casement and take a look at this arm if you would. Can't do much with it, only piss. I suppose a fellow has to be thankful for small mercies, eh? Not much else to do these days but piss.'

'And imbibe strong liquor also, my man,' I said, which will cause mischief to your liver while you are yet a young man.'

'That is true,' he said. 'Take a look at this arm, would you.'

In the thin light which entered the room I perceived Caleb Sawney's face to be much disfigured by pustules, and his person generally to be sorely neglected, though the arm itself was sound enough to wield the scourge. And it lay indeed in my gift as to whether to tell this to the fellow or no.

'The arm is yet weak,' he said.

'It is weak as long as the sinews are mending,' I said. ''Tis the way the human frame repairs, so that a man feeling a limb to be weak will not over tax it.'

'Then the arm is mending?'

'It is mending,' I said, 'and will by and by be as good as new if you respect it and do not put it to bad use.'

'Meaning what exactly?' said Caleb Sawney. And it came to me yet again that indeed I had a window in my head through which men might view my inmost thoughts.

And not getting any answer from me he turned his conversation to the woman who had led me to the dwellinghouse, who he said was named Sarah Bower and was much given to strong liquor, and whom many believed to have left Beckwith as she had not been seen for many a long day. And indeed, she had not said to me during the journey to Beckwith that she was married to Caleb Sawney's father, merely that Caleb Sawney was her son, and that she lamented her motherhood in that he had turned out to be as he was. All of which caused me to wonder whether Caleb Sawney knew she was his mother, for he had much to say about her waywardness; so much that I resolved to go again to her dwellinghouse on my return journey and see how she fared, for I found much goodness in her.

Caleb Sawney continued thus, moving his arm a little now that he knew it to be sound again, and would, I believe, have continued much longer regaling me with the shortcomings of Sarah Bower had not Thomas Hayward entered, walking straight into the pots on the floor as I had done.

'Mind those. By Gad, Hayward, what a clumsy fellow you are.'

Caleb Sawney did not look round to see who had entered.

'You are Hayward, are you? I thought this fellow was you and he wasn't.'

'The arm is restored sufficiently to permit the patient to return to light duties,' I said.

Thomas Hayward was meanwhile laying out on the table a quarter of bread and other wrapped provisions, which I gathered from the depleted look of him he had paid for out of his own pocket.

'Are we to believe this fellow?' said Caleb Sawney. 'Happen he's a charlatan. And a Frenchman and a papist to boot. Do I return to the unit then, Hayward? A fellow might do well to think twice when he has his victuals laid before him, eh, Hayward?'

'You heard what the physician said. You are able for light duties, Caleb,' said Thomas Hayward. 'You'll find the militia billeted in Clywold on account of talk going round that there's mischief abrewing among the machine breakers. This physician here has served you well and taken a dose of your sharp tongue into the bargain, and if you are a gentleman you will thank him.'

Which Caleb Sawney did not, neither did he thank Thomas Hayward. And I could see that the officer had had his fill of Sawney's ill manners and could take no more. For the good Lord ever gives men strength to bear what afflictions come their way and when the burden is too great removes it.

So we left the dwellinghouse of Caleb Sawney, and I told Thomas Hayward where I was bound, namely to see the good woman Sarah Bower, to know how she fared, having believed as she did that the raptor hovering over her dwellinghouse had come for her soul. Whereupon Thomas Hayward confirmed what I knew, that Sarah Bower was Caleb Sawney's mother, and indeed the whole of Beckwith knew that she had borne him out of wedlock; but the fellow himself, though he had heard it said often enough and it was true, did not take it to heart and continued to lay whatever ill report he could upon her. Being no better in the matter himself, Thomas Hayward said, for indeed most of the fellows from the militia did likewise, namely took their pleasure where they could and paid for it, yet with less consequence than was visited upon those who sold themselves. And he had heard it said that Caleb Sawney likewise took his pleasure and exacted it with threats against the poor young women, all of whom had machine breakers among their kindred.

'It is a troublesome world, sir,' he concluded. 'And now I must leave you for my way lies toward Clywold, and Sarah Bower's dwelling is nigh on a furlong south. For it is well known, sir, being a place of retreat among the women hereabouts.'

But Thomas Hayward, though he said he must needs be gone, yet lingered.

'Sir,' he said, 'there is a stranger in these parts seeking you, who says he has called on you in York but has not found you there; but happen there may be many who have ills of divers kinds who are seeking you. He's somewhat after your own appearance, sir, meaning no disrespect, and speaks somewhat in your manner. And I told him if I saw you I would convey that he is searching for you. Which makes me a happy man, for today I have delivered myself of two encumbrances, namely Caleb Sawney and a message, sir, which makes me a happy man. Good day.'

So noticing the lameness in Thomas Hayward's feet I gave him a tincture of nutmeg for the relief of the joints and he was gone.

Then to the dwellinghouse of Sarah Bower, which I found empty, with much evidence of having been made neat and clean. And as I was there looking in the boy Matthias came by, who had conducted me to the house where Liz Horridge awaited her surgery. And I wondered at his being so far from his customary place, yet he said that was his habit, to go from one to another; which was the way generally with the likes of himself in the hill country. And he said also that Sarah was about Beckwith clean of person and in her right mind.

XXII

Before I saw Zephaniah Gaut I heard the rasp of his breathing and his laboured steps. For the hills carried not only the secret converse of men but news of the intimate maladies of their bodies, broadcasting to all what ills might be afflicting them. When the footsteps ceased, which was when Zephaniah stopped to recover his breath, an aimless tune replaced the sound of breathing. Then he would continue his walk and the painful process would recommence.

So I walked thus for some two furlongs down the hill road from Beckwith, knowing that Zephaniah Gaut was near, yet knowing not where, so jealously did the hills conceal those who walked upon them, until joining a fork in the road I espied him on the bridle way making for the same fork. And knowing the poor fellow would talk volubly, as was his habit, and knowing he had insufficient wind for both breath and walk, I bade him be seated on an outcrop of stones, thinking also that the sight of a fellow traveller might have taken him by surprise, but it had not.

'I thought to catch up with you, sir,' he said. 'Tha toold me yonder in Beckwith tha was nigh. Happen tha mus attend thy patients, sir, whosoever they be.' By which I understood that Zephaniah Gaut knew my patient to have been Caleb Sawney.

'You are a fair way from your dwellinghouse, Zephaniah, my good man,' I said.

'Nigh on three days' journey by foot,' he said. 'I go seeking Robert, but happen tha guess that. Thas no folk will tell me where he be, sir.'

Then I bade Zephaniah Gaut take a tincture of digitalis and, to stop his talk for a while so that he might regain his strength, filled the silence with my chatter, telling him of the last time I set eyes on Robert Gaut, namely in the Sheep-close when the master of Clywold mill pleaded with the magistrate to halt the scourge, which he would not; which affliction continued until one came down from the hills and dealt a savage blow to the perpetrator. To all of which good Zephaniah Gaut listened attentively. Then I told him all I knew of how Robert Gaut fared, that he being weakened by his ordeal was the cause of the master of Clywold mill bringing forward his bay mare Yolande, who knelt for the injured weaver to be placed on her back, which same gentle beast conveyed him at an easy pace to where certain good hill folks awaited him and took him thence in a cart, though I knew not where he had gone, nor had I heard any talk of him since. For the hills which broadcast the affairs of men far and wide for all to hear also keep their counsel and do not give up their secrets, which thought I spoke to Zephaniah Gaut, who understanding what I said nodded.

Then observing that his breathing was less laboured I ceased my prattle. But he said nothing.

'And I would dearly like to know where Robert is,' I continued, 'for he had suffered some mischief, though not grievous to his life. But I do believe that the good hill people have sufficient lore among themselves to see that his hurts are tended.'

Which indeed I believed wholeheartedly, for there was much goodness and wisdom in them. And I believed moreover that even those fellows who went out by night with blackened faces had many of them by day the gentleness of angels.

After which Zephaniah Gaut made to speak, beginning his tale as I thought afar off.

'Twas the strangest thing, sir, and I'll remember it rightly if I have a minute.'

Zephaniah took up his aimless tune again, part whistle and part the hiss of the air through his poor lungs.

'See tha, sir?' I followed his gaze across the valley. 'Thas raptor,' he said. 'Tis bird of ill omen but tis heading off and thas good.'

I told Zephaniah I could see nothing at so great a distance, being short of sight through long years spent in the preparation of remedies, but that I had seen the raptor on my way up, and he had flown off, having no business about Beckwith.

'Happen it was tha day I brought my lass Hannah to see ye, sir,' Zephaniah continued, 'though it may have been another. Or happen it was but a dream, sir, though it was real enough, if you follow my meaning. Anyways it was the fair town of York where we was an it was the day of the assizes, for folks was gathered underneath the castle, sir. An we stood thereby having got caught up in the crowd an unable to leave, though we would fain have left, sir. An those poor souls for the hearing was brought forrard in a line, sir, an as white an sickly an pitiful a bunch as I ever saw, an some covering up their faces. An as we was watching, for we could do no other, sir, being constrained by the press of the crowd an unable to leave as I said, sir, we hears a young woman call out, "Robert!" An at first we knew not where the lassie was, for, meaning no offence, for God made all creatures to be different one from another, sir, she was hid in the midst of the crowd on account o her low stature. But certain of them present made way for her so as we set eyes on the young woman, who was an angel from heaven, sir, for the sweetness of her. Yet deficient in her stature, though I know not if angels be tall or otherwise if you take my meaning, sir. An Hannah an myself hearing the name of our own son made to speak to the young woman, sir, an a believe it was our Robert she called, for she talked of him as a musician, until my lass Hannah was all for thinking she was sweet on him. But she said she was not an never would be wi any fellow, being forbid by her weakened frame.'

Having said which and scarcely drawn air in doing so Zephaniah was hard pressed to take even so much as the next breath and stopped his talk. Then little by little when he had come to himself he told the rest, which was not much, namely that they in the crowd, hearing the young woman and seeing her sweet face urged her to go into the assize while there was yet time and follow the fortunes, good or bad, of he they supposed to be her sweet heart, but that the great doors were closed even as she made her way through the throng.

'An the truth is, sir,' concluded Zephaniah, 'that neither my good lass Hannah nor myself could recollect how the encounter ended, being as we were taken up with the notion that Robert our son were up at yon assize, if not tha day then another. For we know now tis the tinnitus my sweet lass Hannah has in her ears, but she has ever entertained the notion tis the building of the gallows-tree she hearkens to and tis never far from her mind.'

And indeed I believed Zephaniah with all my heart, for the gallows-tree in the fair land of England is little removed from the guillotine in the fair land of France, and there had been many a night when in my dreams I was climbing the steps, going higher and higher until I could hear nothing nor see the crowd below, yet I knew they were there; and it was ever the same conclusion, that a most fearful clatter would wake me, which I was hard pressed for the space of half of an hour to believe was not the sound of the blade falling.

So I gave to Zephaniah a tincture of basil to cheer the sweet heart of his wife Hannah, and for himself a tincture of honeysuckle for the breathlessness, and also a further tincture of Digitalis purpurea for when he should go on his way; for I could see that he had not yet finished his discourse.

'Begging your pardon, sir,' he said presently, 'an I pray you not to take the question amiss, but would you be in the same manner as Hannah an myself in that we have a grown son, an that son nigh on a stranger to us? Begging your forgiveness for such impertinence, sir an begging you not to answer if you are not so inclined.'

And though I would gladly have kept all talk away from myself, Zephaniah Gaut's question was so humbly placed before me, and moreover he had ample reason to be feared for his son, I could not but answer. And I told him that I had taken minor orders in the church of Rome in the days of my youth and therefore the homely converse between men and women was forbid me.

Which answer, by reason that it was not withheld, pleased Zephaniah well, though I had no doubt but that he was a dissenter. And he told me then of his son's hostility of manner, of which I knew much, saying that there was many a day when he fancied he had seen murder in his son's eyes, though in his discourse he was the mildest of men. And he did not know but that his present affectation of the lungs and his consequent whistlings and wheezings were vexatious to his son to hear, being of a musical turn of mind. But though the father was vexatious to the son, his mother had never been so, and from early infancy Robert had cleaved more to his mother than his father.

'An it does cross my mind,' said Zephaniah, 'tha the murder I see in my son's eyes, for the very reason that it is kept down so to speak, might yet find its outlet in machine breaking or other such violence. Not tha the folks don't have a grievance, sir, for the work is amost non-existent among the hand weavers i some parts, but recourse to violence, tha never done nothing. As you might well know, sir, being from the land of France an on the wrong side o the divide so to speak, forgive my impertinence. Twas allus my shortcoming to be garrulous, sir.'

By which saying humbly delivered I deemed that the good man Zephaniah Gaut with his failing lungs and clear mind deserved more than silence, so I told him in a few plain words that what he surmised was indeed the truth, for I was considered an enemy of the revolution on account of my orders within the church of Rome; yet an apothecary is not partisan and I had counted many citizens also among my patients in those perilous times. To which Zephaniah merely said, 'Aye,' and I knew that my sayings to him would go no further, for such intricacies of my life I would not have imparted to another.

So I left the good man without telling him that which he most wished to hear, namely that I would inform him if I had tidings of his son's whereabouts. Nor indeed did he press me to do so being a man blessed with tact and a fine intelligence, though of small account in the eyes of the world. And I would gladly have gone with him on his journey, which was towards Clywold, but that I had promised to call upon Grace Born and Rosie Todd at Holmroyd.

Then as the daylight was nearly spent and the lights of the town of Withersedge puttered and glimmered through a cleft in the hills I resolved to lodge overnight at the sign of the Blue Boar. Though not before, as was my habit at the time of night when the sky was a violet blue and the shade of the petals of the Sonchus hesperus, I had reflected on the wellbeing of my patient Liz Horridge, whose sweet eyes were of the same hue, and who was ever in my mind, though I willed it not. For though others perceived a window in my head, and my scribe Luke Bower in particular, through which the inmost processes of my mind might be discerned, yet I saw it not, and to myself the origin of my thoughts was as opaque as the mist clinging to the hills outside Beckwith that same morning. Which recollection brought to me also the bird of ill omen, which had nevertheless left the presence of Sarah Bower with a will in her to continue her life; and which now, as I looked towards the star Sirius, that hung like a drop of water low in the heavens, flew over my head and was gathered into the quiet of the night.

And approaching the Blue Boar as fresh horses were being put into the traces in preparation for the last coach I saw among those waiting to board the musician Domenico Jommelli who had been seeking me these weeks past, and indeed I him, though I knew not why. Who, not seeing me as I was yet a way distant and concealed by the darkness, boarded the coach, which forthwith set off in a smoke of dust, for after the mist of the morning the day had turned to heat.

And indeed the departing call of the coachman was the last human voice I heard that night apart from the meagre civilities of the host, for all within the public room fell silent as I entered, eyeing me with no little suspicion; and I concluded that a meeting of machine breakers had been in progress, for I noted that each face wore the same gaunt look. Which brought to mind the town of Beckwith, how they there were hungered through lack of work, and how when men are desperate the common civilities of humankind are forgot.

And I knew not whether it was my rough reception at the sign of the Blue Boar or the ardours of the day just gone, or otherwise the converse with good Zephaniah Gaut, but in the small hours of the next morning when it was yet dark the same dream came upon me, that I was climbing steps, going higher and higher so that the baying crowd beneath, which was considerable, was silenced by distance, though I could still see their mouths working. And as I looked up into the sun I could see a black shape, which as it approached resolved itself into the bird of ill omen. I continued to climb higher into the sun, yet the raptor, however swift he might have been on the wing, did not reach me; until the dream ended in a great clatter, which was the host throwing back the shutters of the scullery below, and meanwhile conversing pleasantly with the kitchen maid.

For he was a genial fellow and I understood much perturbed by the meeting of the previous night, the presence of which not only closed his hostelry to other guests but depleted his means as the poor fellows who attended had no great funds to lay out on refreshment; indeed, he said, he was obliged to provide for them gratis. And the good host confirmed my speculation, namely that they were for the most part cloth finishers who had lost their livelihood to the mills at Tindercliffe and Beckwith, and even Clywold which was a fair way off; and he pitied them for their hunger and their idle hands, yet he himself had a hostelry to keep.

And while he spoke I surveyed his well-natured face, observing a contracture between the brows which denoted the head ache, and I asked him as much; to which he answered that, yes, he did indeed suffer with the head ache, to the extent that on certain days he must lie down with the shutters drawn to, and leave the operation of the hostelry to his good wife; and at such times also he suffered much with nausea so that he asked himself if indeed he were in the right profession, it having much to do with victuals which were anathema to him while the head ache was upon him. Though he trusted today was not that bad a day and he would get through, yet the troubles of the night before did not help. So I gave to the good man a tincture of betony, and having done so repaired to the parish of Holmroyd.

XXIII

'I have come to meet you, sir,' said Luke Bower.

'I can see that, Luke,' I said. 'Thank you. You are a good fellow.'

'Are you not going to ask why I am come to meet you, sir?' said Luke.

'If I were to ask you, you would only tell me in your own good time, Luke.'

'That is true, sir. But I will tell you nevertheless. Certain folks are not there, sir. Namely him as does not remember his own name. And the two ladies, sir. The two ladies who wear braids in their hair. They are not where you might be expecting them to be, nor are they anywhere that I know of, sir – which is not to say they are nowhere at all, but nowhere that I know of. And having heard of this matter in York, sir, I have come to forewarn you, being bound for their dwelling. Say something, sir, I pray you, otherwise I am like to surmise that you are scattered in your wits; and also there is a limit to how long I can go on rehearsing folks' absences. You have gone a white colour, sir. Say something, I pray you. Do you hear me, sir? You are as white as yonder sheep on Capcarhill.'

The good fellow had caught hold of my sleeve and was pulling me along, for indeed my wits were fled, and I was hard pressed to string a sentence together, or indeed make any thing of the sweet world around me. For the heaven and the earth, painted as they were in bright hues by the hand of God Almighty, had been drained of their colours, and I saw naught but white heaven and white earth, and everything therein turned to white.

'I cannot get a word in edgeways for all your chatter, Luke,' I said. 'What was it? Pray tell me again and I will be more sensible.'

'That certain persons are not there, sir,' said Luke. 'Him as cannot remember his own name, but happen you know that already, sir. Likewise the two ladies with braids in their hair. And hearing such in York, sir, and knowing you to be in Beckwith yet bound for Holmroyd, sir, and ignorant of their absence, sir, begging your pardon for you are knowing in all else, I resolved to warn you, sir.'

All this time good Luke Bower continued to pull me by the sleeve as one would a wayward bairn, from time to time turning round and inspecting my head as if my wits might yet be flying loose.

'I trust the matter has not taken you by surprise, sir,' he said. 'We are bound for the sign of the Ram's Head where you will take refreshment, sir, for you gave your bread to a woman by the name of Sarah on the way.'

'Pray, Luke, what else is news in York?' I said. 'You may let go my sleeve now, thanking you for your goodness.'

'Nothing to speak of in the way of news, sir,' said Luke. 'Nothing to speak of at all, which I will impart to you fully when you have taken refreshment. I liked not the look of you just then, sir. You had about you the whiteness of the sheep on Capcar-hill, and I feared you had also lost your wits like the sheep, which I never knew to say a word of sense yet.'

'So what may be the news in York, sir?' Luke said when we were arrived at the sign of the Ram's Head and were seated in the public room, which at that hour was deserted of all but ourselves, and as if he had asked the question and not I.

'You will answer your question in your own good time as is your habit, Luke.'

'I will answer it now, sir, if it pleases you, for I see that your colour is restored,' said Luke. 'The justice at Tindercliffe has delivered a verdict, the verdict being, sir, that the remains with which you lately assisted and which will forever linger in my nostrils are those of the magistrate of Holmroyd, namely Richard Born.'

'And how come you by this news, Luke?'

'As I said, sir, the news is abroad in York, for the gentleman was widely known among certain in society. And indeed, sir, had the tidings only been known to one person in York, the matter would have been broadcast to all by now. Tis the same thing, sir, if you follow my meaning.'

'And how come you to know that I gave a ration of bread to a woman named Sarah?' I said. But Luke had finished his discourse and there was no more to be had from him on the matter.

And it was indeed a question to which I sought no answer, but that my tongue was wont to fill with words the void in my mind. For never had I been at such a loss, knowing not how to proceed, since I foresaw a grave misjustice in the making, though I knew not how to put it right, save that I might seek the wisdom of my scribe, and afterwards that of good Kit Swain, who had assisted at the retrieval.

'Luke, my good man,' I said, 'since you have been acquainted with this news for some time longer than I, both that of the identity of the remains and the fact that the two good ladies are gone from their home, have you also become acquainted in your mind with the possible implications of these events?'

'Sir,' said Luke, 'you know that nothing happens in this world but that there is a reason for it. Men have known that since our forefather Adam walked in the garden. Similarly, sir, nothing happens in this fair world but that there is a remedy for it, as you know well from your profession of apothecary. Yet we, being but foolish fellows, and I speak only for myself, sir, know not the remedy all of the time, that being in the realm of heaven and not given to the common run of men. But, sir, since there were others with you at the retrieval you might first seek out the fellow Kit Swain who is an uncommon hand at the billiard table, that item of furniture having been restored to its former use save for a few stains of blood and gore, sir, which fairly turn my stomach. That being the case I will leave it to yourself to find him, sir, for I cannot stand the sight of blood.'

Which scruple I knew of already,for Luke Bower was apt to hide himself behind his distaste for such things.

'Meaning, sir, that the fellow is at this moment of time present at the sign of the Ram's Head, and having been informed of your presence by myself, begging you to forgive my presumption, sir, is at this moment awaiting that same presence and has been awaiting so for some time, until such occasion as your faculties should be returned to you, sir.'

Whereupon Luke Bower ushered in Kit Swain and himself departed I knew not where to. And Kit Swain proceeded to deliver his tale beginning from the time when I saw him last, namely when he set off in the cart with the remains bound for the justice of Tindercliffe; and how the justice being abed and a man of uncertain temper withal had ordered the cart to be placed nigh the stable at the rear of the dwellinghouse, where he himself presently appeared, foul of mouth and temper and with the foul stink of liquor upon him; by which turn of phrase I gathered that Kit Swain was of the dissenting community, they being temperate of habit. And having given the remains a peremptory glance, lifting one corner of the sacking, the justice pronounced such to be the earthly temple of Richard Born, magistrate of Holmroyd, God rest his soul, for he had been wearing that same suit of clothes at the last sessions; which being the case he would vouch for the identity himself and so finish the business for the night.

'And with that concluded, sir, we came back on foot, reaching the parish of Holmroyd in the hour before dawn when it was still dark and Orion sinking behind the hill. Yet at that hour they were already astir in the dwellinghouse of Mr Born, and I have not known that to be the case before, though I am often thereabouts in the dawn when the sheep are on the move.'

'What say they in the parish, Kit Swain, my good man?' I said.

'No man durst say aught, sir,' said Kit Swain, 'and saving your presence none have inquired of me about the doings of the night for the magistrate is feared equally from the other world as he was in this. And I know you will tell no man, sir, and therefore I may say this, that the magistrate of Tindercliffe was well under the influence of strong liquor, sir.'

Which indeed Kit Swain had intimated before; and he was on the point of leaving the public room but turned back, closing the door again, saying he had delivered the remedies, but that the magistrate was in no fit frame of mind to acknowledge such, and that his housekeeper would draw his attention to the tinctures on the morrow.

And I knew not how to thank Kit Swain, and I said as much, which he brushed away saying that the billiards was not yet done, and if I wished to know where Luke Bower was, he was there, having said at first that the state of the billiard table had turned his stomach, but he had altered his mind as the play progressed.

So I sat in the public room waiting on Luke's return, which was so long in coming that I sank into a reverie, being fatigued by the journey from Beckwith, and indeed depleted by the news, which I took to be the truth, of the verdict of the magistrate of Tindercliffe and of the disappearances, for in my mind I called them such, of Grace Born and Rosie Todd. And presently I must have fallen into a slumber, though in my mind I was wakeful enough, for I saw the face of the magistrate of Holmroyd looking in through the window, noting that his person, of which I saw but the upper half, the rest being concealed below the sill, was attired in the dress of a common fellow. And being in that condition known at night-time paralysis, though it was but day, I was unable to move from my chair; yet I saw, as if there were no dwellinghouses between the Ram's Head and his own dwellinghouse, that the magistrate, having ceased from looking into the window of the public room, repaired to his own dwellinghouse and took to battering on the door thereof, at which point I awoke to find the host present in the room and making heavy weather of mending the fire, though it was not cold. And asking the host if there had been any person looking in through the window he remarked that I might as well ask him if there were any sheep out on Capcar-hill, for the answer was like to be the same. 'But,' he said, 'in truth, since the doleful episodes of recent weeks there might well be certain folks passing by who would look inside to see if anybody might yet be laid out upon a trestle or if any other mischief was afoot. And happen it was one of those fellows, sir,' he said, 'unless it be yon magistrate arisen from the dead for I wouldn't put it past him, he gave himself such airs, asking your pardon, sir, for my impious speech.'

By which I understood that the word of the magistrate of Tindercliffe, namely that the remains were those of Richard Born, was not doubted, though I knew that the due process of the law had been passed by in that no kinsman or kinswoman had been called upon to identify the remains, and reliance had been placed solely on matters of dress.

Then the good host, rendered talkative by my presence, for I came to the Ram's Head as one ignorant of the most recent happenings, told me what I had lately heard from Kit Swain, namely that in the hour before dawn following the night the remains were taken to Tindercliffe it was noticed among certain folks that lights were ablaze in the dwellinghouse of Richard Born, and that besides Kit Swain a certain ne'er-do-well had seen and taken fright and fled believing that the magistrate was early upon his rounds and would find him loitering in the way; and also a husband come by to call upon a neighbour to assist his wife be delivered of a bairn; they and certain others. And indeed, each witness testified to a sense of fright abroad that night and sounds as of persons being questioned under duress, which were wont to be heard at the rear of the dwellinghouse of Richard Born. Though, the host concluded, these tales grew the more elaborate the more they were repeated and he knew not what was the truth. For what is truth, he said.

So presently Luke Bower came in and asked me what I intended to do, since they whom I had come to call upon were not there, nor did anyone know of their whereabouts for a certainty, though the majority of folks, Luke said, believed they had fled to Mrs Born's kindred fearing to be suspected of foul play now that it was confirmed by the justice of Tindercliffe that the remains were those of Richard Born. Yet, though I did not say as much to Luke Bower, I thought not, since Grace Born had said to me that her kindred had cast her off since her liaison with Richard Born.

'You are thinking that the two ladies with braids in their hair have come to some mischief, sir,' said Luke.

'I did not say so, Luke.'

'Yet you thought so, sir,' he said.

'Then if that be the case, where do I think the two ladies might be?' I said.

'You are thinking that they have been apprehended on suspicion of foul play, sir,' said Luke, 'which is not the same as believing they are guilty, sir, for you do not, but that is what you think.'

'And supposing that is what I think, Luke,' I said, 'what do I propose to do next?'

'Doubtless you propose to find them, sir. They and the others.'

'Others?'

'I have told you, sir, he as does not know his own name. He is gone from the concealed chamber.'

'That is only one other, Luke.'

'And the musician fellow, sir. And two hand weavers who dwelt yonder of Kessle-wood. Their folks have not seen them this sennight gone.'

I said nothing, knowing that as ever, when prompted, Luke would give away nothing, whereas left to himself he would be hard pressed to contain such knowledge as he had come by.

'I would have thought you would have sought more tidings, sir,' he said presently, after the host had been back into the public room and made a great labour of mending the fire again. 'For you know them of old, sir. Tis one Simon Horridge and his violet-eyed sister Elizabeth, as like to each other as if both had been maids or else both lads, whom their kinsfolk seek and who have not been at their dwellinghouse, as I say, sir this sennight gone or longer, as no folks can remember when they were last seen. That being the nature of the hill country, sir, for no folks can remember when they last saw their neighbour.'

By which prattle I understood that Luke knew he had been hasty with his tongue in stating in the public room, which was empty, though the door stood ajar, that I was acquainted with certain hand weavers.

'For indeed, sir,' he continued at a pitch louder than was customary with him, 'I mean not that you knew any hand weavers, sir, for I know you do not nor any folk of the hill country particularly, save that you journeyed to Beckwith on the King's mission to tend the soldier who had delivered just chastisement to an enemy of the Crown.'

And as I looked at Luke, wondering whether it were he or I whose wits were scattered I noticed him incline his head very slightly in the direction of the window, and although I did not turn, yet I saw, caught on a shaft of the declining sun, the shadow of a man lying across the floor between good Luke Bower and myself; and the door of the public room, which had stood ajar but a moment before, was wide open.

Then we left the sign of the Ram's Head forthwith, knowing not but that the walls and the doors and the very casements had eyes and ears as open as any man's. Nor did we exchange a word until we came to the cross roads where we sat to await the coach bound for York, which being a deserted place and none others there waiting Luke continued his discourse.

'Did you notice anything, sir?' he said, and before I could reply he went on as if the question had not been asked. 'There was a fellow looking in at the casement, which is not the principal matter, sir, but that there came with him an assault to the nostrils. And, begging your pardon, sir, the said assault to the nostrils was so like to that which I noticed on your person after you had presided at the retrieval, sir, that I believed the fragrance of the remains yet clung to your person and your clothing; either that or it remained in my nostrils, as an unwholesome fragrance is like to do. But I was mistaken, sir, for it was neither. The fellow at the window whose shadow fell across the floor, as you noticed yourself, sir, took the fragrance away with him.'

'Then likely it was one of the fellows present at the retrieval,' I said.

'But likely it was not, sir,' said Luke. 'Likely it was the deceased come back to look in through the casement.'

'I would beg you not to speak your ideas to any other soul, Luke,' I said, 'lest they should spread like wild fire and be all around the county of York. Nor will I say anything.'

For indeed I had noticed the same aroma accompanying the fellow who had looked in at the casement, but I did not say so to my scribe.

XXIV

'Here comes another,' said Luke.

'How come you see another? Tis nigh on dark by now,' I said.

'That may be so, sir,' said Luke. 'But there is another. I may not see or hear this other, but I know that he approaches, though he may be three furlongs off.'

'One day you will tell me how you know of this person whom you cannot see and cannot hear and who is yet present three furlongs hence, in the same way that you will tell me of the good woman Sarah with whom I shared bread.'

'There is no great mystery in either,' said Luke. 'While you were in Beckwith, sir, I looked at the writings of him as does not remember his own name, being backwards way on, sir, and have made a fair copy which awaits your scrutiny at the dispensary.'

'I thank you heartily, Luke,' I said, for in truth I had forgotten that I had left his writings undeciphered. 'You are a good fellow.'

'That I doubt, sir,' said Luke. 'For though you are always telling me so, the rest of the world is not, and I am obliged to believe the opinion of the majority.'

'This other has not yet arrived, Luke,' I said presently, 'and I fear we may miss the person, for the moon is arisen over the hill and the night coach will surely be here within the next half of an hour.'

'He is here now, sir,' said Luke, then to the newcomer who had come upon us unawares, 'Pray do not be alarmed by two ne'er-do-wells awaiting the carriage, who you might not

180

have been expecting to come upon in this lonely place. How fare you?'

'I fare generally quite well, thank you, Mr Bower,' said the lad Matthias, for it was he, whom I had first seen at the dwellinghouse of Simon Horridge, and who as I understood had no fixed abode, but rather wandered from one to another seeking lodging where he may. 'I fare generally well in these troubled times, sir, though the same cannot be said of all folk.'

'And have you a lodging this night?' I said, 'for Cassiopeia is nigh the zenith and it is late,'

'Thank you, sir,' said Matthias. 'There are those in the parish of Holmroyd who will likely give me lodging and I shall be comfortable enough, though the same cannot be said for all in this troubled world, who do not rest easy this night.'

'And who is it who does not rest easy this night?' said Luke.

'Happen you don't know, sir, you and the physic gentleman, being from over York way, that there are certain who do not rest in their dwellinghouses at all this night but are some place other. And I have asked of many but none will tell me where they are, though I believe all know.'

'Who are these persons?' said Luke

'They are Mistress Horridge and Simon her brother,' said Matthias. 'And I know that they are gone, for one night in the hour before dawn when I had not found lodging, being passed from one to another and none would have me on that occasion, I was making my way yonder, though I am not at liberty to say where, when I came by the dwellinghouse of Simon Horridge, which is hidden from all places other but from a turning at the heel of the hill nigh the sheep walk, and I saw, though it were dark elsewhere, lights in the dwellinghouse and I heard also a mighty clamouring and stamping and snorting of horses, sir, for though I was a way off, sir, all else was quiet and the hills, they take up noises and broadcast them again; so I had no doubt that even they over at Brancliffe and Beckwith might hear. For though men keep their secrets, the hills do not. And presently I saw as I thought those within the house brought forth with no great ceremony and taken round to the side of the dwellinghouse, and so lost to view. For when I reached nearer, but not very near for fright, there was naught to be seen and I wondered if all had been an apparition brought on by fatigue and the lack of food, sir, for such is oft the manner with me if I have not had lodging.'

Whereupon I offered the lad Matthias a ration of bread, which he declined, saying he thanked me kindly but he had eaten that very day.

'And I would likely have said nothing more, Mr Bower,' he continued, 'but that it was noised abroad already that certain souls were away from their dwellinghouses, among them Mistress Horridge and Simon Horridge. Which leads me to suppose that the clamouring I heard by night was true and not what I dreamed up.'

'Is that all thou hast to say, lad?' said Luke.

''Tis not, sir,' said Matthias. 'For when on the morrow I heard them say that Mistress Horridge and Simon were away from their dwellinghouse I told what I had seen in the hour before dawn and they bid me accompany them to the homestead. But fearing the sight of blood, sir,' said Matthias addressing me, 'and you know well, sir, that the sight of blood makes me feel sick in my stomach, I resisted going, yet they impelled me with their banter saying what would I do when I kept company with a maid if I were fearful of a drop of blood; which though I knew not the full import of their sayings I took to be lewd on account of their ribald laughter. And it fair puts me off keeping company with a maid.'

'We need not know the rest, Matthias, my good lad,' I said, for I could see, dark though it was, that the poor fellow was nauseous at the mere thought of what had passed. Yet I asked him who were those who made him go to the dwellinghouse, and he said certain rough fellows he knew not well, but thought them to be from beyond Beckwith, for the majority of weavers in these parts were folks of agreeable disposition, not given to coarseness, and dissenters withal; and moreover he feared for Mistress Horridge and her brother

Simon, having seen blood spattered on the very threshold of their homestead.

Having said which the poor lad took himself off behind the gorse and retched piteously; whereupon I gave him a tincture of bistort for the sickness.

So we fell into silence as the night drew on for the coach was not yet arrived, the poor fellow Matthias showing little inclination to be on his way.

'For in truth, sir,' he said, 'I came this way to flee from the hills, for they were talking among themselves tonight, and though I heard not the words, they being in a language I do not understand, yet I felt the terror upon me and have walked this way out of the reach of them. Not only that, sir, but they were moving sheep around in carts for I saw from underneath the covers sometimes a leg and sometimes a head looking out with its dead sheep's face and it did turn my stomach, and I know tis trouble when sheep are on the move by night. For which reason I am pleased of company, though I am not thus by nature and would willingly lie under the stars without fear if the hills were not talking. Since I know, sir, that whenever the talk is in the air tis followed by troubles, and troubles is followed by folks being taken in for questioning by fair means or foul.'

And I gathered that the lad Matthias knew all, which indeed I had thought before, though many around considered him to be deficient in his wits on account of his wayward life.

'And if it pleases you, sir, I will be on my way for I am out of hearing of the hills and whatever they may be planning.'

So Luke and I settled to await the coach once more, saying little and hearing naught but the wind in the gorse and in the dry grass and around the stones. And it was yet some hours short of the dawn, and the mid night not yet past, when I fancied I saw on the road afar off a carriage, and I saw also as I fancied on the eastern horizon a red glow as of the rising of the sun in winter, which as I watched became the more until the sky was ablaze.

'Tis Clywold way, sir,' said Luke. 'Tis as the lad said, when dead sheep are on the move and the hills are conversing one with another mischief is not far behind.'

'I had thought you had been slumbering, Luke,' I said, though I never yet knew my scribe to take any manner of rest.

'There is a carriage on the road, sir, which happen you have seen, and happen you have noted that it is not going towards York but away from York. Therefore it is going Clywold way. Therefore your mind tells you, sir, as does mine, that it were better to go with the one coach abroad on this night rather than wait like fellows with our wits awry for a coach that may not be running, for if it were running, sir, which you will have reflected upon in the privacy of your mind, there would be other folk awaiting and there are not. Which fact we might have considered before, sir, had our wits been with us.'

'You have looked into the window in my head, Luke,' I said, 'and have read accurately what is writ there, as ever. Yet I have looked in the mirror and have not observed that there is a window in my head, which is not the same as denying the presence of one.'

So we boarded the coach bound for Clywold, being the only passengers therein, the others having disembarked at the Holmroyd cross roads.

'The writing, sir,' said Luke when we were settled within and the coach on the road awaiting the return of the coachman who we understood to be directing those lately disembarked to the sign of the Ram's Head.

'The writing?' I said, for to tell the truth I knew not of what he was speaking.

'Sir, the writing of he who does not remember his own name, who also writes backwards.'

'You have deciphered it, you said, Luke, and once again the matter had gone out of my mind, and it is no good saying to the contrary for you know what is or is not in my mind.'

'Tis a last will and testament, sir,' he said.

XXV

The coachman presently returned and inquired of us what businesss we might have at Clywold that night, saying that if it were all the same to us he would as leave not take the horses there on account of what looked like a conflagration over the hill; then, without waiting for our response, and noting that I wore the dress of an apothecary, the good man begged our pardon and said he would travel as far as he could.

'Yet avoiding the mill if it is all the same to you, gentlemen,' he said, 'for all in the county of York know by now that there is mischief abrewing there one of these nights, and happen it is tonight from the looks of the sky. Though they that travelled with me in this last stage swore me to secrecy, and I know you will not say again what I have said to you.'

Indeed, it was not only the coachman wary to drive to Clywold that night, for even the horses themselves were afeared, laying back their ears on their heads and already showing the whites of their eyes ere the journey began. And out of pity for the poor creatures I would gladly have sat at the cross roads the whole night awaiting the next coach bound for York, but that the coachman, repenting of his former reluctance to make the journey, said he must needs deliver back the coach and horses and have them rested in time for the morrow on pain of his livelihood.

And all this time my scribe Luke Bower kept silence, which was rare enough for him; for it came to me that my scribe, whose name was that of many in the town of Beckwith, was like to carry with him the reticence of the hill folk. And indeed, for all his talk, I knew little enough of him save that he was a fellow of an acute mind and an exquisite hand with the pen, and a good fellow withal; though he said others were not of that opinion, which saying disturbed me not a little, namely for the reason that he thought he travelled through his life with the good opinion of no other.

Then with these reflections in my mind and the sight of the fire on the horizon still before my vision I fell into a slumber; for I was once more in the dwellinghouse in Paris with the baying of the crowd in my ears and the presence of one near me asking again and again the same question, though I knew not what it was; and with each repetition of the question the pain in my right hand increased, namely in the terminal joints of the first and second digits. And all the while I knew also that behind a meagre partition, which served to make two rooms of one, another fellow was, as I thought, undergoing coercion likewise, for I could hear the question asked again and again, and between each the evil whistle of the scourge descending on him. Then all of a sudden there was the cry of "Fire!" at which those questioning fled, leaving myself and the other poor fellow abandoned in the dwellinghouse to escape as we may, or perish. And at that moment all the place caught, for the fire had crept into the rafters from the nearby dwellinghouses, and the beams fell. And with the fire all around I saw not what became of my brother in affliction, but that I was left awandering in the streets of Paris, which were in that quarter but lanes of fire; yet I knew not for whom I was looking, for I had only his cries to know him by, and few enough of those for he was for the most part silent under coercion.

Then I awoke, for the pain in my hand made me, lodged as it was in a crack of the door of the coach and caught fast. And the night was filled with the breath of fire, and the roar of it, and the whinnying of the poor horses as the coachman knocked at the traces; which indeed in a state between sleeping and waking I fancied to be the building of the gallows-tree, the same that my patient Hannah Gaut had described, and to whom I had then said that the condition with her was the tinnitus. But this now I doubted for there is no knowing what the mind may fear and which later comes to pass.

'Tis Clywold, sir,' said Luke, 'and the night is ablaze. Pray be careful how you step down for we are in a godforsaken place and the coachman can take us no farther on account of the horses being frighted, and he fears they will also be lamed if we travel on. Have you heard me, sir? I fear you have that look about you when your wits are awry. Talk to me, sir, else I am prattling to the elements.'

I assured him that I had indeed heard, saying nothing about the dream I was in when the coach came to a halt, for knowing of it would have occasioned the good fellow to start pulling me along by the sleeve, as was his habit when he thought my wits were scattered. Though indeed that was the case, for it was a hard task to decide which direction to take as all were equally ablaze, and I feared there were many dwellinghouses alight that night in Clywold and many poor folk rendered destitute if not reft of their very lives. And we might have remained thus, in a state of indecision, but that a cry went up that Clywold mill was about to be fired.

Then recognising that we were in the locality of the dwellinghouse of Susan Knowles and Jane Pearce, I resolved to go thither, not least to be confirmed of their safety; and finding a back lane my scribe Luke Bower and I threaded our way through flakes of fire falling down as do leaves on an autumn day. And indeed I wondered, as I had no doubt many did in the town of Clywold that night, if we would see again the sweet daylight and the green of the earth, for all seemed consumed with fire as of the deepest pit of hell; which I have ever thought to be of the making of men and not of God Almighty. And with such doleful reflections I would likely have forgotten Luke, but that turning a corner into a secluded alley I could once again hear his voice.

'Talk to me, sir, 'I pray you. I have been asking these several minutes gone, and I have been at pains to keep up with you for you have the advantage of height, sir. Where are we bound?'

'We go to the household of Susan Knowles who has the canker and Jane Pearce who has the bairn with the rickets whom you will remember as numbering among our patients, Luke, for you prepared a record of their remedies.'

'By which I know now for a certainty that your wits are awry, sir,' he said, 'if you came to Clywold, which you will perceive is on fire, to pay a visit to your patients at this time, which you will perceive is the dead of night, sir.'

'All is not well, Luke,' I said.

'Granted that is true, sir,' said Luke. 'Otherwise there would not be fire dropping out of the sky. But nevertheless tis not a time to be affrighting poor folks with a knock at the door. Yet ...' the good fellow continued, '... I see there is no preventing you, as you are about to tell me that you are persuaded that all is not well with your patients. Therefore you intend to see them whether or no.'

'Which is the case, Luke,' I said.

And we fared forwards, arriving presently at the rear way into the dwellinghouse of Susan Knowles and Jane Pearce; finding only Jane Pearce, and she running from one window to the other with her bairn in her arms and distracted to the last degree, and to whom I gave forthwith a preparation of thyme and bade her be seated to recover herself, apologising the while for our peremptory visit; which surprised her not at all for she said she had been expecting Ellie Bright to send some manner of assistance. For indeed she dare not leave the homestead for fear that the fire would presently arrive at her door, having arrived at many others. Then she said also that Ellie Bright had left the homestead, she knew not how long ago for the night watchman was not abroad, and was gone forth into the lanes which were all afire for they were setting alight the dwellinghouses of the mill folk; and Ellie Bright said moreover that she feared for Martin Gathercole, to whom she stood in some manner of relation, though Jane Pearce knew not what. After which, seeing Ellie Bright gone from the dwellinghouse Susan Knowles raised herself from her sick bed, Jane Pearce said.

'For she is as near the next world as ever a body may be, sir. And though she could scarce get her breath, sir, she went forth, saying as Ellie Bright had helped her in her sickness she must lend assistance to Ellie if it were the last thing she did; which hearing her fighting for her breath, sir, might well be the case, that it will indeed be the last thing Susan does.'

And with this Jane Pearce wept long and piteously, saying she would gladly have gone out herself to where the dwellinghouses were alight, and the machine breakers at the mill gate, but the thought of the little bairn prevented her and she must needs stay at home, whether she perish or no for the little bairn would not breathe out yonder with the smoke and all.

'Then I stay with you, Jane Pearce,' said Luke. 'For happen tis my kinsman there in your arms, being as how the fellow who brought this on you is also my kinsman by virtue of our having had the same mother at the beginning of our histories, if you take my meaning.'

To which Jane Pearce assented, showing no surprise at Luke's sayings, if indeed she followed them which likely she did not, so distracted was she, and so convoluted was his talk.

'And happen you will stay here as well, sir,' said Luke then addressing me, 'though I know you will do whatever you will and so I will hold my peace.'

Which he did not, expounding to me for the next quarter of the hour the folly of going forth into the lanes ablaze as they were, and the whole town of Clywold abounding in rough folk that night. 'For happen the machine breakers have cohorts from over Brancliffe-tor,' he said, 'who are uncouth fellows if ever there were.'

So I went forth, minded to come upon Susan Knowles and Ellie Bright, making my way to the mill, for there the fires had not reached for all the talk going about; and all folks were occupied in making safe their dwellinghouses, and few were abroad save one or two of those on the watch who bade me take cover, though I did not, being as I have said minded to set eyes on Ellie Bright and Susan Knowles; knowing that both would face the evils of the night, Ellie for her goodwill towards Martin Gathercole and Susan because she was so far gone from this world that she cared not to save herself.

Then I came to the mill, approaching it by the sluice gate at the back, and I had no wonder that they who fell into contact with the water of the beck lower down the valley came to some kind of grief, for the whole was poisoned with a poison worse than that of the fires. And I asked in my mind whether indeed the machine breakers might not have right on their side, though they pursued it in misled ways. Which reflection was jostling with many others in my mind when, following the path round the side of the mill, I beheld a party there of some thirty or forty as I imagined, being so blacked about the face and dark clad as to be hidden by the night. Which party seemed to heave forward towards the door of the mill but could make no headway. And again they made to enter but were driven back by some agency unseen by me, for in spite of my height there were certain fellows half a head above me. And it was as if indeed an angel of the Lord hindered their way as they tried to press forward.

And then, in a lull in the great voice of the night I heard that of one addressing, as it were, the impediment in the way.

'Though we be rough men,' he said, 'we are not so rough as to offer hurt to a woman, God forbid, and we pray thee to stand aside. Be so kind therefore as to get thee hence otherwise we will be obliged to lay hands upon you and remove you, though as gentle as we can, may God help us.'

To which the answer, if indeed there was such, was smothered by the cracking of timbers, and cries in many places and the roar of the flames.

So I made my way round the fellows, as indeed one of them, for I had no doubt that my face was also blacked from the smoke in the air and the soots raining down. And I saw, pressed against the great door of the mill, through which she had walked on many a day to her labours, the figure of my patient Susan Knowles, coughing piteously in the smoke, whose voice between her coughs yet carried.

'Good men, be gone,' she said. 'The times they change and happen some labour at mill and others in the homesteads, and happen there be room in this fair world for all, and happen ye'll be caught at these capers, which I know not whether they be right or wrong for the good Lord gave me not such understanding. But this I do know, that if any of ye be caught, Zebedee Clark and Tim Bray and George Turnill, that ye'll be aworking neither in the mill nor at the cropping shears, for ye'll be in York gaol awaiting transportation or the gallows-tree.'

At which a fit of coughing stopped the talk of the good woman and in front of the assembled party of machine breakers and bent nigh on double Susan Knowles sank to the ground. Whereupon the company dissipated I knew not whither, and in their place, as I tried to assist the poor woman, suddenly stood Thomas Hayward, the apparition of whom convinced me finally that I would never in this life be surprised by anything again. Not only Thomas Hayward but a company of the King's militia, summoned to defend the mill, and among whom, singled out by his stature, was Caleb Sawney. Then Thomas Hayward, seeing the plight of the poor woman, ordered Caleb Sawney to bear her to her home, a task which he made to undertake with little alacrity but could do no other being under orders, and moreover the man most able on account of his height, for the Lord bestows grace on all men, be they good or ill.

So we came, with what was surely much distress to poor Susan Knowles, for the night was deafened with crashing timber and reeking with fire, to the dwellinghouse, which was yet safe; and Caleb Sawney, seeing my scribe Luke Bower and indeed Jane Pearce, laid the poor woman on her bed and left forthwith saying to me that he had orders to join the men on completion of his mission, though I had heard no such orders given to him.

'Methinks I am surrounded by my kinsmen tonight,' said Luke. 'You will tell me what I might do for the relief of your patient, sir, and you will meanwhile ask her what she most wishes while she may yet speak.'

Which I did, and to which poor Susan Knowles replied as best as she could that she would as soon as the good Lord willed take a walk in Kessle-wood to see the plant growing, the name of which she could not remember but without doubt it would come back to her presently, and she prayed also that if it were the good Lord's will she should not set out on her walk before she had seen Ellie Bright once more in this world.

And Luke, hearing her, whispered that the poor soul's wits were scattered, yet I knew she spoke with perfect lucidity of mind, and I believe also Jane Pearce did, for she bade Susan Knowles take comfort and not speak such doleful words.

Then towards the dawning when the fires in the lanes had sunk down and Arcturus shone clear in the northern sky, drifting in and out of the smoke which yet hung above the town, Susan Knowles set out for Kessle-wood, hearing not the assault on the door of the dwellinghouse, which came but minutes after she had departed; it being good Martin Gathercole come banging on the doors of the homesteads to see what ailed with the mill hands; and hearing of poor Susan Knowles would I believe have wept openly, but that the bairn, awakened by his battering on the door, did so for him. And I perceived also the poor bairn to be anhungered and no doubt Jane Pearce suffering her former malady, so I gave to her groundsel, and also thyme for the sadness, and to Martin Gathercole pulmonaria for the lungs, the good man having been abroad among the smouldering of the homesteads I knew not how long; and by this also to impart to the poor folks the hope of recovery, as the flame of hope which burns ever in the soul had indeed sunk low that night in the souls of all in Clywold, both they who worked the mill who saw their homesteads burn before their eyes and they of the machine breakers who, driven half mad by the hunger of their bairns, would willingly have risked the gallows-tree.

Then Martin Gathercole spoke, saying that the watch and ward of the parish of Clywold had appraised him on the yester day of a mustering of machine breakers up in the hills, having gained the intelligence from an informant, and though he disliked the means, Martin Gathercole said, he was obliged to take note of the message. So on the evening of the night just gone he had stayed himself in the mill, for what purpose he did not know except to reason with the hill people; yet, having made fast the main door, forgot that door at the back through which the mill hands went in. And while waiting he had repaired to the office room where he was seated when Ellie Bright, whom he had not seen for many a day and believed to be in a place of safety, entered.

'She being the natural daughter of my second cousin, sir,' he said addressing me, 'which happen you didn't know, whom I took in, she being a poor lame little creature and much closeted for shame. Then Ellie said she had entered by the mill hands' door, which she had secured from the inside, and also she had been hard pressed to prevent Susan Knowles following her out of the homestead. For she had been living at the dwellinghouse of two mill hands, Susan Knowles and Jane Pearce; and Susan Knowles was not long for this world, having a torment of the lungs. After which I bid my sweet Ellie how she proposed to assist if the machine breakers came, which question she was at a loss to answer, but I had no doubt she would stand before the King himself, though he be in his dotage, and converse without fear if she believed right was on her side. And she said also, by way of making conversation and yet not wishing to alarm me, that certain of the homesteads of the mill hands had been set alight and the lanes were burning. Then we knew naught else, save that none of the machine breakers had as we thought reached the mill, until an officer of the King's men entered, saying that the fellows found gathered at the mill hands' gate had dispersed for the main part though not all, and some were still within abreaking of the shearing frames. And to bring this account swiftly to a close for that I must, sir, certain men were apprehended in the act, though not without mischief for I fear there has been loss of life, sir,' said Martin Gathercole, with the tears standing in his eyes, 'which life, sir, being that of a machine breaker or a man of the King's militia, is worth more than any shearing frame, and I am sore grieved, and at my mill as well, for I had hoped not to see this awful business again on my own doorstep.'

To which we listened all, not wishing to stop the good man. But he had finished, saying that he himself would attend to the obsequies of his worker Susan Knowles, and expedite the apothecary and his assistant back to the town of York. For, by whatever reason we were in Clywold that night (and indeed we knew not ourselves) we had witnessed the misery of the times and that was no mean thing. So finished Martin Gathercole his discourse.

'And happen you'd want this, sir,' he said, thrusting into my hand a rough tract. 'And happen you'll want to know that Ellie Bright is safe, sir, and also my bay mare Yolande, being both at my dwelling which was not this night set afire.'

XXVI

Then Martin Gathercole left the dwellinghouse, saying that he would see to the obsequies of Susan Knowles without delay, and find also a lodging for Jane Pearce, for though her dwellinghouse was as yet untouched by fire she would be there alone with her bairn and would fall into a melancholy deeper than that she was already in; and so many other matters the good man talked of that I begged him not to concern himself with our travel back to York, which we would see to ourselves. So we bade farewell to Jane Pearce and Martin Gathercole, and to the town of Clywold lying as it was under a cover of smoke with the clear air above it;

And I having put the tract in my scrip for want of a better lodging, knowing that the scrip would not leave my person. For the document carried the penmanship, however rough, of some poor fellow who would no doubt be deemed guilty of every felony under the sun, for according to Martin Gathercole there had been fatalities, though we knew not whom and we did not ask; being now some furlongs out of the town of Clywold and under the wide canopy of heaven with the song of larks falling upon us even as the flakes of fire had fallen out of the sky the night before. And we could see yonder in the sunlight and in a cleft in the hills the town of Withersedge, lying innocent as it seemed of all that had passed higher up the valley, to which we made our way, and to the sign of the Blue Boar, which lay but a furlong out of Withersedge.

'Tis nigh on the day of midsummer,' I said to Luke, by way of making conversation, for he had not uttered a word since leaving the homestead of Jane Pearce, and I feared that the melancholy of the scene yet lingered with him.

'That may be so, sir,' he said, 'but tis dark night in my head.'

To which I said nothing, knowing that no purpose was ever to be served by probing the contents of Luke's head.

'Tis rare to see the cow parsley hereabouts,' I said, 'and, look, it grows in profusion though the flowers be done. Tis a sign of a fair summer for the next year.'

'For those of us who will see the next year, sir,' he said.

'Some will and some won't,' I said. 'Tis not for us to question, for the matter lies mainly out of our choosing.'

'I liked it not last night, sir,' he said.

'There were indeed many things to dislike about last night,' I said.

'I liked it not, sir,' said Luke. 'Tis the first time I set eyes on a deceased and I cannot drive it out of my head.'

Which saying perplexed me greatly for I had found Luke seated on the ground fairly in the shadow of the gallows-tree, and I reminded him of such.

'That may be so, sir,' he said, 'and you need not believe me, but I did not look. For I was always led to believe by those in Beckwith that he who had been my father was bound for the gallows-tree, for which reason I attended many a time to be companionship for him, whosoever he might be. But I did not look, sir, for being deceased, it frights me. And before last night I had not seen any person deceased.'

Then I asked Luke what it was he did not like, to which he replied that he did not know exactly but it was nevertheless dark inside his head; and there were certain aspects of his work also that he did not like, namely the fluxes of the body and all things assaulting to the nostrils. Which presented the likelihood to me that my scribe might terminate his hire, and I could do no other than on the bridle path leading to the town of Withersedge, with the larks singing above our heads and the sweet gorse and cow parsley around our feet, offer him his liberty if he wished for such, and make him also a promise of a fine testimonial, for I had never had a better assistant.

'Nay, sir,' he said, 'for where else would I go? And I have had my say. But the fact remains that I do not wish to be a deceased myself, though I know all must.'

And the best I could do was assure Luke that the journey was indeed a lighter one than many a poor soul makes on this earth, and that good Susan Knowles for all her having departed this life had not gone far.

'So we might even now find her walking in Kessle-wood, sir,' said Luke. 'Not wishing to make a mockery, sir,' he added.

'Twas a conversation we had, Luke,' I said. 'Twas nothing real, and she knew it as well as I. Twas a place representing a release from her troubles.'

'Methinks you had a tender place in your heart for her, sir,' he said. 'And methinks also Mistress Horridge and Mistress Born.'

To which I said nothing for there was no disputing with Luke Bower, who was privy to the window in my head, though I did not see through it myself.

'Which is not to say, sir,' he said, 'that anything untoward passes through your mind, for it does not, but tis as I have observed.'

And finding Luke's spirit lightened by such matters I let him continue in his talk, for it pleased him greatly. And thus pleasantly we arrived at the sign of the Blue Boar outside the town of Withersedge, there being but one fellow other in the public room, and an unkempt morose fellow at that, who but grudgingly passed the time of day. Nor was the host any more to be drawn out in conversation, and indeed the accommodation itself was deficient in cleanliness and the bread and cheese old.

'Though I have seen older,' I said to Luke in order to divert him, for I could see that the darkness was like to descend on him again; and moreover the dour presence of the other guest had a lowering influence on me also, and I knew not what it was, whether the fixity of his gaze or his silence or the aroma about his person.

'I have seen older at the sign of Le Chapeau Bleu in Paris,' I continued, 'for there the cheese might well have been used to tile the floor and the bread serve as coping stones.'

And I prattled on thus, inventing many a hostelry in Paris for the benefit of he who sat opposite, for we knew him not. But seeing Luke no lighter and doubtless with thought of mortality still oppressing his spirit I offered him a tincture of thyme and feverfew for the melancholy. Then opening my scrip I beheld, as if for the first time, it having fled my memory, the tract given to me by Martin Gathercole on his departure, which document I replaced in the scrip for I could do no other, trusting that the fellow opposite was slumbering; as indeed he appeared to be, for he made to wake with a start when the host returned.

'If you be the apothecary,' the host said, knowing well that I was, 'you are requested to attend the fellow in the stable out yonder. And I know not what it be and beg you to refrain from asking. Follow me, sir.'

Which I did, seeing on the way, through a door which stood half open and which was quickly closed from within, the double bass standing; and that surprised me not a little, yet on the night just gone, when the militia materialised out of the thin air in the place where the machine breakers had been but a split second before, I had told myself that I could never again be surprised in this life.

'Tis in there,' said the host, stopping before a rude outhouse. 'They are awaiting ye. Tis dark within. Ye'll not see aught to begin with, and very little more to end with I don't doubt.'

And indeed that was the case, for after the dazzling midsummer sun the place was sunk in dark. And for all I knew it could have been devoid of persons, but that after a while, and becoming accommodated to the gloom, and there being splinters of light entering through cracks in the edifice, I understood the place to be well crowded. And all stood silently around a trestle on which lay a form covered with a sheet; and all, which I understood from the fact that I could make out only the whiteness of their eyes, were possessed of blackened faces and dark dress.

I knew not who it was who then spoke, for the voice was as from everywhere.

'We pray you to look to our brother, sir, to confirm that his soul has passed. And tis as well for he would be on a capital charge.'

Then the hem of the sheet was lifted and I beheld the arm of one who had been a cropper, where indeed, as the brethren well knew, the flow of life had stilled. So I prayed also that the good man might allow me to examine the pulse in the neck, and there also I found no sign of life.

'Tis as you suspected,' I said. 'Your brother has departed, and may God have mercy on his soul.' To which most answered, 'Amen,' by which I deemed them for all their rough means to be decent men at heart. And the door was opened for my exit.

Then I sought out my scribe Luke Bower and found him yet in the public room, the other visitor having left.

'You wish me to make a record of the remedy, sir,' he said.

'There was no remedy,' I said.

'Methinks you see no one without giving them a remedy, sir.'

'Yet in this case there was no remedy,' I said, not wishing to increase Luke's darkness of spirit by telling him that the patient was a deceased, as he now called those departed this life.

'Then the patient had no need of a remedy, sir,' said Luke, 'which puts me in mind of a deceased, for my nostrils also tell me that you have lately kept company with a deceased, sir, though I ask you not to say yea or nay. Though if you were to ask me the selfsame question and not I you, if you follow my meaning, sir, I would be telling you that they in the stable yonder were you know whom, having brought hither one of their brethren who was on the night just gone engaged in the mischief at Clywold mill; who likely set off from the mill as lively as you or I and became a deceased on the way, having sustained a gun shot.'

And where Luke had gathered this tale I knew not though I had no doubt of its veracity, and indeed I had conjectured the same myself.

Then we left the sign of the Blue Boar, seeing no more of the machine breakers, and indeed the stable door stood open as if none had been there. And the way being solitary, and none but the larks above our heads to hear, and unmindful that the hills themselves had ears, I thought to ask Luke if he had also seen the casing of the double bass at the sign of the Blue Boar, or was it that my wits were scattered; for I did but glimpse it through an open door which was promptly closed and I saw it no more, if indeed I had seen it the first time.

'You might have seen it and you might not, sir,' said Luke, 'but I did not, which is not the same as saying it wasn't there. Nor did I see the deceased at the sign of the Blue Boar, which is not the same as saying the deceased was not there. Yet I heard tell of the double bass by Jane Pearce while you were away at the mill, sir, for she said two players had been in Clywold at different times, one a gentleman so like the apothecary that she thought he must be a fellow countryman and the other a young fellow from the hills. And though she had not herself heard the music for she had sufficient labour for her ears in hearing her bairn awailing, Ellie Bright had tales enough of the strange music from the beginning of the world which she heard, until Jane Pearce harboured the idea that Ellie Bright was sweet on the young fellow from the hill country, whose name she said was Robert Gaut; and there had been some mischief and he was not talked of, which made Ellie Bright fear that ...'

And here Luke's account broke off for we were past the bridle path and onto the York road, where two others awaited the coach at the finger post.

'Which is to say, sir,' continued Luke, 'that there is a fair chance of a coach, for other folks are of the opinion. Which is not the same as saying the coach is running, sir.'

So we came to York in silence, for in those times none would willingly talk in the presence of strangers save to pass the time of day; and moreover I suspected that the darkness of spirit had fallen upon my scribe Luke once more, though he told me afterwards it was both the swaying of the coach and the presence of the other passengers who offended his nostrils which made him thus silent.

But he recovered the more the nearer we approached to the dispensary and were once more in the familiar and crowded thoroughfares of Conyng-gate and the Ald-walk. Then arriving at the dispensary Luke brought to my mind once more the writings of him as could not remember his own name, as he called the patient Will Cantrell, that he had left a writing writ backwards before taking his leave of the concealed chamber, the transcription of which awaited my perusal.

'For as I have indicated, sir,' said Luke, 'it is a last will and testament, and I know what you are thinking, sir, but I will not tell you, sir, for you will find out what you are thinking soon enough.'

'Indeed, I am not thinking anything, Luke.'

'But you will find out soon enough, sir,' he said, 'for folks always find out what they are thinking sooner or later. For at this moment in time, sir, I am thinking, besides the other matter, that persons untoward have been in the dispensary while we have been in the company of the deceased.'

And indeed I had noticed that the dispensary had been entered in our absence, for all will leave a fragment of their spirit, for good or ill, wherever they go.

'Which you noticed, sir,' Luke continued, 'although you did not like to tell me for fear that the darkness might still be upon me. It has gone away, sir, and I am recovered, for I favour the clamour of the streets above the silence of the hill country, for all that my beginnings were there. And you are going to tell me, sir, that certain persons are still here, for you noticed the spirit of them and were loath to mention to me that their spirit yet lingered in this building.'

'If they are not exactly in the building they have not gone far, Luke, and will be here presently. There is naught else we can do but wait. There is ample room within the Monk-gate where persons untoward as you aptly call them may secrete themselves. Had we but known we might have taken measures to conceal the records which I fear are in the press in the concealed chamber.'

And thus I continued with my make-believe having seen in the mirror a shadow cast across the doorway, which shadow had stayed there for some while and indeed had most likely followed us from the coach to the dwelling. And which shadow, upon our discovery of it, materialised forthwith into a certain man of the militia, yet not of Thomas Hayward's company but a rough fellow as I suspected from the lanes of York, and I doubted in the King's employ at all but hired by some renegade bent on doing mischief, for there were in those times many anhungered who stood sore in need of any manner of labour.

'We'll see this chamber, sir. And if you have a mind to offer resistance there are fellows aplenty in this dwelling who will think naught of refting you of your life.'

Whereupon I took the fellow to the closet whence the effluent was consigned to the gentle river Foss and taken away by and by, and where, for want of a better place, a list of harmless yet ineffective remedies was kept in a locked press, encrypted in Latin by my own hand and indecipherable.

'I'll take a look in there,' said the fellow. 'Unlock it if you would, sir.'

He seized the document. 'We'll take this if you don't mind, sir. Tis enough and more to place you on a capital charge as I see from a cursory glance.'

'Tis even more so if you hold it right way upwards, my good man,' I said. And I was thankful that he understood not the import of my words, for no man is to be despised for his lack of letters.

'I will take a look in them drawers in yonder room now,' he said.

Which he did, my scribe Luke Bower opening them one by one and showing him the remedies, expounding the properties of each in a Latin which confounded me.

'This one being the Atropa belladonna and this the Solanum dulcamara which being deadly poisons are kept shut for once the drawer is opened the room will be filled with a potent mist, and any man breathing it will expire in the instant. Therefore I dare not show it thee, or else thou and thy fellow officers are deceased.'

'I do not ask it of you. Happen this is enough to incriminate you,' said the fellow, glancing again at the confusing list of effete remedies with a contracted brow. And he laid hands also upon my scrip, which was hanging behind the door through which he had entered the dispensary. 'What's this?'

'Tis a scrip,' I said. 'Tis for carrying remedies to those patients who dwell afar.'

'Open it.'

I did so, seeing no alternative, knowing that the tract Martin Gathercole had hastily thrust into my hand was concealed there. Yet it was not. There was nothing save various common remedies, which I described to the poor fellow, dwelling on their associated maladies in as much and as loathsome detail as I might, until his complexion drained of colour and I bid Luke bring him a draught of water. After which he and his men, whom I believed to be there but had not seen, left. For most are fearful of sickness and the poor fellow lately in the dispensary had, of all the men sent thither, the temerity to enter.

'I am surprised that the tract which Martin Gathercole gave me and which I thoughtlessly put in my scrip was not there, Luke.' I said.

'No, sir,' it was not there,' he said. 'Tis in a safe place and will go out with the flux in time, and I knew not what remedy to take but I have taken it nevertheless without asking your leave, which I have never yet done and will never do again, begging your forgiveness, sir.'

XXVII

'I find you also have the spirit of melancholy, sir,' said Luke, 'but doubtless you will keep the reason for it to yourself. It has sat upon you since the time the fellow came who held the paper wrong side up to read.'

'I fear I took advantage of his simplicity, Luke,' I said.

'That may be so, sir, but he was too simple to perceive that we took advantage of his simplicity, for it was I also.'

'That makes no difference, Luke,' I said. 'It is known to me in my heart that I did him wrong and tis also known to the Lord God Almighty.'

'Against that I have no answer, sir,' said Luke. 'But you did likewise to Thomas Hayward in persuading him that he had the plague till it was all around the ridings of the county of York, and you were not then searching your soul.'

'It was to deter Thomas Hayward from discovering the whereabouts of Simon Horridge,' I said. 'And I know not why we have received this visitation unless it is that I had on my person a tract of the machine breakers, if so it was for I did not read it; and tis well said that in these troubled times the very hills have eyes and ears, leastways the walls of the public room at the sign of the Blue Boar.'

'Neither did I read it,' said Luke Bower. 'For that which a man does not know he cannot tell again. Though I know the fellow who attended us as being from the water lanes; yet I know him not well, save that he is the eldest of nine of which six perished in infancy of the scarlet fever and the two yet living look like to follow on presently.'

'Then you shall take me to them, Luke,' I said. 'And we can do worse than carry with us salix against the fever and groundsel for the poor woman, who will no doubt stand in need of it.'

So we made our way to the thoroughfares leading hence from the great river Ouse known as the water lanes, which my scribe Luke did against his will. And indeed he had journeyed farther than I anticipated, leading me to but a few steps short of the poor woman's dwellinghouse, when he observed that the locality offended his nostrils, and if it were all the same to me he would return to the dispensary in the case that any patients should be waiting.

And I was in no doubt that I had arrived at the right dwellinghouse, for the poor woman within bore the same facial insignia as did the young man who had lately visited the dispensary, namely a strabismus on the left side; to whom I said, having lately made the acquaintance of her son I had come to offer what little I could in the way of assistance to her bairns, who indeed were in a pitiful plight, mewing like kittens on a pallet in the corner. And the good woman assented to the remedies, knowing also what the groundsel was for without my having to cause her offence by explaining. So I administered a tincture of salix in a small dose to the bairns, leaving some also for the good woman to give until the fever was passed. And all the while she was telling me of her eldest son, though not by name, who was like to do well for the family, having found employ with a magistrate, though she knew not the name of him, and afterwards begging me to be so good as to sluice my hands at the common pump so as not to carry the affliction abroad in York. Which surprised me greatly, even though I had told myself that I was never to be surprised again, for I knew not that the practice of sluicing the hands was widely known.

Then I made my way back to the dispensary but saw not my scribe Luke Bower, whom I supposed would have been waiting for me in a thoroughfare close by, yet out of the way of the stench of the water lanes. Nor was he at the dispensary, which led me to assume that he had been waylaid by some acquaintance, for he was acquainted with all in the town of York, as I told him many a time. And I knew moreover on entering the dispensary that he had not been back there, for the dwellinghouse was empty of his spirit.

And I was yet pondering on his whereabouts and making in my own rough hand a record of the remedies left at the tenement of the poor woman, the mother of he who had lately inspected the dispensary, whose name I did not ask for they dwelling in the water lanes are much beset by folks looking for ne'er-do-wells, when glancing in the mirror I saw a shadow cast across the door and heard the laboured progress of one on the stairs.

'Pray come in.'

Sarah Bower, for it was she, after passing the time of day and saying she had knocked but heard no answer, then asked if I were alone; to which I answered that I was, yet my assistant might be back at any time.

'I think he will not, sir,' she said.

And I prayed her be seated and take a draught of water, for the dust in the thoroughfares of York at midsummer and the labour of the stairs had tired her greatly, she being as I could see not yet mended from her encounter with the raptor outside of Beckwith. Then being rested the good woman Sarah Bower told of the purpose of her journey, which, she said, had been undertaken on such a cart as carries sheep, or creatures that had once been sheep but not in a month of Sundays, she added.

'Tis a lot to ask of ye,' she said. 'An I know not if ye will see for to oblige but I could bring to mind no other to assist me. I wish to attend the house where they who have departed this life in a violent manner are, sir, thinking as I do that a gentleman such as thyself is permitted there.'

So I told Sarah Bower that I was permitted there in a professional capacity. Then she asked me if it might be possible for me to make a journey on her account; to which I answered Sarah Bower that I was bound there that very day, though I was not, but I could see that the poor woman would have no one put out of their way on her account. And it being a doleful place I inquired of her if she had recently taken bread, knowing that they who go there have no wish for aught afterwards, to which she answered that she had not but had a portion of bread with her which she was minded to share, as I had done the same when I called on her outside Beckwith. By which I knew that she had prepared for her journey, and it was like that she had called before and found none at home in the dispensary, but I did not ask.

And for all her sense of modesty I could see that the poor woman was much distraught, fearing the occasion and wishing to hasten it on in equal measure; so I bade her be seated and take a tincture of thyme, being ever thankful that it grew in profusion in the dispensary garden. For all were afeared to some extent in those days, whether they owned it or not. And I deemed it for the best not to delay the excursion but to accomplish it forthwith and while the poor woman yet had the fortitude, to which she assented.

'I have no need to tell the name of the one I seek, sir,' she said, breaking a silence which had settled on her since our departure from the dispensary until we were fairly in sight of our destination. 'For you will find out soon enough, if you have not already come to your own conclusion. Tis a doleful purpose we have on such a day as the Lord has made. And I pray you, sir, if I may ask, if you will be so kind as to not leave me for I am afeared, yet I must accomplish this meeting.'

For by that time Sarah Bower was indeed frighted, as I could tell by the pallor on her face and the way she drove her reluctant limbs forward, to the extent that she had quite forgot the tale I spun to her that I had a matter to attend to at the morgue. Which gloomy place was opened up for us, and we were shown he whom Sarah Bower named, whose name indeed was no surprise to me, who lay there as if in a slumber with no sign of his late passage out of this world save for a well of blood spreading from beneath his back onto the table on which he lay.

And Sarah Bower, seeing him, wept bitterly, saying that for all his bad ways he was her son and had she been more virtuous he would not have ended so. And the poor woman was bereft of all comfort, lamenting her own life and that of the wayward son she had borne, so that I told her, when she had ears once more to hear, that on the last night of his sojourn in this world he had carried a poor sick woman to her dwelling place and had laid her down upon her bed, assuring Sarah Bower that this act of charity would go with him into the world to come. Then asking if she would like some moments alone with her son, and she assenting, I fell into conversation with the attendant, who told me that the wife of the late magistrate of the parish of Holmroyd and her maid sat in the women's gaol on the capital charge of complicity in his demise, and also another woman of the weaving community, being charged along with her brother of an attempt on the life of one of the King's men, which fellow was the very one whom I had lately viewed, for his days were already numbered following the earlier episode and he had but to wait for one of the machine breakers to meet him in a dark lane in Clywold. 'For our days are counted from the very moment of our birth,' he added.

So presently Sarah Bower came forth, quieter but disabled for any far journey, and I accompanied her to the house of mercy, begging that if the matter were easily accomplished she might be maintained in ignorance of the presence there of poor Jem Bailey, whom her son had grievously wronged. Then as the door of the house of mercy closed behind Sarah Bower it came to me not for the first time that had she not been so blessed with a meek soul many of the troubles of her life would not have visited her, for there had doubtless been many a fellow in the town of Beckwith who had followed after her, not so much for her beauty but because she would not refuse such converse.

But I would say nothing of these matters to any other for they would question how I was in possession of like thoughts, and indeed I wondered myself. And reflecting thus I found myself at the door of the dispensary under the Monk-bar, and my scribe Luke Bower not yet returned; which caused me on a sudden whim to repair to my late destination and ask the attendant what was new among the male inmates of the gaol, but he said that all had sat there upwards of a sennight, the newest being the brother of the said young woman in the female gaol, being a hand weaver by trade.

'That being an odd thing, sir,' he said, 'for in the main the machine breakers are of the finishing trade.' And the matter perplexed him.

And it was towards night and the candles lit when Luke Bower returned, who had left me before noon in the water lanes; and as if but five minutes had passed rather than half a day he continued his talk where he had left it by begging my forgiveness for his not remaining, for it offended his nostrils to be there, namely in the water lanes of York.

'That is no matter, Luke,' I said.

'You do not ask me why I did not return to the dispensary, sir,' he said, 'which I told you I would do in the case of any patients being there, but I did not.'

'There was but one patient, who was not a patient,' I said, 'though I gave her thyme and have writ a record of it.'

'A woman?' said Luke.

'She bid me accompany her to the morgue.'

'And you did so, sir?'

'Yes, and seeing her depressed in her spirits I prayed that they in the house of mercy might care for her, yet I doubt she will stay long.'

'Do I know her?' said Luke.

'Inasmuch as you know all folk in the county of York,' I said, 'or so it seems to me.'

'You talk in riddles, sir.'

'He who keeps the morgue told me that Grace Born and her maid Rosie Todd sit in the women's gaol,' I said, 'on a charge of complicity in the magistrate's demise.'

'Which is a strange thing, sir,' said Luke.

'Why say you that, Luke?'

'For no reason other than that I was persuaded from my infancy that only our Saviour rose from the dead and none other, yet on this very day I was shown evidence to the contrary, namely that the magistrate of Holmroyd is also risen from the dead. Begging your pardon if that is blasphemy, sir, for I would not offend you.'

'So you have been all this day until nightfall pursuing the magistrate of Holmroyd, Luke?'

'I know not if it was he, sir,' said Luke, 'but if it was not it was very like him.'

'So he walks abroad in York? Many must have seen him.'

'He does not walk abroad in York as himself, sir, if you take my meaning, but as some other and not always the same other. But I know him by his hands. Happen you don't know, sir, that the magistrate of the parish of Holmroyd, being engaged in coercion, wore his finger nails pared down for the sight of blood under the nails offended his wife. And I know that for a certainty, sir, for she said as much many a time though to each one it was a secret and each thought themselves privy to her inmost thoughts.'

'If that be so, Luke,' I said, 'it serves only to suggest that Mistress Born is deserving of our infinite pity if she must needs talk to all and sundry of what went on in the intimacy of her dwellinghouse.'

'Indeed, sir,' said Luke. 'I consider myself chastised for loose talk, though I would not speak so to any other than yourself.'

'It was far from my intention to chastise,' I said. 'You have done well this day. Where did you see this fellow you consider to be the magistrate of Holmroyd?'

'He does not keep still, sir,' said Luke. 'And I know not for a certainty that it is he. It was but a thought I had, and happen it was another fellow altogether, and happen it was a dream I had. Which brings into my mind, though I know not why it does, the last will and testament of he who does not remember his own name, which last will and testament is writ backwards.'

'We had better look at it, Luke, for the matter keeps escaping from my mind.'

'I have the transcription here, sir.'

'It is beautifully done,'

'I do my best, sir. If you would be so kind as to read it, sir.'

'… "This being the last will and testament of William Cantrell",' I read. '… "I hereby leave and bequeath all my worldly good to my daughter Jemima Bailey, this being my good name which is all of the good I possess in this world". I knew not there was so much to be read, Luke.'

'Nor was there, sir. I have made of it what I could.'

'Even so, we can do little about it, Luke, for the original is lost. This is but a paper laid on top of the fair copy when the ink was not yet dried.'

'Yes, sir. If you say so, sir.'

XVIII

And the matter weighted on my mind grievously, that Will Cantrell who had been afforded shelter under my roof had gone abroad in meagre health and strength; which brought to my mind also that his first nurse had left in the selfsame manner, which coincidence perplexed me greatly, so that I resolved to ask the good souls at the house of mercy if there could be any answer to my perplexity.

'The spirit of melancholy rests upon you yet, sir,' said Luke, 'which makes me think we have taken advantage of another fellow's simplicity. Or happen it is some other matter on your mind, sir. Happen tis he as did not know his own name.'

'I notice you speak of him as if he were no longer alive in this world, Luke, and you have not done so before.'

'How so, sir?'

'You spoke of him as he who did not know his own name.'

'Twas doubtless because he no longer dwells under our roof, sir,' said Luke, 'but happen tis in your own thoughts that he no longer lives.'

'It is in my thoughts to inquire at the house of mercy, for two good souls have gone out of our midst.'

'As you wish, sir,' said Luke, 'but naught will avail for they at the house of mercy have sealed lips.'

'How think you that, Luke?'

' The reason being that I was some time sweet on one there and all my beseechings for an encounter with this one availed me not at all.'

For which saying I esteemed Luke Bower the more, that being the manner of secret a young fellow does not willingly tell forth.

'But they will not think the same of you, sir,' he added, 'if you take my meaning, sir, for you are above concerns of that kind.'

So I repaired to the house of mercy, which was but a short step from the dispensary yet circuitous, observing that the midsummer season was like to break; and indeed before I arrived at my destination lightning flared out of the blue sky and there fell also a peal of bright thunder, even as my hand was on the door, so that I must needs knock again when the thunder was done. Which I did thrice more, watching in the meanwhile spots of rain the size of florins impaling the carriageway and sending up springs of dust, while all the good folks fled for cover.

Then the door was opened by the sweet soul I knew as Melody, who was truly a doorkeeper in the house of her Lord, as I have noted before, and who seeing me was unsurprised, saying that Mistress Bailey had been asking.

'For Mistress Bailey is intent on leaving us this very day,' she said, 'though we have prayed her earnestly to tarry until her spirits be restored. Which, sir,' continued the good soul Melody, 'is like to be long for she received way back a paper which distressed her greatly, and we know not what it is for none here will ask, being afeared it is to do with the bairn she delivered untimely, for they in here will have no talk of such matters. Though I think not that it concerned her bairn, sir, from the appearance of the gentleman who delivered it, who looked more like a gentleman of the law to me, from the cut of his apparel. And I pray you forgive me, sir, for being a gossip, for I know you would not say again what you have heard, but the gentleman in question for all his fine apparel had blood under his finger nails and an aroma about his person which sickened me greatly; and moreover he was in the house never having knocked, which I know for there are none but I who answer, sir, being the doorkeeper.'

And I believe that the good soul would have continued long in her talk but that Jem Bailey was upon the staircase dressed as if for a journey, seeing whom poor Melody wept inconsolably and Jem Bailey also until, begging my pardon, Jem Bailey brought forth from up her sleeve a fool's cap of paper, which I recognised as that used in the dispensary.

'I put it there for safe keeping from the rain, sir,' she said, 'having in mind to post it in at the dispensary on my way, in the case that you were out. But now you are here and there is no need, for I do believe Melody conjured you up out of the thin air; and I beg you to say something, sir, and let me know that you are here in truth.' Whereupon Jem Bailey dissolved once more into weeping.

And after reassuring her I was there, though I think she heard not, I begged Melody to seek leave for her to rest in the visiting room. And I prayed Melody to ask leave to stay herself by Jem Bailey's side though she would readily have gone away, being humble in spirit and not deeming herself worthy to stay.

Then by and by when Jem Bailey was more settled the good Melody beseeched her friend to show the apothecary that which she had been given by the gentleman who entered without knocking, whose fine clothing stood at odds with the blood under his finger nails and the aroma about his person; which Jem Bailey did, pressing into my hand the paper.

'Pray read it, sir,' she said.

And I did, finding the document in most respects like that reconstructed by my scribe Luke Bower.

'But tis not his,' said Jem Bailey. 'Tis like enough but tis not his. And he would ever write his name with a single "L", sir. Tis not his.'

I then asked Jem Bailey whom she supposed to have written the document, but she said she did not know; only that William Cantrell, who was her father, 'but happen you didn't know that, sir,' she said, had left from the concealed chamber and she feared he had gone aseeking him who had done her wrong. For her good father was mortified of her shameful condition though he had not the tongue to say so, and laid the blame as well on her as on himself also for getting in with certain rough folks of the machine breakers, so as to bring coercion upon his daughter.

Then the good soul Melody in whose talk there was much sense and pleasant humour told of the consternation among the folk in the house of mercy when they knew a strange fellow had been there, who then took pains to look for any means of entry for to block them, as they would for the ants or the mice, but finding none implied that her wits were gone abroad; which thought caused her much merriment.

And I brought to mind that the young woman had said of the fellow that he carried an aroma about his person, which she then confirmed, saying that she liked not to describe it thus, but it was much like the privy; and seeing the subject caused her some measure of unease I left it, resolving to relate her sayings to Luke if the matter were still in my mind, which was not certain, for my mind in those days was busy with many things and forgetful of most; which brought then to my remembrance the intention I had to visit the women's gaol at such a time as I could. Yet it seemed not a kindness to leave Jem Bailey in her melancholy state; and seeing her rise as if to make a departure I bade her be seated, for the coach was not boarding for another hour, and moreover the rain which had begun as I approached the house of mercy showed no sign of abating.

Then as the young woman was seated again I asked her if she had a far journey, for I feared she knew not where she was bound.

'I know not, sir,' she said, 'for they at home took against me when I found myself in that condition, and they said also that I had given word against my father for he was badly used, so they heard. But I did not give word against him. And they here also, sir, although they have looked to my well-being and I love them dearly, they know not about being with child, which ignorance does them even the more honour for entertaining my presence. Melody will tell you how it is with them.'

'Tis so, sir,' Melody said. 'They that are here, although they be angels from heaven, know naught about such matters. They have no wish to drive Jemima away, sir, and indeed all have beseeched her to stay, knowing how it is with her kinsfolk.'

Upon which Jem Bailey wept again piteously and said she feared her father had passed out of this world without a word of farewell, for what she held in her hand was not his but the doing of some other. Who indeed, though he was a good man and she loved him dearly, cared not when she did well, but when ill befell her heaped coals of retribution upon her head.

And in the instant writ upon the sweet face of Jem Bailey was the gracious imprint of her father's, which vanished also in the instant.

'And you might ask, sir,' she said, though I did not, 'why I carry a name other than my father's, which answer I know not, but that she I call my mother goes by the name of Bailey. Who is no mother, sir.'

Then by and by, and the rain not abating in the slightest but falling the more vehemently against the windows and forming great pools on the stone walk outside, and amid the entreaties of her friend, and after a modest request made to me to discover her father, the good young woman laid aside her wrap and consented to stay at the house of mercy, for indeed she knew of nowhere else to go, her kinsfolk having forsaken her. And as she did so the rain abated and a double bow appeared in the sky over the crowded roof tops of the town of York.

And the day having become once more fair I took my leave, promising Jem Bailey that I would do my utmost to fulfil her request, namely to discover her father. And I made my way to the women's gaol wetshod, for the cobbles were yet awash with the recent downpour, so much that a cart turning into the Stone-gate was axle deep in water and the poor horse straining to draw it forwards while they of the crowd made to hoist up the wheel onto drier ground. Among whom I saw my scribe, Luke Bower, for he was ever where there was interest to be found, and would no doubt tell me of it later.

Then the turnkey let me into the women's gaol, whither I had gone on the pretext of delivering remedies to certain of they who sat there. Which on entering I found to be a place more dismal than I had ever seen for the housing of women, for the recent rain had crept in through the high bars and the whole was dark and chill; yet I knew I would be rapidly accustomed to both, as indeed I would to the aroma, for the Lord who made the senses made them also merciful.

But such was the dark at first that had I not known the place to be inhabited I would have had no intimation of such, for I saw no one and all was silence, the melancholy of the place having settled upon all of them there.

'They you seek are in yonder corner,' the turnkey said. 'And happen you will be wanting to leave this dour place betimes, therefore I will return and let you out. For they as can leave should be counting their blessing on their knees before Almighty God.'

To which one or two poor souls answered 'Amen', and I betook myself to the place he had indicated; and finding there Grace Born and Rosie Todd I said, 'How fare thee?' thinking them to be as beset by the darkness as I myself and unknowing of my approach.

'I fare myself better than poor Rosie,' said Grace Born, 'for she has a low fever and is not herself, which you will discern from seeing tis I who have done our braids, and see what a calamity I have made.'

And indeed poor Rosie Todd was not herself but was seated with her head in her hands as if she would that way stop it sinking into the collar of her gown. To whom I gave forthwith plantain for the head ache and salix against the fever. Then the good soul Rosie raised her head, and I discerned that the light, though it was little indeed, caused hurt to her poor eyes, whereupon I gave her in addition urtica and betony to take at her discretion, of which I saw from her dear face that she was still possessed.

Yet by and by under the influence of the gentle salix and also, I believed, because on my entry a draught of new air had been admitted into the room, though the air was tired enough within the gaol, Rosie Todd recovered sufficiently to raise her head the more and look around, though she still guarded her eyes somewhat. And following her gaze I saw other poor creatures, some twenty in number, likewise seated against the walls and none speaking.

'They are like as we,' said Grace Born, 'for we are all of us out of our wits. And they are like us also for they know not why they are here.'

'Tis true,' said Rosie Todd in a voice I would scarce have known as her own. 'They know not why they are here and no more do we, lest it be that we are all here on the capital charge,' by which I knew good Rosie Todd to be in possession of her wits. 'For I was ever told, sir, that this part is for they who have reft another of their life. And I know not the opinion of Mistress Born on the matter for I have not asked her, but much longer in this parlour and I would wish to be out of life myself on account of the head ache, had I not always entertained the hope that some word of our present state would reach you, sir. And we like not to misuse your presence, but a stone may be dislodged up yonder for to admit the air, which he who attends is not of sufficient height to do, sir, but you are, and we would thank you most gratefully.'

Whereupon a murmur arose from those others as I dislodged the stone, by which I surmised that they could both hear and were in possession of their wits. And I saw that Grace Born was bearing up under her afflictions with a good spirit, whereas Rosie Todd, the dear soul, was sunk in a depressiveness which concerned me greatly as being unlike to her true self. And though she spoke she did not so with her former equanimity.

'I have told dear Rosie that she must be strong, if only to braid our hair,' said Grace Born, 'for I can see what you are thinking, sir, and Rosie will not mind my saying, that you have observed the melancholy which has settled upon her these three days since, for she was herself before.'

Then I ascertained that the onset of Rosie Todd's affliction of mind came with the onset of the low fever and the head ache, and with the abating of the fever so might the melancholy abate. For I have known such cases in the gaols of Paris during the terror, when those incarcerated fell into fever and melancholia and after treatment regained fortitude enough to sustain them in their adversities.

'Mr Rivalux says you will feel yourself again, my dear Rosie,' said Grace Born presently, though I had said no such thing, only contemplated the same in my mind.

'And indeed, that is the case, sir,' said Rosie, 'for the head ache is lifting with every minute that passes and I am persuaded that I will braid our hair again this very day. But you came not to talk of braids, sir,' she added.

'It is as fair a talk as any,' I said, 'though I know not whether braids be well executed or no.' Only I knew, though I did not say, that to hear Rosie Todd occupied with braids pacified me, in that her low spirits had come with the fever and would pass with the fever rather than settle on her until her life's end, as I have known of such in my time. And indeed, as I looked around and my eyes became accustomed to the gloom I saw others with braids; for which I could not but be thankful that these poor souls who might yet be bound for the gallows-tree or for transportation to some far land, yet had the delight in their fair looks.

'You may see the hair I braided,' said Grace Born, 'for it is not well done.'

To which I said that I could discern no difference, and to return to the reason for which I was present, for the turnkey would be back, I asked Mistress Born and Mistress Todd once more how they fared.

'We are well enough for the present,' said Grace Born, 'but that is not to say we will fare well in the future for we are on the capital charge of the murder of Mr Born. And it matters not, sir, to talk in the presence of these our sisters, for we know well enough each others' woes; and nothing can happen to make matters worse for they are at their worst already. For we know not how to plead our innocence, sir, as it is well known that Mr Born and I did not agree together and tis noised abroad that I said I wished him no more on many occasions, though I did not say that.'

'And I have told Mistress Born,' said Rosie, 'that I did not believe the remains to be those of Mr Born, as I tell Mistress Born everything and she does me. And the headache is almost lifted now, sir, for which I am thankful from the bottom of my heart. And now I must ask you, for Mistress Born will not and she greatly needs to know, as do we all, is there any aroma about our persons, sir, for we would not know if that were the case.'

To which I answered that there was not, but gave to each present a drop of lavender. And while engaged in the distribution of such meagre comforts I came to one seated on the cold stone against the yonder wall who could scarce lift her head, and being indeed the only one there who had not had her hair dressed in braids.

'I fear you are in grievous pain, my dear,' I said. 'Pray lift your head.'

Which the poor woman did, and I perceived in the instant that the previous malady had returned, brought on no doubt by the debilitating habitation of the gaol.

XXIX

'Tis the old malady, is it not, my dear?' I said. 'I fear you are in grievous pain, for it is writ on your face. If you will, we may ease your pain, though with worse pain in the easing of it.'

Then Liz Horridge, for it was she, whispered, 'If you please, sir.'

'We will ask of the turnkey for some clean water, and we will also conjure up Mistress Todd to help us, for we are full of magic,' I said, prattling as I did with the hope of alleviating a state of affairs in which there was small hope. For the sweet face of Liz Horridge was in appearance worse than I had seen in any with the abscess, being black and swollen and already suppurating through the surface of the flesh.

And Rosie Todd, as if she had heard our talk, which she could not have done on account of the extent of the place and the traffic of carts and horses and of fellows' voices rising up from the street, was forthwith at my elbow looking with interest into the face of the patient, having most precipitately regained her old self.

'Tis a case for the lancet, sir,' she said. 'And without doubt you will have asked the turnkey to boil the lancet, for patients fare better with a boiled lancet, sir, though I know not why. She is not afraid, sir. I see it in her sweet blue eyes that she is not. And she knows also that the physician has performed such operations many times before, and though it hurts for an instant tis but an instant and then the pain is gone.'

To all of which Liz Horridge listened quietly, for she knew the pain would be beyond bearing; and I gave her celandine against the tooth ache and salix against the fever, though she scarce could swallow. Then the turnkey returned with water and the lancet also, saying it had been boiled as hard as any side of sheep, though I knew not what he meant and I feared the hearing of it might cause poor Liz Horridge the more nausea, though it did not. And indeed, I doubted if her dis-ease could have been made the worse for her woes were dire in the extreme. Yet she made not a murmur as I lanced the area. Nor was there any murmur from the other women, though some stood round, and I had not the heart to bid them stand away. For there was great kindness among them, and some there were who proffered kerchieves of their own to stanch the wound, which was as deep as any I had beheld in the buccal cavity. And there were some who would willingly have taken away the bowl of foul matter, though I thanked them and said not, for any poor soul in a debilitated way is like to pick up the least malady around; though I withheld the reason for they were in ignorance of the extent of their weakness, being as I understood for the most part strong in spirit.

Then seeing Liz Horridge with her pain a little abated and a smile on her sweet face, which was yet grossly disfigured and blackened by her malady, I asked her how she fared, to which she replied as well as she could which was but little, that her pain was away, though I knew it was not, and now that she was restored she might yet have the fortitude to face whatever was before her. And I knew she spoke with wisdom, for dis-ease and pain weaken greatly the spirit; as indeed I had observed many times during the terror, and also on that very day with Rosie Todd who, from being greatly reduced by the head ache and the fever, was restored to assist at the recent lancing of an abscess.

'For you cannot know what has befallen us, sir,' Liz Horridge said, to which I answered that I had heard words spoken by those who knew no more than the gargoyle on the fair church in York, yet I would that she could say in her own words, seeing that the swelling was subsiding and that words came more easily. Then she told me, and indeed all, for all

223

were gathered around seeing how she fared, that she and her brother Simon Horridge sat in gaol for the harm done to one of the militia, the place being the Sheep-close in the parish of Holmroyd, and the perpetrator of which according to they who stood by was like to be Simon or Elizabeth Horridge.

'For as you know, sir, we are as the two halves of a wall nut. And I know twas not me though I dare not say for then the blame would fall upon my brother, yet I know he did not the deed either, for though he consorts with the machine breakers he would do no violence to a fellow being.'

Then Liz Horridge asked me if I were going to the men's gaol, but not to importune myself in the case I was not going there, if I would send word to her brother saying she was well. Whereupon others among the sweet souls that sat in the gaol begged of me the same, namely that I would take word to their beloveds; the number of whom were beyond my memorising, and Grace Born bade the turnkey bring paper and ink for the writing of their names. But he said he could not on peril of his life, for how was he to know it was not mischief in the writing and more insurrection whereby the whole of the fair town of York might burn down next as did the dwellinghouses in Clywold, and indeed I myself wished not to bring further grief upon the poor women by the carrying of messages.

So I left the women's gaol under a lowering sky, for the rain which had passed over but for a few hours looked like to start again, and indeed before I reached the gaol apportioned to the men great drops were falling, making the more desolate an already desolate habitation. Which on entering gave me to suspect that all there were suffering the low fever, and indeed the turnkey himself sat with his poor head in his hands, scarce able to perform his office, to whom also I gave salix and plantain, bidding him be still for as long as his duties allowed in order for the remedies to take effect, for I could see that the poor fellow would strive to rise to his feet whether he could or no, for fortitude is to be found among all stations of men.

And presently the salix and plantain began their work, and by the grace of God also, for there is no good work in this world without; and the turnkey recovered inasmuch as he could raise his head and converse. Then I asked him if there were many who suffered as he, and he said all did, though not to the same extent, and he believed where all breathed the same air and drank out of the same pots the matter could not be otherwise. Whereupon I perceived the wisdom of the times, for many can see the ill without seeing the remedy; for the remedy hides itself and is seen by few whereas the ills are there for all to see. And I asked him how many were present there, which he knew not, but said the number had been greatly swelled by fellows who were so called machine breakers, which fellows he said belonged not in York but in their own country, and would no doubt have been dealt with there but that certain among them were bound for the gallows. They being the ones who were afflicted by the low fever, he said, being from the hill country and unlike to fight maladies as they more accustomed to the stench of the towns were.

By which I gained admittance to that place which housed the machine breakers without the necessity of conjuring up a reason for my visit, for such fabrications I dislike but are oft times needful; finding there in one room Simon Horridge and Robert Gaut as well as others, for, as had been said to me, the troubles in the hill country and the sentences meted out had swelled the numbers in the gaol of York greatly. And all without exception had the low fever, suffering with the head ache and biliousness till the pots were flowing over and the floor was sullied with vomitus. Yet most on my entry stood after the courteous manner of the hill folk, though they were hard pressed to stand, yet they did so. And I bade them be seated, asking also how they fared, to which each answered that he fared well enough, 'Thanking ye, sir.'

Then I gave to each salix for the fever and plantain for the head ache, and also bistort for the biliousness, asking as I did if there were any stone high up which might be dislodged for the admission of the fresh air, but they said they thought not. And indeed I saw naught but weeping walls and growths of white mould, and the bars well set into the stones; and it was no wonder that the fever should pass from one to another in so dour a place. Yet the thought entered my mind that the very

225

mould itself might if extracted aid the afflicted, for where nature places an affliction she plants a remedy close by. But I had not the liberty to pursue such a thought, which would no doubt ere long fly away, as is the custom of the thoughts of those advancing in years.

And knowing that I must deliver the message of Liz Horridge to her brother Simon before that also fled away, I said to him that his sister fared well, yet not saying where I had encountered her. Whereupon Simon Horridge said I might speak freely for all were now brethren and had their woes in common. For he knew well that his sister sat in the women's gaol, accused of the selfsame matter as himself, for both were accused of the harm done to one from the militia by the name of Caleb Sawney, who while in the act of laying the scourge on one of the brethren had grievous harm done to him by he or his sister Liz, the perpetrator being a hooded figure and slender of build; and Simon Horridge dared not say he was not guilty of the deed for fear recrimination should fall upon his sister, though he knew she did not the deed, having never in her life laid violent hands on any of God's creatures, not so much as a fly. And as matters went they were like to breathe their last on the gallows-tree, as word had gone round that the fellow Sawney had passed out of this world, some said as a consequence of the wound inflicted that very day in the Sheep-close. And he who had the scourge laid to him that day was present in the same chamber, and might bear witness but that he was on a charge of his own and would not be admitted as witness, being counted as a felon. For though he was in extremity himself and enduring the scourge, yet he noticed the feet of he who laid the attack on Sawney, being shod as a townsman and not as one of the hill country.

And having spoken thus Simon Horridge retched piteously, for the fever was yet on him though abating, and indeed the matters of his discourse drew murmurs from the brethren, for many were but a short hearing away from the gallows-tree.

Then as if I were both judge and jury Robert Gaut spoke, saying what his brother in affliction had said was true, namely that he who assailed Caleb Sawney in the Sheep-close was shod as a townsman. But his witness would be without value, he being on a charge himself, namely that of abetting acts of violence by the transportation of weaponry in the casing of the double bass; and there were those abroad who could testify to his carrying the casing, which was at one time a heavy burden and at another time light as if empty.

As indeed I myself had once seen and remarked inwardly that along the way the case had become less burdensome to carry. Yet I knew not but that it was the double bass within, and indeed I knew not whether the double bass was heavy such that a man could scarce carry it or no.

'Twas not weaponry,' said Robert Gaut. 'I stand not by the use of violence myself, though neither do I condemn those who believe in their hearts that violence is meet if the outcome is a just one. For there are they who stand fast to that opinion and they are also my brethren.'

Then I asked Robert Gaut if I might serve him in any way, for I could see that, even if he were to escape the gallows-tree he was not long for this world, the ancient wound having opened in his neck, which he now took no pains to cover and which would provoke ere long a systemic poison in the noxious habitation of the gaol, whatever remedy were given to him.

'You might if you would, sir,' he said, 'send to my parents, begging their forgiveness and with my best love for they did ever love me with all their good hearts, and I did great ill to my father by oft despising him for his simple ways, may God forgive me, yet he knew not. For, sir,' he continued, 'though I conveyed not weaponry I conveyed on my back in the casing certain souls made in the image of our Lord, who would else have been defaced by coercion at the hands of the magistrate, whom I would not ask to bear witness lest they themselves come to grief, having escaped it once.'

And so saying Robert Gaut fell silent.

'There is yet one other of our brethren,' said Simon Horridge presently. 'For we count him among our brethren as being also accused of carrying weaponry; yet being of an alien land, though I know not which, he is kept solitary on account of the suspicion that falls on such folks. Yet the brethren believe that kinship lies not in where a soul was born but in the striving after justice for they who work by the labours of their hands. Therefore he is our brother. You will have to ask the turnkey if you have a mind to see him, sir; and in the case that you are admitted into his place of confinement we beg you to send greetings from the brethren.'

To which those others who had so far recovered murmured, 'Aye,' though there were some who were yet prostrated by the fever.

And bidding the brethren farewell I went forth to the turnkey to beg of him to admit me to the habitation of that other who was believed to be of an alien land, for likely he also suffered the low fever, as all else did.

Then the turnkey, having so far regained himself, bade me follow him, saying it could well be that the other fellow suffered likewise, for it would be odd indeed if all else in the gaol suffered the low fever and he not.

'I know not his land, sir,' continued the turnkey, 'but he has looks similar to thine own, and speech to match, but whereas thy speech is clear to the understanding his is not and many times I know not a word he says. Though tis also true to say, sir, that I have not set eyes on him many times, having been too laid low to traipse all these tunnels since his arrival.

For it was indeed a far distance, though I conjured up in my mind a manner of labyrinth, and doubted that we went straight but more like turned back on ourselves many times, the air becoming the more exhausted as we progressed; until my feet dragged and I believe those of the turnkey did also.

'Tis because he is from an alien land that he sits far away from his fellows,' said the turnkey, 'for it is thought he brings the revolution with him. Though I say it not myself, sir, he being like to you, but tis what is noised abroad.'

XXX

'Tis here,' said the turnkey, 'and if it pleases you, sir, I will return to my place until you have done with your visit, for I have not the strength to stand. And tis no matter to me to come back, though I cannot stand for the while you tarry here.'

Then seeing the good fellow had gone beyond that which his lowly office demanded of him, I told him I would needs wait upon the patient until the remedies had begun their work, and indeed to make sure that there was no adverse reaction; whereupon the good soul unlocked the door and let me in, and I heard his laboured steps depart, yet I heard not the key turn in the lock.

And I stood within seeing nothing, for the darkness without the place was as nothing compared to the darkness within. Neither did I hear any sound, so that I doubted if indeed the place were occupied by a living being. And fear seized me, that I should have come thus far and he whom I had sought these many years be passed out of this world even while I stood on the very threshold of his dwelling place. And I know not how long I remained so, waiting for the gift of speech, for my habitual prattle had fled.

'John Rivaulx?'

'Tis he. How fare thee?'

'Well enough, my friend. The darkness is not that they wish to drive me mad, for I am treated well enough, but that the head ache renders any degree of light unbearable. There is a high window which the good man who conducted you hither covered, and struggled in the doing of it, for he also is afflicted.'

'All they in here are afflicted. The brethren send you their greetings.'

'My thanks. And I would that you return my greetings if you are passing their way again.'

And assuring Domenico Jommelli, for it was he, that I would convey his greetings when I next delivered remedies to the brethren I offered him also plantain against the headache and salix against the fever.

'I would that you give the remedies to the brethren,' he said, 'for their need is the greater.'

'There is ample of everything,' I said. 'The plants grow freely in the dispensary garden, which the good Lord has made to flourish for the treatment of they who suffer. The supply is without end.'

So I gave to Domenico Jommelli salix and plantain, reluctant though he was to receive such remedies, and presently he bade me uncover the window for his head ache was lifting. Then struggling to his feet, for he was yet weak, he extended his hand after the English manner.

'I have sought you these twenty years and upward,' he said, 'though I knew not who you were, only that once in the time of the terror I was in the same place as one other suffering similar afflictions, both of us being coerced on account of our professions which bade us look on all mankind equally regardless of their station in life. And a cry went up of "Fire!" whereupon they our oppressors fled, the dwellinghouse being well ablaze. After which I saw not my brother in affliction; only I knew that the structure of the dwellinghouse had given and the whole was burning. Yet I was on the outside, I know not how, and it was many hours that I was in the burning lanes of Paris looking for one I knew not, whom I would know only by the manner of coercion meted out. And I found him not. Yet often times in the years I have in my dreams been in the burning streets of Paris searching, yet every dream has ended with my arriving again at the dwellinghouse with the roof fallen I and the windows spewing out flame, and my brother in affliction as I understood still within. Then I heard, and I know not how, of certain insurrections in the fair land of England, so I came hither, and by chance saw he whom I sought, waiting after an audience had departed, knowing it was he by his French mien and the hurt done to his hands. Yet I was already engaged in conversation and he did not tarry. And it was you, my friend. How fare thee?'

All of which was delivered in an English tongue so unlike any other that I scarce could fathom many of the words, yet I dare not beg my brother in affliction to speak in our own tongue lest he be further incriminated.

I said I fared well and that the land of England had been gracious to me.

'Though as the years go on,' I said, 'and I may say this to you for we are of an age, I find not the same passion for this life as once I had, which is no doubt on account of my long sojourn in this world; for indeed the minutes creep and the years fly on swift wings for those of advancing age.'

'And trust you yet in the Lord God Almighty?' he said.

I told him yes, for I could do no other, beholding every day the works of his hand in the plants that grew for the healing of the sick, though I told him there was an occasion not long gone when I was present at a scene of great desolation and, but for an instant, lost my trust in a divine presence, yet I said not what the occasion was. Then seeing my friend somewhat recovered I bade him tell me what he would of his own sojourn in this world, which he did as much as his strength allowed, saying that though his sojourn had been long it seemed but a day, and that day had passed not in the pursuit of the music of the double bass, which had occupied but a few minutes of his one day's journey, but in the search after good, which he had found in many and various places but had never been able to practise himself.

'And even in those that oppressed us, my friend, there was good to be found for the aims were laudable, namely equality and liberty and brotherhood, and I do truly believe for the most part they saw not that the means to such ends were foul. And among those who are known as machine breakers I have found much goodness, and in the turnkey himself. And I believe, for myself, if I could do one good thing in the service of humankind, then I would die happy.'

Which saying surprised me greatly, for the music of the double bass, and indeed of any instrument, is the gift of the angels, and I said as much, though he saw it not himself. For the depression of the spirit may pursue a good man through his life, even from childhood onwards, so that he sees not the goodness in himself but is ever wont to hold himself in low esteem. Indeed, I had observed the same in certain of my patients who, though they manifested divers maladies of the body, yet underlying was a bleakness of spirit and a pitiful turning against their very self, made in the image of our Lord. So I ventured to ask of my brother in affliction if he would consent to the remedy of basil, for the low fever is like to depress the spirit, though I knew from his converse that his malady lay deeper. To which he consented, and I think more to please me than repair himself.

And I knew also that the sense of self reproach he carried for having found himself on the outside of the burning dwellinghouse, believing that his brother in affliction was yet inside, had served to depress his spirits the more. Though I said it not, for I wished not to be seen to be making light of the condition in attributing it to a single instance in the past.

Yet Domenico Jommelli in common with divers others saw through the window in my head, which I myself had stood before the dispensary mirror looking for and not discovered.

'I know not whether it is the remedy, my friend, or that I see him standing here before me whom I thought to have perished in the fire, but I feel my desolation of spirit driven away as the rain clouds on a summer's day. Yet it is but a day in the sunlight and the dark will return,' he added. 'And I trust that when the trial comes the Lord may send a summer's day so that I may bear my tribulation the better.'

Having said which Domenico Jommelli fell silent, for the steps of the turnkey could be heard, and presently an oath as he discovered the door to have remained unlocked for the term of my visit to the prisoner; the arrival of the turnkey preventing me telling my brother in affliction that I had lamented also his loss through the years, thinking myself to have escaped and he to have perished within the burning dwellinghouse in Paris in the time of the terror. And I had not the liberty to speak, for the door of the place was thrown open and the poor fellow stood there aghast, thinking to see his prisoner fled and a heavy penalty falling forthwith on himself.

'You are yet here, sirs,' he said. 'And tis to your credit for the door was not locked.'

Then seeing how great was his distress and also his humble manner I feigned ignorance of the matter, saying he need not fear of the oversight being noised abroad for it would not be; and indeed, I said, had he not told us of the unlocked door we would have remained unknowing. Yet I did not well at my feigning for the poor fellow would not be comforted.

'Sir, you were at liberty to conduct the prisoner to freedom yet you did not do so,' he said.

To which I answered that the notion had not passed through my mind, knowing the frail health of the prisoner and the long and tortuous journey. And I do believe the poor turnkey would yet have been at his self-recriminations had not the malady reft him of further words on the matter, and it was all he could do to make fast the door and conduct me back on the circuitous route whither we had come.

Then, seeing no harm done by his late omission nor was any soul likely to discover it, the turnkey recovered his words, asking me if I knew that certain of they in the men's gaol, and he believed in the women's gaol also, were there when they ought not to be. To which I answered neither yea nor nay, knowing that the good man would have his say whether my answer be yea or nay.

'That surprises me not,' he said, as if I had answered in the affirmative, 'for all the fair town of York knows that certain are here on false report. And there is mischief enough, sir, without adding to it by turning the King's evidence,' which he knew not the meaning of, no more did I, for oft times the sum of the words in the English tongue is more than their several parts, and I knew not the sum of that expression.

And I knew not either by whose evidence my brother in affliction Domenico Jommelli sat in gaol, nor had he said aught, as it troubled him not that he was accused. Yet it troubled me greatly that he was so reduced, which I knew not why, for the low fever and a constitutional depression of the spirit such as he had spoken of had been alleviated by the kind offices of the salix and basil, and also by seeing him whom he thought to have perished standing there before him; yet still he had not laid hold on life. And in the instant I begged of the turnkey to take me back to the prisoner, which I knew he would do, being inordinately thankful that none would hear of his omission in the case of the unlocked door.

So the good man, without asking why, and having already seated himself, struggled to his feet, being yet weak though not in fever, and conducted me thither by a way less circuitous.

'For to tell you the honest truth, sir,' he said, 'I have not the will to go that long way round seeing as I know you will not noise abroad that the foreign gentleman is housed nigh to the machine breakers, we being well enough full up at the present time, sir,' he added. 'The other fellow will return for you when you are done.'

And I found Domenico Jommelli unsurprised to see me, and indeed under the impression that many hours had elapsed since our late meeting, which was but minutes before. And I asked him how he fared, as if indeed it were the next day, and he said that he fared well enough for he could not complain of harsh treatment in spite of the fact that he was incarcerated on a heavy charge.

To which I said nothing, knowing that no weal is served by attempting to hasten the process of a labouring mind.

'For it is a charge of the transportation of weaponry,' he said, 'and who am I to say that I did not without laying the charge on another man. And though I would not, for weaponry is anathema to me, yet I cannot say that I did not, for I suffered a manner of apoplexy on my journey and I have lost the recollection of those days as if I never lived them. And it is well known moreover that my leanings are towards the hill folk for I can see them hungered and without labour, for which I am no doubt accounted guilty of inciting sedition.'

Then I asked Domenico Jommelli his whereabouts when he suffered as he thought an apoplexy, and he said it was an hostelry, the name of which he knew not; and they cared for his weal after the seizure, for which he could not but be thankful.

'And they kept the double bass also,' he said, 'for I know not how long, certain days having been erased from my mind as if I did not live them.'

'Yet it is a strange thing,' he continued presently, 'that when I came to play the bass again the notes flowed readily, as do my recollections of the time of the terror, it being only near events I know not. Which you will discern whether they be the signs of apoplexy or no, my friend. For if it be so it will be followed ere long by another worse seizure which will carry me out of this world before the judge of the assize does the same.'

And I would doubtless have prattled as is my habit, but that I was prevented by the entry of he whom the turnkey had talked when he said another fellow would conduct me out; a rough enough fellow who said he had brought water to the prisoner and was giving to all, whereupon he poured from a pitcher into my friend's cup, and having done so departed, with no words of conducting me out. Then presently came another fellow along, saying he had instructions to conduct the physician out of the gaol, and to please make haste for he had much to do.

So I left forthwith after taking the hand of Domenico Jommelli which he extended in the English manner; and in doing so I knocked down with the sleeve of my cloak the cup of water which stood on the table between us. And I begged the poor fellow who was beset with his labours if he might send in fresh water for the foreign prisoner, to which he assented with scant willingness.

XXXI

'I know not where you have been, sir,' said Luke Bower, 'but my nostrils tell me you have been in some offensive place.'

Then I told Luke I had been in the men's gaol, and before that the women's gaol, which were offensive enough on many accounts, the aroma therein being the least.

'Tis not the aroma of the gaol,' said Luke, 'unless they have mice, for you carry about you the stink of mice, sir.'

'That is possible, Luke,' I said, 'and thank you for making the matter known to me, for your senses are sharper than mine. What conclusion do you draw from my carrying on me the aroma of mice?'

'I know naught else that carries the aroma of mice, sir,' said Luke, 'unless it be the Conium maculatum. For I remember that you showed me it growing nigh the beck and begged me to note the aroma about it.'

Then I told Luke what had passed in the men's gaol in the presence of the foreign prisoner Domenico Jommelli, namely that a rough fellow I thought to be the relief turnkey had attended with a pitcher of water, whom I thought also was there to let me out, but he was not, for another came along presently to let me out, and the first filled the prisoner's cup; which in clasping hands with the prisoner on my departure after the English manner I caught with the sleeve of my cloak and overturned it, drenching my sleeve in so doing.

'Tis a bad stink, sir,' said Luke.

And it came to me that I ever carried with me the stink of some place or other, and I could only thank my Saviour that few had the sharp senses of Luke Bower to notice, or the words to say so.

'It is the musician fellow you speak of,' he said. 'And I always wondered, sir, why he has an appearance so like your own and a name so unlike; and I have asked myself many times the same question but have found no answer.'

'Neither more have I,' I said. 'Yet there have been many who are musicians who have taken Italian names.'

'Then I am no more the wiser, sir,' said Luke Bower. 'Neither do I know why he sits in gaol, for if all they from the fair land of France be put in York gaol for fear of revolution then you would be sitting in gaol yourself, sir. And tis no small wonder that you're not for there are they in gaol on false report.'

'How so, Luke?'

'It is all over York, sir, that there are certain in the gaol on false report.'

'So said the turnkey without giving whose false report it is,' I said, 'and I did not ask of him for they in the gaol have all the low fever and might not be taxed with words, which may be asked of them again when they can least account for themselves.'

'I know not what you say, sir,' said Luke. 'And I fear you are not yourself since you have been in the gaol. Happen you have the low fever coming on and would do well to take those remedies yourself which you gave to all they within, for I know the stocks of salix and plantain in the dispensary are low of a sudden.'

Then I told Luke Bower my scribe that I was indeed not myself and I feared the depressed state of the good Domenico Jommelli had communicated itself to me. For the fair world was of a sudden a place of desolation, and it seemed to me that I had caught the malady of my brother in affliction inasmuch as I might search after goodness all my life and not find it.

'And sir,' continued Luke, 'twas not only the salix and plantain depleted in the dispensary. Which I will tell you another time, sir, for I see my words might be spoken to yonder stone wall for all that you are hearing them. If it pleases you, sir, pray give me your cloak and I will put it into steep; and in the mean while you will do well to take salix and plantain and a draught of clear water then take thee to thy rest.'

So I did that which my scribe Luke Bower said, namely took the remedies of salix and plantain and also basil for the depression of the spirit and took me to my bed; or so I thought for that was where I found myself on awakening, the sun being low over the roof tops of York, and the song of the evening blackbird abroad on the air.

Yet whereas I had entered my chamber alone, as I thought, I was not so on waking for I beheld an angel seated in the ingle nook, albeit an angel in plain dress and with the sweet features of a hill woman, which as I looked the more resolved themselves into the features of Jem Bailey.

'You have wakened, sir,' she said, 'and I beg you to forgive my presence for Mr Bower bid me watch over you, for you were taken badly, sir.'

Then I thanked Jem Bailey as well as I might, which was but little for my tongue cleaved to the roof of my mouth and I could scarce articulate the words; which when they came, and I knew it only by perceiving the bewilderment in Jem Bailey's sweet eyes, were after the gallic manner.

Whereupon Luke stood also in my chamber, though he never did so before, and bid Jem Bailey be not frighted, for my wits were scattered as was oft times the case and would ere long return.

'You are awakened, sir,' he said, to which I answered, I knew not in what tongue, that I believed myself awakened for I saw there my friends around me; unless it be that I had awakened in heaven, yet I believed in heaven none were indicted of having scattered wits for there they did not talk so of the Lord's handiwork however deficient it be.

To all of which sweet Jem Bailey listened in much puzzlement, knowing not whether to be merry or downcast.

'The day is far spent,' I said, 'and I promised those who sit in gaol that I would be back.'

''Tis the second day since your sojourn in the gaol that is far spent,' said Luke, 'and they that sit within may sit there one day more, for you are like to carry to them your malady if you are to return, sir, which you cannot, sir.'

'I can give them no malady they already suffer,' I said.

'Tis true,' said Luke, 'but you might well give them a malady which they do not yet suffer, for it is all about in the lanes of York, being brought up from the drains, they say, by one who had been there much and who it is believed is still abroad spreading the mischief.'

And as my scribe said thus I was visited by a disquieting notion, namely that I had spoken in a delirium and known not what I was saying, which thought troubled me greatly. And it must have been writ on my face, or visible through the window in my head, for Jem Bailey asked if I were vexed in my mind, which I could scarcely say, for if any poor soul had cause to be vexed in their mind it was Jem Bailey herself. Yet the question was so sweetly and sincerely asked that I said what ailed me, namely that I feared I had spoken unwittingly in my fever of those things which I hoped never to speak of, even under coercion.

'Twas all rambling, sir,' said Jem Bailey, 'and I was frighted for I heard that which happen I was not intended to hear, and which you would not have spoken had the fever not been upon you. So I called in Mr Bower, sir, for I was frighted not of you, sir, but of the secrets of those others who sit in gaol and who it may be are bound for the gallows-tree. And also, sir, I am frighted that I have in my hands some evidence, though happen tis too late to help my poor father.'

'Mistress Bailey summoned me, sir,' said Luke Bower, 'her being of a tender and confidential disposition and disquieted that she should be hearing those things about others that she had no right to hear.'

Then I asked of Luke Bower what things I had given voice to in my ramblings, for I feared I had said certain things not only that I had never spoken of, even to Luke Bower my scribe, but which had lain in that part of the mind deeper than thought. For I have oft had a notion of such, that there lies in the mind of man a place of great mystery known only to the Lord God Almighty.

And Luke Bower answering said, 'I have writ it down as best I may, sir, and when I have told you now that your wits are gathering together I will burn the writings.'

Which saying Luke produced like any magician a sheet of fool's cap closely and exquisitely written after his manner; and I bade him read it out, for the words danced and faded before my eyes.

And he read thus:

'... "Concerning the persons, these being by name:

' "He who did not remember his own name, being one Will Cantrell, late resident in the concealed chamber, father of Mistress Jemima Bailey, the gentleman being deceased", whom you understand, sir, though you may not know it yourself, to be he whom you were called upon to certify as having passed from this world.

' "He known as Simon Horridge and his sister Elizabeth, who sit in gaol on the capital charge of the murder of Caleb Sawney, late of the militia, whom you believe to be there on a false charge for he who did the deed in the Sheep-close was shod as a townsman and not as one from the hill country. And indeed they neither of them wish to deny the charge, fearing that the said charge would be laid upon the other.

' "Mistress Born and her maid Mistress Todd who sit in gaol on the capital charge of incitement to murder Richard Born, being the magistrate of the parish of Holmroyd, he whom you believe to be yet alive in this world.

' "He known as Robert Gaut who sits in gaol on the charge of the transportation of weaponry, who wills not to deny the charge fearing that he may in so doing lay the charge upon another.

' "He known as Domenico Jommelli who is a player of the double bass, who sits in gaol on the charge of the transportation of weaponry, who also wills not to deny the charge fearing that he may in so doing lay the charge upon another".

'That is all, sir,' Luke concluded, 'unless it be that in the time between your visit to the gaol and my arriving in the dispensary another had entered, for I found not the Conium maculatum. For, sir, the Conium maculatum, having a foul odour and offensive to the nostrils, was on your sleeve when you returned from the gaol, being in the cup you upturned for you doubted he who came delivering water to the prisoner Jommelli; whether you know it or not,' he added. 'And I know not whether it was in your mind, though you knew it not, that certain others of the accused who sit in York gaol may well have been given water from the same pitcher. For knowing that you would entertain such concerns, though you knew it not, sir, I inquired of the turnkey, who is much recovered himself, as are they of the machine breakers also; and he knew not the fellow who delivered the water to the foreign prisoner, for he knows no such fellow. I have finished now, sir.'

'Mr Bower went to the gaol while you were stricken with the fever, sir, to ask after the well fare of those machine breakers, and they do well, sir,' said Jem Bailey. 'They have not had the water. And the foreign gentleman is not poisoned. For Mr Bower told me that the water which you spilt, sir, was poisoned, which you knew and for that reason upturned the cup to stay the gentleman from drinking, which happen you don't remember at present, sir.'

All of which led me to believe that between them my scribe and the sweet soul Jem Bailey had put to rights this troublous world, during which time I had been travelling as a passenger might, unaware and not engaged with the journey. And I would willingly have continued thus as a passenger in the great world, for my head swam and the sinking sun setting afire the windows smote my eyes; but that Luke Bower, for all that he said a quarter of an hour before that he had finished his discourse, yet seeing me woken determined to keep me thus, saying that gruel was on the way from the house of mercy and bread also; for the time would not be long, he said, given the fever that had lately risen from the drains, when all they in the water lanes of York would be crying out for the apothecary. 'And you are the apothecary, sir,' he said. 'And if that were not all, sir, you have it in your gift to come between the sentence and the execution of it on they who sit in gaol, for tis a short furlong between the passing of sentence and the gallows-tree; the reason being, sir, that he who is the ground of such mischief is not where he is supposed to be but in the town of York; which fellow, sir, will be in your way ere long.'

Then I had no recourse but to go with the busy world again, and indeed the fever was abating and the desolation of spirit which I feared I had caught from my brother in affliction Domenico Jommelli was lifting. And I bid Luke if he would take my gratitude to the house of mercy at the least, for he and Jem Bailey would have none of it, saying they had done not a thing; yet I knew from the pallor of them and the shadows beneath their eyes that they had lost much sleep on my account.

'I wished not to tell you before, sir,' said Luke, seeing me somewhat restored, 'that they have sent from the hospice begging of your opinion on a certain patient. And though I know you will do as you wish, sir, tis my counsel that you should cling on to the fever some days more, for you will catch it again if you go to such a place, knowing what it is like, for my nostrils were greatly offended by they who came searching for you, sir.'

Then I told Luke again that they who have the fever do not catch the same fever again, for the constitution has been fortified against it. 'I know not how,' I said, 'but tis so, which is the reason the physician rarely falls into sickness.'

'That may be so, sir,' said Luke, 'but the sickness which has come up from the drains of York is a bad sickness and happen tis a different sickness. As you will see presently, sir,' he added. 'And if it pleases you, and if it does not please you, sir, I will see you to the door of the hospice, though I will not go within on account of the offence to the nostrils, asking your pardon, sir.'

So on the morrow we fared thither to the hospice of York, which was but a step beyond the Monk-bar, being met there by the keeper; and my scribe Luke Bower left with haste, for the stench seemed even to me such as would extinguish not only a candle flame but all the lanes of Clywold at the time of the burning. By which I knew myself to be yet ailing for I was never in my life so discomfited; and I resolved to see whatever patient I was bidden to and be away, for a physician is of use to no one if he be sick himself.

And the keeper, who was as rubicund and hearty fellow as I have ever met with, and no doubt believing I was as hearty as himself, led me towards the wards for the sick, making all the while observations of divers kinds.

'They that come here find the air noxious,' he said, 'but I know you will not find it so, sir, being a physician and accustomed to the fluxes of the body. For the Lord God made us all the same, sir, and even they of high estate who carry around with them the smell of sweet lavender will emit a noxious aroma with the flux. And that is the sluicing room, sir, and that be the ward for the bairns, for they of tender years have been grievously stricken by this pestilence. And that be for the women, sir, for we believe not in subjecting those that are stricken with the presence of their opposites, if you take my meaning, sir, however sick they may be; and that be for the men; and we come presently to he who is isolated, sir, for tis our belief that he has spread the pestilence around York, for he carried the odour of the privy on him as if he had lately risen from the drains; which may well be the case, sir, for every boy at his mother's knee knows that there is a warren of passages under the town leading to divers places; the same as all of those scarce alive in the water lanes know to wash their hands, if not for what purpose, sir. All but this fellow, sir, who is the patient in question, whom we believe for all his rough exterior and churlish manner of speech to be a personage of some standing.'

Then I asked the good man how that might be, that he was believed to be of some standing.

'Why, tis odd, sir, tis on account of his hands. For, sir, if I were to look at your hands I would know you to be a physician from the neatness of them albeit that I see you have suffered an affliction. And to look at the keeper of sheep in York market, I would know him as such by his hands, and the cropping fellows, for we have seen a few of those in times past, sir; their hands bespeak their trades. Yet this fellow who carries the smell of the privy on him, for he will not submit to bathing ... well, sir, you will draw your own conclusions for we are nigh unto his chamber. And I beg you, sir, be not disheartened if he speak coarsely, for you will know, sir, that sickness makes a man himself; whereas they in health deploy all manner of means to deceive the world.'

And the good man, arriving at the last most door, drew back a shutter in it and after looking through himself bade me also look inside for, he said, much is to be learned of a man's condition by watching him, who knows not that he is being watched. Then, opening the door, he bade me enter, saying that he would be nearabouts, and saying also that an aroma of mice had been detected about the patient.

XXXII

And I entered in, finding myself in the presence of he for whom I had been summoned.

And I saw before me lying on a low pallet a man as all men are, made in the image of the Lord God Almighty and placed on the same earth to make the same pilgrimage as all others, with the same choice between good and evil that all have had since the world began; a rough enough fellow, unshaven, and not bathed, turning in the shallows between wakefulness and oblivion; whose flesh such as was visible was encrusted with running sores, and whose noxious breath filled the room.

'I will open the window, if I may, Richard Born,' I said. 'You will fare better for the clear air.'

'I need not a papist and a charlatan to tell me my name.'

'You sent for the apothecary and I am he.'

'I know not whether you are the apothecary or not the apothecary for I see you not, but you have the papist's voice.'

'You cannot see me, sir, for your eyes are covered in matter and need bathing, and you will let no one near you.'

'What is that to you? I asked you not for your opinion.'

'No, you did not ask for it, Richard Born,' I said. 'Yet I will give it. You carry on your person a virulent fever brought up from the drains of York which has spread grievously among those of low estate in the water lanes and looks to run further, namely into the gaol and the house of mercy and heaven where else you have had your goings on, sir. And for the reason, sir, that you parade as a rough fellow and a vagrant for your own purposes, and a fellow who wishes not to bathe. Yet you betray yourself by your manicure, sir, for you did ever keep your hands neat. Submit yourself to the kind offices of the attendants in this place and you may yet save the fever, dire though it is, from spreading to other poor folks, for even though you be confined they who wait upon you must needs carry the affliction wheresoe'er they go; and though they may in their own constitutions have acquired safety from the fever by familiarity with it, yet others have not.'

And thus I let my prattle run away with me for no other reason than to delay the moment when I must needs tell the poor fellow that there was not in the dispensary a remedy which might help his recovery; which indeed he knew for beneath his rough manner there lay a fear preventing his drawing nigh unto the question, namely would he live or no. Then I thought of poor Susan Knowles who knew well that she was not long to walk in the light of the sun and approached her end with equanimity; yet even she in her simple trust talked of the life to come not as itself but as of a walk in Kessle-wood.

'There is not in the dispensary a remedy to cure this fever, Richard,' I said. 'Fever is common enough and many fall victim to it, yet this fever is an unknown fever. The best I may do is to go in the places where you have been and see if there grows a plant nearby; for where nature sends a malady she oft times plants a remedy close by.'

'I wish not to die, sir,' the poor fellow said.

'You will not die, Richard,' I said. 'No man dies for the soul of man is immortal.'

'Dammit, man, I want to be mortal! Confound your immortality, you cursed papist. Get thee away and search out that remedy, then we shall see if you are an apothecary or a common charlatan, damn you.'

Then I asked Richard Born for an account of his sojourn in the drains beneath the town of York that I might go there, fearing indeed that little would grow on account of the noxious vapours therein; which account he sparingly gave, torn no doubt between the prospect of his certain immortality which he wanted not and divulging the places of the subterranean passages. To which I repaired after telling the good keeper where I was bound and praying him to find an attendant willing to bathe the patient's eyes, for that he would submit to, but no more.

And while my feet repaired to the drains of York, which were but a short step from the hospice, my mind travelled back to Richard Born's visit to the dispensary in the presence of his wife Grace, and his complaint that she wished not for converse with him. And it came to me that which I had entertained fleetingly in my mind, yet had not then given much credence to, namely that he was indeed subject to the Treponema pallidum; which Grace Born knew well and would not say for delicacy. And I remembered seeing from the dispensary window that when they left she did not come near to him, not so much as to permit the hem of her gown to touch him.

And I came to the great Ouse and the steps leading thither from the Lendal-bridge, which were covered all with a manner of wrack and the putrid detritus of the river, at the lower end of which stairs, and scarce visible on account of the overhanging branches of a common ash, was the entrance to the drains; being as dark and noxious as any may have depicted the mouth of hell. For it is a truth that hell exists in many and divers places on the fair earth and tis oft times easier to come upon than heaven.

With these reflections and conjecturing also how any man might enter the drains, the place being but low and narrow, I cast my eyes about to see if there were any footholds; and lodged nigh on the water's edge I saw growing the leaves of the Sonchus hesperus, or a plant so like it as to be a close variant, but without flowers. Then I sought the exit of the drain yonder from the Lendal-bridge and found there a specimen with a single flower extant, bearing on it the blue-edged petals of the Sonchus hesperus. Which I left to grow, both, having established its identity, for there is naught to be gained in plundering the sweet world of its treasures.

And being thankful that the fever had passed from me, either that I had forgotten I was stricken with it, or that it was indeed gone, I returned to the dispensary to put my cloak in steep before my scribe Luke Bower were offended in the nostrils by it; and also to collect the remedy named the Sonchus hesperus of which we had an ample supply, for the good earth is ever open-handed with the plants of her healing.

On the way back to the hospice reflecting moreover that the curious eruptions on the flesh of the patient, blackened as they were at the rims, were a manner of burn. And indeed I knew not why it should be so, lest it be that the noxious effluent from the mill works high in the hills might seep and pool into the great common drains of the towns, though the distance was as I thought some fifty and two hundred furlongs; or happen there might be some other machine works nigh the town of York, yet I knew not of any.

And not least occupying my thoughts was the most desolating truth, namely that I carried on my person that which might stay the mortal illness of he who had brought others to the gallows-tree and inflicted many a gross coercion on certain of those who had aligned themselves with the machine breakers; though they themselves were not without their foul measures, of which I knew not a little.

And by and by the resolve came to me to confide in the good keeper of the hospice, that the Sonchus hesperus might restore to well-being a fellow of bad repute under his roof; knowing that the keeper would understand that which is a mystery to all the world, namely that a physician gives to they who do good and they who do ill without partiality, as the rain falls and the sun throws out his beams and the stars shine down on all regardless of their deeds, for all fall short of the glory of God.

'We did not look for your return so soon, sir,' the keeper said. 'And I must say to you in honesty that we expected the patient's demise ere the remedy be here and thus to be spared the dilemma of prolonging further the life of he who had already done ill enough in the world.'

To which I answered that that which he conjectured might well have been the case but that there was already the tincture from the plant in the dispensary, which I and my assistant had

248

made up to treat a different disorder, but like in that the eruptions of the flesh had all the appearance of burns, being charred and blackened at the edges.

'Then we must offer the patient this same tincture,' said the keeper, 'for we can do naught else. What say you, sir?'

'We can do no other,' I said.

'You say rightly, sir,' said the keeper. 'This fellow is the patient and we must needs preserve him to do ill in the world while they who sit in gaol await the gallows-tree for misdemeanours they did not commit.'

All of which was pronounced the more loudly the more nearly we approached to the room, so deliberate being the communication that I feared the patient was like to hear.

'And while you have been absent searching out the remedy, sir,' the good keeper continued, 'he has arrived here who is the new appointed magistrate in the parish of Holmroyd, having sought you at the dispensary, sir, and having been directed by your young man to the hospice; and he has in his company another gentleman. For the former magistrate of that parish, sir, was grievously done to, and his wife and her maid sit in gaol for his murder. As you well know, sir,' continued the good man, standing now outside the room yet not entering. 'And we must needs accept the conclusions of the justice of Tindercliffe, who was the nearest most justice available on that fateful night, that the remains dragged up from the beck, though the flesh had fallen from the face, were indeed those of the magistrate of the parish of Holmroyd, Richard Born, on account of the fine clothing which yet clung to the remains. And though he was a cruel man given to the coercion of machine breakers, yet death is a fearful thing and at its most fearful for those who die not in a state of grace, and whatever the man be we must needs pray the Lord Almighty to have mercy on his soul ...'

Which oration I fully believe would have lasted out until kingdom come had not a mighty noise issued from within the room, whereupon the keeper opened up the door. And we beheld the patient lately risen from his pallet, who had not the strength to stand and had fallen to the ground. Yet what he lacked in vigour of the body he possessed in voice for on the entry of the keeper he lamented dismally.

'I am the magistrate Richard Born, and I live as you live. He who has taken my place is an imposter. I wish not to die,' which saying he broke forth into piteous weeping.

Then the good keeper and the newly appointed magistrate, who had witnessed the sorry scene, helped the poor fellow back onto his pallet, being both hearty men; and I also, being yet weakened from the fever, and he who had accompanied the newly appointed magistrate, being also badly in health, placing the patient as comfortably as we may. After which I gave to him the tincture Sonch. hesp.

And I bade they who had arrived in my absence, being Martin Gathercole and Zephaniah Gaut, to wash their hands, though they needed no bidding, for the air in the room could scarce be breathed for the stink of it, the patient having long resisted bathing; to which he now made as if to submit as the awe of death had overridden all else. And though I liked not wholly the means, yet the end was worthy, namely that a life was saved; for who is any man, that he should judge the worth or otherwise of his fellow.

Then I mentioned to the keeper my suspicions that the patient suffered also the Treponema pallidum, knowing that he would keep remedies for such in the hospice, and bidding also that we leave the patient in the presence of the bathing attendants while the remedy called the Sonchus hesperus took effect against the fever.

XXXIII

And for all that there was much to say, no one said a word. And we waited there, Martin Gathercole and Zephaniah Gaut, and myself, knowing not if the tincture would restore the patient to sound health; and even if that were to be the case, if he would yet acknowledge his identity, for at the present he had done so only inasmuch as he feared that another fellow had usurped his place in the world.

Then at length Martin Gathercole rose to his feet and went to the window.

'I knew not there was rickets in the town of York,' he said, 'for it is reported as an affliction of they who work the machines, may God forgive us; and I know not why tis so, except it be confinement in the mills, as they tell us. Tis a sorry sight. The young woman yonder is more grievously afflicted than Ellie Bright.'

Then I looked out also and saw the sweet soul Melody, she who was doorkeeper in the house of mercy, scarce able to make progress in the crowded thoroughfare, for she was not accustomed to the outside, and I saw also that she was bound for the hospice and was like to be knocked down in the throng. And the keeper, seeing her also, went down to admit her to the building, for indeed the door was heavy and the handle placed too high for such as she.

All of which we forgot as soon as the witnessing of it, for an attendant came, bidding us to be present in the room of the fever patient who was recovering somewhat. And there outside the ward was the justice of Tindercliffe, arrived in York for the assize and summoned thither by the good keeper, who had sent word also to the assize for an officer of the law to attend a patient mortally afflicted who had on his mind that to which he wished to confess while yet in this world. And I knew not whether Richard Born would wish to lay bare his soul before any living creature, being recovered and no longer in fear of his immortality; neither did I know whether he wished to lay bare his soul before his near neighbour the justice of Tindercliffe, for the fellow had about him an air of irascibility which would not brook death bed confessions. Yet in the officer of the law who accompanied him I perceived a good measure of equity.

Then we entered all into the room of the patient, finding him greatly altered for having bathed, for he looked now neither like the fever patient he had lately been nor the magistrate of the parish of Holmroyd whom I had last seen presiding over the scourging of Robert Gaut in the Sheep-close; and whom Martin Gathercole now asked to give account of himself.

To which the patient answered nothing; and Martin Gathercole, awaiting a quarter of the hour at the least put forward the question again.

'In the name of the King and Regent, make an account of yourself, sir.'

To which the patient answered not; and the same was repeated certain times more, lasting until the lamps be lit, for the patient out of fear of the light had bid the windows be half shuttered.

Then he who was justice of Tindercliffe, being choleric in his constitution, with the colour mounting in his complexion, made towards the patient; and I noted that he did so painfully for the remedies against the gout which I had sent with Kit Swain had long lost their efficacy; and also I reflected that there was naught worse than the pain of the gout to put a man into a foul temper.

'Dammit man, speak out,' he said, 'or there will be used against you those means of coercion you practised on others, For there is many an implement of coercion in the operating ward of this hospice, I'll be bound. I have seen it on the campaign, sir, when fellows have had their legs sawn off and a pretty sight it is too.'

And the poor fellow Born being frighted out of his wits would then have spoken but that the attorney at law, he who had accompanied the justice of Tindercliffe, spoke up.

'This gentleman, if he is to be questioned, sir, must needs have his own representation, for that is the law, and it matters not that the inquisition takes place by a sick bed, it is still the law. You may have your own representation, sir,' he said then to the patient, raising his voice somewhat as if the fellow were hard of hearing. 'Whom would you have to represent you?'

Then the patient found his speech, though little enough of it for he was still sorely shaken by the rough words of the justice.

'I'll have Sawney,' he said. 'He'll speak up for me.'

'If that's Caleb Sawney you're referring to,' said the justice, 'you may have him by all means but his speaking days are done. If someone would please send to the city morgue we may get this business under way.'

'Then get me Hayward if I can't have Sawney,' said the patient.

And the garrison was sent to, in the case that the officer of the men, Thomas Hayward, might be there. Yet for myself I liked not the bantering manner of the justice of Tindercliffe to one who was sick, however bad his deeds. And I prayed the keeper that we might all be shown to the other chamber while awaiting a representation for the sick man and leave him in the care of an attendant. Which suggestion served only to transfer the blunt temper of the justice of Tindercliffe from the patient's ward to the said chamber in which we waited; and indeed he had words enough and more to spare.

'Dammit, the fellow Sawney's dead,' he said. 'Didn't show any surprise, notice that, sirs? There were folks out for Sawney's blood. Born enticed some rebel fellow whose daughter Sawney had violated to do for him but that fellow got Sawney first, ha! If it hadn't been the rebel fellow it would have been another. Only got to go to Clywold to see how many bairns there be out of wedlock. And I can tell you why.

All those mill women have folks among the machine breakers and Sawney got under their petticoats by threatening mischief to their folks.'

Whereupon Martin Gathercole bade the justice be the gentleman he was born to be, and asked also what had befallen the rebel fellow who had done the mischief to Sawney, to which the justice replied that he knew not for the remains had not been found, yet he believed the fellow to have passed from this world and to have been laid to rest privily by the hill folk for he knew no more, if indeed the fellow were deceased at all. But he knew for certain the hill folk looked to their own.

'And I'll tell you another thing,' he continued, 'you can bet Hayward's not in the garrison or else they would have found him by now. Born's playing for time, however sick he makes out to be, you mark my words. He was ever a wily fellow.'

And so he continued, as if speaking to the blank wall for none present would either assent to what he said or otherwise for fear of partiality. Yet the justice of Tindercliffe, being a bluff and outspoken fellow, entertained no such scruples.

Then turning to me he fell to bemoaning the sorry state of his feet and the pains he suffered, and said that on the fateful night they that accompanied the remains to Tindercliffe, the magistrate of Holmroyd being understood to have been murdered and they being his very remains on the road, had brought with them some kind of salve acquired from a physician fellow then at the hostelry.

'And I know not what it was, sir, but it did me some power of good, and I would give a sennight of my life to have the same salve again.'

So I asked the justice of Tindercliffe the appearance of the salve and if it carried any odour, which he remembered not; yet I wished not to reveal that it was I who sent it, although he knew well it was I, and knew also that I could not be asked to give testimony. And presently I gave him the tincture of tansy for which the poor fellow was inordinately grateful; for I knew well that he was in dire pain on account of the gathering pallor on his face and around his mouth in particular.

And the justice being then scarce of words for the pain he was in, the room fell silent apart from his low groans as he paced up and down to alleviate the affliction of the gout. But he was not long thus for presently we were summoned, the justice of Tindercliffe, the attorney at law, Martin Gathercole, Zephaniah Gaut and myself, to wait upon the patient in his room, Thomas Hayward having lately arrived; who by the look of him had done so with scant grace, it being writ all over his face that he would more willingly be anywhere in the wide world but attending the patient Richard Born, which was seen also by the attorney at law.

'Officer Hayward,' he said, ''tis writ upon your face that you are an unwilling participant in these proceedings, and it does you credit that you are here, though it be against your better judgement. You have no role but to attend the sick, who has no representation. Do not let yourself be coerced into words by either party.'

Then taking up the holy book and beginning with Martin Gathercole he bade each state his name and state his case, asking that no one of the company intervene until his fellow had ceased speaking.

'I am Martin Gathercole,' the good man said, 'mill owner in Clywold, and lately appointed justice in the parish of Holmroyd, following on the supposed demise of the incumbent of that office, Richard Harcourt Born; I being also the guardian of a young woman named Ellie Bright. And I have with me Zephaniah Gaut, he being the father of Robert Gaut who sits in gaol on the false charge of transporting weaponry and who has undergone coercion by flogging at the hands of one Caleb Sawney, man of the militia, at the instigation of Richard Born. And I myself was there at the Sheep-close in the parish of Holmroyd, sirs, striving to plead with the magistrate Richard Born, but he was not to be dissuaded. And the young fellow would surely have lost his life but that one came out of a crowd of folks standing on the hill and hurt the militiaman in his arm. And a young fellow and his sister sit in gaol on the charge of murder for it is said that the fellow Caleb Sawney died of the wound to his arm. Now I bid my friend Zephaniah Gaut to have his say.'

Whereupon Zephaniah Gaut stood and I believe would also have bowed, so awed was he by the company, had not the attorney at law bid him be seated and speak, seeing his meagre health.

'I be Zephaniah Gaut, hand weaver up till the time the trade went over to yon mills. An tis my son Robert George Gaut who sits in gaol on the charge of transporting weaponry. An happen he be not afeared for himself, sir, for tis my belief that the lad had ever but a slender grasp on life; but he holds dear the lives of them that stand accused of the demise of Caleb Sawney, them being a brother and sister from yon hill country by the name of Horridge, for the perpetrator of the deed was a townsman from the look o his boots which Robert saw as he was being laid about with the scourge. Though he may not give evidence being an accused man himself. I am done now, sir, thanking ye.'

'You were present also at the Sheep-close you said, sir,' the attorney said addressing then Martin Gathercole. 'What say you about the boots of the perpetrator?'

'I would say if I were able,' returned Martin Gathercole, 'but I am not able, sir, my mind having been fixed on the sufferings of the young man who was enduring the flogging, and I was giving no thought to the foot wear of the perpetrator or of any other present. Yet, sir, I will vouch for the young man Robert Gaut, that he was known to carry folks in the casing of the double bass, so long as they were small folks, you understand, who were afeared of the man Sawney or of any other, for I be not partisan, sir, though I am a mill owner. I will bid the justice of Tindercliffe to give his account.'

'I being Bertram Tesh, justice of the parish of Tindercliffe, and I have said that which I wish to say in the room out yonder, though I cannot for the life of me remember what it was. Suffice to say, sirs, that I was in my cups on the night the remains were brought before me, and called out of my bed moreover with all the devils in Hades stamping on my feet. And therefore I, in the present company, retract any opinion I gave for I was not in my right and sober mind, may God Almighty have mercy on me, for a sloven and a drunkard.'

'Then we are done, sirs,' said the attorney at law, 'for the apothecary John Rivaulx is not bound to give testimony, and the officer Thomas Hayward is not bound, being only representative of Richard Harcourt Born, unless he so wishes.'

Whereupon Thomas Hayward said he did so wish, and the attorney bade him state his case and be not dismayed by the company he was in. 'For we must all use the privy whether we be of high or low estate,' he added.

'I am Thomas Hayward, officer of the militia,' said he. 'And I know not the import of the whole affair, yet this I do know, sir, that whoever it be who delivered the blow to Caleb Sawney in the Sheep-close on the occasion of the flogging did not cause his demise, sir, for he was one of my men and though he was a fellow of ill repute, yet he was still one of my men and I attended him on many occasions at his home in Beckwith until I saw him restored to health of the body. That is what I have to say, sir, and they who sit in gaol for delivering the blow to the arm whether they delivered the blow or not, sir, did not murder Caleb Sawney for I saw him restored to health with my own eyes.'

'Now, sir,' said the attorney addressing the patient, and Thomas Hayward having done, 'you may speak for yourself.'

'I am Richard Harcourt Born, magistrate of the parish of Holmroyd,' said he, 'and though I am thought to have perished by foul means and brought up out of the beck, yet I bear no part in any other fellow's error of judgement, that same error having put my wife Grace Born and her maid Rosie Todd in gaol; and that also I bear no part in for the error is the same one, of which I am innocent. And likewise I bear no part in the confinement of they who sit in gaol for the transporting of weaponry, for I was at the time of their confinement dead, sirs, having been brought up from the beck with my face shorn off and only the remnants of my dress to know me by.'

'How know you that your face was shorn off, sir?' said the attorney.

'There was many a one in the city morgue who entered the next world faceless from the cropping shears,' said the patient.

Then, fearing that his wits were awry for he talked without reason, unless it be that he did so with purpose, I prayed the attorney that he would make for an adjournment, which he did readily, calling those present out of the room and sending for an attendant; saying also that it was not meet for any one of the company to be present lest the patient, whom the attorney deemed to be fully in charge of his wits, bend their will to his purpose. Yet still I doubted the fellow's reason and I prayed the attorney that one might watch the door until the attendant be come. For which Thomas Hayward volunteered himself to be the man, and was no sooner gone than he came aflying back white of face and stupefied. For the patient, while unattended, he said, had administered to himself a poison. Yet such were the sores on his hands that a part spilt out on the floor.

'And twas a mighty stink of mouse,' said Thomas Hayward, 'which I know well for every garrison I have ever laid down in has been running with mice.'

And I blamed myself greatly on account of having spoken of an adjournment, for the first premise of the physician it to do no harm; and though I had done no harm by commission yet I had by omission in that I had overlooked that which I knew well enough, namely that the patient had gained possession of the Conium maculatum; the only recourse being then to administer to the patient allium against the poison, of which he had spilt most.

And the attendant, by then having arrived, was for having the patient fastened into a restraining jacket, but that the permission of the keeper would have to be sought before any such measure were put into place.

Then a debate ensued between the attorney at law and the good keeper as to whether a man in the process of taking his own life were acting with reason or without reason, his life being not his own to take but that which was lent to him by the Lord God Almighty, which to take was theft. And neither could agree. And no restraining jacket was put on, for if he were acting with reason then he could be said to be in his right mind.

And none other than myself saw fault on my own part, unless it were God Almighty, who indeed carries lightly the faults of all.

Only that the good keeper, seeing me at liberty after the hearing said a young lady had been awaiting this hour long and more to pass a message, and had been given refreshment while she waited in the women's ward, for she was a sweet uncomplaining soul with a severe case of the rickets.

XXXIV

And I found Melody, she having been brought out of the
women's ward and seated in that area which served as a
waiting room for the visitors; which room then being deserted
on account of the fever rife in the hospice, she said her
message straight out, as if indeed it had been welling up and
needed no prompting to burst forth, namely that a terrible
malady ran through the water lanes of York.

'You will wonder how I know of this, sir,' she said, 'as I
never stir forth from the house of mercy and have been
doorkeeper there for these two and twenty years. And Jem
Bailey, sir, going to the dispensary to seek you out, and I
know not why, found Mr Bower in a sorry way, so bewildered
in his mind that she doubted he would remember his own
name when she called him by it. And I bade Jem stay with Mr
Bower, sir, while I came to the hospice, where I have never
been in my life, thinking to ask help; yet when I arrived they
said you also were here attending a patient. Who must have
been a poor sad case, sir, for you were occupied a long time.'

Then it occurred to me that Melody might be a woman of
more years than I thought, and indeed her wisdom indicated as
much, yet her small stature gave all to believe that she was but
a girl, for which she must have suffered many a patronising
and demeaning manner, and I feared not least from me, for
which I silently begged forgiveness. And asking her if she
would take my arm, which she did readily and modestly, I
conducted her across the thoroughfare to the house of mercy,
being but a short step; though I would it had been longer, for
the sweet evening air was like a draught of nectar after the

close fever ward of the hospice, and the declining sun shed its benediction on all places in the dusty town of York.

'If it pleases you, sir, I must go now,' said Melody, 'for I have been long away.'

So I thanked her gratefully for being a messenger and for being my companion on the way home, to which she answered with a simple grace that the pleasure was hers; and she said indeed that she loved to be in the sun, for she saw little enough of it, confined as she was to the house of mercy.

'And I know not if I am like this because I am not in the sun,' she said, 'for Jem Bailey has talked of those like me in the hill country who go into the mills before the sun is up and leave after it has gone down. For when they saw I was like this,' she continued, 'they put me in the house of mercy, and there I have been dwelling, sir, first as a child and then as a doorkeeper.'

Then I asked of Melody if she had ever had recourse to remedies of any kind, to which she answered no, for they considered her affliction to be the consequence of sinfulness for she was born out of wedlock; which "they" I took to be her kinsfolk. 'For what God has sent must be endured,' she said.

'And do you hold with that opinion yourself, Melody?' I said.

'I do not know, sir,' she said. 'What think you?'

'I do not know either,' I said. 'But I have found in my life that for every affliction the dear Lord has made to grow a remedy, which may not cure in all cases but may lessen the affliction. And I reason thus, that if the dear Lord intended that all should bear their afflictions then the fair earth would be barren of leaves and fruits and roots and barks and all things growing that with a little preparation may become remedies.'

Then seeing that the dear soul would ask nothing for herself, and indeed had not ever in her life asked for any thing for herself, I prayed her to give consideration to the remedy of tamarisk, which though it would not heal her affliction and make her grow tall, yet it may prevent it worsening, the more

261

so if she could from time to time catch the golden light of the sun.

All this discourse being over in little time, I entered into the dispensary knowing as soon as I did that the spirit of my scribe Luke Bower burned low; finding him as I did in a dark room with the last of the shining eventide shut out and but a single candle alight, by which with difficulty I discerned the sweet presence also of Jem Bailey.

'He will not know you, sir,' she said, 'for he knows nothing at all, not so much as his own name, for I have called him by it often to no avail; and I know not whether he be awake or not, sir, for his eyes are open yet he sees not. Happen he is slumbering, yet his eyes are wide.'

And being by and by accustomed to the darkness I made out Luke Bower's eyes, burning like lamps in the night, yet seeing not, for there was no recognition when I brought near the candle, only that the pupils contracted.

'See, sir, he knows,' said Jem Bailey.

'No, Jem,' I said. 'The contraction of the pupils is a natural response to bright light in all living creatures on this fair earth.'

'Then he lives at the least, sir,' she said, 'for which I am truly thankful for I thought him to have passed out of this world. For he has stopped his speech, which he was speaking incessantly before, sir, but naught of any sense.'

And seeing that the response of the pupils of the eyes was yet present I gave to Luke, my scribe, the remedy of salix by pipette, trusting that the reflex of swallowing was also present, which was the case, and for which I thanked our Saviour. And praying Jem Bailey to return to the house of mercy for her repose for a while, even if she were to come back, I set myself to watch over the patient.

Yet being by then overcome with fatigue and the sorry affairs of the day, and hard pressed to stay awake, I fell into a slumber; and I was once more in the lanes of Paris at the time of the terror, searching as I thought for he who had been in the same building as undergoing coercion, when the cry "Fire!"

arose and all they our tormentors fled. For which reason I was searching the lanes going from one quarter to the next, walking through the flames yet unscathed, and knowing not the other's name that I might have shouted out. Until at length it seemed to me that I perceived one like to myself in height and feature, yet the nearer I thought to approach the farther off I found myself; only hearing from a place outside my dream the voice of one saying, 'Twas me, sir, I was he'; and simultaneously the heavy steps of one on the dispensary stairs and a knocking, even as if the blade might be in the making.

Then opening my eyes I perceived that Luke Bower was awake and sentient.

'There is a fellow on the stairs, sir,' he said, 'and if I could go and see to him I would, yet there has lately been a pretty siren here who has bound me to my couch. I perceive that you know not whom to see first, sir, so I pray you to see the fellow on the stairs for I will not escape, and he on the stairs is making a havoc of my head, and has been doing so the past quarter of the hour with his up and down the stairs and his batterings on the door.'

Having said which Luke Bower fell once more into silence and I went to see him who waited outside the dispensary door, finding there a soul whom I had seen but recently and could not remember where.

'I am an attendant at the hospice,' he said, 'and you know me not, sir, for you had much to occupy your mind, and also, sir, I am in different dress. For I find, sir, that even they whom I have attended in the hospice do not know me when they be well and abroad in York. For I am then in different dress, sir, as I say. He who was lately the patient in the fever room, sir, he has gone and tis believed he went out of the window in which case he should have lain sore wounded on the ground beneath, yet they found him not. That is the message, sir.'

So I thanked the good man, who yet stood by as if awaiting an answer, but I had none to give save that the patient had imparted to me the configuration of the drains that lay below the town of York. It being well into the small hours when he left the dispensary, for I heard the watchman passing by on the last watch; and indeed, light crept already into the eastern sky, and Arcturus was long sunk.

'You were talking somewhat, Luke,' I said on returning to the chamber, for the good man from the hospice had declined refreshment, saying the half of an hour of his visit to the dispensary was stolen from his term of duty, and he must needs be back, for they who attended patients by night were but few, as if the sick were less sick during the hours of darkness when often the contrary were true.

'For if a soul is to pass out of this world,' the good man said, 'it is nigh on three hours of the new day, sir.'

Which saying I took to be true, and indeed Luke Bower must have passed the crisis while I slumbered.

'I was bidding you to attend to he on the stairs who was knocking on my head and like to break it,' said Luke.

Then I gave a tincture of plantain against the head ache and bade him be quiet. For some there be that take slowly to the plantain, and some rapidly, even in the space of minutes.

'I am better now, sir, thanking you gratefully,' Luke said presently. 'For though I dosed myself I knew not the doses and nothing was effective.'

'You were talking and I heard you but indistinctly, for like as you dosed yourself in ignorance, Luke, so I sat for to watch by your side and fell into a slumber, we being both of us imperfect creatures, and recovered in spite of ourselves. I heard you as I thought saying, "I was he," and I know not whether twas you or the fellow in my dream, or yet the fellow on the stairs.'

'It was I, sir,' said Luke. 'For though the siren had bound me to my couch and I could not move, not so much as my eyes to blink or my tongue to speak, yet I could hear, and I heard the watchman passing by. And I knew then, sir, that it was nigh three hours of the day when men pass out of this world into the next, which worried me not a bit, except that I had on my mind that which I must needs say while yet in this world. Which was that which you heard me say, sir. And I believe the saying of it brought me back into the world, but I am still bound to my couch by the pretty siren; and you must needs send for her again, sir, to unbind me.'

Then I asked Luke what he wished to say while he was yet in this world, if indeed he wished to say so, knowing now that he was not shortly to leave the world.

'It is this, sir,' he said, 'that it was I who delivered the blow to the villain Sawney though he be my kinsman, meaning naught but to disable the arm that wielded the scourge; yet there are now they who sit in gaol on the capital charge of murder of one of the militia, which is where I should be, sir. Though at this moment I am bound to my couch and I cannot move a limb, nor could I sit in gaol for I cannot, sir.'

And I told Luke Bower my scribe that there was no charge, since an officer of the militia had testified while Luke was in the fever that he himself had waited on Caleb Sawney at his dwelling place in Beckwith, Sawney being one of his men although one of ill repute, and this same officer bore witness to his recovery. And whatever caused his demise it was not the blow to the arm. And indeed Luke knew that I had attended the patient Sawney yet knew also that I could not give testimony. After which he fell into silence and there was no more speech to be got from him.

And it perplexed me not a little that Luke was yet tethered to his couch by a pretty siren, as he said; and indeed, though he was alert in his mind, yet he suffered a vague distress of the lungs of which he was aware. And it came to me that while dosing himself the poor fellow had ingested also traces of the Conium maculatum.

'I will call the pretty siren to release you from your couch if you will, Luke,' I said presently. 'For she may rid you of the paralysis you suffer if you will but take the remedy she offers you.'

To which he consented for he knew that while the worst of the fever had passed, yet he was left with a stupor of the limbs which was like to pass to the lungs and thence carry him out of this world. And I had not to call on the house of mercy for no sooner was the thought in my mind than good Jem

Bailey appeared on the dispensary stairs and knocked softly on the door, whom I bade take to the patient a tincture of allium against the poison, though I said not to her what it was.

Then Jem Bailey sat down, as I had seen her on the day previous, though I knew not rightly which day it might be, with her sweet hands resting quietly upon her apron, in her own world, yet watchful of the patient, who had fallen into a slumber. And I inquired of her if she had taken refreshment, to which she answered that she had, for they were very good to her in the house of mercy, although they there were women who had never wed and knew not of child bearing; yet they were kind in all ways else.

'And if you please, sir, and have patients to attend I will stay here,' she said.

So I told her I must needs go to the hospice of York for they who had the fever there.

''Tis all around, sir,' said Jem Bailey.

'Then you are not frighted of catching the fever yourself while sitting with the patient?'

'I have heard that they who tend the sick do not catch the fever themselves, sir,' she said. 'Though that is not why I am here.'

'And why think you that they who tend the sick do not themselves catch the fever?' I said. For indeed I had heard it spoken of among certain Moorish peoples when I was yet in France who tended their sick most devotedly without any thoughts for themselves, and I wondered if such a belief might be shared by the hill peoples, that the Lord would watch over them.

'Mr Bower told me while you were badly yourself, sir, that they who tend the sick are fortified against the sickness themselves, though I know not how. And I do not believe Mr Bower caught your sickness, sir, for it was too quick. 'Tis because he was oft among the drains for some purpose known only to himself. But I have no doubt that it was a good purpose, sir,' she added.

'Jem, do you feel tenderly towards Luke?' I said. 'And you may tell me that I am an inquisitive old fellow.'

'Yes, sir,' said Jem, 'meaning that I feel tenderly towards Mr Bower, not that you are an old fellow. Did you ever feel tenderly towards any one, sir?'

Then I told Jem Bailey that I had, but not in the way that she meant, for I had taken orders in the church in France while yet in my youth and converse of that kind was forbidden. Jem Bailey being the second soul I had told of these matters, the other being Zephaniah Gaut, who had said merely, 'Aye'.

Yet sweet Jem Bailey, being in the spring of her life, had words enough.

'I have heard that there be they whom the Lord God forbids to marry,' she said, 'and I believe they in the house of mercy are of that persuasion; and I like not to say aught against the Lord God, but I do think he gives to some of they who serve him best very heavy lives, sir.'

Then reflecting on Jem Bailey's words I made my way across the thoroughfare yonder side of the Monk-bar to the hospice. And my life seemed to me not to be a heavy one, nor the orders I had taken as a young man, for it would have been a heavy life indeed to cleave to only one soul; and I could not think of aught else.

XXXV

Then I came to the hospice of York, finding there already a company of men in the waiting area, and for what reason I knew not for it was yet early in the day and the dew not yet gone from the coats of the horses stamping and snorting in the thoroughfares after the manner of their kind.

And I saw there one or two whom I knew by sight, they and all the others presuming that I was there for the same purpose as themselves, which I knew not. And presently the good keeper arrived in our midst, looking by his grey unshaven face that he had not seen his couch these three nights past; and it came to me that I looked the same, an uncouth dark-browed fellow who cared nothing for his person.

Gentlemen,' said he, 'I thank you for gathering here on this day, for which purpose you may be unaware. Yet nevertheless you have gathered, for which we thank you most heartily. Gentlemen, a patient has absconded from the fever ward, being somewhat restored in himself but still like to carry the fever to all the dwellinghouses of York, and we must needs search him out. And I ask you, gentlemen, that all they who have not fallen prey to the fever or nursed they that be sick with the fever now to leave this company with quietness of mind, knowing that the willingness to do a good deed is equal to the doing of it in the sight of God; for they who have not been in the presence of the fever are like to fall victim to should they come upon this patient.'

Yet no man left the company and I knew not for what reason, whether it was that all had been in the presence of the fever, or that no man wished to be seen unwilling before his fellows.

'We are to spread out, sirs. We are to comb the lanes and the broad thoroughfares. We are to search outhouses and gardens and drains. For we have in our possession the configuration of the drains beneath this town. And we have a good lad of slender proportion who has been sick of the fever in this hospice and who will search out the drains. And I ask for a help for him, not to go into the drains but to watch over his weal. If Mr John Rivaulx were here he would indeed go himself, but he is not here, having his assistant sick with the fever.

Whereupon I raised my hand like any bairn in the school room and the good keeper apologised, saying I was not on the tally of names.

'And we must needs know all they who go out,' he said. 'Here we have the fair town of York mapped out place by place and the names of two fine gentlemen by each, if you would please to consult the chart. And they who might not have brought their eye glasses, if they would please to seek assistance of another to read. Thank you, gentlemen.'

And I saw they that went forth out of the door of the hospice, being for the most part as I thought men from the lanes, with their breeches and their surtouts well worn; and also those of standing, among them a dissenting minister whose name I remembered not though I knew him to be a saintly man. Yet I saw not any young lad of slender proportion meeting the description of the good keeper. And presently all they on the search had gone out through the door, leaving only the keeper there in the vestibule marking them off on the chart, whom I approached, believing him to be in ignorance of my presence, having but lately acknowledged the same.

'Forgive me, sir,' he said, 'for I was duplicitous. I want not every fellow going into the drains and filling up the hospice with fever cases, for I saw that not one left who had not been in contact with the fever; which is to be praised in the fellows, yet there have not been that many cases that all have suffered it or nursed it. The lad is not here. He will await you at two hours before the noon day by the Lendal drain, before which I beg you to take refreshment, sir, for you have had none by the looks of you.'

Then I was conducted to the men's ward whence came the goodly scent of toasted bread, much at variance with the foetor of the fever; for in truth I had not regained my former self such that no odour offended me. And I waited there until nigh on two hours before the noon day, when I set off for the Lendal-bridge, after thanking the good attendants and seeing somewhat of the patients who had divers ills and of whom some were undergoing the remedy of bloodletting. And I thought of my poor assistant Luke Bower, how he would have blanched at the practice thereof; wondering also how he fared, yet doubting not the combined efficacy of the remedies of allium and a pretty siren.

So presently I came to the Lendal-bridge, and seeing many there but not he whom I had been sent to meet, I sat down under the Castanea sativa, leaning back on its fine gnarled trunk and watching the golden circles of the sun filter through its many fingered leaves, until I believe I fell into a slumber. For standing by my side was the lad Matthias whom I had last seen in the hill country, but expected not to meet in the busy town of York, and I said as much, whereupon he told me he was sent to the Lendal-bridge by the keeper of the hospice. And both of us having said little, but enough to realise a common purpose, the lad Matthias and I concluded that each of us was intended to meet with the other to carry out a search for a fever patient; and whether he knew who the patient was or not he said not a thing, and neither more did I.

'I fear you have had the fever as I have, sir,' he said. 'For I was with a cart, as I am sometimes, and I know not rightly what was under the sacking save that there was a sheep's leg to be seen, sir; and I surmise that I caught the fever from the sheep for the stink was very bad.'

Then I asked of Matthias if he were recovered well enough to take up again his nomadic life, lodging in whatever household would have him, to which he replied that oft times they gave him a bed in the hostelry if he would sit on the cart; after which I did not pursue the discourse of the cart.

'We are to look to the drains, sir,' he said, 'for the keeper told me that the gentleman sent to assist me would know the drains. Which I do not, sir, though I may take myself through narrow passages if need be, though I would rather not for the stink here is like to the privy and makes me sick to the stomach. I ever had a weak stomach, sir, which happen the keeper of the hospice does not know and I liked not to tell him for they at the hospice saved me, otherwise I would now be passed out of this world.'

'The pattern of the drains is indeed known to me,' I said, 'and I have found in my life that the senses become accustomed soon to any bad stink as if it were not there.'

Which of a truth I did not believe myself for the air at the entrance to the drain was the most malodorous I had ever had occasion to breathe.

'Happen we are both of us not fully recovered, sir,' the lad said, and I understood those words to be spoken with wisdom, for I knew only of the Sonchus hesperus to heal this fever fully.

So we entered in, finding ourselves on a narrow pathway below which the dark torrent flowed, the air being so noxious that the lantern flickered and was like to fade entirely, but that we reached at length a place where the passage widened and a slant of light crept in through the roof; and indeed fronds of the type of wrack I had observed before shifted there as if blown by the breeze, yet there was no breeze; only in the torrent below there was a disturbance in the flow as if caused by some manner of obstacle under the water.

'The roof has fallen in at this place,' I said. 'Observe the plants stirring, which indicates that the like is to happen again and we know not when. We will do well to retrace our steps and enter the drain yonder of this place.'

'If I go out I will not go in again, sir,' said Matthias. ''Tis best we continue now that we are here, for we will soon enough be past this place.'

'Nevertheless, we must go back,' I said; which with the lad Matthias taking the lantern we did, though he was for going forward.

'I think I see more steps than ours in the mire, sir,' he said. And indeed I had noted the same on the inward journey, yet I liked not to say lest the lad should be frighted out of his wits in so close and desolate a passage.

'Tis only ours, Matthias,' I said. 'There were no others when we came this way. I was seeking other footprints but there were none.'

'Your voice I hear is like the hills speaking, sir,' he said. 'You are one but down here you have many voices. Yet if you will keep talking, sir, for all that you have too many voices for one, I will be the happier.'

So I told Matthias of the fair land of France, of the castles there, and of the gold of the sun like unto the gateway to heaven, and of the vines like those that grew in the time of our Saviour; and of the tumult, for many there were poor and few were rich, and of the fair queen who sat on the throne, who knew not that they in the land starved; and of they who rose up in rebellion with the cry of liberté, égalité, fraternité, and of the hymn they made, which stirred the souls of men and women; yet I said not of the tumbrils and the blade.

Until we came at length to the entrance of the drain by the Lendal-bridge, having travelled as I understood some six furlongs under the fair town of York. And I thought not to see again the sun and the Castanea sativa with her many fingered leaves, nor feel the breeze in my hair nor drink of the clear air. And I feared that my companion Matthias was sunk in gloom, for he said not a word while we made our way out of the drains.

'I thought not to see the world again, sir,' he said presently. 'But, sir, all the time you were talking of the land of France I was resolving in my soul that I would travel there, even should I wait the remainder of my life to do so.'

Then I asked of Matthias what the keeper had bidden him to do once the drains were searched, to which he answered that he thought there were yet more drains, and although the task was burdensome and we liked it not we should see it out for we had not found the patient.

'Or happen you saw him, sir, and liked not to tell me,' he said.

Whereupon I saw that there was no deceiving Matthias and I told him of my conjecture, namely that the cause of the eddying in the water was likely to be that there was some obstacle beneath and it would be well to make an investigation before searching the drains further.

'I saw many footsteps, sir,' he said.

'Likewise did I but I wished not to fright you the more until we were out of that doleful place,' I said, 'for which I beg your forgiveness, Matthias, for you are a brave lad.'

'I thank you that you did not tell me he was under the water for I should have died of fright,' he said.

'We know not that it is he,' I said, 'but we must needs see if there be any soul there under the water.'

'Asking your pardon, sir, but I pray your "we" does not include me, sir, for my stomach will not abide a retrieval,' he said.

Then I assured the lad that none would expect him to attend, and that he had been the stoutest fellow of all in the search party in finding the patient; and indeed he suffered my prattle with patience and a good grace; so thus we came to the hospice, entering by the sluice way on account of the ordure yet clinging to us.

And there was naught to be done but for the keeper to get up a party for the retrieval, which was to assemble by the Lendal-bridge at the hour before the mid night, there being then less likelihood of a multitude of by-standers; all they in the party being bidden by the keeper to mean while take rest and refreshment, for the retrieval was like to be a protracted and nasty business.

Then I returned to the dispensary, finding my scribe Luke Bower somewhat recovered, enough so for him to remark upon where I had been from the ordure that still clung about me. And I put my cloak in steep and retired, being not yet out of the fever, for my limbs were as straw, and every time I closed my eyes I saw naught but the drain underground and the strange movement of the wrack where there was no breath of air, and the seething of the foul torrent with the obstacle beneath its surface.

Yet I woke when the sun was low, finding a light breeze in the chamber, and on the desk a loaf of bread yet warm from the baking of it, which the good soul Jem Bailey said they had sent thither from the house of mercy.

'For they be good women there,' she said, 'although they be women who have never wed and know naught of childbirth.'

And it weighed still on my mind that they from the water lanes stood in dire need of remedies against the fever, though I had taken none in. Then seeing Luke come to himself I asked of him if there had been any word from the lanes which might have been spoken to him by Jem Bailey. To which he answered yes, but was little inclined to say more. And I pressed him on the matter, to which he said only that all had been resolved, after which there was nothing more to be got from him.

'I must tell you, sir,' said Jem Bailey, 'for Mr Bower will not, but they from the water lanes came seeking you while you were stricken with the fever and Mr Bower gave to them the remedy of salix, asking me to bear witness. Yet he would not tell you, sir, for your mind would then be dwelling on they in the water lanes when you were sick yourself.'

'I will ask Mistress Bailey to make my other confessions for me, sir,' said Luke, 'yet not now for my nostrils tell me you have on that noisome cloak again and are bound on a further walk among the drains.'

So we set forth without even the light of the stars to grace the night and give an man an intimation that what he did had the sanction of God Almighty. For a gloom settled upon us one and all, and I had not a doubt that no man among us thought he did well. For the entrance to the drains, dour enough in the blessed light of day, was like unto the mouth of hell under the night sky, and the stench of the torrent underneath overpowering.

And we were making to get ready the lanterns and the ropes and the hooks, there being four men besides myself, who were strangers to me all, when one other was seen on the Lendal-bridge and descending the stairs to the drain; and in whom I recognised the attorney at law who had lately conducted the hearing in the ward of the fever patient. Who arriving in our midst bade each man give his name, that we might at the least be known to our fellows, he said; giving his own as Stephen Clay, and asking each if he had already suffered the fever, for they who had not must return home with the consolation that to offer oneself willingly for such a task were as laudable as having undertaken it.

Yet none went back, there being present that night, besides the attorney at law and myself, Tim Armitage, Geoffrey Spence, Michael Worsley and Henry Pike, which latter made light of himself, saying that he could not but offer his services with a name such as his; and each man looking like an effigy of himself from the flare of the lanterns, even the attorney, whose goodly face was cast in a most unearthly light; and each man was but spare in build for the passage was narrow.

'Which must put us in mind, gentlemen,' said the attorney, 'of what is said in holy writ about the narrow way, for though we are engaged upon the most unholy business, yet we must believe in its ultimate merit if those who sit in gaol are to be delivered into freedom.'

To which one or two good souls answered, 'Amen,' though doubtless they knew not of those who sat in gaol blameless. And we went forth, making but slow progress and each man sickened by the dearth of air and the foetor of the place, until we came, as I thought, to where the roof was open, though seeing but little for the dark outside.

Then the lanterns were shone upon the ceiling, which showed not the fissure, but the growth of wrack drifting on a breeze which was not, and the torrent of water seething as if some obstacle lay underneath. And the search was ended, with naught left to be done but raise the remains, which was effected in little time for all wished to be out under the sweet night.

So we went back, bearing between us he who would no more see the light of day, and we raised him from the mouth of the drains and up the stairs, and laid him beneath the fragrant Castanea sativa. Then the attorney at law, Stephen Clay, being nauseous himself asked of each man how he fared, all of whom were better than he. Yet I gave the tincture of bistort to all, for the effects of such an undertaking are like to last long and become apparent even weeks after the event.

And presently we made to convey the remains to the hospice, it becoming apparent as we communed between ourselves that some score of folks had assembled on the Lendal-bridge, among them poor souls who are of a habit abroad at night being without dwellings, and certain poor women whose pitiful converse is at nights, and folks in their cups who doubtless had mislaid their dwellinghouses and were awandering round and searching; some of whom as we passed crossed themselves and asked the Saviour to have mercy on the departed soul, which to our shame we had not done, not one of us.

XXXVI

Then we entered into a quiet more afflicting than all that had passed in recent days.

For each went to his dwellinghouse bound to secrecy, all they who had been on the search and they who had assisted with the retrieval. And no man spoke a word, not to his good wife at home, nor even to his horse outside the door, nor yet to the breeze that fanned his face. For no matter relating to that night was to be spoken of lest any jeopardy be done to the findings.

While in the meantime the pitiful remains lay within the city morgue. And I went to those who sat in gaol to see how they fared, yet could not say any word of what had passed; finding them resigned as to what fate would befall them, so that none did ask if there be any news. And for the most part they were restored, whether by virtue of the remedies or that the low fever had run its course through the gaol and was done. For each one wore an expression of quiet which I have noted in those who had but to wait for the merciful hand of death and can do no more, not least they who journeyed forth in tumbrils from the gaols and dwellinghouses in Paris at the time of the terror.

'Be not dismayed, sir,' said Rosie Todd, 'for you see, we have done our braids. For you come in expecting us to be in extremity as we were before, yet we are restored.'

'Rosie says rightly,' said Grace Born, 'for there is naught else we can do; and we know that we are innocent of those malefactions they have placed on us. Is that a word, Rosie? If not I have invented it and it will live after I have gone out of this world, for it is a good word.'

Then looking into Grace Born's face I saw in her eyes that she knew, either by that intuit of mind that women have, or that she had seen through the window I wear in my head, which many see through, yet for all that I have searched for in the dispensary mirror I have not seen myself.

'It is indeed a good word, Grace,' I said, and I passed on presently to Liz Horridge, asking how she fared. To which she answered that she fared well, for the pain in her mouth was done and gone.

'And you see, sir, I have braids,' she said, 'for it was not within me to refuse, though the braids do itch my head with the hair being pulled so tightly, yet I can say naught to sweet Rosie for tis her gift to every one of us and tis our saying that we fear nothing. Forgive me, sir, but you have the look of fatigue about you, and I fear you caught the fever.'

Then I asked permission of the good soul Rosie Todd if Liz Horridge might loosen her braids that I may observe the mandible articulating freely, which subterfuge was not lost upon Rosie Todd for she said happen she had done them too tightly as indeed her own head itched also, as no doubt did all the others'.

So leaving the women's gaol I passed on to the men's, finding likewise, namely that all were restored and wore the same expression of quiet. Yet Robert Gaut, although he was over the fever and the lesion on his neck was near healed, was gone as I thought so far on the journey as not to return to this world. And I asked him if there was aught on his mind, to which he said there was. Which I understood to be that he had wished his father out of the world, and I said to him that happen thoughts had come to him unbidden when the spirit of heaviness was upon him, which was no more nor less than that caused by the affliction of depression of the spirit, over which he had no say; for such a spirit visits men and women like an uninvited guest and lodges in the soul unbidden. And I knew not whether Robert Gaut took heed, for he said merely, 'Aye, happen tis so, sir. I thank you.' For Robert Gaut was ever a man of grace and humility.

Then I went to see my brother in affliction Domenico Jommelli, finding him likewise restored from the fever, and with an intimation of the late intended poisoning, which I knew not that he had awareness of.

'I have to thank you for averting that, my friend,' he said, 'though I knew from the aroma of it that is was a draught of hemlock, for we have both of us lived our younger lives in France. Yet I believed it to come from a turnkey and thus a device conjured up from within the gaol for my demise. And I knew not who it was, save that when I was stricken at the hostelry there was another fellow who was a guest but he was not like this turnkey in his person.'

So I said to Domenico Jommelli that I had no more on this matter, knowing that he did not believe what I said, yet he understood that I was sworn to secrecy for a reason other than that of my profession. And the noxious odour of the Conium maculatum was still in the air, for it was in the grains of wood on the table and between the flags on the floor. Yet there was naught else to do but to give Domenico Jommelli a tincture of allium as a prophylactic.

After which he asked how the other brethren fared, they of the hill people who sat in gaol, and I said they fared as he did, for I could say no other; wondering indeed and not for the first time how they of the hills who had lived simply and by the plain music of the seasons should leave their looms and follow the tune of the double bass, which could not but be strange to all their ways.

'It is that they saw the double bass as the pattern of their lives,' said Domenico Jommelli. 'For I said to them ... "See the strings, they are the warp, and the bow as she sweeps across the strings is the weft ..." Then the tune, hard as it was at first, became a cherished thing, for all they who heard it saw in it their lives. And because they could not come to the town of York I instructed a young man in the playing of it that he may continue when I am back in France. Yet because the music became a pattern of the lives of the weavers, it also became a matter of subversion in the eyes of some, and for that reason we have ...'

'... Malefaction,' I said, for he could not find a word.

'Yes, malefactions placed on us, the young man and myself. And now we are both of us confined, and the voice of the double bass is silenced. For it seems that they who brought the charge liked not that music should lift the souls of those oppressed,' said Domenico Jommelli.

Then I perceived that which had crossed my mind before, that my brother in affliction was indeed a fighter in the cause of the poor and cared not that he was on a charge of the transportation of weaponry, neither did he care for his life, for the warp and the weft were gone.

Yet I could not say anything about he who brought the charge who lay now in the city morgue awaiting the findings of the justice. So I bade Domenico Jommelli farewell and found the turnkey outside the door, who being restored again after the fever discovered himself to be as great a prattler as I.

'I tell you this in secrecy, sir,' he said, 'but I have it on good authority that a fellow was drawn out of the river last mid night. For many there were who stood on the bridge and saw. Not knowing rightly who it might be, sir, but twas done in the dark hours for a reason. And some say they at the retrieval were draped head to foot as if the deceased carried the plague, and the deed was done at that time so as not to stir up the people. Yet you know, sir, as well as I, that the night has eyes that sleep not, and tis my opinion that we will shortly see a rebellion if the matter is not made known.'

Then I said to the good fellow that I would have been informed had those at the retrieval been in the presence of the plague, to which he said that would certainly have been the case and he was but repeating the secret as he had heard it. And I said to him that I would keep the secret, for he was a plain fellow and good of heart.

Yet I found the matter to be abroad in all the town of York, the concensus of opinion being that it was indeed one afflicted with the plague who had been brought up out of the river at the dead of night. And a gentleman too, it was said, for there were they standing on the Lendal-bridge when the retrieval party passed by who noted the hand of the deceased, ill covered by the sheet, that it was neat and manicured, yet disfigured by the insignia of the plague. And even on my return to the dispensary I found the same opinion to be held by Luke Bower, my scribe, I know not how, for he was not yet abroad in the world of men.

'I did but hear it coming up through the window, sir,' he said, 'and I know not if it be the truth, but that is what I heard.'

Yet I had not heard ever of news coming up through the window of the room in which he lay, though no doubt it would have done so if the window were open; yet it was not, and had not been opened these many years, and indeed was obdurate in opening.

'I see you studying the window, sir,' said Luke, 'observing that it has not been opened these score of years, though you do not say so. There was a knocking on the dispensary door, sir, which was answered by Mistress Bailey. A lady has been here searching for her husband, and though she was of the hill country by her speech and dress, Mistress Bailey knew her not; yet entering into conversation with her I discovered what news is abroad in York, the lady fearing her husband also sick with the plague.'

And it perplexed me greatly who the visitor might be, yet I wished not to question good Jem Bailey lest she feel herself to be at the inquisition when indeed she had suffered afflictions enough. So I let it pass and went forth, thinking to find any one of whom I might inquire of the findings, short of seeking out the attorney himself.

Whereupon I saw the bay mare, Yolande, tethered to a post yonder of the Goodram-gate, and thought to wait by her until such a time as Martin Gathercole should return, finding her a gentle and quiet companion, and knowing also that Martin Gathercole would be nearby for he cared not to be parted long from his bay mare.

Then presently the good man appeared, thanking me heartily for watching over Yolande, and greeting her tenderly.

And indeed the gentle beast knew him for she nuzzled his face after the manner of her kind.

'You are the very man I was seeking, sir,' he said.

'And I was seeking you, Martin,' I said, 'knowing that where Yolande was you would not be far. She is a gentle creature.'

'We seek out each other for the same purpose, John Rivaulx,' he said. 'We must needs know if there be any findings, which if there have been they have not been conveyed to us. The attorney fellow must be found.'

Which saying Martin Gathercole had unwittingly conjured up the subject of his discourse, namely the attorney at law Stephen Clay who was even at the moment proceeding along the Goodram-gate, and at a brisk pace also for the word had gone around that he who had been retrieved was sick of the plague and few folks were abroad; the day itself also being grey and dour and the leaves flying untimely off the trees, enough to bring any man to contemplation of his own mortality.

'The work is done, sirs,' said Stephen Clay, 'in that the cause of the fellow's demise has been decided, and we need but an unhappy soul to assure the Crown of the identity of the deceased; there being but his good lady wife who sits in gaol on the capital charge of the murder of her husband; who like as not had little to do with his demise, being under lock and key at the time. It is a sorry business to ask such an office of a woman, sirs, and I know not the rightness of asking one on such a charge, but after the last travesty when the justice, without mentioning a name, freely admitted to being in his cups, and doubtless did not view the body though he remembers not, the affair must needs be carried through with probity.'

And the attorney being gone on his way I inquired of Martin Gathercole after the well-being of Ellie Bright.

'I know not,' he said, 'for she was at the dwellinghouse of Jane Pearce seeing after the bairn, for Jane Pearce as I understand from the mill hands, sir, went off to seek her fortune in York among the night walkers, if you'll pardon my saying in your presence, for I know you are not a wedded man, sir. Neither more am I, but I am more wedded than you I'll be bound, if you take my meaning. And matters went not well with Jane Pearce for she is back in the dwellinghouse in Clywold, thank God, not saying where she had been, sir. But Ellie is not there and Jane Pearce knows not where she is. Neither more do I.'

Having said which the good man threw his arms around the neck of his bay mare Yolande, and would I believe have wept were we not in the public thoroughfare. Then recovering himself he said he had much business in York on account of the mill, and begged my pardon for an unseemly display of weakness.

And having naught to do but wait I took myself to the assize, finding there a great throng, for the curiosity of folk outweighed the fear of the plague; there being before the assize that day, it was said, certain of they who were of the fraternity of the machine breakers who were like as not bound for the gallows-tree. For it has ever been thus, that death exerts a fascination for men as long as it be not their own. And many folk were there since early morning, for many had seated themselves on the ground before the great gates. Then all at once there was a rustling among them as folks rose to their feet, as they would in church or before the King, for certain men were being brought forth from the gaol to be led into the court of the assize; and though I was far off with a mighty throng before me, yet I saw they at the front parting as if to let one through, whether a sweet heart or a mother I knew not, for there were more oft than not such women about the assize court. Then presently I saw they who were led forth to the court, the crowd having fallen silent, for they were goodly men and fearless, yet knowing well what fate would be theirs before the day's end. Nor was there any sound, so that the clang of the chains was audible above the crowd. And I knew not whether the good woman, if woman it be who had been let through the throng, entered the assize or no, for the great door was closed; the folk for the most part going on their way but for a number who would sit out the hearing and broadcast the verdict throughout the town of York. And I did not stay, for the sentence of the gallows-tree was always anathema to me. And I went to the women's gaol.

Finding the good souls low in spirits and knowing that a hearing was on. Yet I found not Grace Born, nor did I expect to, nor could I find anyone who said where she might be, for they who sit in gaol have ever believed that the saying of any ill might provoke that very ill to come to pass, which would not happen if silence were maintained.

'We fare well, sir,' said Rosie Todd in answer to a question I had not asked. 'But as you will see, sir, Mistress Born is not here and has not been here since the new day looked in yonder window, and we dare not ask the turnkey lest the ill we conjecture in our hearts come to pass for her.'

Whereupon Rosie Todd fell into silence, and indeed the prattle I deliver when I know not what to say quite dried up also; and I was about to bid farewell and take my leave but that Grace Born was brought back. Then all stood, reaching out to touch her sweet face, yet none said a word.

'You feared that I had gone before the assize,' she said, addressing not so much those present as the stones beneath her feet. 'But I did not. I did not go there. I could not go there for I had not said farewell. They have taken me to see my husband, who let it be known that I and my dear friend Rosie Todd had sent him out from this world and placed him in the beck outside Holmroyd parish boundary. Now he has been retrieved from the drain below the town of York, and I know not where next he will take himself and give good men the arduous task of retrieving him. Yet I pray to God they call not on me to witness for I believe I cannot bear such a calling again.'

XXXVII

And I found outside the gaol my scribe, Luke Bower, not yet recovered of the fever but in the busy world again.

'For I could lie abed no more, sir,' he said, 'for all that there was a pretty siren in my chamber. The lady visitor who is seeking out her husband whom she fears to be stricken with the plague is at the dispensary again, sir, and I bade her wait for I knew there would be but few places in York where you would be at this moment, it being the first I have tried, sir, for which I am thankful as my legs are like straw. And I would as leave sit in gaol myself only so long as I could sit and not stand on my two legs that are turned to straw.'

Then I prayed of the turnkey to give Luke Bower a draught of water and a stool for to rest his straw legs, giving him also a tincture of cowslips and letting him be, for there was naught to be gained in much solicitude, which he liked not.

'You have your wish, Luke, my good fellow,' I said, 'for now you may sit in gaol, and if you are absent at the day's ending I will know you are in gaol for keeps.'

And indeed, I scarcely knew if it was near to the day's ending or not for in the gaol the sun sweeps over the sky and they see but little of it, knowing not the passage of time until the window darkens and the bright belt of Orion tightens around them. Yet it was light still and the dour day had quieted into evening and a red sun had come out to set over the roof tops.

So I returned to the dispensary and found there Hannah Gaut waiting, for whom Jem Bailey had brought potatoes and a gruel from the house of mercy.

'For I liked not to go into your larder, sir,' she said. 'Mr Bower went out searching and he is not yet returned, and he is not well, sir.'

'He sits in gaol, good Jem,' I said, 'which is where he wished to be so long as he might sit down, for his legs are at present made of straw. He will be back ere nightfall.'

'Tis nigh on nightfall now, sir,' she said, 'and he is not returned. Happen we must wait, sir, for I see you are not anxious for him.'

All of which discourse reached Hannah Gaut as she waited, for she had on her when I saw her the fear not only for her husband but now also for my scribe, Luke Bower.

'Tis the way we speak to each other,' I said after bidding her be seated again, for she had risen to her feet. 'Luke will be well and I trust also your husband, for I saw him lately in the company of Martin Gathercole and there is no better man. And if there were plague in York,' I said, 'I would have been informed.'

Which latter I said now with less conviction, knowing that the findings were complete and we were yet in ignorance.

Then Hannah Gaut said that she and her husband were at the assize that very day, and it was not that she feared him missing but that she determined to absent herself from him in order to visit the dispensary on her own account. 'Having been here recently and not found you, sir,' she said.

So I asked Hannah how she fared, in particular in respect of the complaint called the tinnitus, for I could tell by her sunken eyes that she slept but little.

'Tis as you know, sir,' she said, 'that I hear ever the building of the gallows-tree. Yet my good husband took me to the very place and there was no gallows-tree, it being yet the court of the assize and no gallows-tree built and pray God there will be none.

'When I came before I was in the company of Zephaniah, who is a good man, sir, but he will always speak for another, and he well knows it yet there is not a thing he can do about it; likewise his whistling, there is not a thing he can do to contain it, for tis he and tis as the good Lord made him. Yet it fairly drove Robert to distraction so that there were times when I feared he would lay violent hands upon his father. And now he sits in gaol, sir, and we know not if he be guilty of the felony of which he is charged, for it is a grievous crime to transport weaponry, next near to the using of weaponry.

'For I have to say, sir, that there were nights years gone when I knew not of the tinnitus and I have been awakened by what I took to be the weaponry of Napoleon Bonaparte, and the cries of the men at arms and the screams of the horses as they fell; and if not that, the cries of my bairns who were untimely delivered; that, sir, being until my husband Zephaniah, who was ever a good man, said we should have no more converse of that kind, asking your forgiveness, sir, if my speech is vulgar. And for all that Zephaniah could not forgo the necessity in him to answer for every other one, sir, which you have perceived, he had turns of phrase in him which I did not, for he told our son Robert of my plight while he was yet a bairn.

'... "Thy mother," he said, "you see her frame, tis tall; that be the warp; and she be narrow also, that be the weft, and tis how the Lord God made her that her frame be tall and narrow an she canna carry bairns."

'For in those days, sir, with the war on and before the orders of council there was toil in plenty for outworkers such as my husband. And he would say to the lad also when he asked me, is Napoleon good or bad, for Robert had ever a question in him,

'... "Tis not a matter for thy mother, lad, for tis a question only the Lord Almighty knows."

'For our son Robert, sir, he was ever apart and liked not overmuch the company of other lads, nor even the work of the loom to which he was born, for he said to me one day when he was grown, "Mother, I want to do one good thing."

'Yet I know not what he meant and I know not if he did. For he had taken up lessons with the musician and oft times we knew not where he was.

'And you will know, sir, that the musician took up the cause of the hill people for he would say to them about the

287

warp and the weft, so that the music became the song of their lives. Which I have to say, sir, I liked not as well as my husband did, for the casing of the instrument, it brought me in mind of a casket. Yet Zephaniah would say to Robert at the rare times he darkened our door that if he did no better than to play the double bass in his life he had done one good thing.

'And I am shortly coming to an end, sir.'

To which I answered Hannah Gaut that she must have her say, and if it gladdened her heart to know, I had heard my scribe Luke Bower lately arrive in the dispensary. Then Jem Bailey brought in candles. Yet far from coming to an end of her discourse, Hannah Gaut took up the thread of her narrative again as if it were the broken weft she was splicing into the cloth.

'Zephaniah,' she continued, 'for an unlettered man who knows little that is writ but the holy book, has ever said the music of the double bass lifts the soul, which I believe, sir, though it does not so for me, sir, hearing not the flights of it.

'And for the reason that our son sits in gaol we had communication from Mr Gathercole, who though he is a master is a good man. And we care not how it may go with our brethren that we have been in communication with a master, though it is like not to go well for us. I am nearly done with my ramblings, sir.

'For which reason,' she said, 'namely that our son Robert sits in gaol we came to York while the assize was on, sir, Zephaniah in all his life having put by from his wages; that being another sorrow, sir, for whether or not that Robert had been in the company of the machine breakers, yet he knew there was little work and so he took himself away. For oft times when you sent the remedies, sir, we discovered there certain shillings like unto the gold in the mouths of the sacks of Joseph's brethren in holy writ.

'And outside the assize, sir, for there was a throng, we heard the voice of a young woman begging to be let forward. For they to be before the judge were even then being led out, and the place was crowded, even though some feared the plague to be about, and crowded as the place was it was hushed so the drop of a pin might have been heard. Then we saw the young woman like as to an angel whose head was crowned with hair as of fire; but for all that, she was broken in the making, sir, for the Lord God does not bring all his creatures to birth properly and she was stunted in her legs with the rickets. And they at the front would have let her through but that the great door slammed. Yet all the time, and even as she hammered on the door with her hands she was crying out, "Robert!"

'Hearing which, sir, Zephaniah bade me go to her, for once being short of words, and ask in whatever way I could if she were sweet on he whose name she called.

'... "For tha being a wooman," he said, "tha knowest how to ask, but say thas his mother, lass."

'Then the young woman, looking at us, said she knew from the good face of Zephaniah and from my gentle turn of phrase that we were his parents, for she had a sweet way with her. And the question I feared to ask she answered, saying how could a woman such as she be wed and have bairns. And we knew not, sir, who that young woman who was as an angel might be, but that she said she had followed Robert only in the sense of making her way over the hills yonder of Clywold for to hear him play the bass, for the music she did love from the bottom of her heart as did Martin also, whom we assumed to be Mr Gathercole, sir. That is all. Thanking you, sir, for you were ever a kind and patient gentleman, and I fear this is not all new to you for you have had my poor scripts to study.'

And it being far into the first watch of the night I asked of Hannah Gaut how she would find Zephaniah, knowing from the sounds in the dispensary that he had been in the building some little time; for the tinnitus in her poor ears had driven out some measure of her hearing, for which reason I had no doubt that the music of the double bass sounded to her as the harsh squawking of the corvus. Then, seeing her bewildered for she had quite forgot the passing of the day, I bade Luke Bower show Zephaniah up the same stairs as he climbed on his first visit. And indeed his breath was no easier, nor yet was it more laboured; and I gave a tincture of digitalis and bade him be seated, which he did, whistling the while, and in no less anguish than his wife Hannah.

For, he said, despite that they had stood without the assize and seen they who were led in, yet they knew not if their son Robert Gaut was there also, for what the eye wills not to see it is oft blind to. And I reflected again what wisdom there was in the hand loom weaver Zephaniah Gaut, and in Hannah his wife also.

Then I said, for they knew not, that I had with my own eyes seen Robert Gaut their son, and certain others on like charges in the gaol even as the assize was in session, so that they might believe that Robert was yet alive, knowing well that I thereby infringed the honour of my profession. And, telling the good parents as much, Zephaniah said, 'Aye, we thank you, sir.'

So presently they made to leave, saying they were lodging for the night at the sign of the Jester, for they believed the assize court was sitting also on the morrow.

And it was as if the tidings blew in on the storm wind, for in the hour before the mid night a mighty gale arose, sending tiles clattering from roof tops, and groaning in the trees, and setting the bell of the house of mercy clanging. And I prayed that Hannah Gaut could not hear it, for she would surely have found in the night the hammering together of the gallows-tree and the heavy knell of death. Yet I had no doubt that she lay awake at the sign of the Jester, fearing that although Robert was not in the court of the assize on the day just gone yet he would be on the next, or failing that the next day following, or on every other next day until the justice proclaimed a limit on the term of his earthly life.

And it was said afterwards, which I knew for a truth for I heard it, that the knell from the house of mercy sounded out, even though the storm was passed, until the new day crept grey over the roof tops of York, and yet for hours afterwards.

Which next day brought tidings of the heavy judgement passed on those who had been before the court of the assize;

the journey to the gallows-tree being a journey no man of mercy would willingly inflict upon another of his brethren.

For as to the life, the Lord gives and the Lord takes away, from each man at his allotted time.

XXXVIII

And the day brought also a quiet in the dispensary, for Luke Bower, though he had been there on the night of the judgement and indeed was restored to his former self, was gone; and Jem Bailey also on account that her patient was recovered had returned to the house of mercy, saying that there was another lodging there with the rickets, like unto an angel, but though she had the face and disposition of an angel, yet she was powerless to stop the bell clanging, for it continued to do so.

'It frights them at the house of mercy, sir,' she said, 'for word has come to them of the judgement at the assize and they see it as the knell for the souls of they who will walk to the gallows-tree; though no one is there to ring it, sir' she added, 'it being greater than a man's strength.'

Then I thanked Jem Bailey for her sweet kindness to Luke and myself, seeing also that such watching and nursing as she had undertaken had served to restore her after her afflictions, and she said as much, for she was never willing to take gratitude without giving back thankfulness of her own.

'Are there not patients today, sir?' she said.

'We know not from day to day, Jem,' I said. 'Why ask you that?'

'For the reason that the other lady has been nearby, sir, and I thought her to be waiting for the dispensary.'

'Thank you, Jem,' I said, though I knew not whom she meant. 'There will be few abroad today for a judgement ever casts quiet over the town. If you will permit the company of an old man I will walk with you to the house of mercy and see you safe.'

To which Jem Bailey readily agreed, remarking on the way that the bell had near stopped its clanging, and asking if the reason was that the poor souls were already sent out of this world into the next.

'Tis more like to be that the bell has stopped of its own accord,' I said, 'for the bell was set tolling by the storm and continued thus of its own accord by virtue of its weight until it ran out of strength, though I know not why.'

'So it was not protesting against the judgement, sir?'

'I know not the mind of the bell, Jem,' I said, 'what it thought about the judgement,' thinking to lighten her spirit with my foolish saying, yet I saw that her sweet face was fallen into sadness.

'Twould have been my father sooner or later,' she said, 'for he was a cropper, as you know from how his arms were. And I have oft feared, sir, that he gave away word on the brethren for which reason they took him away privily and did what they did to him so that he talked no more. I know not if he was laid to rest in a Christian way if he be passed out of this world, and I know not where to ask.'

Then I told Jem Baily of the time at the hostelry when I was called upon to say if one of the brethren was deceased or no, knowing not if he that was deceased had been her father; yet I knew that the brethren dealt honourably with their own to the last, and I told her of those gathered around who had said the Amen, which word, if none other were pronounced, would surely have sent his soul to heaven. That being the second time I infringed the honour of my profession by my talk, though I said not so to Jem Bailey.

And she said no more until we reached the door of the house of mercy where I waited, saying I would do so until I saw the door opened to her.

And having twice broken the secrecy of the profession I reflected again on the plight of Grace Born, that I might in the last extremity prove the identity of Richard Born her husband, though my profession were in jeopardy, if it were to save her from the gallows-tree.

Then making my way through the Saviour-gate I met good Stephen Clay abroad on a day when few were abroad, and with all the looks upon him of not having ceased his hasty perambulations in three days.

'Thank God I have seen you, sir,' he said, 'for though none are abroad today yet none are at home whom I must needs see. There is no progress, sir. Mrs Born did not identify her husband, saying neither yea nor nay. We must pray that another comes forward who is kindred, though we know not where to seek, for Mrs Born does not say. Otherwise the charges against those in gaol stand. A sorry business, sir.'

And knowing not the purpose of my visit I went to the women's gaol as if my feet would carry me to no place other, finding there a scene so like the one I had witnessed the day before that I doubted any had moved from her place since that time. For Grace Born remained there seated with the others gathered round, reaching each one to touch her hands and her face as if they thus might remember her.

Yet in the instant, though I might have fancied the scene unchanged, I observed that Grace Born had changed beyond knowing, for her face was white as the distemper on the walls was white and her eyes sunken as those of one deceased, which indeed her mien suggested, but that she rose to her feet and held out her hand.

'Mr Rivaulx, my friends believe me to be not long for this world. Pray tell me that I am yet alive.'

'You are alive, Grace,' I said, 'but I fear you are not well. Your sickness is the sickness of melancholy, seen in they who have had too much to bear.'

Then I gave to her tinctures of thyme for the melancholy and sweet rosemary and betony for the affliction of the mind, though I said not to Grace or to any other that I deemed her afflicted in her mind.

'They took me to see my husband, sir,' she said. 'And they brought me back, though I remember nothing between the setting off from this room and the coming back to it. I believe also I had forgot every word I ever knew for they told me they waited while I was in the presence of my husband and

I had no words to say. Which I believe, sir, for he does ever drive the spirit out of me. I would bid Rosie do our braids but I am too wearied.'

'Mistress Born has had naught to eat, sir,' said Rosie Todd, 'though all put by from their own for her, yet she would have naught. I have heard of such in the campaigns, sir,' she continued in a whisper, drawing me aside, 'when they who have seen their comrades fall have gone off their meat, and some not to recover. Have you a remedy, sir, for I fear she is in a decline.'

Whereupon the good Rosie Todd wept a little but not long, and undertook to give Grace Born thyme and rosemary at the eventide, and sorrel for the appetite, though I doubted any would heal the affliction of the spirit.

Then I went out intending to return, meeting Henry Pike in the Walm-gate, though I scarce knew him for the darkness disguises all, and I had but seen him at night.

'You remember me, sir,' he said. 'Pike by name and Pike by nature since our travails in the drain, ha. Though it scarcely is a laughing matter. I met Clay not an hour gone and he says the fellow is not identified. What do you make of that, sir? You saw him as well as I. There is someone who knows him.'

From which discourse of Henry Pike I understood that the attorney at law had made known that the deceased's wife had been taken to see her husband; and I said nothing on the matter, only to remark on the strange silence in the town of York.

'Always so after a judgement, sir. If I am not mistaken you are going my way for your footsteps bend thither. Tis as good a place as any I've no doubt, when trade is bad, begging your pardon for the turn of phrase, sir.'

And I knew not where Henry Pike's footsteps tended but walked with him, and he indeed thought I was leading the way, until presently we reached both of us the city morgue, to his no little surprise.

'Why, sir, we are bound for the same place,' he said. 'For though I am called Pike my name might just as well have been Quill, for I record those deceased who have been required by the Crown or for other reasons for the purposes of dissection, and when I am not doing that I serve as clerk of births, sir; and the latter keeps in my mind that all is not desolation in this life, as I would surmise also in your profession, sir that it would be no great error to think all is malady. I wish you good-day, sir.'

So saying Henry Pike entered in under the arch of the city morgue and was presently gone into its dark interior. And I made my way to the men's gaol, finding there, as I had in the women's gaol, that all were as I had left them, neither better nor yet worse, but for Robert Gaut who was hard pressed to rise to his feet on my arrival; though I would not have wished that of any, for we are all of us of equal esteem in the eyes of the Lord God.

Then I asked of Robert Gaut how he fared, to which he answered that he fared well enough; and indeed the fever had left him and the lesion in his neck which he took no pains to conceal was nigh on healed.

'Yet I am low in my spirit, sir,' he said, 'for I have been ever thus, and tis not to do with the gaol for the brethren are here also and we fear not the assize nor the judgement. Happen you know there has been a judgement, sir.'

To which I answered that all of York knew.

'Aye,' he said. 'All of York knows, and beyond York also. Happen my parents know also, for in my dreams I saw them here for the assize.'

'I also saw them, Robert,' I said, 'for they were in a throng outside the assize as they who were bound for the court were led forth. And I saw also a young woman like unto an angel with hair the colour of fire who cried out a name, and all took pity and let her through the throng, yet the gate was closed, and the young woman then communed with Hannah and Zephaniah.'

'Tis Ellie Bright,' he said, 'called that way for the colour of her hair, for she knows not her father.'

Saying which Robert Gaut fell silent, and I feared that I had committed a grave offence in letting it be known that Ellie

Bright had waited at the assize, though I liked not to tell Robert Gaut that it was his name that she had called.

Then even as I was bidding farewell to the brethren and my hand was on the door he spoke.

'I would please to ask of you, sir, if you are so able, to convey my respects ...'

Then sticking at the word he turned to Simon Horridge.

'Tha mus do better than tha, lad.'

'... to convey the deep love of my heart to Ellie Bright, if you may find her, in those words, for I have but words, having no pen to write.'

'You will write a letter, Robert,' I said, 'for I will give you a pen and a fool's cap of paper; and it will be the better in your own hand.'

And thus I infringed the honour of my profession a third time in conveying out of the gaol a letter, for I knew not what was in it, having sealed it and put it in my scrip, and fully expecting a sign from some malign heaven for my malefaction; yet there was none save a bow in the sky with the dark above it and the gold beneath it, such as I had never seen in my life, which those who saw it said afterwards that they took it to be a sign of the troublous times. For they who had seen the machine breakers led forth to the assize saw not uncouth and violent fellows with blacked faces but goodly lettered men who faced the judgement with equanimity.

Then I went to the house of mercy and gave the letter of Robert Gaut into the keeping of sweet Melody, saying not from where it was, and neither would she ask for she was a good and faithful soul.

And after that to the city morgue for to ask of the attendant the divers diseases that presented, as was my wont; finding there among those brought in from the thoroughfares of York none of natural causes, but one of murder and one fallen under a coach while in his cups.

And finding the attendant also full of talk saying he feared he was that way on account of those with whom he had dealings being for the most part silent; though one time he came in of a night, he said, to attend on one newly arrived and when they who had brought him were departed the building the fellow sat up and said the prayer our Saviour taught us, after which he laid himself down and took his leave.

'To be sure, sir,' he said, 'I have never since heard the good prayer said in church without being frighted out of my skin, wondering if the minister is like to pass on after its utterance.'

'That fellow from the river is still here,' he said presently, 'for his good lady wife was overcome and did not speak, and some there are who say her wits fled on seeing her husband in such a way. Yet to my mind, sir, I tidied him up handsomely so that he was little changed from the last I saw of him.'

Then, as if I had interjected some question, though I had not, the good attendant continued his discourse.

'Yes, I remember the party as if it were the yesterday, for he came to request a cadaver, which is not so rare a request, sir, for there are they who are learning the anatomy; and these poor fellows, who were some of them of small account in their lives, yet when they become cadavers might advance the learning of the anatomy and so save many. And if there be they of the kin who come looking after the cadaver has gone, that is what I say to them, sir, that they might rest contented knowing that the deceased kinsman was of assistance to his fellows at the end. But this gentleman asked not for a cadaver for dissection but merely for a cadaver. And as Mr Pike has been here this very day collecting names of those who have been so taken I remember the name of the deceased, who was requisitioned by the gentleman we have here now, apropos of which he was in truth a gentleman by the cut and the fine cloth of his coat, sir, and he had a gentleman of the militia to assist him, a tall fellow and handsome with it; for the gentleman we have here said he was a magistrate and tis not my duty to question yea or nay. So I handed over the cadaver, a fellow by the name of Harcourt, the name being, as I said, in my mind for the reason that Mr Pike has recently been in attendance. In answer to your question, sir.'

XXXVIX

Then it came to me that those two humble servants of the Lord, being Henry Pike the clerk of births and the attendant of the city morgue whose name I knew not, were jointly and severally in possession of such knowledge as might release into freedom they who sat in gaol, though they knew it not. And I reflected also how many in this world carry within them, though they know it not, that which may assist their fellows, and indeed how many go to their last rest not having done that good which they could have done had they but known it was theirs to do.

Which thoughts hastened my footsteps to the chambers of Stephen Clay, for I was so far gone in dishonouring my profession by speaking unguardedly that I heeded not what other follies I might commit.

And finding the good man slumbering in his chair I was minded to go away, but that the matter was pressing.

'You find me resting my eyes, sir,' he said. 'I do not make a habit of resting my eyes in the broad daylight but that I have walked every street in York three times over in these last days, or so it seems to me. Pray sit down, sir, and don't mind my informal manners, for which I beg your pardon.'

Then I told Stephen Clay of what was but an incidental discovery between myself and the attendant of the city morgue, namely that the fellow whose pitiful remains awaited identification, and whose wife had been unable to identify him, had requested a cadaver whose name was recorded as being Harcourt on a date coinciding with the retrieval of certain remains from the beck nigh on the Holmroyd parish boundary.

All the while of which the good attorney sat nodding, with his eyes fairly closing in fatigue. And I likewise felt the same languor creep over me, until the question of the identity of the remains faded into little importance; and all I could see was the fire flickering in the hearth, until I felt myself sinking into a slumber, and indeed I fought with myself to wake lest the recurring dream of the burning lanes of Paris in the time of the terror should overtake me. Yet I was awake and not awake, thinking that Stephen Clay had risen from his chair and taken his hat and gone forth into York; and as much as I strove to do likewise and be out of the chair in front of the fire I could not, for my limbs were in a manner of torpor. And I knew not how long I was thus, for I started suddenly as the wind threw a patter of rain at the casement, finding my companion yet seated as I had been, drowsing by the hearth.

'Asking your pardon, sir,' he said, 'for I believe I was dozing and you were waiting on me to come to my senses, for which I thank you, sir.'

Then I told the attorney I had likewise fallen into a slumber and had a strange waking dream that he was risen from his chair and gone out into the thoroughfares of York.

'That may be so,' he said, 'though I knew nothing of it. But I am now returned and we have a matter in hand which must be attended to, yet I know not how, save to find another to identify the deceased, who might carry the name of Harcourt. Tis not a name in these parts, sir. In all my years I have not come across a Harcourt, but that the fellow Born had it. To my mind it smacks of affectation, the landed sort of fellow, and we are not of that ilk in the ridings of York. I speak as to a friend, sir, not in the capacity of the law. What think you?'

Then I told Stephen Clay that I had known of the fellow from the militia who assisted with the removal from the city morgue of the cadaver named Harcourt, which militiaman was named Caleb Sawney and was also deceased, having met his end at the machine breakers' uprising in the region of Clywold. And it came to me also that I knew his mother who went by the name of Sarah Bower, who was indeed the mother of my scribe, Luke, though I said not so to the attorney. And indeed I had inquired not at all into Luke's beginnings, knowing only what he told me, namely that he would by habit sit in the shadow of the gallows-tree on the chance that he might there be in the company of his father; it being a fact of the remote places in the ridings of York that many be related in some sense, and indeed there were those who said of the town of Beckwith that when a man had seen one he had seen all. And although I did not relate these thoughts to Stephen Clay, yet he saw through the window in my head, as do all others.

'But it could be, sir, that knowing the name of this militia fellow there are like to be others to be found who are yet alive and may assist. For we must follow every avenue of inquiry if we are to deliver those who sit in gaol.'

To which I assented, deciding in the instant to confide in my scribe Luke Bower, who knew all others and their business but would give away little in the way of idle chatter in his talk. And I bade good-day to Stephen Clay, leaving him to his slumbers and saying I would call on him should there be any soul found who might assist as witness for the Crown.

And arriving at the dispensary and it having gone out of my mind that which Jem Bailey said, namely that there had been a lady nearby, the presence there of Sarah Bower came as no little surprise, as if my having given her thought but half of an hour before had conjured her up; whom I bade be seated and take refreshment, for she was indeed a sorry soul with all the melancholy of a dark world drawn in circles beneath her eyes.

'Nay, sir,' she said, 'for you shared your bread with me and now I share mine with you, and will ever do so when I am in your company,' having said which she brought from her reticule a new loaf and divided it.

Then I asked Sarah Bower how she fared though it was writ on her face that she fared not well.

'I fare well enough in myself, sir,' she said, 'though I see every day the raptor above the hills of Beckwith and I know not whether he comes for me or some other, for he has had

301

chance enough to take me yet he has not, even though I travelled on the way to meet him, sir, as you well know. Happen you don't see the raptor in York for he is a creature of the high lands. Your assistant is not here, sir?'

'No, Sarah,' I said, 'and I know not where he is, for I have these last hours been engaged on visits in York.'

'You are occupied, sir, and I use up your time without cause for I fare well and have no malady.'

After saying which Sarah Bower fell into a silence, gnawing at her under lip and watching the clouds as they scudded by the open casement.

'It is writ on your face that you fare not well, good Sarah Bower,' I said.

'I am not good, sir,' she said, 'for though I am now a woman of fifty and six summers and indeed more like a hag than a woman, yet when I was young the sweet Lord gave me what many considered to be a fair face, though I say not myself. And I will spare you the rest, sir, but suffice to say that I had three sons out of wedlock. Caleb, as you know, sir, I saw in the city morgue of York, and Luke you know, sir, whether or not you know that I am his mother. And I am come seeking my first son Richard, conceived when I was but a girl with one who made himself a gentleman but was no gentleman, being already wed. For the raptor informs me that my first son has been taken and I know not about his father. And like his father, so did my first son, and made himself a gentleman and a magistrate, but he was not a gentle man, sir, in his dealings with the machine breakers.'

'How come you to the knowledge that your first son is no more, Sarah?' I said. 'The raptor is but a wives' tale, which you well know.'

'I did not say it, sir, that he is no more, only that he has been taken and I know not where.'

'Yet you are talking of him in the past, and of his father also, as if you believe in your heart that they are no more.'

''Tis true, sir, that is what I believe. And as for my son Caleb, you told me, sir, that though he was but a coarse man, yet at the last he carried in his arms a poor mill woman to her home. I would that you could tell me of a fair deed done by my first son. But happen you cannot, sir.'

Then I asked of Sarah Bower if she would accompany me to the rooms of Stephen Clay.

'So you cannot tell me, sir, of any one deed he did by which his soul might be shown mercy.'

'He did what he believed to be right, Sarah,' I said. 'And whether right or wrong tis not for us to decide, but for the Lord God Almighty.'

And I knew not what else to say, for all are deserving of mercy and all have fallen short of the glory of God.

And that being not what poor Sarah Bower wished to hear, we took our walk to the rooms of Stephen Clay companionably enough though in silence. For I believed also that Sarah Bower held herself in so low esteem that she would feel abashed by any companion, even such a one as I. And indeed she kept her head lowered lest any should see her, while for the whole journey, which was but a few thoroughfares, I searched in my mind for that which could be said to her of the goodness of her firstborn son Richard, knowing little of him and that not likely to quiet her soul, namely that he had been a man of unbridled habits and a harsh magistrate, delivering coercion among the community of the machine breakers, to women as well as men, and that his good wife would not so much allow the hem of her gown to touch him.

Thus we were until the entry to the Flesh Shambles, a lewd and rough place running with the gore and sinews of the poor beasts for sale there, where one ribald fellow called out from an upper window an unseemly word, thrown down to the street as the contents of a piss pot are, for all and sundry yet for no one in particular.

'Tis not meant for me I know, sir,' said Sarah Bower, 'but tis what my life has been.'

Then I bade her take my arm which she did reluctantly enough, saying that she wished not to do me any dishonour, to which I answered that it was indeed an honour to walk through the town of York with her for I esteemed her greatly;

and thus pleasantly we arrived at the rooms of Stephen Clay, attorney at law, finding the fire burned low in the hearth and the good man yet slumbering, for all that it was one hour and a half since our last discourse.

'I am awoken now, sir,' he said, 'for of a truth I could not open my eyes when you were here lately. Pray leave me to do that, my dear ...' for Sarah Bower had busied herself mending the fire while the good man recovered himself. And I could not but wonder at the trustfulness of the poor soul, for she knew naught of what more in the way of desolation that day had in store for her.

'Mistress Bower knows not why she is here, sir,' I said, 'only that she is at the chambers of an attorney at law. She has come to the town of York seeking her firstborn son Richard. I will let her continue for I am an old man oft times scattered in the wits and I wish not to mistake in this. I will take my leave if I may.'

'Pray do not, sir,' said Sarah Bower, 'for tis nothing I have to say that you know not already. My son goes by the name of Born, sir, not Bower,' she said addressing Stephen Clay. 'For he made himself a gentleman and there be many Bowers of little account in the town of Beckwith, and he wished not to carry that name. Tis noised abroad that his wife and her maid murdered him, for which they now sit in gaol, but tis not true for the night the town of Clywold was afire my son Luke Bower was told by one Jane Pearce who oft times plies her trade in York that she had seen one of his likeness among the stews. And word has since come to me, sir, it matters not how, sir, for tis common knowledge, that a gentleman was brought from the river lately whom they on the bridge when the party brought him up noted by his hands that he was a gentleman. Therefore his good lady wife and her maid cannot have done the deed for they were sitting in gaol. Tis Richard Born whom I seek, sir, and I mind not to view his mortal remains if Mr Rivaulx and, I humbly ask, your good self, go with me, sir. For I viewed the remains also of my son Caleb Sawney and Mr Rivaulx took me there.

'We will go presently,' said Stephen Clay, 'for the poor fellow is not likely to take up his bed and walk. But first, sir, we must both of us look to this good lady, that she taken a remedy to strengthen her against what might befall.'

So I gave to Sarah Bower borage and thyme knowing well that no remedy would be her safety against going into that place for such a purpose a second time. For one time in a life is that from which a soul does not recover and twice is like to provoke profound melancholia and also madness.

And Stephen Clay gave to her a bowl of tea, talking the while.

'Tis more like the puddles of rain that stand outside my door in the Walm-gate,' he said. 'And had I a housekeeper she would have accomplished the task with more excellence than I, but I have not a housekeeper so we must needs make do.'

All of which talk the good man delivered to lighten the spirit of poor Sarah Bower, and though her spirit was not lightened for the sorrows of the world were writ upon her face, yet she made as if she were restored and we went forth into a storm of rain.

And we went under the great arch into the most desolate place in the town of York; and indeed I felt myself a fear overwhelm me, as if I were Sarah Bower entering into the city morgue with the most doleful task awaiting her; finding the attendant not at his post but the clerk of births, Henry Pike.

'You may not remember me, sir,' he said to Stephen Clay. 'Pike by name and Pike by nature. I am bound here until you be sent for, sir, though you are here and the messenger is here and not yet left. For if I leave then the tidings will leave with me, which if you can understand, sirs, you have sharper wits than I.'

So continued Henry Pike until the attendant was heard approaching from afar off, for indeed such was the place that the echo of steps might be heard long before he who caused them came into view.

'Sirs and lady,' he said. 'Tis done. A young man was lately here, being the brother of the deceased who came to this place of his own volition without coercion, saying that though he and his brother were long estranged in spirit yet he knew him as the magistrate of the parish of Holmroyd, Richard Born, they being of opposing views in the machine breakers' matter. Yet the young man said he owed this to his brother, the said Richard, that he had taught him the reading and writing and if he did naught else good in his life he did that.'

Which in the instant, though the attendant knew it not, gave to Sarah Bower that which she craved above the deliverance from the task of identifying her son's remains, namely that she should know that in his life he had done a good thing, which before she knew not of.

Then seeing Henry Pike about to take his leave it came into my mind again, and I know not how, that the attendant and good Henry Pike had in their knowledge that about the name of the remains in the beck, being Harcourt; which though it was but short months ago that Kit Swain had taken charge of the retrieval, yet it was like years of my life, and I felt sick at heart for all that had passed. And looking up through the open casement I saw framed in it, and out of her customary dwelling, that plant called the senecio, yet flowering in the late season like an open hand full of the golden sun. For the senecio is but the humblest of plants and finds her way into the most dismal of places.

And I went back to the dispensary, finding my scribe Luke Bower not there; and indeed as I entered the building I knew that the spirit of him had left.